I0788110

GONE ROGUE SERIES

Rogue OPERATOR

PATRICIA D. EDDY

If you love steamy romantic suspense, I'd love to send you an exclusive short story set in Dublin, Ireland. Castles & Kings is ONLY available for my newsletter subscribers. Visit my website and let me know where to send your free short story! http://patriciadeddy.com.

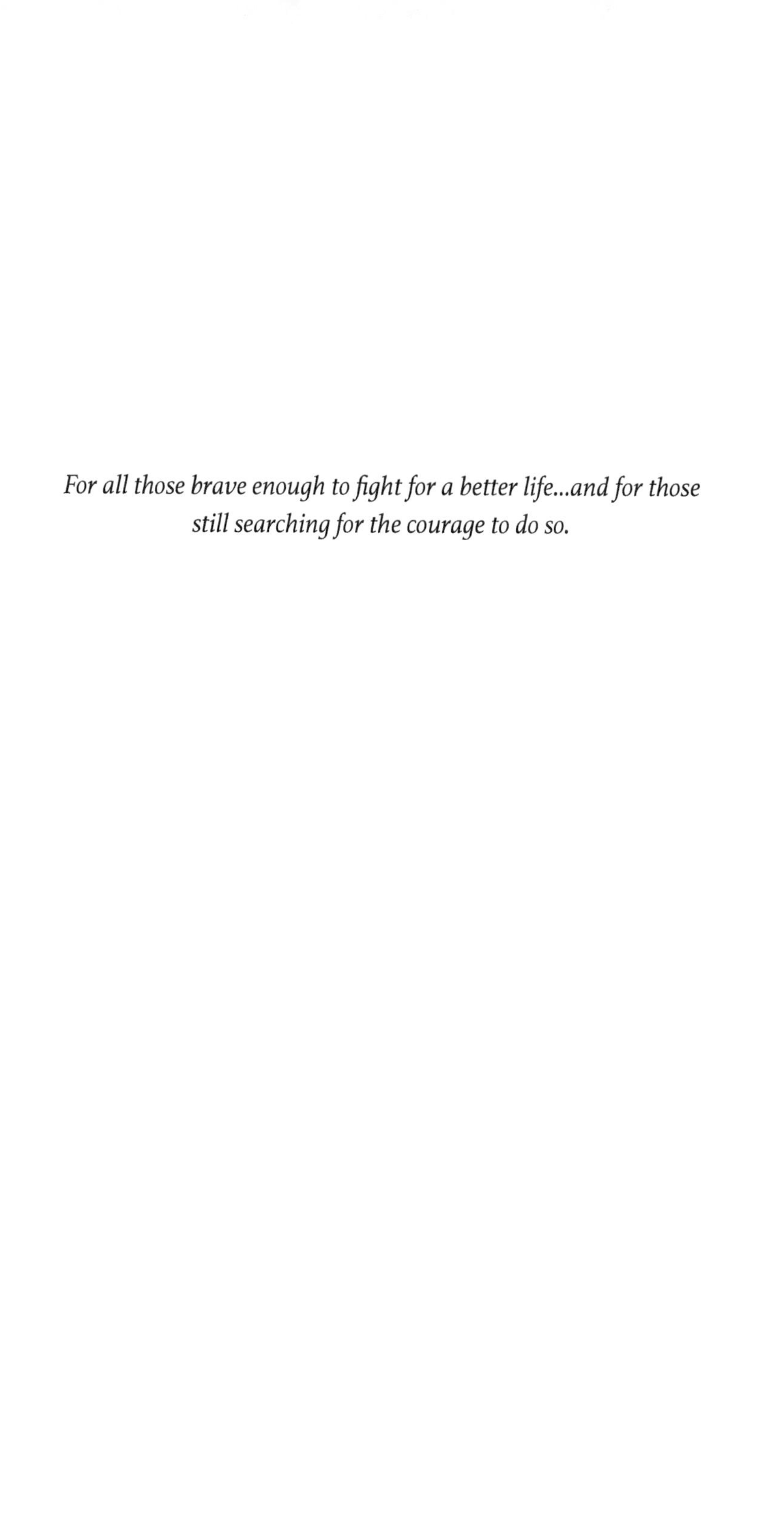

For all those brave enough to fight for a better life...and for those still searching for the courage to do so.

CHAPTER ONE

Three Years Ago

Nomar

FUCKING TIMING. If I'd been twenty minutes faster, I'd be back in the States, nursing a beer at a baseball game. Not in the middle of the fucking Afghan desert setting off on a suicide mission with men I thought I'd never see again.

For ten years, I've woken with the sun every day. No matter what. Except for last Tuesday. When sleeping in meant I was still here to take Ford's call. Now, I'm fastening a button camera to my tunic at oh-dark-thirty in the morning, preparing to breach the most heavily guarded compound in the whole country.

The headscarf makes it hard to see anything in my periphery, and I have sand in *every* crevice.

These clothes—a *gift* from the tribal elders I paid off— will help us blend in, but they're far from clean. Hell, this whole goddamn country smells like horse shit, goat shit, and cow shit, all laced with spices.

The only two men in this world I consider friends stand in front of me, waiting for orders. Trevor Moana, former CIA sniper, and Ford Lawton, a Marine I served with more than twenty years ago.

"Make your way to the back of the compound, and for fuck's sake, stay out of sight," I say, slinging my AK-47 over my shoulder, slipping out of the old barn, and mounting one of the horses.

The ride up the hill is quiet this time of the morning. Only a handful of goats crossing my path, herded by a kid who can't be more than fifteen. But even the animals don't get too close to the compound.

Anyone who's spent even a few months in country knows the name Amir Abdul Faruk. Weapons, drugs, women... The man traffics in them all.

According to our intel, Ford's former fiancée is inside that compound. Faruk had Dr. Josephine Taylor kidnapped from a Doctors Without Borders caravan in Turkmenistan a week ago. God only knows what he's done to her since.

At the front gate, I pass my contact a pouch with five thousand dollars in cash tucked inside.

"You have thirty minutes," he says in Pashto. "Any longer, and I will not be able to get you back out again."

The gate rolls open on wheels that shriek under its weight, welcoming me into the lion's den.

A handful of cars are parked haphazardly along the walls. Good cover. If we need it. But the center courtyard is wide open—except for a group of men on prayer mats near a fucking water fountain? It's the middle of the damn desert.

One of them...tall, jet black hair, full beard, wearing a tunic inlaid with golden threads paces until another exits the massive house pulling a woman behind him.

Joey.

She's panicked, dragging her heels in the dirt, but the brute is almost twice her size.

When she cries out, Faruk strides over to her and slaps her hard enough, *I* feel it. "You are making him worse, not better!"

"No!" Joey cries. "All of his numbers were better last night. You saw the report."

Faruk shoves her, grabs the back of her neck, and forces her head down so she's only inches from a young boy lying on one of the prayer mats.

"Does he *look* better to you? He fell over and he will not get up!"

Her next words are too quiet to hear, but she's defiant. Far from broken, thank God.

Faruk kicks her in the stomach, then rains blows down on her back until another man calls, "Amir Faruk, sir. The doctor cannot cure your son if you...break her."

Straightening his tunic, Faruk steps back. "Zaman! Take her to the lab, along with my son. I expect him to join me for prayers by nightfall, Josephine. If he does not, I will hold you responsible."

I duck behind one of the vehicles as the big man drags Joey back toward the house by the neck of her tunic. Another, shorter man picks up the boy and follows.

"Leave us," Faruk shouts at a woman in a dark blue abaya. She flinches, her gaze pinned to the ground. "Watch over my son or you will be sorry."

"I'm going to try to find out where they took Joey," I whisper. If Trevor and Ford followed orders, they'll be hiding by the back wall of the compound and will have seen everything.

The camera's range is absolute shit, but our comms units—courtesy of Ford's company—are state of the art.

The house looks like a collector's wet dream. Glittering lights, red tile floors, and plush rugs everywhere. The walls are painted gold, for fuck's sake.

Two women dressed in black burkas with full face coverings dart past me, their heads bowed. Shit. I should have left my gun at the door.

Or not. A pair of guys stand sentry at the end of the hall, Kalashnikovs held at the ready. Behind them, a plain room holds half a dozen computer monitors, a simple desk, and a *very* uncomfortable looking stool.

Right. Not going in there. Turn after turn, I commit the layout to memory. This place is a goddamn maze with men everywhere.

Until I find stairs down to a lower level. The hallways here are quiet. Pristine. White tile floors without a spec of dirt.

Muffled voices come from a room at the end of the hall. I edge closer as my watch buzzes. Shit. I've already pissed away ten minutes.

"He will never stop," a woman with a French accent says. "Every good thing about Mateen...Faruk will destroy it."

I pull a small mirror from my pocket and angle it around the door. The kid lies on a narrow bed with an IV hooked up to his arm while Joey takes his blood pressure.

The other woman sits in a chair, fiddling with the sleeves of her abaya.

"Mama? Is Papa mad at me?"

"No, my sweet boy. Papa wants you to get better. Lie back now and let Dr. Joey work."

Another buzz from my watch, and I shove the mirror into my pocket and hightail it out of there.

"I found her," I whisper once I'm back outside. "The kid's hooked up to an IV. I couldn't stick around. Give me twenty minutes to map the rest of the place, then I'll meet you back at the barn. We'll infiltrate tonight."

THE MOON RISES along the horizon as Ford—his hands bound and a hood over his head—stumbles. Trevor doesn't bother to catch him. All part of the act.

I jerk him up and drag him toward the gate.

"Thanks, asshole," my oldest friend mutters.

The guard raises his rifle when we approach. "Stop. What is your business here?"

I answer in Pashto. "This man is responsible for the explosion last night in Kabul. At the auction. Amir Abdul Faruk will pay for him, yes?"

The guard pulls a phone from his belt, dials, and cups his hand around the speaker. Quiet words pass between him and someone on the other end of the call for a full minute.

Two other guards join the first. "Hand him over," one demands.

"No. Not until you pay." I gesture to Trevor, and the CIA assassin pulls a blade from his belt and holds it to Ford's throat. "Ten thousand American dollars or we cut off his head."

All three guards draw down on us, shouting, threatening, ready to drop us in a heartbeat. Shit.

"Abdul Mahmud sent me here!"

The guards fall silent at my declaration, and the first one is back on his phone in seconds. It doesn't take long.

"You go in," phone guy says. "Wait by the fountain for payment."

As we pass the guards, one of them slams the butt of his rifle into Ford's skull. He collapses with a groan, and they grab his arms and drag him away.

Trev and I exchange a glance. This was *not* the plan.

At the fountain, we stand with our backs to one another, surveying our darkened surroundings.

"Two hostiles at each guard tower," Trevor whispers.

"And another two at the gate. But they're high as fuck. I'm going to smell like weed for a week."

After a beat, the man I swore I'd never work with again pats the pocket of his tunic. "I'm getting the package. Set the charges and find Foxtrot."

"Roger that."

He hurries toward the house while I creep back to the gate. The closest car looks like it hasn't run in years. Slipping around the back of it, I drop to the ground and roll under the old sedan.

This might be the first time I'm grateful for the headscarf. At least it keeps the sand out of my hair.

I have enough C4 taped to my torso to blow up half the compound. Pulling a pen light from my pocket, I clasp it between my teeth. Two bricks of explosive should do it. With seventeen minutes on the detonator, I connect the wires and get the hell out of there.

The back gate is harder. No abandoned cars to use as cover. Just some wooden crates. The guards on the watch towers don't pay me any notice. I look like I belong. Move like I belong. The crates are wired to blow in under two minutes.

Fourteen minutes left.

"Tango, you have the package?" I hiss on my way back to the front of the house.

"Not yet. Approaching her door now."

Voices come from the courtyard. Angry ones. Along with a woman's cry.

"Take him back to his room. Now," Faruk snarls.

"No. Mateen is hungry. He needs fresh vegetables and fruit like Dr. Joey says. We are going to the kitchen."

"You will do as I say!"

Faruk's wife—Lisette—whimpers, and I stop in my tracks. Her husband punches her in the stomach. She crumples to her knees in the dirt. But he's not done. Faruk kicks her, cursing her in Pashto while the kid wails next to her.

"I should have ended your life years ago! You make him soft!"

Move it. Now.

Twelve minutes to find Ford and get the hell out of here.

"Papa, stop!" Mateen shouts. The asshole's slap sends him to his knees.

Big mistake, fucker. No one hurts a kid on my watch.

I take off at a run, then spring, landing on Faruk's back and wrapping my arm around his throat.

He's got at least six inches on me—and fifty pounds—but I'm scrappy as fuck and twice as mean. When he tries to flip me, I wrap my legs around his torso and squeeze harder.

"Zaman!" His voice doesn't carry. Much. I'm cutting off most of his air. His veins bulge, but he's not going down. Shit. I reach for the knife strapped to my thigh. The angle's bad, and it tumbles to the dirt.

Still on the ground, Lisette looks from her son to me to the blade. Fierce determination darkens her gaze, and she lunges for the weapon.

I slap my free hand against Faruk's ear. It does the trick, disorienting him long enough for her to drive the knife into his fancy leather shoe.

With a roar, he claws at me, missing my eyes but taking a chunk from below my collarbone.

"You...are...dead..." he grunts. His uninjured foot connects with Lisette's shoulder. The sickening *pop* sends me into a rage.

The faces of all the women I've failed to save over the

years flash through my mind so quickly, I don't have time to blink.

I can't reach my gun. Even if I could, the shot would blow any chance we have of getting out of this place alive.

Harder.

I have to pull harder.

Lisette scrambles for Mateen, her left arm hanging uselessly at her side. Faruk stumbles. Sways. His throat bobs under the pressure. His knees hit the ground. With my feet under me, I hold on until he goes limp, then stagger back.

"Fucking piece of shit." Wrenching the knife from the asshole's boot, I check my watch. Ten minutes.

"You are American." Lisette has her good arm around Mateen's shoulders, and stares at me like I'm the Holy Fucking Grail. "Take us with you."

"I can't. We're here for—"

"Dr. Joey." She comes right up to me so we're almost nose-to-nose. Or would be if she were a few inches taller. "If we stay here, my son will die. And my...*husband* will blame me. Please. At least...take Mateen. Give him a chance to live."

In my ear, Trevor hisses, "Are you on your way to Foxtrot?"

"No. There were...complications." I should be moving. Ignoring the tears brimming in Lisette's green eyes. But I can't.

"Get your ass in gear," he says. "We only have one shot at this and we're not leaving a man behind."

I sheath my blade. "You have to find him. I'm too far away. I won't make it before the charges blow. If you can't, he said..."

"I know what he said, but I'm not letting that sadist have him just because you ran into 'complications.' We're heading for him now. Get to the rendezvous point and pray we show up."

Fuck.

At my feet, Faruk groans softly. I could kill him right now. It would be so easy to slit his throat and let him bleed out all over the sand. But the Afghan theater is so fucking fragile, slaying one of its biggest players could start a goddamn war.

"Amir Faruk!" a man shouts from the far end of the compound. I can't see his face, but the Kalashnikov in his hand glints in the moonlight.

This is a bad idea. But if I leave Lisette and her son here, I'll never forgive myself.

I grab the kid, holding him close to my chest as I meet Lisette's panicked gaze. "Come with me if you want to live."

She keeps pace with me as I take off toward the west side of the compound.

"My exit won't exist for another six minutes," I whisper. "You have any idea where we can hide until then?"

"Go left," she says through clenched teeth.

Dammit. A dislocated shoulder is the worst kind of pain. She'll never be able to run if I don't fix it.

We dart behind some sort of outbuilding, and I set the kid on his feet against the wall. "Stand right here, buddy. Don't move, okay?"

Lisette pats her son's shoulder. "Do what he says, *mon chou*. This man works with Dr. Joey."

That's enough for him, thank God, and I turn to his mother. "Do you know how to fire a gun?"

"Yes."

I stare up at the sky. At the canopy of stars twinkling this far from civilization. They're beautiful. One of the only beautiful things about this country.

If Trevor can't find Ford in time, Faruk will kill him. God. If we did all this to get Joey out and the man she loves dies? My ledger will run red with blood.

Five minutes.

Lisette's lips press flat. She's starting to tremble.

"We don't stand a chance if I don't fix that shoulder. But it's gonna hurt."

"I can handle pain." Her eyes are dry. There's nothing in her voice now but determination.

"Cover your mouth. If you scream, we're dead."

She's brave as fuck. Doesn't make a sound when I snap her shoulder back into its socket. But her knees buckle as I step back, and I catch her with an arm around her waist.

"Breathe for me."

After a beat, she straightens. "I will be fine. Give me the gun."

I pull one of my backup pieces from my vest and pass it to her, butt first. "Safety's off. Stick close to me and be ready to run as fast as you can. We're going out the back gate, but there's no cover for two hundred yards, and we'll be exposed."

"You will take Mateen?" Testing the gun's weight in her hands, she locks eyes with me. "He cannot run like other boys. He is sick."

"I know. I'll carry him."

Lisette kneels in front of the boy. "You have to be quiet now, Mateen. We are going with this man—?" She glances up at me.

"Nomar," I whisper.

"Nomar is going to help us. But only if you are very brave. Can you be very brave for me?"

He nods.

"Up you go, buddy. Hold onto my neck and don't let go."

My watch buzzes with the three-minute warning. It takes almost that long to wind our way to the back gate between buildings and stacks of crates five feet high. Shouts come from every direction.

"Who did this?"

"Find the attackers!"

"They took the Amir's son!"

There's no fucking way we're going to survive this.

Twenty feet from the gate, I pull Lisette against me and put my back to the impending explosion. "Cover your ears and close your eyes, Mateen. This is gonna be loud."

The kid's fine, but Lisette yelps—a sound I feel rather than hear with my ears ringing. "Run!" I shout.

The once hard-packed sand shifts under my boots as we race through the busted gate. Loud *pops* pierce the night. Lisette turns and stumbles.

"Don't look back." I grab her arm. My side burns like someone lit it on fire, and I almost drop Mateen. "Fuck!"

Lisette fires two quick shots. "Zaman will kill us. Go. Take my son. I will—"

"Hell no." I shove her in front of me, pointed toward an old, busted Range Rover. "Get behind the car. On the ground. Cover Mateen's head."

She takes the kid's arm and tugs him with her. The AK-47 I stashed in the back seat hours ago is heavier than it should be. Too much blood plasters my tunic to my skin.

The thirty-round magazine empties in seconds. One man goes down. The other's still firing. Until the final charges blow, and screams come from the compound. "You are dead!" the man shouts before turning and racing back through the gate.

CHAPTER TWO

Lisette

THE STOLEN car bounces over what was once a road, but now is little more than a suggestion. I huddle in the front seat, head bowed, hoping no one will recognize me.

In the back, Mateen clutches his little soccer game to his chest while he snores softly.

The man behind the wheel—the one who saved us—swipes at his brow.

Every hour, he looks worse. Weak. Feverish. The harsh scent of blood fills the car.

"You need medical attention."

"I'll live," he grunts.

"You can barely sit up straight. How much longer until we meet up with your friends?"

He checks his watch, blinking hard like he cannot quite focus. "They'll be hours away by now. But we'll stop in ten minutes so I can get comms working."

"We are not meeting them?"

"No."

My eyes burn from lack of sleep. With every breath, my shoulder aches, and I have no idea where in Afghanistan we are. Or where we are going.

"Why not?"

"Safer."

His one-word answers are getting tiresome, but he saved our lives. If I make trouble, he could leave us in the middle of the desert. Without water, without shelter, without any way to survive. We are driving in circles—I think—which means we are not far enough from my *husband* and his men for me to feel safe.

Nowhere is safe. Not from Faruk. He will never let Mateen go.

Tears burn the corners of my eyes. What have I done? He will punish me for this. Severely.

The one time I tried to escape—only weeks after he brought me to Afghanistan—he broke three of my ribs, my right arm, and my collarbone. When I refused to marry him —to sign the marriage certificate in front of the Imam—he sent me to the old well in the middle of the compound for so long, I forgot what it was like to see the sun. Zaman dragged me out of there covered in scorpion stings, delirious with fever.

For this? For taking his son from him?

He will kill me.

After another ten minutes, Nomar pulls the car behind an old stone hut missing half its roof.

"Stay here." He leaves the engine running, goes to the trunk, and rummages around inside.

My heart races, the seconds stretching into what feels like an eternity. I glance back at my sleeping son, then ease the passenger door open. Nomar is on his knees behind the car, trembling.

"Merde!" I try to get him to his feet, but he hisses out a

breath and shakes his head. "You cannot die on us. Let me help you!"

"And do...what? You're...not a doctor."

"My son has an incurable illness and his father *rarely* allowed him to be treated at a hospital. And I have eyes. It is obvious you are losing too much blood."

Dropping down next to him, I pull up his tunic. His black shirt is plastered to his side. If he dies...we will be alone. I cannot let that happen.

"Off with this."

"Not here. Not yet."

"*Zut alors!* Not yet? How much longer do you want to wait?" I unpin my headscarf, the soft, black material sliding through my fingers.

Only the best for the Amir's wife. The best clothes, the best food. The best beatings.

"Get up. Lean against the car."

It takes him three attempts to stand, but when he does, he meets my gaze. His dark eyes are full of pain.

Passing the silky fabric behind his back, I step close enough to scent him. Sweat, blood, but something more. Something comforting and *real*. I have not been this close to another since Faruk took me. He would fly into a rage if I even *looked* at anyone but him. Yet with Nomar, I feel safe in a way I have not felt in more than ten years.

"This will hurt."

"No shit. Do it." Nomar grits his teeth and braces his hands on the trunk.

I pull the headscarf until he groans and his ruddy cheeks pale in the starlight. The knot will hold—for a time—but will it be long enough to get us to safety?

If not, I pray my death will be quick.

Nomar

"We're blown. On the move in five." The call drops before I can end it. Ford has the sat phone and my mobile barely has a single bar. I don't even know if Trev heard me.

How the hell did they find this place? It's little more than a shack on a goat herding trail. From the dust the caravan of vehicles is kicking up a few miles away, Faruk's men are heading right for us.

"Do you have a phone?" I snap. "Hand it over."

"I do not. He would never let me..." Lisette pulls Mateen closer to her, trembling where she sits against one of the crumbling walls.

"Check your pockets. Your clothes. They have to be tracking you or the kid somehow." I angle a glance up the hill. Ten minutes, max, and they'll be on top of us.

"He will never let me go." A sob wells up in her throat. She's about to lose her shit, and that'll put us all in danger.

"Lisette?" I soften my voice. "Faruk's men have been on our tail for hours. We've traded cars twice, and we're not following roads on any map. I need you to check your clothes. Mateen's too."

Reaching for my go bag, I lose my breath and crash into the wall next to them. The fever set in not long after we left the compound, and my whole body aches. If I don't get medical soon, I'll be in a world of hurt.

"Nomar!" Lisette's delicate fingers flutter over my cheeks. "You are burning up."

"I'll live. Unless they find us. Please...check your clothes." Getting up exhausts me, but I have to keep it together or we're all dead.

"*Mon chou*, come here." She drops to her knees and starts running her hands over Mateen's sleeves and down the sides of his little tunic. "Do you have anything in your pockets?"

"Just my rocks, Mama." One after another, the little boy pulls out half a dozen smooth, black rocks. "See?"

"Is that why you weigh so much?" I wink at the kid—as much to distract myself from the pain as to reassure him. "Or is it all those muscles?"

"My muscles! I'm Superman!" He raises his arms over his head, fists clenched like he's about to fly.

"There is nothing in his clothes." Lisette squeezes her loose sleeves, brushes along her neckline, and reaches for the hem of her abaya. "*Merde!*"

"What?" I pop two ibuprofen and take a long swig from my canteen. We need more water. And food. But I can't risk stopping again until I know Faruk won't be able to find us.

"Here." She pulls up her abaya, revealing a pair of loose blue pants underneath the flowing material, and points to her left ankle. "Feel."

Something hard—and smaller than my fingernail—is sewn into the hem. Using my knife, I slice through the fabric and force the piece of plastic into my palm.

"Is that it?"

"We're about to find out." I tuck the tracker into a hole in the wall, then stagger to my feet with a groan. "Let's go. The moon's about to set. If we're lucky, they won't be able to see us until we're close enough to civilization to blend in."

Lisette

"Mama? My head hurts." Mateen rolls over on the blanket and rubs at his eyes. He has been so good since we fled the compound, but he is getting sicker. Nothing I do gives him any relief.

We have been running for more than twenty-four hours.

Three stolen cars, short rests in abandoned houses and once in a tent with four old men. They did not speak to me or Mateen, but gave us bread, rice, and water as we hid from the heat of the day. Nomar paid them. A fat wad of cash from deep inside his duffel bag earned us six hours of refuge. Now, we are on our own again.

The faded paint on the walls of this deserted mosque makes me think it was once a happy place. Bright colors form intricate designs all the way to the ceiling, but rats have devoured most of the prayer books piled in one corner, and the floor is covered in a thick layer of dirt.

After setting tripwires along the outside of the building, Nomar passed out a few feet away. His fever spiked hours ago, and I fear for him if we do not get to his friends—and Dr. Joey—soon.

We are less than two hours from them, but after Nomar almost fell asleep at the wheel, we stopped in this little town to rest until sunrise.

Mateen whines again and rubs his belly. "I don't like it here, Mama."

"We will leave in the morning, *mon chou*. Have some more water." I tip the canteen to my son's lips, but there are only a few drops left.

Next to us, Nomar moans in his sleep, then jerks up with a shout, eyes wide open, gun in hand.

I throw myself over my son. "No!"

Mateen cries out and wriggles under me. "Mama! You are too heavy!"

"Fuck! God. I'm so sorry." The bitter edge to Nomar's voice sends goosebumps racing down my arms. I turn as he pushes up with a grunt and staggers outside. Blood stains the dirty tile floor, shiny in the light from the small lantern next to Mateen's head.

With a heavy sigh, my son flops over onto his side. "When are we going home? Papa will be mad I missed prayers."

Tears prick at my eyes. My heart cracks into a thousand pieces. Mateen is a smart boy. He knows Faruk hurts me. But, like any son, he wants to please his father more than anything. How do I tell him we are never going home again? Will he forgive me for taking him from all he has ever known?

His eyelids flutter closed before I can answer him. With trembling fingers, I brush the soft curls from his clammy forehead. Dr. Joey was treating him twice a day, but even if we find her tomorrow, with his body so weak, will she be able to do anything for him?

I have to believe she will. Otherwise, I will not be able to go on.

Saying a silent prayer to the God of my youth—the one I was forbidden to pray to or even speak of once Faruk took me —I press a kiss to Mateen's temple, then tiptoe out of the makeshift shelter to find the man who saved us.

I do not have to go far. Nomar sits against the crumbling facade, gun in hand. He scans the street, his eyes never still. An engine thrums in the distance, getting closer. I drop to my knees, out of sight behind a low stone wall surrounding the old mosque. The vehicle passes, the sweet scent of tobacco lingering in its wake.

"Come back inside," I say quietly when the old sedan turns the corner and disappears. "You need to rest."

"Safer for you and the kid if I stay here."

"I do not believe that." My entire body aches as I sink down next to him. "You are exhausted, Nomar. Your wound is infected, and I am worried about you."

"I've had worse."

"*Mon Dieu.* Where? When?"

With a heavy sigh, he lets his head fall back against the

wall and stares up at the glittering expanse of stars stretching all the way to the horizon. "We'd be here until dawn if I told you about all the times I've almost died."

I use my sleeve to dab at the sweat beading along his forehead. He touches my wrist briefly, like he is not sure I am real. "Is your job that dangerous? Or are you not very good at it?"

His chuckle reassures me. He still has his faculties. His sense of humor. But for how long?

"I'm the guy they send in when shit goes sideways. I go in alone. No team. No support."

"But you were not alone when you came for Dr. Joey..."

Nomar winces as he leans forward and watches a dog trot down the center of the road. "I retired five days ago. Should have been stateside by now. But Ford—he and Joey were a thing twenty years ago—called me when she went missing and asked for my help. He brought Trevor with him, though I've worked with the guy before. He used to be CIA, and we had a couple of ops together."

We sit in silence for several minutes, close enough I can feel the heat rolling off him. It has been ten years since I have been able to sit in comfortable silence with a man. Since I have not been afraid of saying the wrong thing. In the wrong way. At the wrong time.

I want to ask about his job. His skills. The way he carries himself—like there is nothing he fears—and how he managed to get into Faruk's compound in the first place.

But I also want him to rest so that in the morning, he can keep us safe until we meet up with Ford, Joey, and Trevor.

"I can't let myself sleep, Lisette," he finally says, his words so quiet, I strain to hear them. "I pointed a gun at a six-year-old boy because this fucking fever made it too hard to understand I was having a goddamn nightmare."

"You stopped yourself."

"What if next time, I can't? You asked me to make sure Mateen *lived*. The only way I can do that is if I stay awake."

I lay my fingers over his hand—the one *not* holding a weapon—and squeeze gently. "Come lie down. Give me the gun. I can stay up. If I hear or see anything, I will wake you."

Nomar checks his watch, and from the way he sighs and the set of his shoulders, I think I have convinced him.

But when he tries to get to his feet, he groans and his back hits the wall of the mosque.

"*Merde.* Let me help you."

His one-armed embrace is born of necessity, not desire, but it makes me feel more alive than I have in a decade. He does not hide his pain, or how difficult each step is, but we make it back inside and I lower him down to the floor.

"Dizzy," he whispers. "Need to leave...at sunrise." His fingers find mine, and he holds on tight. "Can't be...late or... they'll leave...without us."

"I will wake you." For a moment, he stares at me so desperately, the world stops, and it is just the two of us on this dirty floor. Until he shudders and his grip goes slack. "Please, hold on for me," I murmur. Leaning closer, I press my lips to the back of his hand. His skin is clammy and his breathing shallow. "Mateen needs you. And so do I."

CHAPTER THREE

Nomar

"You are too sick to drive," Lisette says after settling a barely conscious Mateen in the back seat.

She's right, but we're heading into a Taliban hotbed. If anyone sees a woman behind the wheel, we're fucked. "It's two hours. I'll make it."

Her green eyes narrow. "*Merde.* Why will you not let me help you? I know the risks, Nomar. I can cover my hair. Do you have a hat? Or I can tear material from my abaya."

"No." Pointing to the back seat, I grit my teeth as a spasm of pure agony racks my torso. "Mateen needs you. If he throws up again…"

The poor kid vomited only minutes after trying a bite of one of my protein bars, and there's a sickly sweet scent oozing from his pores. I don't know what's wrong, but it's serious.

"And you could pass out and crash the car."

"I won't. I know my limits, Lisette. Get in." Every minute we spend arguing is one I might not have before my body gives up completely. We have to drive through half of Mazar-i-Sharif to reach the safe house or I might have let her take the wheel.

The engine protests as I turn the key. This old compact is a piece of shit, but it had almost a full tank of gas when I boosted it yesterday afternoon.

"Keep it together," I whisper, patting the dashboard. I don't know if I'm talking to the car or to myself—or both.

CITIES ARE UNIVERSAL. Crime. Poverty. Drugs. Then rich, opulent areas with luxury cars, gleaming storefronts, and the ability to disappear. For a price.

Every kilometer ratchets up the tension in the car. Lisette holds Mateen close, rocking him gently and singing to him—*Au Clair de la Lune*, I think. I only catch a few words here and there over the sound of the engine.

I meet her gaze in the rearview mirror. Fuck. She's terrified. "We're almost there. Mateen's going to be okay." I don't think she believes me.

Less than five minutes later, I pull the car into an alley.

Trev's boss hooked us up with this safe house. A two-bedroom apartment with a private garage and only one other tenant in the building. If I were alone, I'd waltz right up to the front door. But with Lisette and the kid...that's a bad fucking idea. Even in this neighborhood.

There's no one around so early in the morning, but the smells of cooking waft through the air as I brace my body against the trunk and reach for my duffel bag. The damn thing feels like it weighs two hundred pounds, and I almost drop it twice before I sling it over my shoulder.

Lisette tries to pull Mateen from the back seat, but the little boy whines in protest. "*Mon bébé*, I need you to help me now. Please. We are going to see Dr. Joey."

"Nuh-huh," he says loudly. Lisette begs him again, but he's not having any of it.

"I'll take him." I wrap my fingers around her upper arm, and she flinches.

Shit.

She's bruised everywhere, dumbass. Be careful.

A wave of dizziness hits me, and I lean against the rear quarter panel.

Lisette narrows her eyes at me. "Can you even stand without assistance?"

"No. But I won't drop him. I promise." Having a purpose is the only way I'll make it inside. It's how I managed to get us here. How I've managed to keep us safe for two days.

I give Lisette the duffel bag, then scoop Mateen out of the back seat and kick the door closed. The motion almost sends me to my knees.

"Stick close." Each word is harder than the last. When we reach the front of the building, I grit out, "Need you to get the radio. Trev...won't let us in...without the code."

She fishes the handheld device out of the duffel bag, holds it close to my lips, and presses the button.

"Open the damn door," I manage.

Ford's voice is the best fucking thing I've ever heard. "Authentication code: Nine-Seven-Alpha-Oscar."

"Foxtrot-Charlie."

The locks disengage seconds before my vision tunnels. Lisette's firm grip on my arm is all that keeps me upright as she ushers me inside.

"Oh, my God," Joey cries. "Mateen!"

I'm shaking, but Lisette hasn't let go, and I lean against her while the doctor checks the kid's eyes, then leans down and sniffs him. "Lisette, why didn't you tell me he was diabetic?"

"He isn't. But last night, he started to complain that everything hurt. And now..." She shakes against me, her voice weak and trembling.

"He's in ketoacidosis. His liver is malfunctioning. That's why he smells like a bottle of rotten perfume. Mateen? Do you remember me, kiddo?"

"Dr. Joey," he says softly and turns his head into my chest. "Nomar? Can we go home?"

After all I've seen—all I've done—these past twenty years, I didn't think anything could touch me. But a six-year-old kid's desperation is enough to crack my heart into pieces.

"Get him onto the couch." Joey points halfway across the room, but I can't focus. All I see is a patch of brown in the middle of a sea of beige.

"Nomar, please..." Lisette's whisper close to my ear—and her grip on my arm—urge me forward until my shins hit the cushions.

Once I lay Mateen on the sofa, I blink hard, searching for somewhere I can rest.

The fucking room tilts on its axis and my knees wobble. Joey says something, but my heartbeat is so loud, she sounds like some demented *Peanuts* character. Lisette isn't holding onto me anymore. I stumble. My fingers close around the back of a chair.

"Trev!" Ford shouts. "Get the fuck out here. Now!"

The last pinpricks of light fade away, and I fall.

Lisette

I tug at my abaya, helpless to do anything for Mateen *or* Nomar.

"What happened?" Ford asks.

"He was shot. By Zaman as we were fleeing the

compound. But he would not let me do anything to help him. We had to keep moving. I used my headscarf to tie around the wound. He kept us safe. Two days, he kept us safe."

Another man bursts into the room, wild eyes and hair sticking up at all angles. I stifle my yelp as he growls, "What the hell is this? We're not running an escape train here. Our mission was Joey, Ivy, and Mia."

"Shut the fuck up," Ford says as he lifts Nomar's shirt. "Joey, it's bad."

There is so much blood. More than one man should be able to lose, I think. If he dies after everything he did for us… Silent tears stream down my cheeks.

"Lisette? Can you get Mateen some water?" Dr. Joey asks, then kneels next to Ford. "Nomar? Tell us what happened, okay? You need to keep talking."

"I...had to," he whispers. "Saw them...as I was...trying to escape. Faruk was...wailing on her."

Dr. Joey presses on his side, right above his wound. The other man—Trevor—brings a first aid kit in from the next room, and she pulls out...tweezers? *Merde.* She cannot...?

"This is going to hurt. A lot," she says as she unbuckles his belt, folds it in half, and offers it to him. "Bite down."

She is so efficient. So fearless. I could never be that brave. Retrieving a glass of water for Mateen, I crouch by his side and try to get him to take a few sips.

The harsh scent of vodka mixes with blood in the small living room. Nomar screams, but the belt muffles the worst of it.

"Good. Just one more thing, and then you can rest." Joey turns to Ford. "Hold his shoulders. He needs to be very, very still."

I cannot watch Joey dig the bullet out of his body. So I focus on my son. He is crying now, and I gather him in my arms. "Shhh. It is all right, *mon bébé*. Nomar will be fine. So will you."

"Got it," Joey says, holding up the tiny piece of metal. "We have to get both of them to a hospital. Mateen needs insulin and chelation. Nomar...I'm not a surgeon. Even if I were, this isn't the place. But now that the bullet's out, as long as we can keep his fever down and stop the infection from getting worse, he should make it."

Relief sends a shudder through me, and I swipe at my wet cheeks. "Nomar saved our lives. He picked up Mateen and told me to come with him if we wanted to live."

"Seriously? He pulled a Terminator on you?" Ford asks.

"A what?"

"Sorry. It's...a movie thing. I'm Ford, by the way. Joey's... um..."

"Fiancé," she says, getting to her feet and wiping her bloody hands on the towel Trevor offers her. "Pack up, Marine. We need to get Nomar and Mateen to a hospital. As quickly as possible. Or we could lose both of them."

I clutch my son close to my chest. Did I make a mistake when I begged Nomar to free us from our desert prison? Would Mateen have been better off with his father?

As Ford, Joey, and Trevor spring into motion, grabbing bags, bottles of water, and weapons, I stare out the window at the bright blue sky.

A pair of birds soar toward the horizon, moving almost as one.

No. Whatever happens now, Mateen and I will be free.

I JERK AWAKE FROM A NIGHTMARE. One in which Faruk could not see past his own prejudices and self-righteousness to *ever* take Mateen to a hospital. Or listen to the advice of the doctors he threatened or paid off.

But this nightmare was very real. One I lived every day.

My entire body aches, I am exhausted and hungry, but my son is sleeping peacefully. Nomar, though... He needed a transfusion, and his heart stopped. But he is stable. For now.

This tiny medical clinic in the middle of nowhere is not well staffed, but we are in a private room, with Ford and Trevor taking turns on watch. At dusk, we will head for a boat that will take us to Uzbekistan.

Ford and Trevor believe all will be well once we reach the hospital in Qarshi. That Mateen will get the help he needs. But without a bone marrow transplant, this disease will kill him.

"Lisette?" Trevor pockets his phone and pulls up a chair next to mine. He keeps his voice low so he does not wake Mateen. Or Joey. "My boss got in touch with your family. Your sister, Noele, will meet us in Qarshi."

"Noele? *Mon Dieu.* I never..." A sob wells up in my throat. My little Noele. I have not seen her since she was fifteen. All freckles and braces. She will be an adult now. Grown with a career. Or a husband. Or both.

Trevor passes me a tissue, and I dab at my eyes. I can only imagine what Noele looks like now. Tall? Like our mother? A full head of raven black hair? But her eyes...we have the same eyes.

"Thank you," I whisper and throw my arms around him. Touching another man should feel wrong, and Trevor does not move. I am not even sure he breathes for a full minute until he pats my back twice and pulls away.

"Your parents wanted to come, but there aren't any direct flights from Paris to Qarshi. Noele has twenty hours of travel ahead of her. When we get you and Mateen to Boston—"

"Boston?"

"Shit. I thought Joey would have told you. She works at St. Jude's. With kids. They have the largest bone marrow donor database in the world. If there's a match out there for Mateen, she'll find it." He stifles a groan as he pushes to his feet. "We leave for Uzbekistan in an hour. Get Mateen ready. This is almost over."

CHAPTER FOUR

Lisette

"You should get some sleep," the nurse, a slight woman named Anora, says as she replaces the bag of fluid hooked up to Mateen's IV.

The narrow cot the hospital staff set up against the window beckons me. For two days, I have barely slept. Constantly worried about Mateen. About Nomar. About Faruk finding us.

I tear my gaze away from the pillow and focus on my son.

"I cannot. If he wakes, he will not understand where we are and why his...his *father* is not here."

The nurse peers down at me, touches my chin, and tuts softly at my black eye. "He will understand. And you will not be far away."

Tears lend a soft glow to the room. "Maybe...later."

"A shower, then? You must want to change out of...*that.*" She gestures to my ripped and stained abaya.

The stale scents of sweat, blood, and vomit cling to me. Anora is being...delicate. She could have told me I stink.

I glance back at the door. Two guards stand outside—courtesy of Ford and Trevor's boss. We are safe here, Ford says. But...are we?

"You will stay with Mateen? I will be quick."

Anora pulls up a chair next to Mateen's bed and offers me a gentle smile. "Take your time."

In the small bathroom, I strip out of my abaya and turn away from the mirror. I refused to let the doctor examine me. My shoulder is swollen and tender, but no one needs to see the evidence of a decade of Faruk's cruelty.

I will heal. I always do.

The water runs brown at my feet as I let the spray soak into my long locks. I should have asked Anora for a pair of scissors. Faruk never let me cut my hair, and I hate it.

But as I spill shampoo into my palm, I shove the thought away. My needs can wait until my son is far from Afghanistan. Back in France—or in Boston, I suppose—with a new name. Somewhere his father will never find him.

How am I supposed to tell him he has to be...*someone else*? Matthew? Mattie? Marcus?

And what about *my* name? How can Lisette Moreau disappear if Noele Moreau does not? If Jacques and Anna Moreau can be found as easily as Ford's boss found them?

By the time I wrap a towel around my body, my worries have consumed my every thought. I am no good to Mateen if I cannot calm down. But without answers...

The new clothes feel like heaven against my skin. The long, flowing dress covers my ankles—even in Uzbekistan, women must dress modestly—but leaves my forearms bare, and it is so freeing to go without a headscarf, a small smile curves my lips until all my worries take over again.

I do not know how Trevor managed to get all the right sizes, but even the tennis shoes fit.

Anora has a magazine in her hands when I emerge from

the bathroom. "You look so much better!" she says, keeping her voice low.

"I am certain I smell better, at least." Too nervous and tense to sit with my son, I move to the window. The city lights twinkle across a large expanse of darkness—a river runs next to the hospital—and the whisper of freedom tickles my panicked thoughts. Along with the face of the man who brought us here.

"Where is Nomar?" I ask, turning with the sudden need to know if our rescuer is all right. "The man who came with us. He had been shot."

"Oh! The handsome one?" Anora's cheeks flush crimson and she grins at me. "I...am not allowed to tell you. Hospital policy."

"Please." I twist my fingers together, two of my knuckles cracking and sending little jolts into my palms. "He saved us. I have to know how he is. Mateen will ask when he wakes up."

Anora glances down at my son. A pang of guilt tightens my throat. I have no idea if he will ask about Nomar. He was so sick, I cannot even be certain he remembers the man's name. But in this moment, I need to speak with Nomar more than I need anything else.

"If I decided to go for a walk—down the hall—would you suggest I go left or right?"

The nurse's eyes narrow. "Right. But...do not go past room 247." She checks her watch. "I can give you another fifteen minutes. After that, I must check on my other patients."

"Thank you." I want to hug her. But instead, I reach out and squeeze her hand. "If Mateen wakes up—"

"I will come for you."

Nomar

Every time I move, another one of the wires and tubes attached to my body catches on *something*.

I don't remember much of the past thirty-six hours. Pain. Gentle hands on my face. Lisette calling my name. Ford and Trevor carrying me. The rocking of a boat. Someone yelling at me to breathe.

Trev stopped by a couple of hours ago. Told me to rest up. That Lisette and Mateen were safe. He, Ford, and Joey are spending the night at a JSOC apartment building with more security than the White House, full amenities, and a goddamn concierge. By the end of the day tomorrow, they'll be on their way back to Boston, but the doctor won't spring me until the end of the week. Something about the bullet almost nicking my liver and the raging infection that followed.

At least this hospital room is halfway decent. If it weren't dark outside, I'd even have a view.

I close my eyes and tug the blanket higher. The sheet skims over my piercings, sending goosebumps rising along my arms. In the field, I don't notice them. But here...with nothing else to distract me...

It's been too fucking long since anyone but me saw them. Or cared about them.

Dragging my hand down my chest, I flick one of the heavy gauge nipple barbs. My fever broke, but my skin is still ultra sensitive, and my dick twitches in response.

With my eyes closed, I try to call up the memory of the last woman I slept with. We weren't an item. Hell, we'd only known each other three days. But the night we shared was the stuff fantasies are made of.

So why is Lisette's face the only one I see?

"Fuuuuuck."

"Nomar?" Her voice sends me jerking up. The stitches in my side pull taut, and I hiss out a breath. "Are you all right?"

Pinpricks of light hide her face as I try to calm my racing heart. When they finally fade, she's standing next to the bed, concern drawing her brows together in such a way, I'd reach up to smooth away the furrow if not for all these damn wires.

If she'd been five minutes later, the sight she would have seen... I bend my left leg, hoping she won't notice the tent in the blanket.

"I...wasn't expecting visitors."

Her cheeks tinge pink. Damp hair falls over her shoulders, all the way down to her elbows. Several old scars dot the pale skin of her arms, and deep finger bruises peek out from under the sleeve of her dress.

"Mateen is sleeping. No one would tell me how you were." Lisette drags a hard plastic chair close to the bed and sits, her hands clasped in her lap.

"He's not alone, is he?" She flinches at the harsh edge to my words. "Trevor was supposed to arrange for guards—"

"He did. And the nurse is with him." Her back is so straight and stiff, and she won't meet my gaze now. "I should not have come."

"Wait." I'm too damn weak to do more than brush her fingers, but the touch relaxes her enough to flick her eyes to mine for a single moment. "I'm sorry. I didn't mean to snap at you. I'd blame the morphine, but..." I shrug, "Really, I'm an asshole."

Her laugh does more for me than any drug. Warmth settles in my chest. Even the stitches don't hurt anymore.

"An 'asshole' would not have stopped Faruk from hurting me. Or put his life in danger to save us," she says softly. "And you are right to worry. Mateen will not be safe until his father is dead. I...a part of me wishes you would have—"

I squeeze her hand. "Amir Abdul Faruk is one of the

richest and most powerful men in Afghanistan. His death would have started a war. I couldn't risk it."

"What is one more war in a country full of them?" Tears shimmer in her eyes. "Mateen has a chance to grow up because of you. But we will have to hide...forever."

For a full minute, I scramble for something—*anything*—I can say to comfort her. But she's right. Afghanistan is so fucking patriarchal, if Faruk *doesn't* get his son back, he'll lose the respect of his men. And once that's gone, so is his empire.

"The mission to rescue Joey was—is—illegal as fuck, Lisette. We had to get in and out fast. If anyone in the United States or the Afghan government found out what we were planning—what we *did*—we'd *all* end up in some black site where we'd never be heard from again. But if we'd had any idea what he was doing to you..."

A single tear tumbles down her cheek, landing on the back of my hand. "My family must have looked for me, yes? I was only supposed to be gone for two days. Not...ten years. Faruk said he wanted to take me to Morocco for a film festival. But once we were in the air, he told me we were going to Afghanistan. And that I would never see my family again."

All the women I've saved in my career, and I'm still shit at this part of the job. At comfort and reassurance. At restoring a sense of safety. I'd give anything to go back ten years and stop that asshole from ever touching her.

"We should have known. And I should have slit his throat while I had the chance. Damn the consequences."

A SHAFT of sunlight angles through the window, warming my legs. I couldn't sleep a wink after Lisette left. I wanted to go after her. To promise she and Mateen would always be safe.

But I can barely manage to take a piss by myself. And this hospital gown leaves nothing to the imagination.

The door to my room opens with a bang, and Ford stalks in.

"'Bout time, asshole," I say when he drops into the chair. "You couldn't have brought me some clothes? Or a coffee?"

"You were unconscious last time I checked. Cut me some fucking slack."

Something's up his ass in a big way. Is it Joey? Or me? He won't meet my gaze, so I'm betting it's me.

"I screwed up, man. I put everyone in danger by grabbing Lisette and the kid."

Ford flops back and runs a hand through his hair. "I would have done the same thing. Though...weren't *you* supposed to be the one getting me out of that damn basement?"

"Fuck..."

He chuckles, but stress lends a raspy quality to the sound. "Your loss was my gain. Joey got to half carry my ass out of there."

"We should have known about her, Ford. About what he was doing to her. Lisette and Mateen should have been part of the plan from the get-go."

"You almost died." Exhaustion makes him look so much older than his forty-eight years. "There was no way we could have planned a triple rescue with only three people. Ryker would have gotten involved and there'd be a hole the size of Boston in the Afghan countryside."

"But Faruk would be dead. Lisette, Mateen, *and* Joey would be a hell of a lot safer because of it."

Anger flashes in Ford's eyes. "Don't you think I know that? Trev's been on the phone with Dax all morning. Faruk won't get his hands on any of them ever again."

He's so certain. I can't blame him. Dax Holloway is a

legend. He and Ryker McCabe survived more than fifteen months of torture in the Taliban's most notorious prison—Hell Mountain. Then escaped and blew the fucking place off the map. They've been doing their damnedest to save people ever since.

If anyone can protect Lisette and Mateen, it's Dax.

Ford checks his watch. "Do you have the video surveillance you took of the compound? Wren wants to run any faces through her software. She'll watch the airports—both in Boston and France—for any sign Faruk's on the move and coming after his son or Joey."

I raise the bed a little more, but when I try to sit up, the room starts to spin. Fuck. The morphine's wearing off in a big way. "My bag's hidden under the corner of the mattress. Get it for me?"

Ford passes me the oilskin pouch. With the IV taped to my left hand, it's awkward as fuck to unzip the damn thing, but I pull out a small data card. "This should have everything you need. Video from my initial recon and from when we broke Joey out."

He nods and tucks the card into his wallet. "Thanks, man. When are they springing you?"

I shift in the narrow bed, then hiss out a breath. "Three or four days. Total bullshit. I've had paper cuts worse than this."

Throwing his head back, Ford laughs hard enough to shake the chair. "You need to get out of the field. It's warping your mind."

No shit.

"Listen, you think there might be some work for me at Second Sight? Never gave much thought to what I'd do after this. But...seeing Lisette's face when I told her I was taking her with me..." I rub my chin, staring out the window at the horizon. It's beautiful. In a desolate, dry, unemotional sort of way. The kind of beauty you'd appreciate if you weren't neck deep in the worst of humanity. "I want to help people, Ford. But hell if I can do it in this part of the world anymore."

Ford claps me on the shoulder, squeezing once before he straightens. "Normally, I'd run a new hire by Dax. But pretty sure he'd be thrilled to have you join the team. Call me when you get back to the States, and we'll make it official."

CHAPTER FIVE

Lisette

Mateen pushes the fruit around in the bowl. "I want mantu. Oranges are gross."

The beef and onion dumplings have been his favorite food for a year. My heart aches knowing the heavy breakfast was only making him sicker.

"Oranges are good for you. Remember what Dr. Joey said? You need them to grow up big and strong. The nurse promised if you ate all your fruit, she would bring you sugar-free pudding for lunch. Chocolate."

The mention of the forbidden treat—Faruk rarely allowed us anything decadent or foreign—has him spearing the tiny piece of citrus and shoving it into his mouth with all the speed a six-year-old can muster.

"Chew, *mon bébé.*"

Smoothing my hands down my thighs, I savor the feel of denim under my fingers even as I worry someone will burst in and demand I cover my hair. Or beat me for my bare forearms.

A brisk knock sends me lurching to my feet, panicked, until I see Trevor through the small window in the door. He motions for me to join him in the hall, and I nod.

"I need to talk to Dr. Joey's friend. You can play games until I come back. Then we will work on your letters, *oui*?"

He wrinkles his nose, but the moment I hand him the little gaming system, he forgets all about the threat of lessons.

Worry keeps my eyes pinned to the floor as I slip into the hall. Until a shriek comes from behind Trevor.

"Lisette!" My sister throws her arms around me, holding me so tightly against her, my shoulder and ribs send shooting pains down my back. "I did not believe it. Not until now. *Ma belle. Ne nous quitte plus jamais!*"

Never leave us again.

"I will not, Noele. I promise." It has been so long since I spoke French—since I was *allowed* to speak French—I wonder if I still can.

Tears swim in my eyes as I meet Trevor's gaze over my sister's shoulder. "*Thank you,*" I mouth. He grins, then pulls his phone from his pocket, ambling down the hall and giving us some privacy.

I hope I can keep that promise. But until we are far away from Afghanistan, we are still in danger. Even then... Faruk has more money than anyone I have ever known. Enough to charter private planes, pay off the police, and make us disappear.

"When that man called—the one from Boston?—I could not believe it. Maman and Papa...they cried the entire time I was packing." Noele draws back, holding me at arm's length and looking me up and down before she skims her fingers along my cheek. "Your...*husband* did this to you? Oh, Lisette. Why did you stay with him?"

I shy away from her touch. Can she be this naive? To think I had a choice? The woman in front of me is all grown up. Twenty-five years old. Poised. Confident. Beautiful. I remember that age. Until Faruk stole me away, I thought the world was kind and good. But I was so very wrong.

"Please, Noele. I know you must have questions. But I have to be strong for my son. He almost died when we escaped. Until he gets a bone marrow transplant—"

Noele gasps. "A transplant? What is wrong with him?"

Suddenly exhausted, I lean against the wall for support. "He has Alpha Thalassemia. It causes severe anemia. His father refused to allow any doctor to see him for years. We had to give him blood transfusions weekly. But now...even that is not enough."

"*Mon Dieu.* Why would his own father not want him treated?" Noele peers around me, her eyes shimmering when she catches sight of Mateen through the little window.

"Transplants are forbidden here," I say, my gaze pinned to the floor. "But even once we get to Boston, I am not a match for Mateen."

My little sister takes my hand, squeezing gently. "I am family. Maman and Papa too. One of my friends at school had leukemia. Everyone in the class was tested. Can the doctors in Boston access those records?"

The briefest spark of hope flares to life in my heart. "I do not know. Maybe? When Mateen's doctor comes by, we will ask." I brush away a single tear and pull her closer. "I missed you so much, *mon petite fleur.*"

"I am taller than you are," she teases. "Maybe I should be *grande fleur* now?"

"No! You will always be *petite* to me." It feels so strange to laugh. To smile unbidden. For ten years, I lived in fear. But even though I will worry for the rest of my life, today, I am free. "Wait here? I must talk to Mateen for a moment, and then you can meet your nephew."

When I slip back into the room, Mateen waves the little gaming system over his head. "Mama! I got four goals!"

"Four?" I cover my mouth with my hand, my brows shooting up. *"Mon Dieu.* Such skill. One day, you will score four goals on a *real* field."

His lower lip juts out and he stares at the game. "Papa would not like that. He wants me to be like him."

Anger and sorrow battle in my heart. "We do not live with Papa any more, Mateen. If you want to play football, you will play football. Or paint. Or be a doctor. Anything. And when you get better, you can have chocolate every week."

His eyes go wide. "Really?"

"Yes. Every week." I lean down and brush a kiss to his forehead. "But right now, there is someone outside who wants to meet you. Can I bring her in?"

Mateen nods, but his little body tenses under the blankets. He has been so brave, but every child has his breaking point. He knows nothing of my family. Of his *grand-maman* and *grand-papa*. Of France. Faruk forbade me from speaking French at all, though I managed to teach Mateen a few words here and there.

I wave Noele in, then take her hand and lead her closer to the bed. "Mateen, this is your aunt. *Tante* Noele."

She crouches down and smiles at my son. "You are so big! Your *grand-maman* will weep with joy when she sees your beautiful curly hair."

He burrows deeper under the blankets, pulling them up to his chin.

I want nothing more than to hug Noele and never let her go. But instead, I slide a hip onto the mattress and gather my son as close as all the wires and sensors allow. *"Mon bébé,* you have been so good for me the past few days. I know you are scared, but Noele is my sister. She is family."

"What about Papa?" Mateen asks. "He is family too."

My fingers shake as I trace the swelling under my right eye. "He hurt me, Mateen. All the time."

His big eyes water. He's solemn when he whispers, "I know, Mama."

Guilt curves my shoulders, and I touch my forehead to his. "Papa is staying in Afghanistan, but we are taking a big plane across the ocean tonight. Somewhere the doctors can make you better and no one will ever hurt us again, okay?"

Mateen considers for a moment, his lower lip wobbling. "Okay."

NOELE HAS NOT STOPPED TALKING since she sat down. I think she wants to tell me *everything* that has happened since I disappeared. Before lunch. "Maman and Papa hired a private investigator. He even went to Afghanistan to look for you. But he never found you. The *Direction Générale de la Sécurité Intérieure* said he was the best." She huffs out a breath. "Did your *husband* pay him off or something? God. He was a bastard, yes? Why did you go to Afghanistan with him in the first place?"

If I told her the truth, would she believe me? That Faruk tricked me into getting on that plane. That he locked me away in the middle of the desert with no hope of escape. That he beat me and starved me and threatened me until my spirit was broken. That every day I feared he would snap and kill me.

"Lisette?" She touches my arm, her big green eyes bloodshot, no doubt from the twenty-hours she spent on planes to get here from Marseille. "Did you hear me?"

"Je suis désolée." The apology tumbles from my lips

without thought. *How can she think this is a good time to talk about what Faruk did to me? With Mateen so close?* "He does not need to hear this, Noele. Please." The words wobble and catch in my throat. I cannot cry. Faruk punished me for my tears. But now that I am free, it is all I want to do. I am afraid if I start, I may not ever be able to stop.

"Oh." Noele sits back. Her eyes flick to Mateen. His full lips are twisted into a frown as he frantically jabs the buttons on his game. "Then I will tell you what you have missed. Papa retired six years ago. Maman had to take up bridge to get out of the house every day. He wanted to talk to her nonstop."

I laugh, picturing my mother and father bickering about the dishes or whose turn it is to buy scones at the market. Such mundane things, but still, I am enraptured at the thought.

A brisk knock startles us both, and a dark-haired man enters the room. "Starfire."

The code word calms my racing heart. Trevor assured me every one of the guards would use it so we would know they had no ill intent. After the man finishes his security check, he leaves us, and Dr. Joey peeks her head in. "How's my favorite patient?"

Throwing my arms around her, I hold on for so long, Dr. Joey pats my back and pulls away with a nervous smile.

I step aside and gesture to my sister. "I am so happy you could come. This is Noele."

The two embrace, and Noele kisses her on each cheek. "I owe you a debt I can never repay. We had given up hope. Maman and Papa cannot wait to meet their grandson."

A blush creeps up Joey's cheeks. "You don't owe me anything. Except maybe pictures once in a while? Of Mateen growing up big and strong?"

The two exchange email addresses, and Joey eases a hip

onto the edge of Mateen's bed. "Football again? Who's winning?" she asks.

"I am! Want to play?"

One of the machines beeps twice, then hisses as it delivers a small dose of fast-acting insulin through the pump attached to my son's side.

"Okay, kiddo. One match, and then I have to go. But I'll see you in Boston in a day or two."

With a pout that will certainly break many hearts one day, Mateen passes her the game. The two giggle and laugh as Joey tries to get her player to do what she wants, and I sit back, a soft smile curving my lips.

The moment would be perfect if Mateen were not still so sick. If we were in a flat above a bakery on Rue du Panier. If I knew Faruk would never find us.

Noele yawns. "I am going to the café for a coffee. Lisette, would you like one?"

"No. I do not drink—" What am I saying? In France, I loved coffee. I *do* drink it. Freedom tastes like *cafe au lait*, and I will have as much of it as I wish. "Yes, please. With milk."

The small step toward reclaiming a piece of the woman I used to be makes me smile, but I am so tired. By the time I returned from Nomar's room, it was after 3:00 a.m., and while I tried to sleep on the cot, the hospital is not a quiet place.

I close my eyes, listening to my son babbling happily. Dr. Joey should hate us. Faruk had her friends killed. Zaman locked her in a small box and smuggled her across the border to Afghanistan. When I first met her—only five days ago—she was bruised from head to toe. Yet, she cares for Mateen. And I think...for me too.

It has been so long since I had a friend. Maybe—

The door hits the wall behind me. I jump up as Mateen's doctor stumbles into the room.

Behind him, cold, black eyes lock onto me.

"Zaman..." I can barely force the word from my lips. Fear tightens a vise grip around my chest. He slams the butt of his gun into Dr. Simms's head, and the doctor collapses to the polished floor.

The scent of blood mixes with antiseptic, burning my nose. Joey makes a tiny, choked sound.

"I know there are American security personnel in the hall," Zaman says, pinning me with his glare. "If you alert them, I will kill the doctor. And we will wait right here for your sister to return so I can have my way with her."

I cannot move. He is the worst of Faruk's men. The biggest. The meanest. He will follow through on his threats.

"You are *not* going to hurt them again," Joey says, stepping in front of me. Mateen whimpers and pulls the blankets over his head.

The sickening sound of the gun hitting Joey's cheek brings tears to my eyes. She slides to the floor next to the doctor and curls in on herself with a small sob.

"We will not go back with you." I straighten my shoulders, hoping if I *look* brave, I will feel something other than terror. "My son will not grow up like his father."

He lunges for me. My scream dies when his fingers dig into my throat. "Amir Faruk was very clear. The boy and the doctor are my priority. You...are expendable."

Two men rush into the room, guns drawn. "Let her go!" one of them barks.

A wave of relief washes over me. Zaman cannot fight them both. But I hear a strange sound. Almost a *plink*. Then a second. A hint of hot air. The men collapse. All hope vanishes when I stare down at the blackened hole where the taller one's left eye used to be.

Mateen is crying now. I cannot even speak to comfort him.

"Wait!" Joey staggers to her feet, sways, and braces herself against the bed. "I'll go with you. Me and Mateen. I won't fight or scream as long as you don't hurt Lisette."

I struggle against Zaman's hold. My breath wheezes in my chest. How can she betray us like this?

Joey holds up her hands. She stares between me and the doctor on the floor. Once. Twice. Long, meaningful looks. I follow her gaze to see the man peering up at her before he closes his eyes again.

Is this a ruse? Some plan I cannot figure out?

"No one else has to die," she says. "Let me unhook Mateen's monitors and IV the right way. Otherwise, he won't survive the journey back to Afghanistan."

Zaman's fingers flex against my windpipe. I have to fight not to cry.

"Lisette, I'm so sorry," Joey whispers. "But think of Noele. She's just down the hall, remember? Visiting that man in two-four-seven? If she hears us and comes back in..."

Two-four-seven. Nomar's room. Is Ford here too? And Trevor? I flick my gaze back to the doctor. He gives Joey a barely imperceptible nod. That is what she was trying to tell me. He will find Nomar if Zaman leaves the room. If *we* leave the room with him.

I sag in Zaman's grip. Mateen needs me. If we can delay long enough, someone will find us.

"Ready him. Now. You have one minute," Zaman snaps. He shifts his hold to the back of my neck. Swallowing hurts, but I can breathe again.

Joey turns to my son and starts removing his IV. "You have to be very quiet now, Mateen. We're going for a ride. Do you understand?"

He stares up at me, confusion in his brown eyes. "I want to stay here. Mama, you said—"

"I know, baby. Hush now and listen to Dr. Joey. Everything will be okay."

I can only watch as Joey turns the various machines off one by one. She gathers Mateen in her arms and carries him to a wheelchair in the corner of the room. "Someone will notice his heart rate monitor isn't working soon. We have to leave now."

The gun presses to my side. "Anyone you ask for help will die," Zaman warns and wraps his big fingers around my upper arm.

"I get it, asshole," Joey mutters.

I cannot speak at all. Fear keeps me silent.

The hall is mostly empty. Where is the security guard who is supposed to be outside our door? Did Zaman kill him too?

Before we reach the elevator, a nurse rushes up to us. "Where are you taking him?"

Oh, God. Can she see the gun? Zaman could kill her right here and it would be all my fault.

Joey clears her throat and gestures to Zaman. "The doctor wants him to have an MRI. We're going to radiology. Mateen didn't want to be alone."

How can she be so calm? My entire body is shaking.

"But Dr. Joey—" Mateen says.

"Remember what I said about these tests?" She crouches down so she's eye level with my son.

I wish I could comfort him, but I am too frightened to move. Yet with a few words, she does what I cannot.

"They won't hurt at all." Peering up at the nurse, Joey shrugs. "It has to be so hard on them to have all these procedures one after another."

"It is." The nurse pats Mateen's shoulder. "When you're done, I'll bring you some sugar-free Jell-O. Okay?"

Mateen looks up at me, as if he doesn't know what he's allowed to say.

"That'll be great," Joey replies. "Thank you."

Less than a minute later, the elevator doors slide shut, sealing us inside. Zaman orders me to press the button for the basement. My stomach drops as we start to descend.

Will I ever taste freedom again?

CHAPTER SIX

Nomar

"I SHOULD GO CHECK on Joey. I stepped in it this morning. Big time." Ford rubs his hand over his hair. "I don't deserve her, but I'm going to spend the rest of my life trying to make her happy."

Ford has been broken for as long as I've known him. Until today. He's found a piece of himself that's been missing since he lost Joey all those years ago.

"I'm happy for you, man." My ass is falling asleep, but I sit up and offer him my hand. Pain slices through my side. "Fuck, that hurts."

"Next time, don't get shot, dumbass." He grins like a damn fool and pushes to his feet. "Rest up. I'll see you at the end of the week."

"Ford? Do me a favor, will you?"

"Anything." His expression sobers, and he shoves his hands into his pockets. "Anytime. For the rest of my life."

"Shit. Is this going to be a thing?" I don't know why I'm

asking. Of course it's going to be a thing. "Don't answer that. Just...call me when everyone's safe in Boston."

"Everyone? Or—?"

An alarm cuts through the low hum of hospital noise. A man in a white coat lurches through the door. Blood drips down his temple.

"The American woman said...to come here..."

Ford grabs the doctor by the arms. "What happened?"

"He had a gun. Made me bring him into the little boy's room. He took them." The doctor's eyes roll back in his head and Ford eases him down to the floor.

I swing my legs over the side of the bed. The world tilts and spins until my feet hit the cold floor. "I'm right...behind you," I manage. "Fuck." Ford's already out the door.

The IV rips from the back of my hand when I shove at the mattress to find my gun. I stumble into the hall. Two guards almost mow me down racing toward Mateen's room.

Ford crab walks back into the hall and shouts, "Stay down and away from the windows! Where did the boy go?"

A young woman rushes around the far corner. My God. She's the spitting image of Lisette, but taller and curvier. "The boy? Mateen? What happened? Where are they?"

One of the nurses pops her head up from behind a desk. "His doctor wanted him to have an MRI." She points toward the elevator. "They went that way."

"Parking garage." Ford jerks as I grab his arm to stay upright. "Get the fuck back in bed, Nomar."

"The hell I will." We haven't worked together in twenty years, but I have an idea what he's planning. "Go. I'll cover the elevator."

Taking off at a run for the stairwell, Ford calls for the two guards to follow him. "We go first," one of them says.

"No. I'm a former United States Marine..." The door to the stairs closes softly, cutting him off. I jab the elevator call button again and again. It's stuck one floor down. Shit. This is taking too goddamn long.

If I didn't think I'd die trying, I'd follow Ford, but we're three flights up. Where the fuck is Trevor? The spook wasn't supposed to leave the hospital. Not until Lisette and Mateen were in the transpo to the airport.

The doors whisper open with a *ding*. Thank fuck. I brace myself against the back wall and check my weapon. The edges of my vision dim. A spasm wracks my torso. If Faruk gets them out of the garage...

No. Ford will get there first. Joey's with them. He'll do anything to save her. Including get himself killed. He's been out of the field for too long. I'm the deadliest operator in the Afghan theater and I'll die before I lose anyone else.

Lisette

My knees slam against the floor of the dirty brown van. "Mama!" Mateen whines from behind me.

"It will be okay, baby. Quiet now," I manage through my tears. Joey stares wildly around the garage, but no one else is here. Where is Trevor? Ford?

Zaman pulls a zip tie from his pocket. "Hands. Now."

"Please... I will not make trouble," I whimper.

He growls and advances on me. "You have already 'made trouble.' Any more, and you will not be worth keeping alive."

Expendable. I...am expendable.

Squeezing my eyes closed, I offer him my wrists and cry harder. Faruk will throw me into the well for weeks for what I have done. The scorpions come out at night. Their stings bring on such terrible fevers, I will promise Faruk anything to let me up. *Anything.* It is how he *persuaded* me to marry him.

The hard plastic is so tight, my hands start to tingle in seconds. My scalp prickles as Zaman grabs my hair and slams my head into the side of the van. Dazed, I do not fight when he gags me.

The greasy cloth is sour against my tongue. Nausea crawls up my throat. Mateen watches me, his big eyes full of tears.

"You next." Zaman holds up another zip tie and gestures to Joey. "Behind your back."

"You can't," she says. "Mateen's sick. He's going to need fluids during the trip. I can take care of him. What do you think will happen if you bring Faruk his son...dead?"

He punches her in the face. The move is so quick, his arm is nothing but a blur.

"Dr. Joey!" Mateen tries to get up, but Zaman shoves him back into the chair.

"Do not touch him!" I scream, but the words are muffled by the gag. I throw myself at Zaman. My nails rake down his cheek, leaving my fingers slick with blood.

"Bitch!" He picks me up and tosses me back into the van. I land on my bad shoulder with a sharp cry.

Joey struggles to her feet, fire in her eyes.

"Get the boy into the van," Zaman orders. "Now."

She glares, but does what he asks, picking up Mateen and setting him next to me. His tiny hand flutters along my cheek. "Mama?"

I want to put my arms around him and sing his favorite lullaby, but all I can do is hold his gaze and touch my forehead to his.

Metal clatters. Shots break the silence, and I push up on an elbow.

Blood spurts from Zaman's shoulder. The gun clatters to the concrete a few feet away. Joey leaps for it, but Zaman lands on top of her.

"Joey! Fight, baby!" Ford shouts.

The sound of his voice gives me hope. Until more shots come from a different direction. Angry shouts in Pashto, English, even Dari. Faruk's men.

"Please...I can't," Joey whimpers. "Don't hurt me. Don't... put me in there..." Her voice sounds different, and her eyes are glassed over. Like she is somewhere else. Trapped in her memories.

Yanking her by the hair, Zaman drags her toward the van. I can see Ford now. He's on his knees, Nasir's arm around his neck. He starts to twitch, all color draining from his face.

Joey screams. Something snaps, and she drives a blade into Zaman's leg. The two struggle, but no matter how much she twists, he will not fall.

Get up. Do something!

I scoot closer to the edge of the van and pull the gag from my mouth. "Stay down, Mateen."

A tire iron rests behind the front seat. It is so heavy, and my hands shake. Joey grabs the gun and slams it into Zaman's head. But he is so much taller than she is, the blow glances off his cheek.

I swing with everything I have. Impact sings up my arms. With a sharp cry, I rear back, ready to try again, but Zaman collapses onto the concrete and doesn't move.

Heavy footsteps approach. Joey whirls around. Another one of Faruk's men races for us, a large rifle in his hands.

We are dead. All of us. Mateen will never get his transplant. Joey will live as long as Mateen does, but then she will die too. Faruk will blame her. And me...? He will make my last days so terrible, I will pray for the end long before it comes.

A shot rings out from the elevator. The rifle clatters to the ground. Half of the man's face is...gone.

"Ford. Get...to...Ford..." Nomar wheezes, stumbling toward us.

Joey takes off at a run. I drop the tire iron and pull Mateen against me so he cannot see Zaman or the dead man only a few feet away. "I love you, *mon bèbè*. Eyes closed now."

"Lisette... Hold on to him." Nomar drops to his knees, pulls the knife from Zaman's leg, and shoves the man onto his side. "Don't...look."

I turn away. A slick sound is quickly followed by weak gurgles. Then Nomar's groan as he collapses next to me. The plastic tie around my wrists snaps in two. He's folding a pocket knife against his thigh when I wriggle back around to face him.

I peer over his shoulder, then quickly avert my gaze. A pool of blood spreads out from Zaman's neck. His eyes are open and staring up at nothing.

My son cries softly, his little arms tight around my waist.

"Is Mateen...hurt?" Nomar asks.

"No. Only scared. But you are. Let me see." His hospital gown clings to his side, a bright red stain spreading all the way to his hip.

He cups his free hand over his crotch. "Hell, no—"

Joey cries out. "Ford. Oh God, Ford. Open your eyes. Look at me!" Nomar tenses until she sobs once. "You're okay. You're going to be okay. Just...keep breathing."

Men shout in Uzbek. A radio squelches from nearby. Nomar takes aim until a man in a security uniform calls, "Starfire!" Then he drops the gun and rests his hand on mine.

"We need a doctor here. Now!" I call. My fingers are still numb. My wrists ache and my shoulder feels as if someone is trying to pull it from its socket. But I have my son in my arms. Nomar saved us. Again.

CHAPTER SEVEN

Three Days Later

Nomar

THE DRIVER PULLS AWAY from the curb, leaving me staring up at St. Jude's Children's Research Hospital wondering what the fuck I'm doing.

I left Uzbekistan at oh-dark-thirty this morning, and after almost fifteen hours, landed at Logan a little after 5:00 p.m. Ford arranged for a car service to pick me up from the airport and take me to a hotel, but I had other plans.

By the time I figure out what floor Mateen is on, the twinge in my side has grown to a full-blown ache. The doctor didn't want me flying this soon, but Ford's updates have been few and far between. Fucking nine-hour time difference.

He's taking care of Joey. Calm down.

If only I could. Faruk is too smart, too rich, and too well connected to settle for failure. He'll come for his son again. Even here. Six thousand miles away.

Two mountains of muscle stop me as soon as I emerge from the elevator. "This hallway is off limits."

"Starfire."

To the men's credit, knowing the code word isn't enough. They demand to see my passport, paw through my duffel bag, and spend five minutes on the phone verifying my identity with someone from Second Sight before they let me pass.

"Third door on the left," the taller one says, but before I reach Mateen's room, Lisette slips into the hall.

All the tension I've carried with me since I left Uzbekistan melts away in a single breath. A red t-shirt clings to her curves, and flowing black pants end just above her ankles. With her hair in a ponytail and no fresh bruises, she looks ten years younger.

She doesn't notice me, moving to the nurse's station and smiling at the woman behind the desk. "Mateen is hungry. Is he allowed to have more food tonight?"

The nurse checks her tablet. "Let me guess? The corndog was a hit?"

Lisette's laughter soothes my soul. "He has never had one before. Pork was...forbidden. I fear he will never want anything else ever again."

"The cafe is open for another hour. I'll call down for you."

"Oh, thank you. He was nauseous most of the day. I want him to eat while he is hungry."

Lisette turns, and shock sends a flush darkening her cheeks. "Nomar!" I don't get a chance to say a word before she rushes over to me. But she stops short of touching me. "I worried for you. We had to leave so quickly after..." Her hand goes to her throat, fingers fluttering over fading yellow bruises.

"Got the all clear this morning and took the first flight out."

The doctor didn't give me anything *close* to an all clear, but she doesn't need to know that.

Lisette's eyes narrow on my duffel bag. "Did you come straight from the airport?"

"Not...exactly."

Gritting my teeth so she won't see the pain it causes me, I bend down and retrieve a small box from my bag. "A buddy of mine works for Nintendo. Mateen's going to be here for a couple of weeks, right? I thought he might enjoy this."

Her eyes shimmer. "You brought my son a gift."

"Trevor told me his old gaming system didn't survive." I shrug, staring down at my feet until Lisette's arms wind around my waist. She smells like something warm, soft, and sweet. "It's nothing—"

"It is everything." With a little sigh, she relaxes against me. "Come in and give it to him? He asks about you every day."

I draw back enough to tip her chin up so I can see her eyes. "Me?"

"Why are you surprised? You saved us, Nomar. You are his hero. Mateen..." she shakes her head. "He loves his father. As all little boys do. But he knows Faruk hurt me. And after what happened...in Uzbekistan, he does not want to go back there ever again."

The sorrow in her voice has me sliding my hand down to the small of her back and holding her against me. The contact isn't enough to ease my guilt *or* her pain. There's nothing in this world that can. She'll carry the memories with her for the rest of her life. Mateen might forget. One day. He'll have the chance for a normal life.

"Please," she says and threads her fingers with mine. "Come say hello. He had a bad day, but he is feeling better now."

"How bad?" Holding fast to keep her at my side, I scan her

tired gaze, the bags under her eyes, the slump of her shoulders. "He's getting the transplant, right?"

"In one week, yes. But first, his immune system must be... destroyed." The word catches in her throat. "He has chemotherapy every day. By the weekend, he will no longer be allowed visitors. Even a simple cold could be life threatening. I will need to wear a mask and gloves at all times..."

Her eyes glisten with tears, but she blinks them away. "I will not be able to stay in the room with him at night. He will be all alone."

I cup her cheek, skating my thumb just under her eye. Up close, I can still see the fading bruise, but it's barely more than a memory now. Lisette stiffens for a beat, then leans into my hand. Shit. I don't have any right to touch her. Not after everything she's been through. And if she really knew me, she'd run—*should* run. If only I could help myself.

"He's a strong kid, Lisette. And Ford...I've never met his boss, but he's a legend in my world. No one's getting to Mateen."

She nods absently, but I can tell my words don't do a damn thing to reassure her. She's barely holding on. There's a hollowness to her cheeks and a pallor to her skin that worry me.

"Who's taking care of *you*, sweetheart? Are you sleeping? Eating?"

Lisette pulls away, angling her gaze to the floor. "Noele and my parents are here. Ford gave us an apartment three blocks away. They dote on Mateen."

"That's not what I asked." I guide her to a padded bench against the wall and urge her down next to me. "When was the last time you slept?"

She still won't look at me. "He has nightmares. All the time."

"Can your sister stay with him? Even for a few hours? You need rest."

The little shake of her head sends my frustration through the roof until she whispers, "To Mateen, she is the woman who brings him coloring books and looks like his Mama. He does not know her. When he napped yesterday, I went to the apartment to shower and change, but he had a bad dream. He cried for me until I returned. Noele was heartbroken. My parents even more so."

"So you haven't had a break. At all." The harsh edge to my voice has her shoulders curving inward.

Fuck. Be a little more sensitive, idiot.

Gentling my tone, I ask, "What can I do?"

Lisette swipes at a tear glistening on her cheek. "Come say hello to Mateen. Maybe...he will feel safe knowing you are here."

"What about you?" I shouldn't press her, but I have to know. "Do you feel safe? With me here?"

For several seconds, she holds my gaze. "I feel safer now than I have in ten years. Because of you."

Wrapping my arm around her shoulders, I breathe in her scent. Try to memorize the feel of her relaxing against me.

I'm not this person. I go in, do the job, and get the fuck out. I've been the deadliest operator in the Afghan theater for almost twenty years. But with Lisette, I see a chance for something more.

If only I were brave enough to take it.

"The nurse is probably going to kick me out soon. But I figure there's just enough time for Mateen to beat my ass at FIFA."

Lisette laughs and twists out of my embrace. "He beats everyone. If you can hold him off until the café sends up another corndog, I will be impressed."

"Do I need to wear a mask and gloves? I can. Whatever he needs."

I'd put on a full hazmat suit for this woman, despite only knowing her for a few days. For the kid too. They're...important in a way I don't understand, but can't deny.

Her eyes soften, and she reaches up to touch my cheek briefly. "No. Not for a few days. Come."

I tuck the new gaming system under my arm and pick up my duffel bag, following Lisette into the small hospital room. Bright blue walls surround us, with yellow stars painted all along the ceiling. The whole solar system glows from behind the bed, some fancy light-up art panel that the kid probably loves.

Mateen doesn't look up from his coloring book until I take a seat. "Hey, buddy. Fancy new digs you've got here."

"Nomar!" The kid shoves the book aside and launches himself at me, climbing right out of the bed and into my lap. "Mama said you might not be able to find us here."

"I can find you and your mama anywhere, kiddo." My stitches ache where his knee digs into my side, but I grit my teeth and ease him back onto the bed.

"Even on the moon?" His eyes go wide.

I cast a quick glance to Lisette, who's leaning against the wall across from me. "Anywhere. But I'm not just good at finding *people*." I set the box on his lap. "Since you had to leave your old one behind..."

"Mama, look!" Mateen tears into the package and pulls out the bright blue device. "It's the same color!"

"I can see that, *mon chou*. What do we say to Nomar?" She sits on the other side of his bed and brushes a few of his curls away from his eyes.

"Want to play?" The kid peers up at me as he turns the game on. Music pours from the tiny speakers.

"Say 'thank you,' Mateen."

"Thank you," he says with a sheepish smile, then passes me a controller and launches a squad battle. Lisette looks on, and in under a minute, he scores his first goal.

"You know," I say, gesturing to the big red *S* on his pajamas, "you're not supposed to tell anyone about your secret identity."

His cheeks flush bright red, but in the next second, he straightens his shoulders. "Superman told Lois Lane. Because they're family. So I can tell Mama and Aunt Noele and Mémé and Pepe and you."

Shit. Hearing him lump me in with the rest of his family does something to me I can't explain. Makes me want more than I have any right to expect.

"What about the doctors and nurses?" As soon as I ask the question, I regret it.

Mateen looks to Lisette, uncertainty twisting his lips into a frown. "Mama, I need a disguise!"

She worries the edge of her t-shirt with her fingers. "I can ask *Tante* Noele to bring you a different set of pajamas in the morning. But visiting hours are almost over. She cannot come tonight."

"But what about *now*?" His cheeks redden like he's about to cry. The game lies in his lap, forgotten. Shit. I have to fix this. Reaching into my duffel bag, I find my bandana and fold it lengthwise several times.

"Hold out your hand, kiddo." He does, eyes watering, as I tie the handkerchief around his wrist. "Black glasses would be better, but this'll do for now."

A nurse breezes in, carrying a tray with a corndog nestled in a red and white checkered cardboard boat. "I have Superman's dinner—"

"You just missed him," I say, hoping the woman gets the hint. "This is Clark Kent. You can tell by the wristband. Superman had to go save the world. Again."

She stops short, looking from me to Mateen for several seconds before understanding dawns in her eyes.

"Oh my. You're right. Well...maybe *Clark* is hungry? Otherwise, this corndog is going to go to waste. If Superman comes back later, he can call me, and I'll bring him another one."

THREE MATCHES LATER, Mateen's eyelids are drooping. Lisette sleeps in a recliner next to me, and I don't want to wake her to say goodnight.

"I'll see you tomorrow, kiddo," I say quietly, easing the game from his hands and tucking the blanket around him. "Let your mama sleep, okay? You're both safe here. I promise."

"You will come back tomorrow, Nomar?" he asks, his voice slurring.

"Yeah, buddy. I will. Now get some rest." He's out before I even reach the door.

I wave to the nurse at the desk, nod at the two security guards, and pull out my phone as I step into the elevator.

Ford: Get your ass to my place. Shit's going down.

Fuck. The message came in twenty minutes ago, and before I reach the ground floor, he sends another one.

Ford: I mean it. Get. Here. Now.

CHAPTER EIGHT

Nomar

FORD WON'T ANSWER my calls, and I spend the whole ride to his place kicking myself for putting my phone on silent. I've been up for more than a day, and all I want is a hot shower and a bed that doesn't come with a nurse checking my vital signs every four hours.

All the curtains are drawn, but when I knock, Ford answers in under ten seconds. "Get inside."

"What the hell is going on?" My gaze lands on Joey, huddled on the sofa with her knees drawn up to her chest. Her bloodshot eyes are swollen and bruised, and a cup of coffee wobbles in her hands. "What's wrong? What *shit* is going down?"

Ford passes me his tablet. On the screen, a drone flies over—holy fuck. "Why am I looking at footage of Faruk's compound?"

"Because Dax, Trevor, and Ryker's entire team are preparing to breach. Wren—she's Second Sight's hacker and Ry's girlfriend—is on comms from our offices."

"Want to tell me why they decided to wait until *now?* And isn't your boss *blind?* He's not field ready."

"Try telling him that," Ford mutters. "As for why..." He runs a hand through his hair, exhaustion in his red-rimmed eyes. "When we were headed out of the compound, one of Faruk's guys stopped us."

"So you killed him, right?"

Joey flinches and digs her fingers into her forearm so hard, the tips turn white. "Isaad was the one who...*erased* me," she says. "My bank accounts, my driver's license, credit cards...he made me disappear."

Ford covers her hand with his. "You're here, buttercup. Wren fixed everything."

"I know." She leans against him, relaxing by inches. "He was terrified. Broken. I can't imagine what he's been through. If they can get him out—"

"They *will* get him out. Dax and Ryker aren't leaving Afghanistan without him," Ford says.

My frustration is about to get the best of me. "I haven't slept in more than twenty-four hours. Explain this to me like I'm five. Who is this Isaad guy and why are Dax and Ryker on a fucking suicide mission?"

"That's...a hell of a story." Ford nods at the kitchen. "Get yourself some coffee. You're going to need it."

The constant throbbing in my side that hasn't let up for hours is made worse by my stomach growling loudly. I fill a mug, then notice the pizza box on the counter. "Do you mind? The last thing I ate was an apple in Uzbekistan."

"Knock yourself out."

I slide the last two pieces of pepperoni and extra cheese onto a plate. As I take a seat in the recliner across from the couch, a beep comes through the tablet's speakers.

"Alpha Team to Foxtrot. Stay available. We go in ten minutes," a man says.

"Roger that," Ford says.

The rich scent of coffee helps me focus, and after the first sip, I'm almost awake again. "Ryker?" I ask.

"Yep. He'll be the primary one you hear. We're listen only unless Wren says otherwise or Ry asks a question. Fewer distractions that way."

I nod. Smart. I've never met the man, but the way Ford talked about Dax—about both of them—Ryker's capable as fuck and twice as scary.

"Six years ago," Ford says, "Ryker's Special Forces team was ambushed outside Fallujah. Four of them survived the attack. After a couple of months, the Taliban sent them to Hell Mountain." He stares into his mug and shakes his head. "Fifteen months later, only Dax and Ryker were left. Ry broke himself out, but by the time he got a team together to go back for Dax, the fucker who ran the place had poured drain cleaner in Dax's eyes."

"Goddamn. I heard the rumors, but you know how shit like that gets exaggerated..."

"In this case...what you heard probably wasn't even the half of it."

Despite all I've seen, from the look on Joey's face, I don't want to know what comes next.

"For almost a year of their time in Hell, there were three of them. Until one of the fuckwits threw Ripper into the hole. They told Ry and Dax he'd broken his neck."

My tired brain puts the pieces together mid bite, and I drop the crust onto the plate. "This Isaad...he's American? He's *Special Forces*? What the hell was he doing working for Faruk?"

Ford gives me a look that says I'm not firing on all cylinders. "You know better than any of us how to break a man."

"You're telling me Faruk turned a fucking Special Forces operator and kept him prisoner for six years?"

"That's exactly what I'm telling you. This guy helped us get out, Nomar. Without him, none of us would be here. Not even you."

"Lisette had to know," I say, dropping my head into my hands. "Why didn't she say—"

"No." The strength in Joey's voice shocks me enough to look up. "Lisette was a prisoner too. He—Faruk—controlled *everything*. His men walked around like they owned the place, but the women...I saw seven? Maybe eight? They weren't free. Someone escorted Lisette and Mateen to the lab in the basement twice a day. And waited outside until we were done. Even if she did know about Ripper, she couldn't have done... anything."

Fuck. Joey's right. I know better. I've seen, firsthand, how years of conditioning can break a person.

Ford picks up his mug and heads for the kitchen. "Need more coffee, buttercup?"

She shakes her head and wraps her arms around her knees. If I knew her better, I'd try to comfort her. But I'd just make things worse.

The tablet beeps again. "Last call," Ryker says. "Thermals show twenty-three signals, but we don't know how well the scanner penetrates into the basement. We could be looking at double that number."

Joey stifles a small sound and shrinks further into the leather cushions. In two seconds, Ford's back at her side. "Nomar can monitor comms. Let's go into the bedroom. You don't have to listen to this."

"Yes, I do," she whispers. "I know the compound. And shit, Ford. Faruk had me for six days. Isaad's been there for six *years*. I need to see this through."

The two link fingers as Ryker's voice comes through the speaker again. "Let's go get our brother back."

"Hooah," another man says.

Followed immediately by two more voices. "Hooyah."

Ford taps the screen and adds, "Oorah."

Army. Navy. Marines. Their battle cries are legend, and though my Army service record is so fucking classified, there are only ten people in the whole goddamn country who know about it, I add my own quiet "hooah."

The minutes drag so slowly, every second feels like an hour. Joey's gaze is pinned to the tablet, where half a dozen green blips move around the property. Ford keeps rubbing her back, deep lines etched around his eyes. We're getting too old for this life.

"He's not out here." On screen, Ryker's green blip moves toward the house.

"Wait," Wren says. "Stop. There's...something. Where are you, Team Leader?"

"Twenty-five meters west-northwest of the front door."

"Hold position." On the right side of the screen, the view changes. Thermal imaging shows a faint reddish glow not far from Ryker's location.

Joey jerks, sitting up so quickly, Ford loses his grip on his coffee cup and it tumbles to the floor. "I need to talk to her. Right now," she says.

Ford opens a private comms channel. "Wren, Joey needs to talk to you."

"Go for it, doc."

"Um...Faruk has a well," Joey says, her voice trembling. "The first day, he showed it to me. He said if I didn't help Mateen, he'd throw me down there. With...the scorpions. There were marks on the walls. Like...someone had been tracking the days. So many days..."

"Oh God." Wren says softly, then clears her throat. "Team Leader? Right in front of you. Maybe half a meter. Is there some sort of cover? Like you'd find on a manhole?"

"Affirmative."

"It's…a well. Faruk threatened to put the doc down there. Keep her there if she didn't cooperate. And there's something really faint on the thermals. Like…actually underground."

After another minute, Ryker swears softly. "Package located. Bravo Team, prepare for infil. My position. Hold until I have proof of life."

"There's a rope ladder," Joey says. "And a stake in the ground a few feet away."

"Alpha Team Leader," another man says, "Enemy target secured. Office. Southwest corner of the main floor."

Fuck. They've got Faruk. And they're going to kill him.

"Mateen will not be safe until his father is dead. I…a part of me wishes you would have—"

"Amir Abdul Faruk is one of the richest and most powerful men in Afghanistan. His death would have started a war. I couldn't risk it."

Our conversation rattles around in my head for too long. Lisette and Mateen will be safe now. For the rest of their lives. No more fear. No more running. No more hiding.

"Base, put the doc on," Ryker demands, pulling me out of my own head.

After a beep, Ford nods. "I-I'm here," Joey says.

"His heart's racing. One-sixty at least. There's an empty water bottle with him, but I don't know how long he's been down here. He ate some of the scorpions, I think. And he's burning up."

"Oh my God." Tears spring to her eyes. She balls her hands into fists so tightly, her knuckles turn white and Ford whispers something in her ear. After a few seconds, she stammers, "Y-you have to…to get fluids into him. And sugar. Lower his core temperature. His kidneys are probably shutting down. Beyond that…get him to a hospital."

"Roger that."

I'd give anything to see what's going on. And then as if the

Universe heard me, the thermal image disappears and a grainy video takes its place.

"What the fuck?" I scoot closer to the screen.

"Dax is wearing a camera," Ford whispers.

Joey swipes at her cheeks when Dax kneels next to Ryker. The man on the ground between them is barely breathing. Blood stains his lips, and his closed eyes are sunken.

Joey covers her mouth with a trembling hand. "He's been down there for days. Because he helped us. Faruk knew…"

On screen, Ryker orders Trevor and Dax to get Ripper to the truck, then takes off at a run toward the house. Less than two minutes later, the big man's voice takes on a tone that scares the fuck out of me—even from six thousand miles away.

"You took our brother. If our truck wasn't full, I'd bring you with us and spend months making you bleed until you begged for death. And then I'd let you heal up and do it all over again. But instead, I'll grant you this one mercy."

After a muffled moan, Ryker's back on comms. "Bravo Team? We're on our way. Faruk will never hurt another person again."

Joey breaks, turning into Ford's embrace and sobbing quietly. She's been through too much. I meet Ford's gaze over her shoulder and nod at the door. The two of them need to be alone, and I need a double shot of scotch and a soft bed. Because tomorrow, I have to tell Lisette her bastard of a husband will never hurt her again.

CHAPTER NINE

Lisette

Noele breezes into the hospital room, a large coffee in her hand. Her smile fades when she sees me slumped in the chair next to Mateen's bed.

"Did he have a bad night?" she whispers. Beautiful as always in a soft white sweater and flowing black pants, she takes a long sip from her to-go cup. The scent makes my mouth water.

"He did not have a single nightmare." My spine cracks, loudly. Thankfully, Mateen doesn't stir, and I brush a few curls from his forehead. "He woke up half a dozen times, though. The port in his chest itches him."

"Pauvre bébé," Noele says softly. "You should go to the apartment and sleep. I sent Maman and Papa on something called a 'Duck Boat ride.' They will be gone at least four hours."

"What is a 'Duck Boat ride' and why would you send them anywhere but here?" Our parents have come to the hospital every day, and Mateen is starting to look forward to their visits.

Noele crouches in front of the chair and covers my hand with hers. "Because at breakfast, Maman said you were keeping too many secrets. She wants you to tell her about your time with...*him* and I know you are not ready."

My heart pounds painfully in my chest, like someone is squeezing it to the point of bursting. "She agreed to wait until Mateen was better."

Noele sighs—one of those deep exhales that shakes her entire being. "I know, *mon fleur*. I do not think she realized how long that would take."

I link our fingers. Noele's are so pale, while mine are the only part of me besides my face that hold any color. Courtesy of the abayas and hijabs I was forced to wear every day for the past ten years. And the relentless Afghan sun. "One of my last memories from...before was of you sneaking back into the house at six in the morning. Do you remember that? You had been out with a boy, I think. Maman was so angry."

"That was Frederick." She shakes her head. "*Quel idiot.* His scooter ran out of gas. We had to walk home from the rave. Maman wanted to take my phone away, but you reminded her that without it, I would not be able to call her if I needed help." Noele smiles, such warmth in her green eyes. "You were always protecting me."

"And now you protect me." We embrace, and I do not fight the tears burning my eyes. "How are you so wise beyond your years?"

"I wanted to be like you. Always." She swallows her sob. For several minutes, we hold one another.

If we were alone, I would tell her everything. No matter how long it took. But with Mateen sleeping so close, confessions will have to wait.

She rises with the grace of a dancer. "I told the security

guard with Maman and Papa to bring them *here* after the boat tour. You will be safe at the apartment until dinner time. Rest. Read a book. Watch television. Do something...you enjoy."

"I do not know what that is any more. We had no movies. Only local television. No modern books." The realities of my life with Faruk are too terrible to relive with Mateen still so sick. "I suppose I could call Nomar. He came to see us last night."

"The hot guy who saved you in just his hospital gown?" Noele's eyebrows shoot up. "I thought he was still in Uzbekistan?"

"He was. Until yesterday." Nodding at the new gaming system my son has clutched under his arm, I add, "Mateen likes him. I think...maybe that is why he slept better last night."

Noele steals a glance at my son. "He has several treatments today, yes?"

"Only one. Tomorrow, though...he has three. By the weekend, you and I will be the only ones allowed to see him. We will need to wear protective equipment at all times so he does not get sick."

"Then for today, you should be only Lisette, *mon fleur*. If Mateen asks for you, I will call. I promise."

She's right. Even if I do not know how to be...me. I stop to press my lips to Mateen's forehead. "Be good, *mon chou*," I whisper. "Mama will be back this afternoon."

Noele settles in the chair next to his bed and pulls a book from her purse. She gives me a little wave through the window in the door, and I clutch my phone to my chest and practically run for the elevator.

THE APARTMENT IS UTTERLY SILENT. Vasquez, one of Ford's men, insisted on checking the bedrooms and bathrooms for any threats, but then tells me he will wait outside for as long as I want to stay. I am safe here. The building is the most secure I have ever seen. There are cameras in the hallways, panic buttons hidden in every room, and we each have one on our phones.

Despite my exhaustion, I cannot sleep, so I make myself a *cafe au lait* from the fancy machine in the kitchen and sink down onto a plush, beige couch with a view of the Charles River.

"You should be only Lisette."

I have not been "only Lisette" since I let Faruk steal me away. I was a prisoner. A wife. A mother. No possessions of my own. No privacy. I made the best of that life, but it was not *mine.*

I used to love to paint. My talent was only passable, but it made me happy. I gave tours at the *Musée des Beaux-Arts de Marseille*—one of the few uses for an art history degree as I had no desire to teach at university. Perhaps after a shower, I will ask Vasquez if we can visit a museum. And an art store.

I STARE AT THE CLOSET, the bright colors and modern styles overwhelming and exciting at the same time. Choosing a pair of flared black pants and a striped sweater that exposes my collarbones, I stare at myself in the mirror. This little bit of rebellion should not make my palms damp.

Do not be silly. You are not rebelling against anything.

Except, I am.

"Cover yourself!"

I can *feel* the balled-up abaya hit me in the chest. *Hear*

Faruk's harsh words. *See* his dark eyes flash with the threat of barely controlled rage.

"No. This is what I want to wear, and no one will stop me. He cannot touch me here."

I would give anything for that to be true. But I know better. Once Mateen can travel, we will need to disappear. Ford mentioned Switzerland. Canada. Panama. He said he would find a way for us to see Maman, Papa, and Noele. But I do not know how he can make such promises.

I fill a small purse with my wallet, lip balm, and keys, but before I pick up my phone, someone knocks at the door.

"Vasquez?" I ask.

"It's Nomar."

He looks so serious when I invite him inside. Lines tighten around his eyes, like he has not slept. "What is it? Something is wrong." Snatching up my phone, I check for any messages. "Is Mateen—?"

"He's fine. Shit. I didn't think. I should have called." Nomar sweeps a gaze around the flat. "Is anyone else here? Your parents? Noele?"

"Noele is with Mateen, and my parents are on a 'duck boat' for the morning." His tone worries me. Desperate for something to do, I gesture to the kitchen. "Would you like a coffee?"

"What? No." He's at the window, staring across the river with his hands shoved into the pockets of his jeans. "Come sit down. There's something we need to talk about."

I sit a respectable distance away, my hands folded on my thighs and my gaze pinned to the floor until Nomar slides closer. "You're not *there* anymore, Lisette. You can look at me."

The power in his dark brown eyes makes my heart race. Only a week ago, I was certain I would die in Afghanistan. By my husband's hand. Now, I would give anything to know the feeling of Nomar's lips on mine.

"Do you remember a man who worked for Faruk named Isaad?" he asks.

"Yes. I was not allowed to speak to him. Or he to me. His room was at the far end of the house. It was the only one—besides mine—that had a lock on the outside of the door." My voice falters, and I run my fingers over the hem of my sweater.

"Do you remember when you first saw him?" Nomar's voice is gentler now, but his stare is icy cold.

"Five years ago? Perhaps longer? After Mateen was born." My cheeks heat, and I have to look away. "I did not leave my room until he was almost six months old. Faruk *bought* a girl —Damsa—to be Mateen's *au pair*. She would bring him to me when he needed to nurse, but she changed him, played with him. I cried whenever I saw him, knowing he would grow up—"

"He won't." Nomar takes my hands in his, holding on tight. "I promise you, Mateen will never see his father again."

I jerk back, swallowing my sob. "You cannot know that! Faruk has enough money to find us anywhere. He will *never* stop searching for his son. One day, he will take Mateen. And he will kill me."

"Lisette."

Nomar says my name so gently, I want to listen. To believe we will truly be safe for the rest of our lives.

"He won't come for you. He can't. He made a mistake, sweetheart. Six years ago, U.S. Special Forces Sergeant Jackson Richards disappeared from a Taliban prison called Hell Mountain. Faruk threw him into that fucking well, and kept him there for so long, he forgot his own damn name."

I suck in a sharp breath. "The scorpions come out at night. The pain..." Lifting my sleeve, I run my fingers over the small, round scars on my arm. "Even my abaya could not protect me."

Nomar takes my hand again. "Hell Mountain had two other prisoners when Jackson disappeared, Lisette. Both Special Forces. One was a mean son of a bitch named Ryker McCabe. And the other...was Ford's boss, Dax."

His words sink in. "Is that why you came for Joey? Because of Isaad?"

With a sound that is part laugh and part snort, Nomar shakes his head. "Ryker and Dax didn't know a damn thing about Isaad until four days ago. I paid off one of the guards to get me into the compound the morning before we breached. I needed the lay of the land. And I was wearing a body cam. As soon as they saw the footage...they knew their brother was alive. And last night, a team of the six deadliest operators on the planet—besides me—pulled Richards out of that fucking well. Right before Ryker slit Faruk's throat."

I start to shake, ten years of pent-up fear and terror escaping in a weak, thin cry.

My world shrinks down to twin pinpricks of light. I feel myself falling. Sliding. Until strong arms band around my body. "Shhh, sweetheart. You're okay. Everything's going to be okay."

Jagged edges of relief slice through me, opening wounds I kept buried so I could survive another day. A hand cups the back of my head. I breathe in his scent. Clean, woodsy soap. A hint of vanilla. His neck is soft under my lips. Muscles flex as he shifts me into his lap.

"Let it out. All of it. I'm here," he murmurs. "I'm here."

Nomar

Lisette sobs in my arms until my t-shirt is soaked. "Talk to me, sweetheart. Say...something. Anything. Please."

It takes her another two minutes to manage a shaky breath. "H-how can y-you be sure?"

Easing Lisette back, I cup her cheek. She turns into my touch. "I was on comms—with Ford—for the operation. I heard everything."

"You heard him die?" At my nod, she adds, "But you did not *see* it."

"There's no fucking way Ryker and Dax would let him live, Lisette. Not after what he did to Richards. Faruk was dead the second they knew their brother was still out there. But if you need proof, I'll get it for you."

Leaning back against the cushions, I urge her to relax against me.

"You don't have to be afraid of him anymore. No one does. After Ryker and his team left, he called in some guys he'd worked with before. They burned half the compound to the ground. Everything that had to do with his business, the computers, the offices...gone. The women are all with a local aid organization. Half of Faruk's men surrendered. The rest are dead."

She doesn't say a word. Shit. I'm making a fucking mess of this. But when I'm about to let her go and give her some space, she nestles closer to me.

"Before Mateen was born, every time he punished me, I would pray he would go too far and kill me. After...I had no such hope." With a shudder, she adds, "Thank you."

I should tell her I didn't do a damn thing. That if I'd known about Richards—hell, if I'd known about *her*—that I would have killed the shitstain a week ago. But then her breathing slows, and her entire body relaxes into sleep.

For an hour, we stay locked together. Lisette's legs are draped over mine, her head on my shoulder, and her soft breaths ghost over my neck. God, she smells like the sweetest flower. My hand rests on the small of her back, and her sweater rides up enough for me to feel several thin, raised scars over her creamy skin.

I should wake her. Or carry her into the bedroom. But this is one of those rare, perfect moments in life, and I won't do a damn thing to ruin it.

Too soon, Lisette jerks awake with a little gasp. Her lips are only an inch from mine.

Don't do it.

My inner voice—the one that's kept me alive through some of the most dangerous operations no one's ever heard of —screams at me, but Lisette looks up at me with such raw need, I slide my hand up to the back of her neck.

My first taste is heaven. Velvet lips. A hint of coffee mixes with the salt from her tears. Her tiny moan promises so much more. A future. A home. A *life*.

Until my phone—jammed in the front pocket of my jeans —buzzes, the pattern one I can't ignore.

Easing Lisette off my lap, I check the screen.

AP: Need you in Kabul, STAT. Call me.

Shit. The world knows Amir Abdul Faruk is dead, and there's going to be hell to pay.

I thumb out a quick reply, telling him I need five minutes, then shove the phone back into my pocket. Lisette stares down at the floor, her cheeks flushed bright red.

My fingers curl under her chin, and I urge her to meet my gaze. "I can't stay, sweetheart. I want to. More than anything. But..."

"You do not have to explain."

The way she shies away from me makes me want to kill that bastard all over again. He did this to her. Doused the spark that now lives as a ghost in her eyes.

Sliding my hand back to her neck, I hold her in place. "Yes, I do. Remember what I told you outside that mosque? That 'I'm the one they send in when shit goes sideways'?"

She nods. Then in the next breath, her green eyes widen. "His death would have started a war. You said that too. And now it has?"

"I don't know, but if the head of the United States Joint Special Operations Command is calling me, it can't be good. Can I take you back to the hospital? You shouldn't be alone right now."

A tiny tremor skates down her spine. "I cannot let Mateen see me like this. He will know something is wrong. Go. Vasquez is outside. He will take me back to St. Jude's when I am ready."

My phone buzzes again. I should tell Pritchard to fuck off and stay with Lisette. I'm retired. But if shit *is* going down in Kabul, I can't walk away.

I pull Lisette closer and seal my lips to hers in a hard, desperate kiss full of everything I wish I could say.

She walks me to the door, her hand in mine. "You will not leave without saying goodbye, will you?"

"No, sweetheart. I won't. I promise."

CHAPTER TEN

Lisette

Standing at the second-floor window, I watch Nomar approach a black car and pull out his phone. He's tense, shoulders hiked up to his ears. Will he really have to go back to Afghanistan? He was shot less than a week ago. I wish I had asked for his phone number. Or given him mine.

I can still taste him on my lips. Feel his hand cupping the back of my neck, his fingers tangling in my hair. For the first time in ten years, I let myself *want* someone, and now…he gets into the back seat of the car, and it pulls away from the curb. Away from me.

Sinking down onto the sofa, I dig my fingers into my temples, trying to make sense of everything that happened after he walked through my door.

My husband—the man who took me away from everything I loved and turned my life into a never-ending nightmare—is dead. My son no longer has a father, and he will be better for it.

Briefly, I wonder if I am a terrible person. If there is something wrong with me because I am *happy* he got what he deserved. But then I remember the night we escaped. How he dislocated my shoulder because his six-year-old son wanted a snack.

So many nights, I would lie awake after he forced himself on me, watch him sleep, and imagine sneaking into the kitchen, taking a knife, and...driving it through his black heart.

But that would have been a death sentence. For me and Mateen. Trapped in the middle of that godforsaken desert, no hope of escape, of a future, I had accepted my fate. I would die after watching Faruk bleed every ounce of goodness from my son.

But now, I am free. Zaman, Ehsan, and Nasir are dead—killed in the hospital parking garage in Uzbekistan. They were the worst of Faruk's men. The ones who would have hunted us even without their beloved Amir.

"Half of his men surrendered. The rest are dead."

No one will come for us. Faruk will never again whip me for speaking out of turn. Never order me to fast because I was late for prayer time. Never lock me away because I accidentally exposed my ankle or wrist with another man present.

My son will grow up with a loving family. He will play with other children. Go to school. But most importantly, I will teach him that women are not possessions. He will see his mama happy.

NOELE WATCHES as Mateen races around St. Jude's play area, chasing another little boy who is also wearing *Superman* pajamas. When she sees me, she rushes over. "What is wrong? You were crying."

I touch my cheeks. *Merde.* I spent half an hour lying down

with tea bags over my eyes so Mateen would not know anything was wrong. But when my son sees me, he waves, then asks his new friend if he wants to draw.

"Lisette? You were supposed to relax today. What happened?" My sister squeezes my fingers, and I draw her over to a bench on the opposite wall where we can sit.

"Nomar came to the flat. He had...news about Faruk," I say in French.

Her grip tightens. "Do we need to worry? The guard did not say anything to me when he escorted us down here."

Do I simply blurt out the truth? Or tell her the whole story?

With a deep breath, I lift my eyes to hers. "Faruk did many bad things."

"That is a colossal understatement," Noele mutters. "You have told me almost nothing, but I saw the scars on your back."

My cheeks flush. I study the bright blue tiles that form a dotted line from the play area to the cafe at the far end of this floor. "When?"

"The first night we were here. You went into the bathroom to change clothes. Mateen was crying and I came to get you."

"Shit. Please do not tell Maman and Papa." Desperation lends an edge to my voice, and from the low table in the play area, Mateen looks over at me, his little brow scrunched up with concern. "Draw something for *Grand-Maman* next," I say in English, forcing a smile.

Noele stares me down. "You are stalling."

"I was not the only one he abducted, Noele. There was a man. Six years ago. I did not know who he was or how he had come to be there. Faruk never let me speak to him. But Nomar told me he was a member of the United States Special Forces. He served with Ford's business partner. Last night,

Trevor and some of his friends went back to Afghanistan to free this man. And they killed Faruk."

"What?" she shrieks.

Everyone within earshot turns to look at us. A little girl knocks over her tower of wooden blocks and starts to cry. A nurse glares at Noele. "Miss, please keep your voice down."

Mateen's lower lip wobbles. He runs to me, crawls into my lap, and regards my sister with wide, watery eyes.

"Oh, *mon chou*, Auntie Noele did not mean to frighten you. Everything is all right." I rub his back, rocking him gently. "You can go back to drawing."

He shakes his head. "I'm hungry. Can I have another corndog?"

My laugh brings a lightness to my chest I have not felt in years. "That depends. Did you eat all your fruit at breakfast?"

"Uh huh. Even the yucky 'taloupe," he says, looking so serious, I fight my smile.

"Well, any boy who suffers through cantaloupe for breakfast should get whatever he wants for lunch. Say goodbye to your friend, and we will go back to your room and look at the menu, okay?"

As soon as he climbs off my lap, I lean closer to Noele. "We will talk more when Mateen has his scans this afternoon. Until I find a way to tell him about his father, no one else can know."

Nomar

Major General Austin J. Pritchard, in full dress uniform, stands when I walk into his office at Fort Liberty. Medals and awards line his bookshelves, along with photos of him with the President, Vice President, and half the Joint Chiefs of Staff.

"About damn time." He tucks a folder under his arm and heads for the door. "Follow me."

"Listen, Pritchard, I got on the damn plane. The least you could do is tell me what the fuck is going on."

"I could say the same thing to you," he calls over his shoulder. "Hurry up. If you keep him waiting, POTUS will have both our asses."

The President? Fuck.

Three turns later, Pritchard shoves through the door to an empty conference room.

"So much for POTUS waiting on *me*. Why am I here, Pritchard? I'm retired. Or didn't you get the memo?"

He takes a seat near the head of the table, and points to the chair next to him. "Men like us don't retire. You know that."

The bitter edge to his voice sets me off. "Men like *us*? We are *nothing* alike. You sit in your plush leather chair in your private office, drinking ten-dollar coffee your secretary brings you while *I* go after terrorists, drug runners, and rapists, then spend a month cleaning sand out of everything I own. Which isn't much."

He levels me with a stare that warns I'm on thin ice. "I did my time until my brother...died. So when I had a chance to get out, I took it. Don't be a dick because you stayed in the field all these years. You knew what you were doing."

Pritchard's holier-than-thou attitude usually drives me up a fucking wall. But he's right. I could have retired. Gotten some cushy consulting gig. Maybe even an appointment like his.

"I didn't know about your brother," I say, stifling my wince as I drop down into the chair.

"Only half a dozen people in the world know. And it's

going to stay that way. We clear?" His blue eyes narrow on me.

"Crystal. So what's the deal in Kabul?" If he suspects I was involved in Faruk's death, I could be in a world of hurt—or prison—before the end of the day.

"Cut the crap, Nomar," Pritchard says. "You and I both know where you spent the past week. Getting Faruk's wife and son—along with one Dr. Josephine Taylor—out of Afghanistan. And if you say one goddamn thing about it to any of the men about to enter this room, I will personally shitcan you so fast, you won't know what hit you."

Fuck. I need to warn Ford. But before I can pull out my phone, the door opens, and the President of the United States walks in. He's followed by the CIA's Deputy Director of Operations and another man I don't know.

Pritchard and I both snap to attention. Technically, I haven't been on "active duty" for more than ten years, but some things are beat into you. "Mr. President," Austin says. "You remember Nomar Garcia?"

"Unofficially, yes." President Campos unbuttons his suit jacket and takes his seat at the head of the table. "On the record, I've never seen the man before. He's not here in this room right now."

Of course not. Because I'm a ghost.

"Amir Abdul Faruk. His name ring a bell?" the President asks, his gray eyes locked on me.

"One of the biggest human traffickers in Afghanistan. He also runs drugs, weapons, cash. If it's illegal, he's got a hand in it. I've had run-ins with his men a time or two over the years."

"He's dead." Alisha Collins, Deputy Director of the CIA, slides folders in front of each of us. "These photos came over the wire this morning."

This is it. The moment I have to choose between my

friends and my country. If there's a single picture of the team that took out Faruk, we're all fucked.

My hands are steady as I remove the first shot. Amir Faruk sits in a leather chair, duct tape over his mouth, zip ties securing his wrists. Blood bathes his beige tunic in a red so dark, it's almost black. The gaping wound where his throat used to be is clean, the mark of someone who didn't hesitate. I'm not surprised.

The other photos show more than a dozen men. Necks broken. Shot. Stabbed. And a room full of computers burned to a crisp.

"It was a goddamned massacre. Do we have any idea who did this?" the President asks.

Alisha shakes her head. "No, sir. But we do have a rough idea of the timing. At 3:36 a.m., one of our assets texted the Chief of Station. Message read: *Under attack.* A few hours ago, we found the asset and five others locked in the basement of Amir Abdul Faruk's compound. They claim two men wearing full balaclavas broke in and gave them a choice. Surrender or die."

"Accents? Eye color? Any identifying marks?" I ask. Next to me, Pritchard holds his breath. If he doesn't have at least *some* idea Ryker McCabe was involved, I'll eat this whole fucking folder. But if I don't ask questions, all eyes will be on me.

Alisha shakes her head. "Nothing definitive. Four of the survivors woke up with knives to their throats. The asset couldn't give us anything beyond 'tall and well-armed.'"

Relief leaves my hands tingling, but I don't let it show. I should have known McCabe wouldn't let anyone see his face and live, but even the best make mistakes.

"Mr. Garcia."

I turn to the man no one's bothered to introduce. "Finally going to tell me why I'm here? And who the hell you are?"

"My name isn't important. The fact that I'm in this room should tell you all you need to know." He leans forward, steepling his fingers in front of him, elbows on the table. "Ms. Collins has a small team in the area guarding the compound, but they won't be able to hold it for long."

"So? Faruk's dead. His empire can't survive without him. Torch the place and forget it ever existed. I'm retired."

"For fuck's sake." Pritchard runs a hand through his short-cropped hair. "Tell him."

Alisha pulls out another folder. This one is only for me. "There are two major players in the region who could fill the void left by Amir Faruk's death."

I flip open the folder and freeze. Shapur Khan. "You've got to be fucking kidding me."

"So the rumors are true," Mr. No Name says.

I shoot the man a look that could freeze hellfire. "Eleven years ago, Shapur was an up-and-coming hacker. Reckless as fuck. With Amir Musa's cartel. He stole a hundred thousand dollars from Faruk's coffers, and the asshole put out a hit on him. The *CIA* thought they could turn him, so they sent me to keep his ass alive. I did my job."

No Name stares me down. "It's time to collect on that debt."

CHAPTER ELEVEN

Lisette

Outside the window of my son's hospital room, night blankets the city in a dark blue cocoon. My stomach will not settle. I had hoped Nomar would call. That he would tell me what was so important he had to walk out on me this morning. But my phone remains stubbornly silent.

Mateen has asked about him more than once. He wanted to play FIFA and show Nomar something called a "back heel kick." But after his treatments, scans, and a game of Monopoly with his Mémé, Pépé, and Auntie Noele, he fell asleep with a stuffed duck in his arms—courtesy of the boat tour his grandparents raved about.

"Lisette," Maman says softly, her hand on my shoulder. "We need to talk."

Shit. I had hoped she would leave me be. I should have known better. I tug at a lock of hair and switch to French in case my son wakes. "I will not talk about *him* in front of Mateen."

"*Ma chérie,* you have said nothing about your time...away.

We cannot keep on like this. When you left us, there was such light to you. Now…"

Tears prick at my eyes. "When I *left*? I did not *leave*, Maman. I was taken. By a terrible man who did terrible things. Is it so strange that I do not wish to share what he did to me?"

I dart around her to turn up the white noise machine next to Mateen's bed, then hold up my hand when she follows.

"No. Not here. When we can return to France, I will tell you what I can. Until then, please…"

"I am your mother, Lisette. I am not allowed to worry for you?"

The judgement in her tone crushes me. "Of course you are. But you can see that I am safe. That my son is getting the best care. I cannot focus on myself when he needs me."

She closes her eyes and smooths a hand over her white hair. Such a simple motion. As a teenager, I learned it meant I had won whatever argument we were having. I hope that has not changed.

"We go home tomorrow," she says, such sadness in her voice. "And I keep thinking… What if I lose you again?"

I throw my arms around her. Ten years, and she smells exactly the same. Like her beloved L'Occitane shea butter with a hint of gardenia. The soft fragrance cuts through the harshness of antiseptic and bleach and lets me breathe again.

"You will not lose me, Maman. You can see how well protected we are. I do not know why Joey and Ford are doing so much for us, but I am grateful for it. For them."

"As am I," she whispers.

Drawing back, I offer her a weak smile. "I am not trying to hide from you. Or shut you out. When Mateen is better…" A lump swells in my throat as I glance over at my son. He looks so tiny in the hospital bed. So fragile. "*Then* I can heal."

Maman cups my cheek. "One of the hardest lessons a

mother must learn is how to put her children first, but not lose herself in the process, Lisette. Do not ignore your own needs for too long. Promise me."

How can I not? This morning, when Nomar told me about Faruk's death, I let myself feel. And I broke into a million pieces. If he had not been there to hold me, would I have been able to put myself back together again?

Her pale gray eyes hold mine, and I know she is waiting for an answer. All I can do is nod and change the subject. "You and Papa should go back to the apartment for the night. I fear he is buying every stuffed animal the gift shop has."

She laughs, her cheeks turning a delicate shade of pink. "I suppose we should not spoil Mateen too much until you come home. Otherwise you will need an extra suitcase just for his toys."

"It will not be long. Three months. Then you can spoil him all the time."

"I will miss you, *ma fille.*" Her eyes glisten with unshed tears. "If you wanted...we would stay."

My emotions threaten to drown me. There is a part of me —the daughter who will *always* need her mother—that wants her to cancel her flight. But I must figure out who I am in this new reality where I am not a prisoner. And I can only do that on my own.

"No. You and Papa should go. If you stayed, you would have to isolate with us until Mateen's immune system recovers. Can you imagine all that time in such a small apartment? No sightseeing, no restaurants, no visitors? We will talk on the phone, though. Every day if you want." I give her hands a gentle squeeze. "Besides, we will need a place to live when we return. You can help Noele find somewhere for us. And decorate Mateen's room for him."

"We will do that, *mon chérie.*"

Maman leans down and brushes a kiss to her grandson's

forehead, then embraces me. "We will see you in the morning before our flight. Sleep well."

I sink into the chair next to Mateen's bed and watch him sleep. His cheeks are pale, today's treatments so very hard on him. We will be all alone for months. In a city I do not know. Adjusting to a life so different from anything my son has ever known.

Ford and Joey are here. And Nomar. The memory of his kiss warms me against the chill in the room. He will be close. Would he be able to see me? To play games with Mateen? He was ready to put on a mask last night. Surely he would do so again? So we could spend time together?

For the first time in ten years, I imagine a future where I am...happy.

***

"Talk." Noele says after walking our parents back to the apartment. "Tell me everything that happened this morning."

Mateen is sleeping so soundly, he does not wake when the nurse comes in to take his vital signs, and once she is gone, my sister unzips her large bag and withdraws a bottle of Champagne and two plastic glasses.

"Noele!"

"What? We are adults." She laughs. "Besides, you missed my eighteenth birthday. You owe me a drink."

A wave of guilt slams into me. "What else did I miss?"

Pain flits across her delicate features for a brief moment. But the *pop* of the cork chases the darkness away. Such a happy, familiar sound amidst the whirring and beeping of the machines monitoring my son.

"Well, Maman walking in on me and Leonardo the last day of school. Naked. My first truly broken heart. Choosing a university. Moving into an apartment on my own. Receiving my degree." A single tear balances on her lower lashes. "But that is the past. You are here now."

I wrap my arms around her, the bottle trapped between us. "I am so sorry, *mon petite fleur.*"

"You have nothing to be sorry for." Noele hugs me back, then wriggles free and pours the wine. She holds her glass aloft. "À ta *santé.*"

"À ta *santé.*" The light, earthy flavor bursts over my tongue, and I savor the simple freedom of choosing what *I* want to eat and drink. "I am sorry we could not talk earlier, but Maman and Papa came too quickly. What else do you wish to know about...this morning?"

"Everything. You have been free for more than a week. Why did it take so long? If you knew about the American—"

"I did not. Faruk kept me away from the men. I spent most of my time with the other women."

"What other women? *Mon Dieu*, Lisette. How many? Did he take all of them?" She pales, and the glass wobbles in her hand.

"Some, maybe. The girls who cooked and cleaned were so young. The others were wives of his men. I learned quickly not to ask questions. We talked about our children, spent afternoons on knitting or bead work. It was a very...lonely life."

Noele swipes at her eyes. "How did you stand it?"

Before I can answer, there is a soft knock at the door. Nomar slips into the room, but stops when he sees Noele and the open bottle of wine. "I...shit. Can I talk to you, Lisette? It won't take long."

His shoulders slump, exhaustion making him look ten years older than he did this morning. "Stay with Mateen. I will be right outside," I say, handing Noele my glass.

Nomar takes my hand, linking our fingers and squeezing gently as he leads me into the hall. It is quiet this time of night—only a single nurse at the desk and the guards standing outside the elevator.

"I have to go away for a while."

"Where? When?" My heart aches, and an icy knot tightens in my stomach. He is so serious. Angry, even.

"Tonight. There's a plane waiting for me at Hanscom Air Force Base. It takes off in an hour."

The pain in his eyes terrifies me. Bringing his hand to my chest, I breathe in his scent. "How long will you be gone?

"A while." Nomar wraps his free arm around my waist and drops his forehead to mine.

"What does that mean? A week? A month?" I try to pull away, but he holds me close.

"Six months. Maybe a little longer," he says softly. "What I have to do...and where...it's classified."

"But you will call. To let me know you are okay?" Fear lends a tremble to my voice. I have only known him a week, but how can I let him go? He risked his life for me—for *us*. He calms me when nothing else can. I need him. So does Mateen. This new reality terrifies me, but with Nomar, I am safe.

"No, sweetheart. I won't be able to call." He brushes a kiss to my lips. "In an emergency, Ford might be able to get a message to me. But it wouldn't be quick."

"Do not go. Please?" I hate myself for asking. I should be stronger. I have Noele—for a short time. Joey and Ford. A place to live. Mateen is getting the best care. But without Nomar, how will I survive?

"I have to." His hand slides into my hair, twisting the strands around his fingers. "I'm so sorry."

Crushing his mouth to mine, he backs me against the wall. The rest of the world falls away. There is no gentleness to the kiss. His tongue sweeps over the seam of my lips, desperate, searching, begging me to let him in. I slide my hands up his chest, and something in my core warms when I feel the metallic barbs running through his nipples.

His hard length presses against my hip. "I wish we had more time," he whispers. "Goodbye, Lisette. Tell Mateen... fuck. Tell him we'll play FIFA together again one day. Tell him...I didn't want to go."

Nomar leaves me with one last, swift kiss, links our fingers in a tight hold, then lets them slip free. He walks backward to the elevator, his gaze on me the whole time, and when he steps through the doors, the anguish etched on his face sends my tears spilling over.

CHAPTER TWELVE

Nomar

Tension wraps a tight band around my temples, squeezing to the point of pain. The long, dusty drive from Kabul to Mazar-i-Sharif put me in a shitty fucking mood. Faruk's compound is the *last* place I ever wanted to see again.

Every time I clench my jaw—who am I kidding? I've barely *unclenched* it for thirty-six hours—I can feel the sand stuck in my teeth.

Mateen's in isolation now. Lisette's parents returned to France sometime yesterday. And I have no idea if she's okay.

The burner phone in my duffel bag is programmed with only one number. An exchange in Kandahar staffed by a CIA asset I'll never meet. I'll call in regular updates, but once I leave here, any contact with the rest of the world could blow the whole operation—and get me killed.

Walking away from Lisette was the hardest thing I've ever done. Harder than finding a shipping container full of trafficked women at a port in Dubai. Harder than infiltrating Al

Jihad in Egypt. Harder than crawling three miles—with malaria—over the mountains in Pakistan to evade Al Qaeda.

I've known her less than ten days. I shouldn't feel whatever-the-hell-this-is for her. I *definitely* shouldn't have kissed her. It was too soon. She was too raw. And it made leaving her that much harder.

Fuck. I slam my open hand against the steering wheel. The pain isn't enough to calm me. Not even close.

"Do not go. Please."

I'll hear her voice in my dreams every night until I can see her again. But by then, will she even want me?

She shouldn't. I'm the worst kind of asshole. My whole life is a lie. Hell, if I hadn't been with Ford and Trevor when I met her, she wouldn't even know my real name. In the field, I go by Guillermo Forza.

A drop of sweat stings my side. The doc in Uzbekistan told me to get the stitches taken out in two weeks. But that's when he thought I'd have access to regular medical care. Guess I'll be removing them myself. It won't be the first time.

Adjusting my headscarf and glasses—no one can know I'm here—I get out of the truck and head for the house. The guy in the foyer holding an AK-47 is army. But dressed in the traditional tunic, pants, and turban, he can *almost* pass for a local.

Blood trails smear the tile, all the way to Faruk's office. Shit. The carpet in front of the desk chair is stained almost black. Slitting a man's throat makes a goddamn mess.

Someone—one of Ryker's men, I bet—drilled his hard drive, but I take photos of his ledger and all the notes in the margins. They're gibberish to me now, but I'll study them once I have some privacy. No other files. No bank information. I'm not surprised. All that shit would have been in the burned-out server room.

I'm not supposed to know my way around, so I wander for

a few minutes before I enter the private living quarters off the kitchen. Mateen's toys litter one corner of the main room. Wooden cars, a rough-hewn train set, some dolls with hand-made clothes. A Dari and English letter book is open to the letter D. *Dukhtar.* Daughter.

I pick through the train cars until I find the engine. It's the most worn, the paint gone, the wheels smooth and almost shiny. He's had to deal with so much in his short life. If the CIA can get this to him, maybe it'll help.

I feel like an intruder when I enter the bedroom. A woven blanket in reds, blues, and golds covers the mattress. A mirrored dressing table holds an ornate jewelry box over-flowing with chains, bangles, and rings. Rubies and emeralds wink in the sunlight slashing through the barred window. The asshole lavished her with gifts. Probably thought they made up for beating the crap out of her on the regular.

This wasn't Lisette's sanctuary. It was her prison.

"Fuck!" With a sweep of my fist, I send the baubles tumbling to the floor. The motion disturbs the long strip of silk covering the table, and something glints from underneath.

The bracelet is simple. A chain with an engraved silver plate.

"Il n'est rien de réel que le rêve et l'amour."

Nothing is real but dreams and love.

The French words send a chill through me, despite the heat in the air. I squeeze my eyes shut, seeing the photo Lisette's parents gave Interpol ten long years ago. She's smiling. Holding a bouquet of flowers in her left hand. With *this* bracelet around her wrist.

I can't leave it behind. He took everything from her. He won't take this.

Back in Faruk's office, I find an envelope and pen.

Lisette Moreau

St. Jude's Research Hospital
Boston, MA

I slide the bracelet inside, seal the flap, and head to the foyer. Slapping the envelope against the sentry's chest, I stare him down—even though he's got at least six inches on me. "If I find out this didn't get delivered, I'm holding *you* personally responsible. Understand?"

His eyes widen, fear stealing the color from his cheeks. He's heard the rumors. All the shit I've done over the past twenty years.

"Y-yes, sir!" he snaps.

I press the train car and envelope into his hand. "Smart man. I'm done here. Blow it all to hell."

Twenty-four hours later, my mood hasn't improved. The serving girl hovers in the doorway, waiting for me to try the overly sweetened green tea. I hate the stuff, but it's all you get in Afghanistan in the summer.

How long is Shapur Khan—the little shit adopted the most pompous surname on the planet a couple of years ago—going to make me wait? I saved his fucking life. He could show some goddamn respect.

Six months. Collins and No Name said I'd be done in six months. I could be home by Christmas if I play my cards right. Or...maybe I'll spend the holiday in France. If Lisette will even talk to me.

"Guillermo!" Shapur breezes into the room. The years haven't been kind to the kid. If I didn't know better, I'd think he was closer to fifty than thirty. His face is puffy, his skin greasy in the heat of June. "*Salam alaikum.* I thought you were dead, my friend."

"That's what I wanted you to think." I rise, my right hand

over my heart, and nod. Shapur returns the gesture. "Abdul Faruk put a price on my head. I had to lie low in Zanzibar for a while. Lucky for me, most of his men were idiots."

He chuckles, his head thrown back. The thick scar across his throat came at the hands of two of Faruk's goons, and it didn't heal well. "Now, you have returned. Who told you of the Amir's death?"

"I have my sources. Any idea who finally got to him?"

"Much has changed since we last saw one another, Guillermo." He sweeps his gaze over the richly appointed sitting room. Plush, embroidered cushions surround the low table. A thick rug adorns the polished tile, and I've seen no less than *four* servants in the thirty minutes I've been here. "The Amir ceded much power these last few years."

"To you?"

He answers with a smile.

For fuck's sake. Shapur is going to take credit for Faruk's death. Stupid on an epic level. Or...shit. No. It's brilliant. The CIA needs him to take over running guns, drugs, and girls in the region. If I can help sell his bullshit story, half his potential competition will run screaming.

The young girl brings a fresh pot of tea. Shapur refills my cup—as is tradition—and offers me a bowl of sugared almonds.

"*Manana*," I say and pop two of them into my mouth. My teeth are practically buzzing now.

"Your Pashto has not suffered for your absence. To what do I owe the honor of this visit?"

"I've kept tabs on you, Shapur. After I helped you in Kabul," I gesture to his neck, "I felt...it was my duty. With Faruk gone, the opportunities for a man with *ambition* are endless. And all who stand behind such a man will share in the glory."

Shapur's brown eyes light up, and he leans forward. "I owe you my life. Whatever you want, you have only to ask."

"I've been out of the game for five years. I want back in."

***

Eleven Months Later

THE TRUCK JERKS to a stop outside a small warehouse on the outskirts of Kabul. The five men under my command heft their Kalashnikovs and form a semicircle behind the vehicle.

I lower the tailgate and loosen the tarp hiding a dozen women from view. "Out! Quickly." Repeating the order in Pashto and Dari, I glare at Shapur's latest *shipment*. They're terrified. And way too goddamn young.

The men shove at them, herding them into the warehouse where they'll be stripped, photographed, and held for days before going to auction.

I can't protect them. Not here. But tomorrow, I'll lose myself in Jalalabad's shopping district and leave the auction address at a dead drop. I don't know if the CIA can save the girls or not. But Pritchard swore they'd do their best.

Inside the warehouse, the girls huddle together, eyes downcast, utterly silent, as one of Shapur's grunts kicks a box of white bras and panties at them. "You will put these on. Now."

Another sets up a digital camera on a tripod in front of a black tarp.

The closest girl has green eyes that haunt me. She's not local. I can't watch this.

"Don't let me lose my soul, Pritchard. That's all I ask."

It's too late. With every shipment, every competitor Shapur asks me to threaten or kill, another piece of me dies. It doesn't matter that this is the job. That Shapur Khan is the least of all the evils in Afghanistan. That the CIA might be able to use him—if he'd ever take a goddamn meeting with them. I'm still here. Five months after No Name promised they'd get me home.

Every night, I dream of Lisette. I wonder what she's doing. If Mateen is healthy. If she's happy. If she's thinking about me.

"Now, *kussi!*" Obalesh shouts. The slap reverberates through the warehouse, and I whirl around to see the green-eyed girl on the ground, holding her cheek.

"Do not damage the merchandise!" I shove him back, waving at Jaabir to take his place. The girl weeps, her abaya bunched up around her knees, and her headscarf askew. "What is your name?" I ask, taking a knee next to the girl.

"Veda." Tears carve pale rivulets down her dirty cheeks. She's trembling so much, she can barely speak.

"I know you're scared, Veda. But if you do what you're told, you won't be hurt here. Change. Let the men take your photo, and then you will get food and water. Okay?"

Behind my back, Obalesh and Jaabir whisper to one another. They hate that I'm kind to the girls. That I don't let them have their way with the *merchandise*. But the buyers will only pay for virgins.

Veda nods and turns around before she takes off her abaya. If the CIA doesn't get her out, I'll track her down and free her myself. I'll free all of them. One day.

SHAPUR SITS on a stone platform in the center of the steam room, a towel around his waist. Water is scarce here, even for the rich, but this decadence keeps his most trusted men happy. The public bathhouses are always packed.

"Was the merchandise acceptable?" he asks, dipping a

large cup into the wooden bucket on the floor, then pouring warm water over his head.

Rage crawls up my throat.

They're women. Not property, fuckstick.

After a breath, I nod. "More than adequate. Where did this batch come from? They didn't look local."

"Pakistan." Shapur leans back on his hands and crosses his legs at the ankles. "They came in with the heroin. We saved a fortune on transport costs."

Did he seriously pick these girls because he got *free shipping*? Fucker. I could end him with a single blow. Crush his windpipe and let him suffocate to death. No one's allowed in here this late at night without an invitation. I'd be in Uzbekistan before any of the servants discovered his body.

Shapur rambles on about his new distribution network for heroin, cocaine, and meth, but I tune him out. I'm the one who set things in motion. Introduced him to the right people.

The steam starts to relax my muscles, and for a moment, I forget how much I hate this life. Until I lower my gaze and catch sight of the French words winding around my bicep.

"Il n'est rien de réel que le rêve et l'amour."

Nothing is real but dreams and love. The memory of Lisette's bracelet haunted me for weeks. So much so, on one of my days off, I found a back alley tattoo shop in Jalalabad and paid a small fortune for the permanent reminder of why I'm doing this. For her.

Tattoos aren't common in Afghanistan. In Islam, it's haram—forbidden—to mark one's body. Thank fuck for long-sleeved tunics. Shapur didn't see the ink until it was healed, and I convinced him it was old. The result of a drunken night and a long-lost love from my youth. The best lies have a kernel of truth to them.

Deep cover is risky. Reality blurs, and the line between

who you are and who you need to be can disappear in a heartbeat. This...helps.

I should have been gone months ago. But Shapur's empire is still too fragile. His biggest rival—some asshat named Musa out of Kandahar—has cornered the market on opium, and until the CIA takes him out, I'm stuck. They claim they're working on it. That it'll happen any day. Hell, I told them exactly how to do it. But they're dragging their feet, and my patience is wearing thin.

Shapur peers down his nose at me. Fuck. I want to punch the judgment right off his face. Between the tattoo and the barbs through my nipples, I'm a heathen of the highest order. But he needs me, and he knows it. If only he knew about the *other* piercing. The one hidden under my towel.

After a sigh, he runs a hand through his black hair. "I must ask you for a favor."

"Name it. You've made me a very rich man. How can I repay you?" I'd vomit at my tone, but in Afghanistan, posturing will get you *everywhere*.

"Retrieve my betrothed and her father from Sarawbi tomorrow and escort them here. We are to be wed in two days."

I sit up straight. "And you're only telling me *now*? I thought we were friends."

His chuckle should reassure me, but I'm supposed to be his right-hand man. The one he trusts with all his secrets. If he's hiding things from me, I'm fucked.

"I only agreed to the union this morning. Her name is Hajira, and she is the most beautiful woman I have ever seen."

I study him, searching for any evidence he's lying. His fingers drum against the stone. Nerves. A hint of worry. But underneath, excitement. Dilated pupils, a smile curving his lips. The man is legitimately smitten.

"How did you meet her? And when?" I don't give a fuck, but I have to pretend I do.

"You will laugh," he says.

Well, shit. Now I *am* interested. "On my life, I won't."

Leaning forward with his elbows on his knees, he shakes his head. "I am a rich man. Fathers demand outrageous dowries when they learn my name. But though we embrace the old ways for many things, you know we are not without technology. I used...an app."

I snap my mouth shut before I laugh myself into a beheading. When I wrestle control of my shock, I ask, "You swiped right?"

With a chuckle, he trails his fingers through the water. "I did. The negotiation was over before Hajira's father learned my name. Bring them here quickly, Guillermo. I have many enemies, and now that we are betrothed, I will fear for her safety until we are wed."

With a nod, I push to my feet. "May you and Hajira have a lifetime of happiness, Shapur. You honor me with your trust. What time are they expecting me?"

***

An hour outside of Jalalabad, I pull over to relieve myself behind some large tufts of desert grass. I'm far enough from the truck, so I take a risk and call the Kabul exchange.

"Bank of Raman," a man says in lightly accented Dari. "How can I help you?"

"Extension seven-eight-six. Deposits and loans."

"May I have your name, sir?"

"None of your damn business." The passphrase was my idea, and the asset on the other end of the line hates it. He sighs and, after a series of clicks, securing the call, tells me to proceed.

"The next auction is in six days." I rattle off the address. "Eight packages, untouched."

"Anything else, sir?"

"Yeah. Tell Constellation she broke our deal. I was supposed to be done in December. It's fucking May. Next time I call, have an exfil plan for me. I need my goddamn life back."

WE'RE HALFWAY TO JALALABAD, and my control is slipping. The moment I met Hajira's father, Yar, I wanted to kill him. He hasn't stopped berating the poor girl the entire drive. She's too slow. Too ugly. Too fat. Her very rich, very powerful husband-to-be is going to reject her, and she'll bring such shame to their family, her life will be less than worthless.

The icing on the cake? She's barely eighteen. I'd bet my left nut she's having second thoughts—if she even consented to the marriage in the first place.

We stop for water under the shade of a large, broadleaf tree, and Hajira sniffles quietly while her father continues his tirade. "You do not know what is good for you. I find you a husband who does not care how stupid you are, and you do nothing but cry."

"Papa, please do not sell me to him," she begs. "I want to go home to Mama."

Fuck. I should have known. The weight of everything I've done the past eleven months hits me so hard, I can't breathe. Digging my fingers into my bicep over my tattoo, I turn away. I *have to* deliver this girl and her father. If I don't, my life won't be worth shit. And neither will hers.

Shapur has trackers on all of his vehicles. He knows where I am, how long we've stopped for...hell, he's so paranoid, he'll probably be waiting at the gate when we arrive.

But I look at Hajira, and I see Lisette at twenty-four. Her fear when Faruk took her. The utter terror of not knowing what would happen to her. If she would ever see her family again.

Yar shuffles around to the other side of the tree to take a piss. I lean closer to Hajira and lower my voice. "When did you learn about this marriage?"

She sinks down to the ground, covering her face with her hands. "This morning. I thought...I would marry a man in my village. Not one...so far away I will never see Mama again."

Her father curses, yanks her to her feet, and slaps her hard enough blood spatters the ground in front of her. "You do not speak to anyone until I have signed the marriage contract." Turning to me, he curls his lip. "We are ready to go. Get back in the car, outsider."

What choice do I have? Subdue the asshole and set off for Uzbekistan with an underage girl in tow? If anyone catches us together—without a chaperone—she could be stoned. Whipped. Branded a whore. Barbaric as fuck, but that's what happens here.

This damn job isn't worth it. The CIA's been "working out" how to kill Musa for months—despite me telling them exactly how to get to him. Stringing me along, telling me they're close. But with every auction, every shipment of drugs and guns, my hope of ever being whole again fades a little more.

I'll deliver Hajira to her new home. For all his faults, Shapur might make a halfway decent husband. She'll want for nothing. Except her mother. And her freedom.

But I'm done with this life. I can't wait for an exfil plan. Before sunrise prayers tomorrow, I'm gone.

CHAPTER THIRTEEN

Nomar

Shapur waits at the front door, smiling like he's just won the goddamn lottery. "Hajira. My jewel. You are twice as beautiful as your picture." He does not touch her, but bows with his right hand over his heart.

Yar shoves the girl forward. "Do not just stand there like an idiot."

Darkness flickers in Shapur's gaze. "She is not an idiot, and you will not speak to her that way in my home." He waves to one of the serving girls, who rushes to Hajira's side. "Esin will show you to your room, my jewel. Then take you to the kitchen for a meal. If you want for *anything*, you have only to ask her. My wife will always be taken care of."

Hajira smiles for the first time. As soon as she disappears into the house with Esin, Shapur snaps his fingers. Three of his men surround Yar.

"Bring him to my office. Now. I will pay off the marriage contract tonight and he can find his own way back to his home."

Yar sputters a weak protest as the men prod him in the back with their weapons, but Shapur ignores him and turns to me. "Was he that...disagreeable the entire trip?"

I snort. "That was nothing. Hajira only found out about the marriage this morning. She thinks she'll never see her mother again."

Genuine pain fills Shapur's gaze. "I went to college in England. You knew this, yes?"

I nod. This is a side to him I haven't seen before. Introspective. Almost...morose.

His shoulders heave with a heavy breath. "This is how we have done things for centuries. But that does not mean it is right. Or best. I knew many couples in England who married for love. I always thought...perhaps one day I would too."

"So why did you pick Hajira? We could have found a way for you to meet women. Your name holds weight, but not many know your face."

"A leader without a wife is no leader," he says, a hint of sadness to his voice. "Thank you for bringing her to me. I will pay her father, sign the marriage contract, and send him home. She will not suffer his anger a moment longer."

Before he walks away, I clasp his arm. "Shapur? Be gentle with her. If you are...she might one day grow to love you."

I wait until 2:00 a.m. The house is utterly silent. Unlike Amir Faruk, who built his compound in the middle of fucking nowhere, Shapur lives on the outskirts of the city. A tall fence surrounds his property, and he bought the two houses on either side so he could have most of his men close. But there's only one guard on patrol outside.

His office is dark. There's just enough light from the hall for me to turn on his laptop. I've watched him for eleven months. Carefully. Never staring. Memorizing his password a character or two at a time. He's never changed it. Why would he? I'm here for the money, and it never stops.

He keeps impeccable records. Spreadsheets for everything. All organized and cataloged. I pop a thumb drive into the laptop and copy two years' worth of records in seconds.

It's not enough. I can't leave without the names of every man who has ever attended one of the auctions. For all I know, the CIA might have freed all of the girls—or none of them. But I fear it's the latter. Shapur's reputation would be in the gutter if every girl he'd ever sold *disappeared* weeks later.

He built the auction site himself, and when I try to access the source database, an error pops up on the screen. Fuck. It's encrypted, and I don't have the key.

My tech skills are only passable. I search the desk, but Shapur is too smart to write the key on a Post-it note under his keyboard.

His bedroom is at the other end of the house. This is a huge fucking risk, but I don't have a choice. Pulling out my phone, I call the one person who might be able to help.

"Hello?" Ford's voice is wary. Mine would be too if an Afghanistan number showed up on my mobile.

"I don't have a lot of time, Marine. Any way you can conference in your hacker?"

"If you tell me where we first met, yes."

I'd laugh, but if Shapur wakes up, I'm dead. "Al-Faw Peninsula. I've got less than an hour to disappear. If she's not available—"

"Wren?" Ford says. "Got a friend who needs your help."

"All right...Friend. What do you need?"

I'm unprepared for her immediate acceptance. "Uh...I'm looking at a HyperCrypt login screen securing a triple hashed database. And I need in."

Wren whistles over the line. "I like you, Friend. I haven't

had a challenge like this in a while. If you have internet access on that box, type in the following address…"

I do as she asks, but see only a blank screen with a single file in the upper left. "What is this?"

"Double click that file. It'll give me access to the hard drive. That level of encryption isn't something I can break in twenty minutes. It's going to take hours," she says. "I'll work as fast as I can, but—"

"I don't have that long. Not if I expect to live to see tomorrow." I lean forward, peering into the hall. It's still quiet, but every minute I'm here is a minute closer to death.

"Run the program," she says. "I'll turn off the screen. No one will know the computer's on, and you can get out of there. When I decrypt the data, I'll upload it to a secure share and you can access it from anywhere."

"You're sure no one will know?"

"Flippin' flapjacks. Ford, tell your *friend* I know what the hockey puck I'm doing."

I'm having a stroke. That's the only explanation for what I'm hearing. "Uh…?"

"Wren gets creative with her profanity," Ford says with a chuckle. "She's also one of the top three hackers in the world."

"*One of*…?" The delicate sound that carries over the line is definitely a snort. "Puh-leeze. The last time I went up against ZedHorse and Daystrumer, they crawled back to their mothers in tears after I zeroed them."

She's so confident, I click on the file. A black window flashes on the screen for a few seconds, text scrolling by too quickly to read, and then it's gone.

"I'm in. Get out of there, Friend. When you're somewhere safe, call Ford and he'll connect us."

"I can't repay you for this—"

"You saved Joey's life," Ford says. "You don't owe me a damn thing."

The call drops, and I stare at the phone until the laptop screen flickers off. I didn't even get a chance to ask about Lisette. To find out if she's okay.

Stop it. You don't have time for that now.

I rush back to my room, shove a single change of clothes, a wad of cash, and a pair of Berettas into my duffel bag. It has to look like I'm coming back.

The single guard patrolling the grounds stops me before I get into the truck. "Where are you going?"

"Got a call from one of Musa's guys. We did a couple jobs together ten years ago. He says he's got info we need. I'll be back by noon."

He nods, then opens the gate. If this plan doesn't work, Shapur will never stop hunting me. But staying here another day? That would kill me.

FORTY-EIGHT HOURS LATER, I stagger into an abandoned house on the outskirts of Kandahar. Blood stains my tunic, my hair, my fingernails. None of it mine. For now.

I dumped Shapur's truck in north Jalalabad, stole another, left it in Kabul, and wound through the streets for three hours before I boosted the one I'm using now. Other than the cash, pistols, and USB drive, I kept nothing I took from Shapur. After finding that fucking tracker in Lisette's abaya last year, there was no way I could take that risk. I smashed my CIA-issued phone and bought a new one before I left Kabul.

I trust no one—except Ford and Trevor—so I sink down against the wall and dial the former Marine.

"Foxtrot Charlie," I say before he can get a word out.

"It's about damn time. Another six hours and I was going to send McCabe's team to look for you."

"Why?"

"Because we're friends? Because without you, I wouldn't be meeting Joey for lunch in an hour. Because Pritchard told me where you've been since you left Boston."

"Fucker. Wait, how do you know the head of JSOC?"

After a long pause, Ford blows out a breath. "You've been under a long time, Nomar. Austin was shitcanned months ago. He's a civie now. And Trevor's in love with his sister."

My low whistle echoes off the mud and stone walls. "Shit. What about Collins?"

"Who?"

"Deputy Director of the CIA. Alisha Collins. I've been sending her my reports for months. If she's gone too..."

"Hang on..." After a few seconds, he continues. "According to Wikipedia, she's still there. But I can have Dax make some calls."

"Don't bother. I'm out. Or I will be in a few hours." Saying the words aloud makes them real, and I pull my knees up and drop my head into my hands. "Fuck."

"Ask, and I'll call McCabe." Ford's confident the K&R firm out of Seattle can help me, but he doesn't know the shitstorm I'm about to be caught up in.

"After what he did to Amir Faruk? If McCabe or any of his people step one toe over the border, they're signing their own death warrants. Besides, I still have work to do."

"What work?" The strain in his voice belies the casual question. "You had Wren decrypt a hell of a lot of data, Nomar. Names. Bank accounts. Routing numbers. Payment amounts that are suspiciously familiar. Shapur Khan took over the flesh trade after Faruk's death. And you're his right-hand man."

"Was," I snap. "And it was fucking killing me. The

goddamn President of the United States asked me to work the kid. So we'd have a friendly face in Afghanistan. And I did it. I've moved guns, drugs, and so many girls, I'll never be whole again. They've been stringing me along for months now. Telling me they're working on an exfil plan. That they just need another few weeks. But three days ago, I had to deliver an eighteen-year-old girl to Shapur's house because her father *sold* her off to be married sight unseen."

"Fuck."

"Yeah. Thing is, he's actually a halfway decent guy. I think he'll worship that girl for the rest of his life. But there was one with green eyes in the last group to go to auction, and all I could think about..." My voice falters, a lump clogging my throat.

"She's back in France," Ford says softly. "The transplant was a success. Mateen's healthy. He's been working with a private tutor the past few months so he can start school in the fall with other kids his age."

I don't have any right to ask if Lisette's happy, so I settle for the next best thing. "Does she have everything she needs?"

He huffs. "If you'd bothered to call more than once in the past year, maybe you'd know the answer."

"Ford..."

"For fuck's sake," he mutters to himself. "After Faruk... *died*, Wren spent weeks siphoning money from his accounts. The ones she could find, anyway. Ripper emptied the rest of them in September. Ry and Dax sent two million to Lisette and there's another five million in trust for Mateen."

"Five...million?"

"It would have been more, but Lisette told us if we put any more money into her accounts, she'd stop sending Joey pictures of Mateen." He sighs, and I wonder how much the kid's grown since I left. "You should call her, man."

God, I'd give anything to hear her voice. To see her. To hold her. But until I've atoned for every one of my sins, I don't deserve to even *think* about her, let alone talk to her.

"I need the data Wren got off Shapur's hard drive."

Ford gives me the hacker's number, and I program it into my phone in case I need it after tonight. "Come back home," he says when I tell him I have to go.

"There's so much blood on my hands, I'm drowning." The words crack, and my eyes start to burn. "Don't look for me. Don't send McCabe. Promise me."

"Can't do that—"

I slam my head back against the wall, using the pain to fuel my resolve. "Goddammit! I'm not fucking around here, Ford. As soon as I get what I need from Wren, I'm going dark. I have to. Let me do this. Please."

"On one condition," he says. "Non-negotiable."

Exhaustion hits me so hard, I can barely speak. "What is it?"

"Every six months, without fail, you send up a flare. Let me know you're alive. If you're even a day late, Ry and his team will drag you back here trussed up like a Christmas goose."

I don't have a choice. Ford's as stubborn as I am, with a whole family of men and women willing to risk their lives because he asked them to. So I agree, and when I end the call, I wonder if I'll live long enough to talk to him again.

AFTER A FEW HOURS OF SLEEP, half a canteen of water, and the last of the dried meat I bought at the market in Kandahar, I connect to a secure email server and upload a single photo, along with two words.

"You're welcome."

Musa's death wasn't pretty, but it was quick. I severed his carotid artery while he slept. The bastard bled out within seconds of opening his eyes.

Now the CIA has no reason to wait. They can wrap up Musa's assets in a pretty pink ribbon and deliver them to Shapur's doorstep. Hell, he thinks *Musa* killed *me*—thanks to the carefully staged pictures I took of myself, bloodied, in a shallow grave in the middle of the desert. And sent from a phone I stole off one of Musa's men a few months ago. If Shapur really did consider me a friend, he'll be so fucking grateful to the CIA, he'll listen to anything they have to say.

Wren set up a website I can access from anywhere— secured by a sixteen-digit passphrase. Buyers' names and addresses. Photos of the girls they purchased. The price they paid. Hell, she even organized it by region. As if she knew exactly what I was going to do.

Of course she did.

She's part of McCabe's team. And any black hat worth her salt knows the shit that goes on in this part of the world.

Outside, I build a small fire and burn my bloody clothes. The next auction is in two days. If I have any hope of saving those girls, I need to get out of here tonight.

But as I kick dirt over the last red embers, I hear Lisette's sweet voice.

"Do not go."

"I have to, sweetheart," I whisper into the darkness. "Or I'll never be whole again."

CHAPTER FOURTEEN

Present Day

Lisette

THE PATTER of raindrops on my umbrella keeps me company as I walk along Rue du Parc. The school bell trills, harsh, yet happy at the same time, and I turn to wave before Mateen disappears inside.

But his head is bent towards his best friend, Philippe, and he does not see me.

I miss the days he looked to me for everything, though I knew they could not last. The long, strange months isolating in Boston while his new bone marrow took hold. The loud, cramped weeks sharing a single room in my parents' house in Marseille. The exciting year we passed in a rented apartment with private tutors so he could attend school with other children his age.

Toulouse was the start of a new adventure. A place only for us. A duplex I own, bought with funds I did not want, but am grateful for.

I called it blood money. Joey called it restitution.

The city suits me. Busy, but not frantic. Close enough to Marseille we can visit Maman and Papa every few months, but far enough away for me to figure out who I am now that I am...free.

Ten minutes later, I push through the door of *Pétales de Fleurs*. "*Bonjour*, Fleur," I call, breathing in the fresh, sweet scent of roses, carnations, and peonies.

"Lisette! Come sit." With a warm smile, Fleur pats a chair at the small bistro table in the corner of the shop. "I bought *Pain au Chocolat* and *cafe au lait* on the way in. I thought you could use a treat today."

Dabbing at my eyes with a tissue, I swallow the lump in my throat. "Mateen was so happy to see his friends again. You would think we spent three *years* in Marseille, not three weeks."

"Time moves slower for children." Fleur opens the simple, white box and offers me a chocolate croissant. "Did you have a good visit with your parents?"

I tear off a piece of pastry. "Maman still thinks I am too thin. She baked fresh bread every other day. Mateen learned how to swim. He is like a fish now." Pride tugs at my lips. "I think he grew three inches this summer. Another year and he will be as tall as I am."

"Do you have pictures?" Fleur asks. "I have not seen your sweet boy since June."

"*Mon Dieu.* I did not know it had been that long. He was so busy this summer with his tutors. But he does not need them anymore. His French is almost as good as mine now." I pull out my phone and we scroll through photos until our coffees are nothing but a distant memory, and it is time for the shop to open.

A LITTLE AFTER THREE, I carry my last arrangement of the day to the cooler and tuck it neatly inside. Before I can wash my hands, my phone beeps in my pocket. The tone is one reserved for Ford and Joey. I hold my breath as I check the screen.

Joey: He's in Pakistan. Sending you the number he used to call Ford. Maybe this time, he'll answer?

My eyes burn. He will not. He never does, but I have to try.

In the back room, I sink down onto one of the storage crates. My fingers shake as I dial.

Please pick up.

The call rings four times before it goes to voicemail.

"Be quick," the message says. His voice is raspier than I remember. Strained. But still so familiar. I hear it in my dreams most nights still.

"It is...me." I do not dare use his name—or mine. "It has been so long. A lifetime, it seems. We are...happy here. But I still hope that one day I will see you again. You made me feel safe when my life was in ruins. I...miss you."

If I say more, I will start to cry. For months, I held out hope he would return. That the kisses we shared meant as much to him as they did to me. But as the days stretched into a year, then two, and now three, I locked my feelings away so they could no longer hurt me.

"Lisette?" Fleur knocks softly on the storeroom door. "Oh, honey...what is wrong?"

Fleur took a chance on me a year ago. I had no work history. No experience. No confidence. But she saw something in me she recognized. She knows I escaped something terrible. That there was a man who saved me. A man I thought could be a part of my future.

"Every six months, I call him," I say, staring at the darkened phone screen. "But he never answers."

She folds me into her embrace and lets me cry in her arms. After all this time, I should be stronger.

"I built a life for myself, Fleur. For Mateen. We are happy here. I should be able to let him go."

Patting my back gently, she sighs. "When two hearts come together, distance and time mean nothing. If it is meant to be, he will come back to you."

Nomar

"I...miss you."

Fuck.

I shut the phone off, tuck it into my vest pocket, and secure the flap. Her voice leaves my hands shaking. I should know better by now. Every six months, I contact Ford. Usually a call or a text. Email's too easy to spoof. And within half an hour, I get a message from Lisette.

The first one, there were tears. The second...anger. After that, resignation. She knows I'm never coming back. Yet she asks. Every time.

If I were stronger, I'd tell Ford to stop giving her my number. But I'm not. I *need* to hear her voice. To know she's okay. To remind me why I'm hiding behind a burned-out car in the dark, for the third straight night rather than booking the first flight I can get to France.

On my knees, I slam my fist into the hard-packed dirt. Pain sings up my arm. It's not enough. It's *never* enough. Since I faked my own death and left Shapur, I've been shot, stabbed, and tortured with a car battery. I've gone months without a proper meal, a full eight hours of rest, or any semblance of a home. But every time I fall asleep, I dream of her.

That last kiss...sometimes, I can still taste her. I hear her voice in the wind. In birdsong. In the moments between the screams.

Fifty meters north, a man slings a Kalashnikov over his shoulder and lights a cigarette. The reddish glow flickers over his beard and his dark eyes. He's the only one guarding the exterior, but there could be up to five armed guards inside the Karachi warehouse. Along with more than two dozen men, women, and children trafficked into forced labor.

I creep closer. The moon rises in an hour, and I'll lose the cover of total darkness. Crouching down behind a Land Rover that's seen better days, I check the smoker's position.

He's staring at his mobile. Idiot. Some of these assholes make it too easy. Flicking my wrist, I send a stone skipping along the edge of the asphalt. Smoker tenses and turns.

In two seconds, I have my arm around his neck, cutting off his air. His cigarette tumbles to the ground as he claws at my sleeve, but he could gouge half my arm away and I wouldn't let go.

His body goes limp. Fuck. He's heavier than I expected. I drag him back behind the Land Rover, zip tie his wrists and ankles, then press my knife to his throat. After a few seconds, he groans softly.

"Not another sound." His eyes snap open, but to his credit, he remains silent. "How many inside?"

His gaze darts to his left, but I jerk the blade, opening up a shallow cut. "They can't help you, asswipe. How. Many?"

"Three," he whispers.

I can handle three. Hopefully they're as poorly trained as this idiot. Pulling a scrap of cloth from my pocket, I smile at him. "Open wide."

"Please," he says through clenched teeth. "If you leave me alive, Rayan will kill me. Slowly."

"Not my problem." I dig my fingers into either side of his

jaw. A weak cry escapes his lips, and I shove the rag into his mouth. But before I can tie a length of rope around his head, I see the fear in his eyes.

Shit.

His boss has taken over the flesh trade in both Afghanistan *and* Pakistan. Flexing my shoulder, I wince as the long scar across my chest pulls taut. Rayan's men gave it to me. Before they waterboarded me and tortured me with live jumper cables for two fucking days.

"Tell us who you are working with!"

Joke was on them. I work alone. If they'd believed me, maybe they would have kept their intestines *inside* their bodies.

I yank the rag from Smoker's mouth. "You have a family?"

He nods.

"What about the guys inside?"

Another nod.

I drag him back to the warehouse and prop him up against the wall.

"Call them out here. Make it easy on me, and no one suffers. You have my word. But if you warn them, not only will I keep you alive, I'll drop you on Rayan's doorstep with a thank you note and a dozen cookies."

"M-my phone," he stammers. "The first number."

I dial, then drop the ancient device in his lap and take aim with my M4.

"Someone's coming. Two trucks. Get out here. Now!" He lowers his head onto his bent knees as the door bangs open.

Three shots, and the threat is neutralized. Another three to make damn sure no one gets back up again, and I return to Smoker. "You sure about this?"

Tears shine on his cheeks as he peers up at me. "It is the only way to keep my wife and son safe."

"Close your eyes."

One hundred and six. No, one-oh-nine. I don't regret any of my kills the past two years. Every single one of them would have ended my life given half the chance. This guy is no different.

So why am I hesitating?

Because I'm tired. Because no matter how many lives I save, it'll never be enough. Because when I heard her voice, I remembered what it was like to feel.

The shot tears through Smoker's skull. He jerks once, a single, gentle breath escaping his lips as his heart stops.

Inside, the women and children huddle in one large cage, the men in another. Unwashed, with tear-stained faces, ripped clothing, and almost identical expressions—shock mixed with fear.

"Safe," I say in Urdu, Pashto, then English. "You're all safe now."

TWELVE HOURS LATER, I dump the van on the outskirts of Hyderabad and sling my duffel bag over my shoulder. It took forever to get the twenty-seven men, women, and children I rescued across the border to India. But they're safe now. Delivered to a former member of the SAS I met while rescuing Lisette, Mateen, and Joey. Matt will get them back to their homes or set them up with new identities in India.

Finding an internet cafe, I pay for an hour, and sink into a shitty chair in a cubicle that looks like it's about to topple over. It took me nine months to work my way through the list of buyers I stole from Shapur. In the eighteen months since, I've found the worst of humanity all over the Middle East, and picked them off one at a time. So many that I've made a name for myself. Or a nickname, anyway.

The Viper.

I should be using my time here to pull up a map of Multan. Familiarize myself with the terrain around Rayan's home. Instead, I connect to a secure email server and find the photo Ford sent me six months ago. Lisette stands on the bank of a river, her arm around Mateen's shoulders. The kid has grown almost a foot. Lisette's dark hair—once long enough, it brushed her ass—is now cut in a short, angled bob. Her smile lights up her whole face. She's no longer rail thin, with soft curves under her black sweater.

They look so different. So...happy.

"Enough." The word sticks in my throat. Nothing will ever be enough where Lisette is concerned.

I log off, wipe the browser history, and head for the nearest pub. Alcohol won't silence my demons, but if I drink enough, maybe I won't dream.

CHAPTER FIFTEEN

Lisette

"*Mon chou*, pick up your socks, please. Your aunt will be here soon!"

Cheers come from the television as Liverpool scores a goal. My son slides off the sofa and sinks to his knees. "No! Offside! Offside!"

"Mateen," I call.

"Maman, the match only has thirty seconds left!"

His whine should grate on me, but he has only recently started calling me "maman" rather than "mama" and the change warms my heart. Even if he is only doing it because that is what his best friend calls *his* mother.

At my sister's brisk knock, I lean over the breakfast bar to peer into the main room. "Now, young man. Or I will turn off the internet for the rest of the day."

He huffs, swipes the dirty socks off the floor, and stomps up the stairs to his room.

When I open the door, Noele thrusts a covered, cast iron

pan at me. "Thirty minutes at two hundred degrees. Start it now, so the champagne does not go to our heads."

"Bonjour to you as well, *mon petite fleur.*" I love my sister dearly, but she treats me as if I am a broken doll, even now.

A flush creeps up her neck, and she leans in to kiss me on each cheek. "*Je suis désolé,* Lisette. It has been a long week, and the bride I met with today wants to get married at *Domaine du Beyssac* in less than six months!"

"Did you tell her to pray for a miracle?" Peeking under the lid, I smile. Noele's cassoulet is better than our mother's, and I dreamed of Maman's cooking for years while I was... gone.

"She would have found a new wedding planner." Noele pulls the bottle of champagne from the refrigerator and gives the muselet ring six quick turns. With a few twists of the bottle, the cork pops free. "Where is my nephew?"

"Sulking in his room after I made him miss the end of the football match." I slide two glasses across the counter and call for Mateen.

"*Tantine!*" he shouts as he skids down the stairs. "What did you make for us?"

Throwing his arms around my sister, he lowers his voice. "Maman tried to make quiche last night and it was terrible."

"Mateen!" My cheeks catch fire. "It was not that bad."

"It was," he whispers. "She burned it."

I pick up the glass of champagne and stalk out to the patio. The rain earlier in the week left everything fresh and clean, and my plants are thriving. Brushing my fingers over an orchid blossom, I stare at the city spread out in the distance.

My son is not wrong. I am a terrible cook. I mastered corn dogs in Boston. Mac and cheese. Even pizza. But French cooking eludes me. Maman tried to teach me how to bake bread over the summer, but my attempts all stubbornly refused to rise.

"I told Mateen he could play video games until dinner," Noele says as she slips out the door to join me.

"He has been disagreeable all week." Stress weighs on my shoulders. The tiny bubbles dancing over my tongue bring only the barest hint of a smile. Every Saturday, Noele drives an hour from Carcassonne—with dinner—we enjoy a bottle of wine or champagne and catch up on bits and pieces of our lives. "Philippe's mother says all children are overwhelmed when they start school, and that it will pass. But it is hard. I miss the sweet, loving boy he used to be."

Noele brushes a leaf from the bright red patio chair and sits. "Was he like this last year?"

I think back, then shake my head. "No. But it was his first time with other children. He had tutors to help with his homework, and *everything* was new and exciting. He played football and sang in the choir. Now...he still loves being with his friends, but there is more responsibility."

"Then be patient with him for a time," Noele says after a sip of champagne. "He knows you love him."

Nodding, I focus my gaze on a flock of birds streaking across the sky. My sister means well, but she is not his mother. He does not slam doors with her, refuse his chores, or close himself in his room for hours because I asked him to tell me about his day.

I know I am lucky. Mateen is kind. Smart. Strong. He makes me laugh—when he is not making me cry. And most importantly, he understands the rules we must live by to stay safe.

NOELE FLOPS BACK on the sofa, her arm flung across her forehead. "We must find Maman a hobby."

"Why? Is she asking when you will give her a grand-child?" I lean against the cushions, enjoying the relative quiet of late night. Mateen is asleep, the dishes are done, and my sister spent an hour telling stories of the last overly dramatic bride she took on as a client. "You and Marcel have been together for two years now. It is only natural."

"No, Lisette. She wants to play matchmaker for *you!*" Noele peers over at me from under her arm, a devious smile on her heart-shaped face.

I sit up straight. It is all I can do not to laugh. "She is not serious?"

"She is. You have been back for three years now and you have not been on a single date."

"That is not true! There was one. A man who came into the flower shop a few months ago. He asked me out for coffee." I scrunch up my nose at the memory. "It did not go well."

"You said nothing to me!" She feigns offense—or perhaps hurt—and punches my arm lightly. "What happened?"

My palms dampen. Rubbing them on my thighs, I stare out into the darkness beyond the patio doors. "He saw my scars and reacted...badly." I do not tell her that he grabbed my hand, pulled my arm halfway across the table, and demanded to know what had happened to me.

"Then he was an idiot. But there are plenty of men out there who are not. You should try EuroMatch. That is how I found Marcel." She pulls out her phone and taps the screen a few times. "See?"

"*Mon Dieu*, Noele. Why do you still have that app? You *live* with Marcel now. I thought you loved him!"

"I do. But I could never figure out how to delete my profile and...sometimes I like to look. I never *contact* any of them."

She angles the phone and scrolls through photos of a dozen men, many smiling, all of them no older than thirty. "I could make you a profile. You can chat with anyone you like online before you meet in person."

"No." I shake my head, reach over, and turn off her phone. "I am not ready. I may *never* be ready."

Her sigh sends a prickle down my spine. "You have to forget about that man, Lisette. He is never coming back."

My heart threatens to crack in two. She is right. All I will ever have of Nomar are memories. But after I swallow a sob, anger chases away the sadness. "I will never *forget*, Noele. I cried over him when he left Boston, and *you* told me I had to focus on myself. That I could not love another man so soon after what I had been through."

"*Oui.* I was right." Her green eyes narrow at me. "You did not know who you were, Lisette. How could you after what Faruk did to you?"

"I survived for ten years. The only time I let myself feel anything was with Mateen. But Nomar changed that. With him, I found something I had lost. If he had stayed, perhaps we could have made it work. Perhaps not. But it was not your place to stop me from trying."

I tug the blanket from her lap, stand, and fold it neatly.

"I am tired. I think...it would be best if you went home. Thank you for dinner. Next Saturday, I will make us pizza."

She wants to argue with me. I can see it in her eyes. But though she knows more of the world, I am still her older sister. At the door, she kisses me on each cheek, then wraps her arms around me.

"I love you, Lisette. I only want the best for you and for Mateen."

A weak smile is all I can manage as she rushes down the path to her car.

"MATEEN! Hurry. Philippe's mother will be here soon!"

I rifle through his backpack, worried I have forgotten something he will need over the next four days. His class is going to Barcelona—part of a Spanish immersion program he *begged* me to sign him up for—and I do not know how to let him go.

He thuds down the stairs, his curls sticking up in all directions. "Maman, did you pack my Nintendo?"

"Your teacher said no electronics." At his pout, I ruffle his hair. "You will survive. I promise. Now come sit with me for a moment."

He lets me tug him over to the sofa, where I wrap my arms around his slight shoulders.

"Maman..."

"Hush. I need a long hug to get me through this week." Tears lend a shimmer to the room, and I blink them away before they can fall. "You know the rules, *mon bébé, oui*?"

"I am *not* a baby!" he whines.

"No, you are not. You are so big now. So grown up. But you will always be *mon bébé* to me. Rules, please."

"No social media. Tell a teacher if anyone asks for my full name. Stay with my class and listen to Philippe's parents."

"And what is the code word?"

"Firefly," he says against my neck.

A little of my panic fades, and I draw back to tame his unruly locks with my fingers. "You will have so much fun this week, Mateen. But I will miss you every minute. You are my whole world, and I love you."

His big brown eyes water, and he sucks his lower lip between his teeth. The tremor only lasts a single breath before there's a knock at the door. Then, his boundless excitement returns. He leaps from the couch, stopping only when I call his name.

"Mateen, check the camera first!"

"It's Philippe," he says, flipping the locks and throwing the door open.

The boys start talking so quickly, I can barely understand a word they say. After I swipe at my tears, I offer Amelie a wobbly smile. "You will watch out for him?"

She kisses me on both cheeks, then wraps her arms around me. "*Oui,* Lisette. And I will call you every night so you can talk to him."

"Thank you," I whisper. Not long after the two boys met last year, I told Amelie and her husband Laurent a little about our past. Though I do not let Mateen have an email account, mobile phone, or any social media, not all parents are so strict.

"You spoke to the teachers too?" Amelie peers over her shoulder and nods as Laurent picks up Mateen's backpack.

"At the beginning of term. They know to keep his face out of any photos that will be shared, and they will speak to the other chaperones." I run a hand through my hair, feeling silly for insisting on all these rules. "It has been three years. I do not think there is anything to worry over, but..."

"You are protecting him. Do not feel guilty. I would do the same." We embrace once more, and Amelie turns to the boys, who have their heads bent together, practicing the few Spanish phrases they have learned in the past three weeks. "Mateen, say goodbye to your maman. We do not want to be late for the bus!"

He runs over to me, wrapping his arms around my waist and squeezing tightly. "Love you! Bye!"

In the space of a minute, they are gone. What am I supposed to do with myself now?

I SCRUBBED the floors until I could see my reflection in the tile, went through Mateen's dresser for all the clothes he's grown out of in the past few months, paid the bills, and pruned the plants on the patio.

The bus ride to Barcelona is a little over five hours, and they should be arriving shortly. So I open a bottle of Orangina and pull out my phone.

Mon Dieu! Over thirty new emails?

They all have the same subject: *You have a match request.*

What? I open the first one. A man's face stares back at me. He is in his thirties. A wide smile. Blue eyes.

Etienne wants to hear from you. Open a chat in the Euro-Match app.

Each message is from a different man. Jules. Baptiste, Alain. Benoit.

After the fifth one, I am shaking.

"Noele...what did you do?"

My heart hammers against my ribs as I install the app and go through the steps to recover a lost password and log in.

A full profile stares back at me.

Lisette M.

Age: Forty-one.

Lives in: Toulouse.

Interested in: Men.

Likes: Long walks, romantic movies, flowers, museums.

Dislikes: Cooking.

Other: One son, age nine.

Noele used a photo of me taken on the river bank last year. She'd planned a picnic, and Mateen flies a kite in the background while I smile at the camera. His face is blurry, thank God. If she'd picked any other photo from that day...

Swiping away my tears, I call her. "How could you?"

"Lisette? What is it?"

Her confusion only makes me angrier. "You set up a profile for me on EuroMatch! Do you have any idea what you have done?"

"Oui. Something you refused to even think of. You should be happy, *mon fleur.* Not alone for the rest of your life!"

"I told you no," I say, my voice trembling so much, I do not trust myself to pick up the bottle of Orangina. "Faruk is dead. But Ford warned me not to take any chances. That means no pictures. No social media. Nothing to draw attention to myself—or Mateen. He is *in the photo*, Noele. How could you be so reckless?"

"It has been three years," she says softly. "No one will be looking for you."

"You cannot know that! Take it down. Now!"

Noele stammers, "I d-do not know how... Why do you think I still have my profile after being with Marcel for so long!"

I sink from the sofa to the floor, fresh tears burning my eyes. "Fine. I will call Ford. He can help me. But Noele, stop trying to 'fix' me. However broken I am...that is how I want to stay."

CHAPTER SIXTEEN

Nomar

THE SUN STREAMS in through the curtains, slashing across my face. I hiss out a breath. The headache blares through my skull like a fire alarm. I only fell asleep three hours ago. I shouldn't be awake. Why am I awake?

Ford's ringtone spills from my phone's speaker.

Well, that explains the fire alarm.

I roll up to sitting. "What? I called in. As ordered. And yet again, you gave her my number—"

"How fast can you get to Toulouse?" the former Marine says.

Jerking to my feet, I tug on a t-shirt. "I'm in Karachi. It's an eight-hour flight. But there's only one departure a day, and it's not until 9:00 p.m."

I shouldn't know the fastest way to get to her. But I do. Always. No matter where I am.

"I'll have a plane waiting when you get to the airfield. You won't have to mess with commercial."

Pants, boots, jacket, guns, passport. I don't ask how he can afford this. No, there's a much more important question I need answered.

"What happened?"

"Maybe nothing. Maybe everything. Lisette's sister set her up on one of those online dating apps—without her permission. Wren deleted all traces of her name, photo, and information, but she hacked into the company's back-end database, and at least a dozen users accessed her profile from Afghanistan."

"Fuck! But Faruk's dead. Along with all his men. Or did McCabe miss someone?"

"Breathe, man. Ryker doesn't leave loose ends. And users from other countries aren't uncommon. Scammers, rich SOBs looking for a trophy wife, kids with too much time on their hands... They could all be harmless. But Second Sight doesn't have anyone free right now, and you're closer than Ry's team out in Seattle."

For all I know, Ford's lying to get me to talk to Lisette again. But I won't take that chance. If there's even the smallest possibility someone found out about her and Mateen, I'll sit outside her home every night for the rest of my life, watching, waiting, keeping her safe.

"Don't tell her I'm coming," I mutter as I start wiping the room clean. "I'll keep an eye on her until you can send someone else, but I can't stay. Promise me, I won't have to stay."

"Nomar, she needs you. She's always needed you," Ford says quietly. "For three years, she's done everything she can to get you to talk to her. To get you to come home. And you've been so wrapped up in your fucking *mission*, you've ignored what's right in front of you."

"There's *nothing* right in front of me. Nothing but death, blood, and darkness. She doesn't need that in her life, and I don't need the constant reminder of what I could have had..."

My knees hit the floor. If I'd stayed... If I'd told Pritchard and the President to go fuck themselves, maybe I'd still be a part of her life. Or...more.

"You *chose* to become the Viper, man. No one forced you. I know why you did it, but you could have stopped any time. You could have come home." Ford's heavy sigh carries over the crackly connection. "And if you think Lisette needs—or wants—a guy who shits unicorns and rainbows, you're a fucking idiot. She needs someone who understands what she went through. Someone to love her. To love Mateen. He builds model robots now. Wants to be an astronaut. Or an engineer. He plays soccer. He's good, too. Averaged two goals a match in summer league."

I can't get up. Can't finish wiping down the room. Can't move. For three years, I've shoved what could have been down so deep, only my dreams could touch it. And with all the shit I've done? I've ruined any chance we could be together.

"Even if you're right," I manage over the grapefruit-sized lump in my throat, "I shut her out. Ignored every one of her messages. I left her *alone*. And it broke my fucking heart. There's no coming back from that."

Rage crawls up my spine at his chuckle.

"You think this is funny, asshole? Fuck you."

"I think you should remember who you're talking to. When Joey refused to see me after she was...*hurt*, I wrote her a letter. Every two weeks. She returned them all. Unread. Until we broke her out of Faruk's compound. I'd saved them for twenty fucking years because I always knew. She was it for me.

"Life is full of broken things, Nomar. Doesn't mean you can't put them back together. And hell... How many times did we use chem lights in Iraq? You have to snap 'em to make 'em work."

"I'm not a fucking glow stick."

"No, you're not," he says, more laughter coloring his tone. "But maybe...that broken heart can be put back together. All you have to do is try. Get to the airfield ASAP. You'll be in Toulouse by midnight."

I push to my feet, staring around the small, dingy room as I rub my thick beard. "Any chance you could get a razor and a change of clothes on that plane before it takes off?"

"Consider it done. Call me when you make contact."

"Ford?" I ask before he can hang up. "Does she know you called me?"

"No. I didn't want to get her hopes up if you told me to fuck off. Pritchard has a friend, Griff, who's in Ireland on vacation with his girlfriend. He was my Plan B. But now, I'll send him to Barcelona. Mateen's on a school field trip there for the next few days. Griff can keep an eye on him. No point disrupting the kid's life when we don't know if there's even a threat. He's been through enough."

I run a hand through my hair. It's too long. Too wild.

"Mateen's not the only one, Ford. I won't let Lisette see me, but I'll keep her safe."

FORD IS A MIRACLE WORKER. When I make it through security and onto the private jet, I find a deluxe shave kit, two pairs of jeans, three t-shirts, a jacket, new boots, a black beret...even a package of briefs and socks. All packed away in a leather duffel.

"We do not have a shower on board, sir," the flight attendant says as she sets a mug of coffee on the tray table next to me. "But the toilets are large and fully stocked with washcloths and towels. When we reach our cruising altitude, you are welcome to do...what you can."

I snap the seatbelt in place and stare down at my blood-stained boots. "Thanks. Sorry if I smell."

She smiles. Probably sees all kinds in this job. "You are not the first. And you will not be the last. Have a good flight, sir. If you need anything, press your call button."

I *need* a do-over of the last three years. A priest to hear my confession. A fucking miracle to absolve me of my sins. The pretty blond can't help me with what I need.

Pulling out my phone, I pop in an earbud and play Lisette's messages one by one. I saved them all. Like Ford's letters to Joey, I suppose. I couldn't bring myself to delete them.

The third—sent eighteen months after I left her in that hospital corridor—is the one I listen to the most.

"I should be grateful when I hear you are still alive. For a year, I was. Now, I am angry. Ford told me you are no longer working for the government. That you could have chosen to return to the United States. Or...visit me here. Mateen still asks about you. About why you left. I hope one day, I will have an answer for him."

By the time I've listened to every message, the seat belt sign has winked off, and the coffee's gone. I grab the duffel bag and lock myself in the well-appointed lavatory.

The counter is big enough for me to lay out the two razors —one electric, the other with a silver handle and four blades —soap, brush, and comb.

The Viper had to blend in. I let my beard grow and stopped cutting my hair. It's long enough to curl over my ears and my collar now. I don't recognize the man in the mirror. But it's not only his distinct lack of personal grooming. It's his eyes.

They stopped being my eyes when I walked away from Lisette.

Picking up the electric razor, I stare at my reflection until the wild, feral look fades away, leaving only sorrow in its wake.

***

Lisette

"We went to the science museum," Mateen says. "There was a long tunnel, and it was dark and scary, but on the other side, there was a rainforest!"

"*Quelle surprise!* I have never seen a rainforest. Did it rain inside?" I pace the main room, unable to sit still, even now that I know my son is safe at the hotel in Barcelona with his class.

"No, Maman. A rainforest has fish and turtles and birds and plants and it smells like dirt. After we fed the turtles, we went up to the top floor. Mademoiselle Benoit showed us how they make the big robot arms that build cars and boats and airplanes."

"Did you tell her *you* built a robot?"

"She knows. She said I should ask you for a book on circuit boards. Can you get me one? I need to know how they work so I can make my next robot do more things. I want it to be able to pick up my socks for me."

My laugh eases some of the stress of the day. As does the text message that pops up on my phone.

Ford: Griff is in Barcelona, and Wren has tapped into the security cameras at Mateen's hotel. If anyone goes near his room, we'll know.

"When you come home, we will get all the books on circuit boards you want. Ask Mademoiselle Benoit if she has any recommendations, okay?"

"Okay. We have to turn out the lights soon and I still need to brush my teeth. I love you, Maman. Bye!"

He hangs up before I can say the words back to him. Before I can tell him to be careful. To remember the rules. But he is a good boy, even when he sulks. Amelie will watch out for him, and this Griff—this man I have never met—will be close by.

For the tenth time in the past few hours, I check the doors and windows. The drapes are drawn, the locks secure, but I cannot settle.

Ford: If you want, Griff can bring Mateen home in the morning, then stick around until we know there's no threat.

It would be so easy to say yes. But Mateen has been looking forward to this trip since last term. I cannot take it away from him. Not when he has a former CIA officer looking after him at all times.

I message Ford to thank him, then apologize again for all the time—and money—he is spending to keep me safe. Within minutes, the phone rings.

"Ford?"

"Joey's on the call too. How are you holding up?"

"Fine." The lie slips out easily, but perhaps if I say it enough, I will no longer want to throw up. Or scream.

"Lisette," Joey's voice is so patient, I want to cry, "you don't have to be okay. Not with us."

"We have been so careful." The first tear slips down my cheek. "Moving here has been an adventure. Noele is only an hour away, Mateen loves his school, he has made friends. So have I. What if we have to run?"

"You won't. Your profile was only up for three days," Ford says. "I doubt anyone recognized you or Mateen. Even if they had, we tracked down every one of Faruk's people after we got Ripper out. The only ones left alive didn't give a flying fuck about the man or his empire. They were only in it for the money. We made sure they had plenty of it in exchange for them 'forgetting' everything they ever knew about him."

He sounds so confident. So certain there is no danger.

"By tomorrow, I'll have someone in Toulouse. Just in case. They'll stick close for a couple of weeks—though you'll probably never see them. Wren added your name and Mateen's to her monitoring programs. If *anything* pops, we'll protect you. Even if I have to fly over there myself."

"I do not know how I can ever repay you."

"Without you and Mateen," Joey says, "Ford and I would never have found one another again. We're family, Lisette. And family doesn't keep score."

THE AIR CONDITIONING carries the scent of cinnamon through the flower shop, and I tuck one of the dark brown sticks among the roses, dahlias, and peonies.

I should be home by now. Darkness fell an hour ago. But Fleur sprained her ankle this morning, and this order will pay the shop's bills for months.

Counting the vases in the walk-in cooler one last time, I smile. My fingers ache, as does my back, but creating something so beautiful brings me peace, even today.

Once I sweep the floor and dim the lights, I peer out the front windows. The street is still bustling. I will be safe walking home. At least until the last few blocks. There, the trees hang low over the sidewalks, casting long shadows this time of night.

"I can do this. There is no reason to worry." All day, I have ignored the fear squeezing my heart. Amelie texted me three times, and I spoke to Mateen an hour ago. He went on and on about the walking tour they took today. The candy shop, the Spanish stories the guide told—only half of which he understood—and the play in a public park at the end. He is safe. And I can be brave.

I stop at the local market for fresh nectarines, a wedge of brie, snap peas, and prosciutto. Walking through the aisles, I cannot escape my nerves. Not even when I pay, when the clerk smiles at me, when I pass by a group of girls Mateen's age giggling at an ice cream shop.

I turn down my street, keys in hand. Walking quickly, I try not to panic. But by the time I reach my door, I am so very tired—and so tired of being scared—I am crying.

The keys tumble from my hand. Followed by the groceries. A nectarine rolls into the dirt. *"Merde!"*

I fall to my knees, scrambling for the bruised fruit. A rock slices my palm. The first drop of blood shatters what is left of my sanity. I should get up. Go inside. Lock the door. But I cannot move.

"Lisette," a man says from the shadows.

With a yelp, I scramble back, my hands in the air. "Do not hurt me!"

"Fuck, sweetheart, I'll never hurt you again. I promise." He steps forward slowly, until the light bathes his face—the face I see in my dreams every night—in a gentle glow.

"Nomar."

CHAPTER SEVENTEEN

Nomar

For several seconds, we're frozen in time, Lisette's cheeks shimmering with tears, my hands balled into fists, and a small bag of groceries between us.

I should have stayed in the shadows, but the minute she started to cry, I was done for. When I landed last night, I spent an hour wandering the streets around her two-story duplex, familiarizing myself with the blind spots, pinch points, and fastest ways in and out of the neighborhood.

Until I looked up and saw her standing at the patio doors. She was so beautiful, she took my breath away. In that single second, every choice I made from the moment Pritchard texted me three years ago flashed through my head. If I could take them all back, I would. In a heartbeat.

Move, idiot. Get her inside.

"Lisette, I'm going to help you up, okay?" She peers up at me, fear churning in her eyes. Despite shaving, cutting my hair, and doing my best to scrub months of dirt and blood from my body on the plane, I'm still the Viper. Still more ghost than man.

She nods, and I pluck her keys from the flagstone before I offer her my hand. She stares down at her palm. A thin line of blood wells on her pale skin.

"You're hurt." I did this. If I'd knocked on her door last night, this wouldn't have happened. It's just a cut, but I can't take my eyes off the wound. Crouching down, I curl her hand into a fist, then wrap my arm around her waist and help her to her feet.

God, she smells the same. Like shea butter and gardenia, with a hint of rose. For a breath, she wavers, then sinks against me.

So soft. My hand fits perfectly along the curve of her hip. "I'm going to come in with you. Once I know it's safe, I can leave—"

"Because that is what you do." She jerks back, fire in her green eyes. "You leave. Always. Ford sent you, yes?"

I nod, unsure how to admit I've been here for almost twenty-four hours. She's so angry. I deserve every harsh word —and more.

"Why even come, if not to stay?" she asks, a tremble in her voice. "Go back to Pakistan, Nomar. I do not want you here."

"I was going to say, 'I can leave *if you want.*' I fucked up, Lisette. I know that. I didn't have a choice. At first. And after…"

A fresh tear balances on her lashes. Across the street, a shadow flickers almost out of sight. Fuck.

"Get the bag." I unlock her door, shove the keys into my jacket pocket, and grab my Beretta. Six steps lead up to the main floor, and I only pause long enough to flip the deadbolt before I sweep through the kitchen, living area, and bathroom. Lisette holds the brown paper bag like it's a shield, watching me the whole time.

"I have to check upstairs. Don't move." I'm being too harsh, but I can't stop to comfort her until I know we're safe for the night.

My boots make almost no sound on the steps. I shouldn't be here. In her bedroom with its happy yellow duvet and framed photos of her and Mateen with Noele, her parents, even Ford and Joey. In the kid's room with bright blue walls, a poster of France's national football team, and a Red Sox cap hanging from one of the posters of his bed.

A foot-tall robot sits on his desk, a little lopsided, with one "hand" dangling from a pair of wires.

"He builds model robots now."

Fuck. I wish I could stay. Get a little place of my own nearby and be a part of their lives. But I can't. I'm too broken. My darkness would block out her sun.

"Stop. This is a life you can never have."

"Why not?" Her voice startles me, and I drop the robot hand back onto the desk. She stands in the doorway, a towel clutched to her injured palm. "That is Henri. He talks. Ten different phrases. Mateen says the next one he builds will be able to pick up his socks so he does not have to."

"He's a smart kid," I manage.

Lisette's smile lights my entire world. "He is. But the socks. He leaves them everywhere."

I holster my weapon and take a single step toward her. I'd give anything to hold her again, but I haven't earned that right. She doesn't retreat, but the fear and uncertainty return to her eyes.

"Why is this a life you can never have, Nomar? What did we do that was so terrible—"

"Fuck, sweetheart. *You* didn't do a damn thing. Is that really what you thought? That I didn't want you?"

"Why else would you refuse to call? To return any of my messages? You talked to Ford. So...the problem must be me."

I surge forward, wrapping my arm around Lisette's waist and pressing her to the wall. My free hand tangles in her short, silky locks, tipping her head so I can slant my lips over hers.

She tastes like coffee and cookies and the promise of home. Her tiny moan sets me on fire. The new jeans don't give my dick an inch to breathe. I hope she can feel how much I want her. How much I need her.

"It was never you, sweetheart," I whisper against her mouth. "You were—are—perfect."

"Then why?" She touches her lower lip, fingers shaking.

"I'm not...who you need. I can't be. Everything I've done in my life—hell, in the last three years—I'll never escape it. You deserve a good man, Lisette."

I drop my gaze. To the soft swells of her breasts under her striped sweater. To the bracelet clasped around her wrist. The one I returned to her.

Taking her hand, I press my lips to the silver.

"Il n'est rien de réel que le rêve et l'amour," I whisper.

Lisette rests her cheek against my shoulder. "Nothing is real but dreams and love. I dream of you, Nomar. Almost every night. But my bracelet is wrong. Dreams are not real. If they were, you would have come back to me."

We stay locked together for several long moments. I can't let her go. Not yet. Not when this is all we'll ever have. But every second I spend with her makes it harder to walk away.

"As long as you stay inside, you're safe. My car is parked across the street. I'll keep watch from there," I say, my lips brushing over her soft locks.

She pulls back with a frown. "You do not need to sleep in your car. I have a sofa."

I don't tell her I wouldn't be *sleeping* in my car. I'd be sitting in it. Watching her front door all night long. Taking a lap around the block every hour to check for surveillance. Drinking too much coffee. Pissing in an empty water bottle.

"If you're sure..." She'll be safer if I'm inside. And maybe, I'll have a few more memories to carry me through once I'm gone again.

With a nod, she turns and heads down the stairs. I'm frozen watching her go. The sway of her ass in the fitted red pants. The tilt of her head. The light brush of her fingers over the railing.

Stop staring, idiot. Follow her.

When I force my feet to move, I find her in the kitchen, setting a wedge of brie on a plate with fresh bread, a bunch of grapes, and fig jam. "Have you eaten?" she asks.

"No. But I need to get my bag from the car and walk the perimeter first. Lock the door behind me. I'll knock four times when I'm back. Do you have a weapon?"

"No." The knife wobbles in her hand. "Guns are not common here."

Dropping to one knee, I yank up the leg of my jeans, slide my back-up piece from my ankle holster, and chamber a round. "Take this. Safety's off. I'll be ten minutes at most."

"You really think someone will come after me." All the color drains from her cheeks. She backs up until she hits the sink, her gaze fixed on the gun I set on the counter.

Fuck. Think before you speak.

I skirt the counter and mold my hands to her hips. "I don't know. But that's the problem. No one does. So for the next few weeks at least, you and Mateen are going to have protection twenty-four-seven."

"And after?" She peers up at me, and her sultry tone sends all the blood in my body rushing south. "You will disappear again?"

"No." The answer escapes before I can stop it. Some of the light returns to her eyes, and I kick myself for what I'm about to do. "I can't be who you need, Lisette. I can't...stay. But I won't disappear. You'll be able to reach me. No matter what."

Her shoulders heave, and she twists out of my grasp. "You do not know what I need, Nomar. Once, perhaps. But not now. Go get your things. I want to be done with dinner before Mateen calls in an hour."

The *thunk* of the lock is like a hammer to my battered heart. Ford's wrong. Some broken things simply can't be fixed.

Lisette

When he returns, Nomar looks...beaten. That is the only word for what I see in his eyes. But he forces a smile as we sit across from one another at my small table.

"When did you move here?" he asks, spreading a bit of brie over a slice of bread.

"Last July. After we left Boston, we lived with my parents for a few months. Being alone...I was not ready yet. Then, we had an apartment in Marseille for six months. It was a nice place. Close to my parents. But I always wanted to live in Toulouse. When I was young, I loved it here. I still do. My parents did not understand why I had to move so far away. But at least they no longer ask when we are coming back."

Regret, bitter and thick, clogs my throat, and I chase it away with a slice of sweet nectarine. I hated hurting Maman and Papa, but if we had stayed, they would have smothered us.

"And Mateen? Is he happy here?" Nomar asks.

"*Oui.* Very. He has many friends at school, and he loved the tutor he had last year."

"Was he that far behind in school?"

"*Oui.* Boys in Afghanistan do not start school until age seven—and only then if they live in a city. Faruk—" The wine glass wobbles in my hand. It has been so long since I said his name. "He forbade me from speaking French. Mateen knew some Pashto and Dari letters, but no English or French. No science. No math. No history. Nothing of the rest of the world. He hated his tutor in Marseille. She was so strict, and he had so much to learn."

I take a sip of the chilled Chardonnay, but it threatens to turn my stomach. Pushing back from the table, I stumble into the kitchen and pour the wine down the drain.

"Lisette?" Nomar comes up behind me. I would give anything to lean into his warmth. To take comfort in his arms. "What's wrong?"

I sidestep him, go to the refrigerator, and pull out a bottle of Perrier. "I dreamed of being free for ten years. But the reality of it was terrifying. Every day, there was something new. Mateen's first sore throat after his transplant. The first time I shopped for groceries by myself. The first time my son told me he wished his papa were still alive..."

Nomar says nothing. But the anguish in his eyes speaks volumes.

"I did not tell him until after his transplant," I whisper. "He cried only a little then. More when he realized we were never going back to Afghanistan. He knew his father hurt me. But he was the only son. Faruk treated him like a prince."

"What—" Nomar clears his throat. His hands are balled into fists at his sides. "What about now? Does Mateen still talk about him?"

I force a deep breath, lifting my gaze to his. "No. When I told him we were moving here, he asked me why we could not go back home, and I told him some of the things Faruk had done. That he had taken me from France without my permission. That he would not let me talk to my family. That he hurt many people all over the world. Children understand so much more than we give them credit for, I think. He has not spoken of his father since."

My appetite is gone, so I pick up my plate and take it to the sink. "Mateen will call soon. Eat as much as you like. I will clean up when I come back down."

Before Nomar can say a word, I grab my phone from the counter and hurry up the stairs to my bedroom. So many nights I dreamed of him. Of being able to see him again. Talk to him. Tell him about my life. But now that he is here, I can think about only one thing.

How will I survive when he leaves?

CHAPTER EIGHTEEN

Nomar

Lisette barely ate, so I wrap up a plate for her and set it in the small fridge. Being in her space—alone—feels wrong, but there's no way in hell I'm leaving now.

After I do the dishes, I set up an infrared motion alarm over her front door. The sensor is a piece of shit. I cobbled it together from spare parts in Kandahar two years ago. But it'll make enough noise to wake me if anyone tries to break in overnight.

My eyes feel hollow. If I sit down, I'll be asleep in under a minute, so I stand at her patio door and stare out into the night though a part in the drapes. A dozen plants grace the small, outdoor area, along with a bistro table and chairs. In the glow from the street lights, pale pink, purple, and yellow flowers shudder in the light breeze.

My phone buzzes with a U.S. number, and I pop in an earbud before answering the call. "Only one person in the States has this number, and you're not him."

The pause is long enough, I'm about to hang up. "Nomar. This is Griff Hargrove. Austin Pritchard gave me your number."

"Pritchard doesn't have my number." I'm being a dick. I know it, but I can't stop myself.

"For fuck's sake. Is it that hard to believe *he* got the number from Ford Lawton? It's been a long damn day and I need some shuteye. The kids are leaving the hotel at 8:00 a.m. tomorrow to go on *another* walking tour of the city."

"Sorry. I've been up for the better part of thirty-six hours myself. Any sign of trouble there?"

There's another long pause, and I stare at the screen. "Griff? Are you there?"

"Yeah. The cell service here is shit and my glasses are charging."

I touch the earbud. "What the hell do your glasses have to do with anything?"

At this point, the pauses don't bother me as much as the fear I've lost all my faculties—or that this man Ford trusted to protect Mateen is an idiot.

"Ford didn't tell you anything about me, did he?"

"Just that you were CIA and somewhere close. Ireland?" Almost everything about the past two days is a goddamn blur. If I don't get some sleep, I won't be good for shit tomorrow.

"Pritchard and I worked together in Pakistan two years ago. We were escorting the U.S. Ambassador when our convoy was attacked. There was an explosion." Griff's voice roughens. "I lost my left arm, and I'm mostly deaf."

I sink down onto the couch. I don't know who to eviscerate first. Ford or Pritchard.

"Are you blind too? Otherwise, you still need to explain the glasses."

Griff swears under his breath. "Fuck, no. Speech to text. The glasses have state-of-the-art speech-to-text software built into them. They 'listen' to what's going on around me. Conversations, noises—like car horns, alarms, gunfire—and even texts from my phone appear on the lenses in almost real time. When I have to rely on my tablet's shitty 5G to translate, it's slower."

"And the arm? Can you shoot? Fight? Because if anyone comes after Mateen—"

"Have you ever been punched by a piece of titanium?" he asks. After a beat, he adds, "If you had, you wouldn't ask me that question. Yes, I can shoot, fight, and button my own damn shirt. My prosthetic is the most advanced in the world with full articulation of all five fingers. Now can we get back to what's really important here?"

"Look, man. I don't know you. Hell, I barely know Pritchard anymore. The asshole didn't even bother to tell me he left JSOC. But Ford and I are going to have words."

"Fuck you. I can do the job."

My patience is slipping away, and I close my eyes. "I believe you. Ford's on my shit list because he didn't say a goddamn word about *any* of this."

This pause is the longest yet. "Oh."

"Lisette's on the phone with the kid now. It was quiet here today, and I'll be staying with her until Mateen comes home. Any trouble following the kids?"

Griff chuckles. "Following? No. Keeping up with them? I've never felt so old. Or slow."

A door opens upstairs, and I push to my feet. "I'll check in tomorrow, Griff. Get some sleep."

"You too."

Lisette pads down the stairs, wearing a soft pair of dark blue shorts and a tank top. No bra. Fuck. It's only a little after 10:00 p.m. Last night she was up until midnight. How much of an asshole would I be if I fell asleep on the couch mid-sentence?

"You cleaned."

I bristle at the surprise in her tone. "I've been alone in the desert for three years. But I still know my way around a kitchen."

"Do you cook?" Lisette pours two glasses of sparkling water and gestures toward the sofa.

"I used to. But it's been a while. I miss it, sometimes. It's damn near impossible to get a good tamale in Afghanistan. And don't get me started on what passes for ceviche in Kabul. Worst decision of my life. I almost died."

Her laugh soothes some of my rough edges. "I can make mac and cheese, pizza, and corn dogs. Noele says I fail at being French."

We sit in silence for a few minutes, until she sets her empty glass on the side table. "Where did you go when you left me in Boston?"

I flinch. Not "when you left Boston" but "when you left *me* in Boston." She's right. I did leave her. It didn't matter that the President of the United States asked me to go. I could have said no. I *should* have said no.

"I can't tell you, Lisette. It's classified."

She huffs. "You left after a year. Ford told me so. What did you do after?"

"Don't ask me that, sweetheart."

"Is that classified too?"

I stare up at the ceiling, searching for something— anything—I can share with her that won't make her run or put her in danger. "No. But it was illegal as fuck."

"Please, Nomar. I need to know why you left. Why you refused to return my calls for three years. I do not care what you did. Or how many men you killed."

I suck in a sharp breath.

"You were the one who told me you were sent in when

'shit went sideways.' I know you have killed. Do you think it bothers me?"''

I drop my head into my hands, elbows on my knees. "It should."

"I have seen death, Nomar. I know the world is a dark, violent place." Her gentle fingers stroke up and down my back. "Talk to me."

"I can't. If I tried...you'd never look at me the same way again."

"*Espèce d'homme têtu!*" she mutters.

"Stubborn? I'm trying to protect you, Lisette! You're too good. Too...perfect. Too...pure. If I told you all the things I've done, you'd run away screaming. And you'd be right to do so."

Lisette jerks up. "You saved my life. You killed *for me*. And yet you think I would run? How can you think so little of me?"

She stalks upstairs, then returns a minute later with a pillow and blanket. "Be ready to go tomorrow by 9:30. Good night, Nomar."

The sound of her bedroom door slamming shut severs my last nerve, and I punch the pillow hard enough it flies across the room. I'll never deserve her. I know it. She knows it. So why can't I walk away?

Lisette

"Good? Perfect? Pure? He does not know me at all."

Because he left. Because for three years, he refused to answer my calls or respond to my messages. And now, the man I longed for, the one who made me feel safe when nothing in my life made sense, is in my home.

He acted as if he wanted to know me. But why, if he will not let me know him?

I should sleep. The stress of the day has left me physically exhausted. But I toss and turn in the darkness, unable to forget the haunted edge to his voice.

"You'd never look at me the same way again."

I roll over and stare at the light seeping in around the door. "You are being ridiculous. He is here. Not ten meters away. *Make* him talk to you."

It is quiet when I tiptoe down the stairs. A single lamp bathes the living room in a gentle glow. Nomar is stretched out on the sofa, the blanket bunched around his waist. He removed his t-shirt, and my God. A long, thick scar stretches across his chest. Others—smaller, almost round, and shiny—dot his torso. A deep bruise yellows on his left arm.

My gasp startles him awake, and he is on his feet in an instant, gun in hand, a feral look in his eyes.

"Fuck. What's wrong?"

If only I could remember why I came down here. But upright, his torso is like sculpted granite. Both of his nipples are pierced with heavy silver barbs. Tattoos wind over his chest. A broken heart. Flowers and feathers and leaves. Mountains and clouds.

His jeans leave little to the imagination, and my mouth goes dry.

"Lisette?" He sets the gun down and, in two steps, stands in front of me, close enough, I run my fingers over the thick scar.

"What happened? This...is less than a year old."

Nomar lowers his gaze to my hand. "You don't want to know."

"In your world, do people often ask questions they do not want answered? Because that is not how we do things in France."

His laugh causes my anger to flare, bright and hot. Until he smiles. It brings a lightness to him I have never seen.

With a shake of his head, he covers my hand with his. "You really do want to know, don't you?"

"Yes. I am not fragile, Nomar. I spent ten years the captive wife of the most feared man in all of Afghanistan. He did not get that reputation by being...kind. Or gentle."

I link our fingers and guide his hand under my tank top to the scars criss-crossing my back.

"He gave me these only hours after I signed the marriage certificate."

A low sound rumbles in Nomar's chest. Almost a growl. His eyes darken, and the veins at his temples throb with every beat of his heart.

"They were nothing compared to what he had already done to me," I say, my voice threatening to fail at any moment. "You know how few rights women have in Afghanistan. But Faruk still needed me to agree to the marriage in front of the Imam. For two months, I refused. He locked me in a small room first. Starved me. Made me beg for anything more than tea or water. When that failed, he sent me down into the well."

Tears gather in my eyes and I step back to hold out my arms. "The scorpions come out at night. Even in winter. Their venom causes high fevers. He kept the well covered. It was dark. All the time. He would send down water and bread and medicine, but only at night. Every time, he would say, 'If you agree to marry me, I will let you out.'"

"Lisette—"

"Please." I swipe at my cheeks. "Let me finish."

His palm is warm against my back, and the touch helps center me enough to draw in a trembling breath. "I spent many years wishing I had been brave enough to pour out all the water and die of dehydration. But I was still so naive I believed someone would come for me."

"Someone should have..." he mutters.

My stomach twists into a knot. I taste bile, bitter on my tongue, and swallow it down. "Time had no meaning there. But later, I found out it took him five weeks to break me."

He pulls me close, wrapping his arms around me and holding on tight. I rest my cheek against his shoulder.

"I know what true evil is, Nomar. I have seen it. Shared a bed with it. Stood by its side while it ordered the deaths of hundreds of people. So whatever was done to you—whatever you have done since I saw you last—I promise you, it will not change how I look at you. Because you are a good man."

His chest heaves, and he brushes his lips over my hair. "You don't know what you're asking me to do."

Drawing back, I find oceans of pain in his eyes. "Talk to me? It is not hard." My hand molds to his cheek, and I draw my thumb over his lips. "You open your mouth, and words come out."

"It's so much more than that." After a sigh, he drops his forehead to mine. "I told myself I could walk away. That I'd come here, follow you around for a few days—maybe even a week—and once I knew you were safe, I'd go back to being... alone. But I saw you tonight, scared, and all I could think about was holding you."

"Is having your arms around me really so horrible?" I ask with a smile. "Do you hate my shampoo? Do I smell?"

"God, no. You're perfect, sweetheart." Nomar nudges my chin up and slants his mouth over mine. His hand tangles in my hair. He deepens the kiss, his tongue darting over my lips until I part them on a breathy moan.

He tastes of mint. Of strength. Of safety. But most of all, of a promise made three years ago, and only now kept.

My nipples ache, so tight and hard, when he cups my breast, I cry out.

"Lisette...the things I want to do to you... Fuck."

I reach between us and stroke my hand over the hard bulge in his jeans.

"Take me upstairs, Nomar. And show me."

CHAPTER NINETEEN

Nomar

Each step is pure torture. Whoever invented skinny jeans should be shot.

I barely had the presence of mind to grab my phone and duffel bag before she was pulling me up the stairs. As much as I want to tear Ford a new one for not telling me about Griff, the man thought of everything else.

Shaving kit. Deodorant. Condoms.

What the fuck am I thinking? We shouldn't do this. *I* shouldn't do this. She's been through hell. Being with me—even for tonight—could drag her right back under. It doesn't matter that I've spent the last two years trying to atone for a fraction of my mistakes. My darkness could still destroy her.

She hasn't let go of my hand. Is she worried I'll bolt? Probably. Can't say I blame her.

There's no coming back from this. If I taste her, I'll never be able to even *look* at another woman for the rest of my life.

"I need a minute," I grit out when we reach her bedroom. Kneeling threatens to crush my balls, but I reach into the duffel bag, palm a single condom, and slide it under the pillow before setting my Beretta on the nightstand.

Lisette's hands smooth over my back. "What do you want to do to me, Nomar? Tell me. *Show* me."

I spin around, hauling her into my arms so fast, she's only a blur of dark hair and soft skin. My lips find hers. Downstairs, our kisses were slow and sweet. Almost chaste. Not now. She's my oxygen.

"Off with this," I manage and tug her tank top over her head. Her breasts are heavy in my hands, nipples dark pink and begging to be touched.

I pinch one between my thumb and forefinger, rolling it around until her breath hitches and she arches her back with a whimper.

The scent of her arousal fills my nose. "God, sweetheart. You smell like heaven. Do you taste as good?"

I sink down onto the bed, my hands molding to her waist. Nestling her between my thighs, I suck a nipple into my mouth. My teeth score the tight bud. She cries out, and her legs start to tremble.

She's so fucking perfect. Curvy in a way she wasn't three years ago, soft, yet so strong.

Stroking my fingers over her hips, her ass, I find the hem of her shorts and then her panties. Her heat brands me.

"Can I?" I ask, my lips trailing lower. She nods, but I stop. "I need you to say it, sweetheart. Nothing happens here you don't want."

"I want this, Nomar." Her voice cracks, and she leans into me. "I want *you*."

An inch at a time, I lower the silky shorts and her bright blue panties until they fall to the floor.

Lisette rests her hands on my shoulders, ducks her head, and kisses me. Three years ago, she was afraid. Uncertain.

Timid. Not anymore. I take her with me, maneuvering us until we're on our sides, legs tangling together.

"When did you get these?" she asks, pressing her lips to one of the silver barbs piercing my nipples.

God. No one's ever touched me like she does, and I'm not even naked yet. "Maybe ten years ago. I was in Germany. One of the guys I worked with dared me."

"*Mon Dieu!* And you kept them all this time?" Despite her words, I think she likes seeing them. Likes it even more when she laves her tongue over the piercing and I shudder.

"Those were an afterthought. The dare...you haven't seen yet."

Her eyes widen and she reaches for the button on my jeans. But I'm so hard, I'm afraid lowering the zipper could kill me. "Let me."

She watches as I get to my feet and work the tight denim over my erection. The black briefs don't hide the outline of the heavy gauge ring piercing the head of my dick.

"Show me," she whispers.

I shouldn't be nervous. But it's been five years since I've been with anyone. Longer since I had more than a one-night stand with a woman I picked up in a bar.

The briefs land next to my jeans. I'm so hard, I'm leaking. Lisette's gaze is pinned to my piercing.

"The ring should feel...like...*more* when we..." I say, taking a single step closer. "But...if you don't like it, I can take it out."

In truth, removing the damn thing as aroused as I am right now would be excruciating. But I'd do it for her.

"I...have no idea what I like," she says. "There has been no one since..."

Fuck me.

"We'll figure it out. Together. And if you need to stop—at any time—all you have to do is say the word."

At her nod, I crawl up the bed, positioning myself

between her legs and easing her onto her back. Her dark curls glisten with need. My lips blaze a trail from her knee up one thigh, then down the other, avoiding the one place I'm desperate to be.

Our eyes lock as I feather a kiss to her mound. Her eyelids flutter. Hips shifting closer, she tightens her fingers in the duvet.

I press my lips closer to her clit, and she whimpers, "Please."

Gently, I part her lower lips. My tongue traces a lazy path through her arousal. She's so sweet, so very wet. I need more. Flicking her tight nub, I'm rewarded with a sharp gasp.

"I could live on the taste of you," I murmur against her folds. One stroke, two, three until I find a steady rhythm. She writhes under me, and I wrap my arms under her thighs to hold her still.

Her little moans are the melody I'll carry with me for the rest of my days. I memorize every sound, every sensation, every moment I have with this woman who means more to me than I ever thought possible.

I pick up the pace. She quiets, her muscles vibrating. She's wound so tight, she's about to snap. "Oh...God... Nomar!"

Her release is like a summer storm, flooding me with her essence, sending shockwaves all through her.

I flutter my tongue gently one last time, then ease back until I can slide up her body. Tears glisten on her cheeks, and she turns into my embrace.

"Breathe for me, sweetheart. I've got you."

Lisette shifts closer, and my dick aches. I want to bury myself deep in her slick heat, but I need to know she's okay. That she's ready. That I won't hurt her.

Pressing kisses to her hair, I draw the duvet up to cover her against the slight chill in the room. If this is all we have tonight—if this is all we have forever—it'll be enough. It has to be enough.

Lisette

Never in my life did I think it could be like this. My core still trembles, and I nestle deeper into Nomar's embrace.

I still cannot believe he's here. In my bed. Naked.

Pierced.

My arms and legs are so heavy. I could sleep for a week if not for this emptiness inside of me only he can fill.

"Kiss me," I say, tipping my head up to find his eyes. He'll taste of me, and my heart beats faster at the thought.

His hand cups my cheek. The pads of his fingers are rough against my skin. His lips are gentle. Slow, languid kisses that leave me wanting more.

I wish I were brave enough to take him into my mouth. I wonder what his piercing would feel like? For him *and for me.*

Laying me down, he trails his lips along my collar bone. Up my neck. His teeth score the shell of my ear, sending shivers all through me.

"We can stop...if you want," he says. I believe him. Nomar would never hurt me. I think it would kill him to do so. But if he stops now, I might not find the courage to ask—to demand —he touch me again.

"No." I run my fingers over one of the bars piercing his nipples. A low sound rumbles in his chest. "I want this, Nomar. I want you."

He shoves the duvet down, baring me to him. "You're so fucking beautiful, Lisette. Seeing you come...I'll never get enough of you."

His hands are everywhere. Pinching my nipples, cupping my breasts, stroking over my sides. And his lips... He consumes me, and I him. The salty tang of the skin at his neck, the way his abs flex when I flick one of the piercings with my tongue, the sounds he makes...they are intoxicating.

I kiss my way across the thick scar, my gaze fixed on his erection. "Can I touch you?"

Nomar takes my hand and guides it to his shaft. "You can do whatever you want to me, Lisette. I'm yours."

He's so smooth. Hot and hard. My fingers still when I reach the thick ring at his crown.

"It's all right, sweetheart. Touch it. You won't hurt me." His lips press to my temple. The scent of him surrounds me, salty and rich, and I think maybe...I want to taste him. But for now, I circle the piercing, find the thick vein at the underside of his length, and feather a light touch up and down.

"God, yes. Just like that," he groans.

A drop leaks from his tip, but I don't shy away. I kiss my way down his chest to the neatly trimmed, wiry hair, and finally, to his crown. I cannot take him in my mouth. Not...yet. But with the briefest taste, I find something I thought I had lost forever.

"Fuck. I need to be inside you."

Nomar eases me onto my back, slides his hand under the pillow, and pulls out a condom.

Watching him roll it over his length should not make me ache inside. It should frighten me. He's thick, and it has been so long.

I hook one leg around his waist as he positions himself over me. "Please," I whisper, though I do not know what I need—other than him.

Slowly, Nomar slips inside me, stretching me, filling me until I cry out. His muscles tense, a look of horror in his eyes, but I cup the back of his neck and pull his lips to mine.

His kiss sends a burst of warmth over my skin. I grab his ass, and with a gentle tug, bring us as close as two people can be.

"Lisette...tell me what you need."

"All of you."

He lifts his head, and in his gaze I find so much more than arousal. No words pass between us as he moves his hips. With each thrust, my body comes alive. His piercings amplify every sensation—from the barbs scraping against my nipples to the ring sliding deep in my channel.

His pupils dilate. The veins at his temples swell and pulse with each beat of his heart. I want to live in this moment. In the pleasure cresting inside me.

"I can't...God. I'm so close." Nomar reaches between us, his fingers slipping over my sweat-drenched skin to find my clit.

The world around us fades away. There is only his touch, his heat, his voice whispering my name.

I fly off the edge, pleasure rolling through me in endless waves. Nomar groans, long and low. His cock swells, and he slams into me one last time before he lets go.

***

I FEEL it when he starts to pull away. To shut himself off from me. As if this one night of passion—of connection—will destroy him if he gets too comfortable. Too close.

He climbed back into bed and turned off the light after disposing of the condom, but rather than holding me, he laid on his back staring up at the ceiling. The hint of light from downstairs lets me study his profile, and I turn onto my side. "I thought maybe...you would stay."

"I'm not going anywhere," he says, but there is no emotion in his voice.

"You already have."

He flinches, and my heart fractures. No denial. No protest. Only acceptance.

"When you left Boston, I did not know how I would survive on my own. You were my..." the right word eludes me until I pull the duvet up to my chest, "my anchor. With you, I did not have to be strong."

"But you are." He sits up, his back against the headboard, and takes me in his arms. "You amaze me, Lisette. I know Navy SEALs who wouldn't have survived what you did."

"That is not my point." I can still feel the wall he has built between us, though his heart *thumps* steadily under my palm. "I had to learn how to be *me* again. I was no one for a very long time. Then, I became a mother. But that is *all* I was. There was no Lisette. I found myself in those long months of isolation. We were all alone in that apartment. Mateen's body could not fight off infection, so we had to stay away from everyone. I learned how to be strong. What I liked. What I did not. I read books. I painted. I tried to cook—and almost started many fires. I made Mateen cry when I sang along to the radio."

Nomar chuckles with me. I like hearing him...happy. Lighter. I think he has not had much reason to laugh of late.

"I know who I am now. And I know what I want in my life. *Who* I want in my life." He stiffens, and I cup his cheek so I can kiss him. His walls start to crumble when my tongue traces the seam of his lips. Will they fall completely? Or in the light of day, will he build them back up once again?

With a groan, Nomar pulls me into his arms. He consumes me, and I him, until exhaustion drags us under.

CHAPTER TWENTY

Nomar

I WAKE UP ALONE. In a bed that smells like her—like *us*—with my dick tenting the sheets.

I didn't dream it. Lisette and I shared something perfect. Real. But she doesn't know anything about me, and I'm too much of a fucking coward to tell her the truth.

I've been in love with her for three years. If I lose her now...it might kill me. It's only a little after 8:00 a.m., and through the open bedroom door, I hear her moving around downstairs.

My scar pulls tight as I sit up. The memory of the blade is still so fresh. And the *sound* it made tearing through my shirt and into my skin. How can something so quiet still ring in my ears?

Tugging on my hair to the point of pain, I will the dark thoughts away and search for my clothes. I need a shower. Need to wash her scent from my body before I beg her for more than I have any right to ask for.

So why am I going downstairs?

She sits at the table, a silk robe wrapped around her body and a cup of coffee in her hands. Exhaustion lingers in the slight bags under her eyes, but when she sees me, she smiles. "Good morning. I have very little for breakfast. Only what is left from last night. And Cheerios."

"All I need is some coffee. If that's okay."

She waves her hand toward the kitchen. The fancy machine reminds me of the one from her apartment in Boston, and I push the button for a double-shot of espresso.

The first sip brings a jolt to my system, and I sink into a chair next to her. "If I never see a cup of tea again, it'll be too soon."

Her laugh brings such a lightness to her expression—her whole body—I'm determined to find a way to get her to do it again and again.

"One of the nurses in Uzbekistan brought me tea the first night we were there. I did not want to offend her, so as soon as she left, I poured it down the sink. But I did not think to have coffee until Noele came. That first *cafe au lait* was the best thing I have ever had. I thought...it tasted like freedom."

"The first cup of tea I had when I went back to Afghanistan was pure sugar. I almost threw up all over Sha— my host's shoes."

She frowns, as if she wants to ask, but then shakes her head. "In Islam, there are close to ninety days a year one is expected to fast. During those times, the other women—they were wives of his men, mostly—would drink so much tea. The common rooms reeked of it. They claimed it helped with the hunger. But it only made me nauseous. I spent many of those days alone in my room."

"Did you convert?"

Lisette flinches, a soft inhale accompanying the motion. "I had to. Or...pretend to. Faruk gave me a year—enough time to learn long passages from the Quran—then demanded it.

But I was raised Catholic. I found a priest at St. Jude's and gave my confession a few days after we arrived in Boston."

"And Mateen? He'd started to pray with the men. Was he—?"

Her expression warns me I should back off, but before I can tell her not to answer, she sighs. "In Islam, a child born to Muslim parents is Muslim. But they are not required to pray until they reach puberty. Faruk was...a zealot. He wanted his son to be just like him. A few days before Joey was taken, Mateen tried to stop his father from beating me. That was when Faruk made him start joining the men for prayers. He thought it would teach him...submission."

Fuck. With everything I learn about her time as his prisoner, I wish I'd been the one to end him. McCabe was too easy on the asshole. He deserved to be carved up in to tiny pieces. Slowly. Over days. Weeks, even.

I move so I'm crouching next to her, my hand on her arm. "I'm sorry. I shouldn't have asked. Any of it."

Sorrow wells in the depths of her green eyes. "It is—*was*—my life, Nomar. As much as I hate what Faruk did to me, as much as I hate *him*, if I had never been taken, my son would not exist. I am alive. Safe. As is Mateen."

My God. I'm in awe of this woman. Of how she's changed since I left her back in Boston. How she's found herself. She's still everything I've ever wanted. And don't deserve. But now, she's even more.

With a half smile, she continues. "Life is not meant to always be beautiful. Or kind. We are not owed happiness. We have to find it, claim it, and do whatever we can to hold onto it. I am happy here in Toulouse. I have a job, a few friends, a life. And I have Mateen." She reaches out and touches my cheek. I can't help but lean in. "But I think...you have been searching for happiness for a long time. I hope you find it one day."

Before I can reply, she rises with her coffee cup held close to her chest. "I need to shower. You can join me, if you want. Or relax. The patio is beautiful in the mornings."

My inner voice screams at me to follow her, but my feet are rooted in place as I watch her climb the stairs. Ford would tell me I'm being an idiot. That I don't have any right to decide what's best for her. That if she wants me, that's *her* choice.

He's right. I know he's right. But one day, my past is going to catch up to me, and she's the one who'll pay the price.

Lisette

I sit on my bed, holding Nomar's pillow. Every time I think we are making progress, he shuts down. I have so little time left with him. Once my son comes home, I will not allow Nomar to share my bed. Not unless he agrees to stay and give us a chance.

Mateen asked about him for months after he left. Nomar was his hero. His protector. If he sees us falling in love—acting like a couple—only for the man to disappear again, he might never forgive him. Or worse. He might never forgive me.

I bury my face in the pillow and breathe in his scent. Whatever happens tomorrow, we will have today. I will not waste it.

"I hoped I'd find you naked." He grins at me from the door jamb, heat smoldering in his dark brown eyes. "You said something about a shower?"

Loosening the belt on my robe, I stand and let it fall away. Nomar rummages in his duffel bag and comes away with a strip of condoms.

"We only have an hour! You expect to use all of those?"

He shrugs. "Hope springs eternal."

His shirt lands next to my robe. I could look at him forever and not tire of the view. He's nothing but sculpted muscles and tattoos, coiled energy on the prowl.

In three steps, I'm in front of him, running my hands over his chest, his shoulders, down to French words inked on his bicep.

"*Il n'est rien de réel que le rêve et l'amour.*" My eyes start to burn.

"Nothing is real but dreams and love," he says, holding my gaze. "I got it a couple of weeks after I found your bracelet at Faruk's compound. I needed something of you I could keep with me. Always. I thought about you every day, Lisette. You *and* Mateen. If I'd had a choice, I never would have left you."

Pressing my lips to the flowing script, I taste the salt of my own tears. I thought he'd abandoned us. I was so very wrong.

"Lisette? Fuck. What is it?" He tips my head up and kisses my tears away. "Talk to me, sweetheart."

My heart swells at the fear and concern in his eyes. Maybe there is still hope for us. For a future where he does not disappear again. "There is nothing wrong. Nothing at all. Except for those jeans."

WE WALK hand-in-hand down Rue du Parc. The chill in the air warns that autumn will be here soon, and I shiver. Nomar shrugs out of his leather jacket and drapes it over my shoulders. Such a simple gesture, and it brings more of his woodsy scent to my nose. "No one has ever done that for me before. Thank you."

We stop at a light, and he cups the back of my neck, leans down, and kisses me. The stirrings of something more than passion, more than friendship, more than...everything warm my heart. He plays with a lock of my hair, pressing his cheek to mine.

I relish in his closeness as he checks behind us. Every time we stop, he finds some excuse to touch me. And though he is always watching for threats, he is still tender.

Studying his face when we start walking again, I give voice to the question that has been bothering me since our shower. "Do you *always* travel with condoms?"

Shock widens his eyes, and he chuckles. "Nope. But *I* didn't pack my duffel bag."

Now, I am confused. Did he plan on sleeping with me? If so, why did he push me away so many times the previous night. "Who did?"

"Ford. Or...someone he paid." Nomar squeezes my hand, the gesture reassuring. "I was in Karachi when he called. All I had with me were a couple of tunics, a set of black fatigues, some tech, and weapons. Ford had a private plane waiting for me at the airfield. Along with clothes, a razor, a couple of burner phones, a hell of a lot of cash, and...a box of condoms."

"But...why?" I am truly grateful Ford thought of...everything. But, still confused. "Do you sleep with women wherever you go?"

Nomar stops, takes my face in his hands and holds me so I cannot look away. "No, sweetheart. I haven't been with anyone in more than five years. Ford put the condoms in the bag because he figured it out before I did."

"What?" I hold my breath, unsure if I can dare hope he feels the same way I do.

"There isn't anyone else for me, Lisette. I can't give you forever. My darkness would consume you. But I can give you my heart, and I don't ever want it back."

Nomar

I told her. In my own way. She's it for me. I'm in love with her, and though I don't expect her to love me back—or even want me if she ever finds out what I've done—we have this time together. Today. Tonight. Part of tomorrow.

Once Mateen is back, Griff can take over the day-to-day surveillance. I'll stick around for a while. Maybe even date her. Pretend to be a normal guy. One whose sins don't eat away at him every minute of every day.

Even now, in the middle of a flower shop, surrounded by so much beauty, I can feel them. Crawling up my throat. Choking me. I've spilled enough blood to drown a hundred times over, and nothing will ever wipe my ledger clean.

We fill cart after cart with arrangements from massive, walk-in coolers, the large order destined for some big convention happening tomorrow.

The bell over the door rings. I shove one of the vases back into the cooler. My hand finds the butt of the Beretta under my jacket. Lisette sidesteps me, her fingers squeezing my bicep.

"Nomar, this is Fleur. She owns this shop."

A petite woman with white hair leans heavily on a cane with a walking boot on her right foot. She looks from Lisette to me.

"Nomar? *Est-ce la vérité?*"

She knows who I am? Lisette...talked about me? I shouldn't be surprised. Not with everything she's shared. But I am.

"*Oui.* You should sit. The three of us should...talk." Lisette switches to English as she moves to Fleur's side and takes her arm. "Come. I will make you a cup of coffee."

Fleur gives the carts a passing glance as she limps slowly through the shop. "Beautiful work, honey. I knew you could do it. The drivers will be here to pick these up in half an hour."

Thirty minutes? Plenty of time for me to do a perimeter check. I wait for the older woman to sink into a chair in the back room, then clear my throat. "Lisette? Can I talk to you?"

Sliding my arm around her waist when we're out of Fleur's line of sight, I inhale her scent. It's body lotion, I found out this morning. Something French. Sweet and soft and very much *her*.

"Fleur will want to know why you are here," she says. "Why you think it is acceptable to sit in the shop all day while I work. We should tell her. She...already knows about me."

"The *official* story?" I helped Ford craft it. It's more or less the truth, minus the part where Faruk was a powerful trafficker of guns, drugs, and people.

"Yes. I can tell her about the dating app, and she will understand that you are here to protect me."

I don't like anyone knowing who I am. But Lisette's right. There's no way in hell I'm leaving her alone until she gets off work.

"Okay. Tell her. I should go for a walk. Make sure no one's watching the shop. But I need you to lock the door and stay inside until I get back."

"We opened an hour ago," she says with a frown. "What if someone needs flowers?"

"They can wait. I won't be long. If I go now, I won't have to leave you again today. Please, Lisette. I didn't see anyone following us this morning, but whenever I'm with you, I'm... distracted."

"So it is *my* fault you cannot do your job? And now you will make it so I cannot do mine?" She huffs, wriggles out of my grasp, and crosses her arms over her chest. "Flowers may seem unimportant to you, Nomar, but they are not to me."

"That's not... Fuck. None of this is your fault. *I* should have been more careful this morning. And your work *is* important. I'm not asking you to give it up. Just take a break for a few minutes. Can you at least lock the door behind me? Keep the open sign on. If anyone comes by, let them in. But text me first and I'll head straight back."

She holds my gaze for several seconds before her frustration fades. "All right. You have twenty minutes. I will not make the hotel staff knock. This is the biggest order Fleur has ever sold. If they are happy with her—my—work, she will be able to hire more people. Take vacations. Enjoy herself."

The way she talks about this woman, they share a bond. Friendship. Respect. "You care for her."

Lisette nods. "I met her a few weeks after we moved here. It was Mateen's first day of school and I was crying on the street outside the shop. She brought me in, made me a cup of coffee, and by the time I left two hours later, she had offered me a job. I had no resume, no experience, no references. Fleur took a chance on me. She is...like...my godmother."

"I'll be quick. I promise." Leaning in, I brush a light kiss to her lips. "Keep your phone *in your hand*. Got it?"

She pulls her mobile from her pocket. "Hurry back. Fleur will have many questions for you."

Great. Interrogated by a godmother. That'll be a first.

CHAPTER TWENTY-ONE

Nomar

Rue du Parc is far enough from the city center, the sidewalks
are mostly empty at 11:00 a.m. Too late for breakfast, too early
for lunch. A dark-clad figure darts around a corner, but for all
I know, he was a businessman in a black beret and suit jacket.

By the time I reach that same corner, he's nowhere to be
found.

I'd give anything for proper surveillance equipment.
Cameras over the shop's front and back doors. Panic buttons.
And a handful of French National police officers on standby.

Dax is supposed to be working on that one, but I haven't
heard a peep from him *or* Ford since I landed.

At least Griff is checking in regularly. The kids are off on
their walking tour until 3:00 p.m., then back to the hotel for a
few hours before they go stargazing at one of Barcelona's
observatories.

I glance at my texts, and chuckle.

*Griff: I run five miles, three days a week, and these kids are in
much better shape than I am.*

I almost tell him he'll have an easier time when he gets here. The flower shop is all of two kilometers from Mateen's school and three from her home. But that would imply I'm leaving.

Staying is dangerous. Stupid, even. But with every minute I spend with her, leaving becomes more and more of a fantasy. A bad one.

At the shop across the street, I place an order for three *cafe au laits* and a box of macarons. Maybe if I show up carrying sweets, Fleur will go easy on me. The few minutes also gives me time to watch the pedestrians through the window.

A man and a woman walk arm-in-arm by the flower shop. I've seen her before. Haven't I? Not him, though. He's new.

I snap a photo, but I already know it's not going to be clear enough for facial recognition. She's wearing dark glasses, and her bangs slant over one eye.

"I'll be right back," I say to the barista. "My parking is about to run out."

The young woman nods and waves at me to go. "Run. I will keep the coffees hot for you!"

She's getting a fat tip when I return.

I'm out the door in seconds, running back the way the couple came. If I'm fast enough, I can circle the block before they disappear.

But when I turn the final corner, the street's empty. There are a dozen businesses here. Clothing shops, a butcher, two restaurants, and a book store. If I took the time to check them all, I'd be over an hour.

Fuck. I text the blurry photo to Wren, along with the street address of the flower shop. She's worked miracles before. Maybe she can do it again.

If I hurry, I'll have just enough time to pick up the coffees and macarons before my twenty minutes are up.

Lisette

We walk along River Garonne at sunset, long shadows painting the water in an orange hue. Fallen leaves tumble over the grassy banks. Nomar keeps his hand at the small of my back, but he has not relaxed since we left the flower shop.

At dinner, he sat with his back to the wall, tensing every time the door opened. We talked about nothing important. The weather, Mateen's love of soccer, Ford and Joey's visit last spring.

I ache to press him for more. To demand he finally open up to me. But we need privacy. Locked doors. Safety.

"It's beautiful here," Nomar says. "Have you taken Mateen on the ferris wheel?"

I shake my head, staring across the left bank at the wheel all lit up. "No. I...do not like heights. I took Noele to Disneyland Paris when I was twenty, and I almost passed out on the tamest of roller coasters. He has always wanted to go. Noele will take him, eventually. But she is a wedding planner—did you know that?"

"I didn't."

"Summer is her busiest time. The wheel closes in the middle of October." I do not like admitting my failings as a mother. Mateen is my world, and I would give anything to find the courage to take him.

"I could...uh...if you want." Nomar will not meet my gaze. "I know he comes home tomorrow, and I'll understand if you want me to stay away. But..."

I fiddle with the hem of my sweater, unsure how to explain Nomar's presence to my son. "You will stay? Even after the other man—Griff?—is here?"

He stares down at the sidewalk for several steps, and I fear I have his answer.

"I'll stay as long as I can."

I stop and let go of his arm. "What does that mean? 'As long as you *can?*' A day? A week? A month?"

The pain etched on his face should deter me. But not this time.

"If you are only going to disappear again, I do not want you around my son." The first tears prick at my eyes, and I step into his path so he cannot help but look at me. "Mateen asked about you almost every day when you left the last time. I will not put him through that again."

He nods slowly. "I should have told him myself. Or...told the President to go fuck himself. I thought...they told me six months, Lisette. I believed them. Six months, and I'd be done. I could come back. See you and Mateen. Try...for something real with you."

"Why didn't you?" I do not know how to feel about his admission. Happy he thought of me—of us? Or angry he did not return?

"The CIA fucked it all up. Kept stringing me along. 'Just another month. We're almost there.'" He shakes his head and huffs. "At a year, I'd had enough."

"And what of the next two?"

Nomar's shoulders hunch, and he takes my arm. "We should head back to your place. We're too exposed."

Shaking off his hold, I glare at him. "You have not answered any of my questions, Nomar. I have trusted you with some of the worst parts of my past, but *you* do not trust *me.*"

With a ragged breath, he runs a hand through his hair. "I trust you, Lisette. I swear it. I'll tell you everything. Just not here. Not...tonight. Please. Let me have this one, perfect day with you."

The desperation in his voice sways me. Today *has* been perfect. In every way. "All right. But tomorrow...there can be no more secrets between us."

Relief eases the lines bracketing his lips. "I won't disappear again. Even if...fuck. Even if you decide you don't want to see me again after tomorrow, I'll always answer the phone if you call. Always."

⁂

"You ARE JOKING," I say as he takes my keys and unlocks my front door. "Trevor always seemed so serious."

"Oh, he is. Now. But fifteen years ago, he pulled some epic pranks." Nomar removes his gun from the holster and holds up his hand. "Lock the door. I need to clear the house."

Most of the night, I have managed to forget the potential danger. We laughed over dinner, stuffed ourselves with Coq au Vin and Tarte Tatin, and kissed along the banks of the River Garonne. Only our fight marred the perfection of today.

I hear nothing as he moves around upstairs. His footsteps are utterly silent, and it reminds me how dangerous he is. How deadly.

"All clear," he says. "I need to do a perimeter check and move my car. Lock the door—"

"Mateen will call soon. Take my keys." I start for the bedroom, but turn after two steps. "I am not ready to tell him about you, Nomar. Not yet. Please, stay downstairs when you return?"

Pain fills his gaze for a moment, but then he blinks it away. "I wouldn't tell him about me either," he mutters to himself. "I'll be back in fifteen minutes."

I almost stop him.

He said he would not disappear again.

Is that enough? I want it to be. I want Nomar to kiss me

and tell me he wants me as much as I want him. That nothing will ever tear us apart again. But I know he will not. His time in Afghanistan haunts him, and he believes it will destroy whatever this is between us.

When the video call rings, I settle myself on my bed. "Mateen! I miss you so much, *mon chou.* What did you do today?"

"We walked forever. At least five kilometers! But then Mademoiselle Benoit fell and the ambulance came!"

I sit up, panic tightening my chest. "She fell? Is she all right?"

"She got her foot stuck in a drain. The police came too, and then the fire truck. They had this big saw and they had to cover her with a blanket and there were sparks everywhere. She's okay now. But she can't come to the observatory tonight."

I have to steady the phone with both hands as my adrenaline fades. Only an accident. Mateen is safe, and all he will remember of today is an adventure—and maybe the big saw with sparks.

"Are you excited about the observatory? What are you going to do there?"

"Maman..." he rolls his eyes. "Look at stars and stuff."

"And stuff?" I laugh. "I love you, Mateen. I cannot wait to hug you tomorrow."

Amelie whispers something to my son, and he nods. "I miss you too, Maman."

Tears burn my eyes. He may have needed prompting, but he speaks the truth. "Next time you have a school trip, maybe I can go with you."

His whole face lights up. "Really?"

"Yes. Really. Be safe tonight. See lots of stars."

"Love you, Maman." Before Mateen can hang up, Amelie snatches the phone from his hand.

"Go put your shoes on," she says. "Laurent? Get the boys' coats."

She looks exhausted—and frazzled—when she focuses on the screen. "The children were upset when Mademoiselle Benoit fell, but as soon as the fire brigade came, all they cared about was the big saw. She sprained her ankle, but was able to join us all for dinner tonight."

"Oh, good. I am so glad you and Laurent were able to take off work to chaperone. One day, maybe I will not worry every time Mateen is out of my sight."

"I do not think that ever goes away, Lisette. My niece is twenty-two and my sister still worries all the time." She lowers her voice. "How are *you*?"

"Better than I thought I would be. This is the first time we have ever been apart. I feared I would cry the whole time."

I wish I could tell her the truth. That while I miss my son more than I thought possible, I am not alone.

"This weekend, you will come over for dinner and we will show you all the pictures we took of the boys. They have had a wonderful time. They even know some Spanish now."

"Please tell me they learned more than swear words."

Amelie's cheeks flush pink. "They may have heard more than one of those from the firemen today."

"Time to go," Laurent calls.

Mateen waves at the phone. "Bye, Maman!"

"Bye! Have fun!"

Amelie blows me an air kiss and ends the call. The rest of the night is mine, and there is only one thing I want.

Nomar.

CHAPTER TWENTY-TWO

Lisette

I FIND him on the sofa, staring at his phone.

"How's Mateen?" he asks.

"I will not be surprised if he wants to be a fire fighter now." I snuggle against Nomar's side. He wraps his arm around me and presses a kiss to the top of my head.

"I talked to Griff a few minutes ago. Heard about his teacher's fall. He said the fire captain gave the kids a tour of the truck, even ran the siren for them after the ambulance left. Mateen was fascinated."

"He used to watch for the ambulances out the window of his hospital room at St. Jude's. He had never seen one before. But he is only nine. Every week, he wants to be something new. I tell him he can choose anything—or everything."

"He's a smart kid. Griff can't get too close, but he says Mateen is constantly asking questions. Good ones. He pays attention. And he looks out for the other kids."

Heat blooms in my chest. "He was so sick for so long. I think it taught him to be kind."

"Or you did," Nomar says. "You raised him, Lisette. Three years ago, he was a little kid obsessed with FIFA and Superman. He didn't speak a word of French, and he'd never seen the inside of a classroom. Now, he builds robots. He's on a school trip with his friends. *You* did that." He sweeps his hand around my living room. "You did all of this. You're amazing, sweetheart."

Blushing, I run my hand up and down Nomar's thigh. It feels so *right* to sit and talk with him. To have him in my home. As if we are a normal couple.

"There are moments where it feels like no time at all has passed since we met," I say softly. "And others where it feels like a lifetime ago."

He nudges my chin up and slants his lips over mine. The kiss sets me ablaze. Desperate to ease this ache in my core, I straddle him.

His hands sink into my hair. The hint of pain pricking my scalp pulls a moan from my throat. I should not feel this much this soon. But I think...maybe...I have loved him for three years, and only now understand. I *needed* him then. But I *want* him now.

"Lisette..." He rolls his hips, and I shiver at the feel of his hard length. "Naked. Now."

Nomar cups my ass, stands, and carries me toward the stairs.

"Put me down before you hurt yourself!" I beat my fists against his back, but cannot stop myself from laughing as he feigns huffing and puffing all the way to my bedroom.

"I could carry you all day, sweetheart. But I'd much rather strip off all your clothes and spend the next few hours showing you just how much you mean to me."

I thrill at his words. At the depth of emotion welling in his dark brown eyes. At the way he cups my chin and skates his thumb over my lips.

My hands shake, and I reach for the hem of his t-shirt. "I need to ask you for something."

"Anything, sweetheart." Nomar kisses me again, and I take strength from the promise in his tone.

With my fingers hooked in his belt loops, I back up until my thighs press against the mattress. "Take off your clothes."

He still wears his gun on his hip, and works the holster free from his belt before stripping off his blue t-shirt. His boots, jeans, socks, and briefs form a pile on the floor.

My gaze lands on his cock, and I lick my lips. "Come closer."

"You don't have to." Nomar sinks to his knees in front of me, his hands sliding under my skirt to skim my thighs. "The piercing can be a lot to handle."

"I want this." The room takes on a subtle shimmer, and I brush a single tear from my lashes. "I did not think I could... ever again. But with you... Even if I cannot finish, I want to try. Please."

He nods, then kisses each bit of skin he uncovers as he helps me out of my clothes. My nipples get extra attention from his lips, teeth, and tongue. By the time I sink down onto the mattress, my core is drenched, and I am ready to beg.

"Go slow, sweetheart. If you need to stop, squeeze my ass. Okay?"

I peer up at him, unsure if I want to smile, cry, or come. I am giving him everything. A part of me I thought would never be whole again.

My fingers curl lightly around his shaft. He twitches in my hold, and his scent fills my nose. Closing my eyes, I curl my lips over my teeth and lean in.

The piercing slips along the roof of my mouth, and his flavor bursts over my tongue. He's salty and strong, but also sweet. With him, I have no fear—except perhaps that I have forgotten how to do this—a worry that his soft groans quickly dispel.

"Oh, God. Just like that, sweetheart."

I cannot take him deep. He is too big, too thick. But I work his crown, my tongue pressing to the thick vein on the underside of his shaft. My free hand finds his balls, cupping them gently as I continue to lick and suck. He lets me set the pace, only rocking back and forth on his heels in small, slow movements.

I try a hum. He sucks in a sharp breath, and his entire body stiffens.

"Gonna come, Lisette. Stop...now...if..."

Another low sound in the back of my throat sends him over the edge. I thought I was prepared, but I almost choke on him. Until he strokes my cheeks and calms me with a single touch.

Laying me down on the bed, he brushes his thumb across my lips, and comes away with a drop of his release.

"I thought I needed you, Nomar," I whisper when he stretches out next to me and covers us both with the duvet. "For three years, I hoped you would come back because I thought I needed you. But I was wrong. I do not need you. I *want* you. I think...I could love you. Maybe I already do."

Nomar

My heart shoots straight for my throat. I know the exact moment I fell in love with Lisette. But I never expected her to love me back.

She swallows a sob and wipes a tear from her cheek. "I lost so much of myself in Afghanistan. Faruk would force me...like that. It is how his men broke the women he trafficked. At the beginning, he made me watch. I never thought I would want to touch a man in that way again. But with you—"

I sit up, reality slamming into me so hard and fast, I can't breathe. Faruk raped her. For ten years. Forced her to watch other women being violated. And she trusts me enough she *asked* to go down on me.

"You hadn't given head since…"

"I had boyfriends when I was young. But only two were serious. I had not done…that…with anyone in thirteen years." She skims her hand down my chest, but I stop her before she reaches my dick.

"Wait. Please." I can't let this go any further without telling her everything. By tomorrow, I'll be so far gone over her, I'll never be able to walk away. "Yesterday, you said you thought I'd been searching for happiness for a long time."

She nods. "I remember."

"You were wrong. I haven't been searching for it. I gave up on it a long time ago."

"No one should give up on happiness," she says, her green eyes shimmering with emotion. "Please. Tell me why."

I almost lose my nerve. I could beg her to leave me to my secrets. *Maybe* she'd still talk to me once in a while. But I can't. She deserves better than a broken man whose guilt eats him alive every second of every day.

"When I left your apartment in Boston three years ago, I ended up in a meeting with the President of the United States, the head of the Joint Special Operations Command, and the Deputy Director of the CIA." I stare up at the ceiling, unable to watch as I destroy any possibility for a future together.

"Faruk controlled the lion's share of weapons, drugs, and people trafficked through Afghanistan. His death left a big fucking hole. There were three other players in the region, and the CIA had their eye on one of them. Shapur Khan. They thought he'd be open to funneling them information. Maybe help prevent the next 9-11.

"Years ago, the guy had gotten on Faruk's bad side, and I saved his life. He owed me. The President ordered me to find him and get him to hire me."

"What did you have to do?" Her voice breaks, and fuck. I don't know how to do this. "Nomar? You can tell me. Whatever it is...I have seen worse."

Sitting up, I swing my legs over the side of the bed and rest my elbows on my knees. "I trained his men. Advised him. But I also moved shipments. Drugs. Weapons. And...women."

Lisette sucks in a sharp breath. "Women? You... No. I refuse to believe—"

"I did it, Lisette. More than two hundred of them over eleven months. I didn't take them. And I *never* touched them. But the men who guarded them worked for *me*. I fed the CIA the location of every single auction, but they only managed to free a handful of the girls. If they'd gone after too many of them, the whole operation would have been fucked. I didn't have a choice. Those women...were sold because of me."

She scrambles out of bed, her movements frantic and jerky as she pulls on her skirt and sweater. "I cannot hear this. Everything you said. You would have stopped him if you'd known about me. You should have killed him for hurting me. Yet, you condemned others to an even worse fate?"

"Lisette..."

"No. I cannot... I...I need you to go." Tears spill down her cheeks. "Leave. Now."

I push up, but she backs away from me. "I can't. I won't. Not until we know you're safe. I promised to protect you."

"How can I think—how can I possibly find a way to accept this when you are *in my bed*? When everything I see, everything I touch reminds me of you?" Lisette shakes her head. "If you will not leave, I will. I will go to a hotel tonight. In the morning, maybe...we can talk. But not tonight."

She's out of the bedroom before I can snatch my jeans from the floor.

"Lisette! No. It's not safe." I almost fall on my face before I get the denim over my hips, and thud down the stairs barefoot. "Don't!" I shout. She's nothing but a blur through the front door.

I don't care that I'm not wearing a shirt. Or shoes. Or briefs. But my gun. Shit.

Her scream pierces the night air.

Fuck the gun.

I bolt after her. On the street, a man drags Lisette toward the corner. She twists and kicks, finding his shin. He swears and shoves her—hard. Her head hits a parked car, and she slumps to the ground.

The fucker's dead. He just doesn't know it yet.

I tackle him, and we crash to the pavement together. Blows rain down on my torso. He's got six inches and at least a hundred pounds on me, but he doesn't know how hard I'll fight for the woman I love—even if she can't love me back after what I've done.

My knee lands on his family jewels. I wrap my hands around his throat, squeezing the life out of him.

He thrashes, arms and legs flapping helplessly as he struggles to breathe. I release him seconds before he passes out and slam my fist into his cheek. Blood spurts from his lips. A second hit. Then a third.

His body goes slack.

I punch him again for good measure before I spring for Lisette and pull her into my arms. "Sweetheart, talk to me."

With a little moan, she collapses against me. Fuck.

Picking her up, I hustle back inside and deposit her on the sofa. "Don't move. I'll be right back."

Leaving her is the last thing I want to do, but I can't take a chance that shitstain on the sidewalk has friends.

Her attacker leaves a bloody smear on the concrete as I drag him to her entryway and let him fall roughly onto the tile. He's still out cold—thank God—but that won't last long.

I lock the door, race upstairs, and grab my gun, clothes, and duffel bag before returning to the entryway. Flipping him over, I zip tie his wrists behind his back, then secure his ankles and pat him down.

Markov, switchblade, phone, and wallet with more than five hundred euros in it.

"Nomar..." Lisette sways at the top of the entryway stairs. "Who...is he?"

"Stay there," I grit out. He's not going anywhere for at least a few minutes. After that...I'm going to kill him for touching her.

A knot the size of a golf ball swells on Lisette's forehead, but there's no blood. She stands stiffly, and when I try to wrap my arm around her waist, she pulls away. Fuck.

"I know you hate me right now—and you have every right to—but I need you to listen. Go upstairs. Pack three days of clothes for both you and Mateen. Your passports. Any medications you need. Stay up there until I tell you it's safe to come down. We're leaving in twenty minutes."

"What about Mateen? He is still with his class..." Tears gather in her eyes. God, the fear in her voice is going to break me.

"I'll text Griff now, and we'll call him as soon as we're clear. Now, go. Please. I don't want you to see what I have to do next."

CHAPTER TWENTY-THREE

Nomar

I PULL ON MY SHIRT, socks, and shoes, then kneel next to the asshole. He doesn't have ID. Only money and a handful of prepaid credit cards.

A hard slap rouses him, and he lets loose with a string of curses in Dari.

I lean down so my lips are only inches from his ear. "Who do you work for?"

"Fuck you."

"Have it your way." I cover his mouth with one hand, and dig the fingers of the other under his collarbone.

His scream doesn't carry. Much. Sweat beads on his brow.

"That's one of the *least* painful pressure points. There are seven more, and I know every single one of them. Who do you work for?"

The asshole bucks and tries to slam his body into me.

"Not too bright, are you? Or maybe you're just a masochist. I can work with that." I shift my right thumb to half an inch in front of his ear. This time, his scream is two octaves higher. His eyes roll back in his head. "You're not getting off that easy," I mutter and let up on the pressure. "You're gonna be awake for all the pain."

Tears stream down his temples. His breath saws in and out of his chest in shallow pants.

"Ready to tell me now?"

He manages a weak nod. Pathetic. I lift my hand from his mouth.

"Raziq...Ali."

"That name supposed to mean something to me? Why does he want the woman?"

Asshole shakes his head.

"We've already established you don't like pain. And I can cause you an endless amount of it. Try again."

"His...brother! She was his brother's wife! He wants the woman and her son returned to Afghanistan."

Fuck me.

Something crashes upstairs.

"Don't move." I punctuate the order with a sharp kick to the man's nuts, and he howls in pain.

In the bedroom, Lisette curls in on herself, her arms around her knees. A small rolling suitcase lies on its side a few feet away, empty. All the color has drained from her face. She tugs at the hem of her sweater with trembling fingers. "He said his brother was dead."

"You *knew* Faruk had a brother? Did you tell Ford? Wren? Anyone?"

"Why would I tell them about a dead man?" she whispers.

I drop to one knee and take her arm. Her flinch cracks my heart into pieces. Half an hour ago, she had her lips wrapped around my dick. Now, she doesn't want me to touch her.

"You have to get up, Lisette. We can't stay here. Finish packing and wait for me to come get you. We leave in ten minutes." I can't be gentle with her. Not now. There could be more of Raziq's men outside. Thank fuck Mateen is in Barcelona. But if they know about him...how long until they find him?

She nods and pushes herself up. I'd give anything to be able to wrap my arms around her. Hold her for even a few seconds. But I can't. There's no time.

Downstairs, I stop in the kitchen to grab the sharpest knife I can find. Raziq's thug is flopping around on the tile like a dying fish trying to get his bound hands under his ass.

"I told you not to move." His eyes widen at the sight of the blade. "You have exactly sixty seconds to tell me everything you know. Or you'll find out what your own dick and balls taste like before you die."

I spin the knife in my hand like I'm a goddamn circus performer, and the fucker whimpers. "I do not know anything! He paid us fifty thousand dollars to bring the woman to him in Kabul."

My blood runs cold. "Just the woman? What about her son?"

"The boy is in Barcelona!"

Grabbing the asshole by his jacket, I haul him up and slam him against the wall. "How many men in Barcelona?"

"F-five." The scent of piss burns my nose. He's shaking in my grip. Amateur.

"And here?"

"Three."

Before I can ask where they are, the front door shudders. The second hit makes it bow, and the third busts the lock completely.

Lisette screams my name.

I plunge the knife into the asshole's chest, twist, and yank it free. It finds a second target in a blond thug aiming a pistol at my head. The gun clatters to the floor seconds before his body. The last man turns on his heel and runs.

"Stay upstairs!" I shout. Precious seconds pass as I muscle the two dead men to one side of the landing and send a quick text to Griff.

Get Mateen and run.

Taking the stairs two at a time, I find Lisette hiding behind the bedroom door. "We're leaving. Now. Stay close and do exactly what I say."

I don't wait for her to acknowledge me. We don't have the luxury of time. I take the suitcase and, at the bottom of the stairs, grab my duffel and pass it to her, along with my keys. "Got to keep one hand free. Don't stop for anything. My car's a black Fiat parked on the other side of the street. If I tell you to run, drive to the Hotel Rêve, get a room—there's cash in the bag—and call Ford. Do you understand?"

"Y-yes. What about Mateen?"

Fuck. I can't tell her yet. That these assholes know where he is. She'll shut down. "We have to go. Now."

Lisette flinches, but when I head for her broken front door, she follows—and sees the dead bodies on the floor. "You...killed two of them?"

"Yes. And I'd do it again to keep you safe." I cut my gaze to hers. Too pale. Too calm. Too detached. But until we're in the car, it's better this way.

There's no sign of the third man on the street. If he's smart, he ran as far and as fast as he could. But when have I ever been that lucky?

"Call Griff," I say when my phone connects to the car's Bluetooth. Three rings. Four. Fuck. Lisette huddles against the door, crying quietly. "Do you have any emergency contact numbers for Mateen's teachers? Chaperones? Anyone?"

"Amelie and Laurent. Their son is Mateen's best friend." She pulls her phone from her pocket, but the screen is a spiderweb of cracks. "I...it won't unlock..."

"We'll clone it as soon as we get to the hotel. I have a

couple of burners in my bag." I want to tell her everything will be okay, but I can't promise that now. Not knowing this Raziq fucker has at least eight men on his payroll.

I try Ford, but the call goes straight to voicemail. "Call me back, Marine. Now!" I snap, then pull up the only other number programmed into this phone. Pritchard fucked me over when he got shitcanned, but he's our last hope.

"Nomar? Why the hell are you calling me?"

"Because I can't reach anyone else. Someone tried to snatch Lisette outside her house, and the guy guarding Mateen isn't answering his goddamn phone. Faruk had a brother, and *he's* behind this whole fucking thing."

"Where are you and what do you need?"

"We're heading to Hotel Rêve. I need a location and status on the kid right fucking now. But unless you have some other way to reach Griff, there are two dead hostiles in Lisette's entryway and her front door is busted. You have any contacts in the French National Police who can clean up the mess?"

"No, but I can get one. Might be able to track Griff, too. Give me ten minutes."

He hangs up before I can reply.

"What do we do now?" Lisette asks, her voice barely a whisper.

"We go to the hotel, barricade the door, and wait for Austin to call us back. I sent Griff a text before we left and told him to take Mateen and run. If we're lucky, he's not answering because they're on the move."

"Mateen would not go with him unless he knew the code word."

"Firefly? He knows it. We all know it, sweetheart."

She stiffens. "Do not call me that. Not now. I do not know if I can ever trust you again after what you have done."

"Lisette, there's more I need to tell you. About what I did *after* I stopped working for Shapur."

"You *sold* women. Nothing else matters." She returns to staring at her broken phone, one tear after another slipping down her cheeks.

Lisette

"The Hotel Rêve is one of the few places in the city where you can still pay cash," Nomar says as he leads me down the hall to a room on the fourth floor.

Blues and grays dominate the space with a double bed, extra pillows, and a view of the street through the thick velvet curtains.

"Sit," he orders, then muscles the dresser in front of the door. "I need to check your head."

"I am fine. How long has it been since you spoke to that man?"

Nomar checks his phone. "Twelve minutes."

"Why are we here? We should be going to Barcelona. To get Mateen. It is only a few hours. What if Raziq sent men there too?"

I suck in a sharp breath when he meets my gaze.

"He did. You *know* my son is in danger! *Putain!* How could you not tell me?" I can barely see through my tears. "If anything happens to him..."

"I needed to get you somewhere safe," he says. His arms band tightly around me, his lips close to my ear. "If we don't hear from Griff in the next half an hour, we'll go. But Ford and Austin have connections I don't. The kind that get you places on private planes. We could be in Barcelona in ninety minutes."

Ninety minutes. Not four hours. Ninety minutes. I stop fighting him, and suddenly, everything hurts. My head. My shoulder. My hip. "Promise me," I whisper. "In thirty minutes, we will go."

"I can't do that, sweetheart. I don't know a damn thing for sure right now. But in thirty minutes, we'll have a plan. Please trust me. This is what I do. What I've always done."

It feels so good to be held. To have strong arms around me, his voice in my ear. I cannot trust him with my heart. Not now. Maybe not ever. But I trusted him to save our lives once before. I can do it again.

"Okay."

Nomar leads me to the sofa and eases me down next to him. "I need to check you for a concussion." He pulls a small flashlight from his duffel bag and flicks it on. "Look straight ahead for me."

The beam is unbearably bright as he sweeps it from the outer corner of each eye inward.

"How much does it hurt? Scale of one to ten?"

"Three—*merde!*" The pain increases tenfold when Nomar probes the swelling. "Stop." My heart pounds, and I jerk away from his touch. "My head is not important. I need to call Amélie."

With a nod, Nomar pulls a canvas pouch from his bag and sets a phone, a black metal disc, and two cables on the low table in front of us. "Give me your mobile."

The screen lights up at my touch, and Mateen's smiling face peers back at me from under the hundreds of cracks in the glass. "You can retrieve my photos? They are all I have..." Hot tears spill down my cheeks. If anything happens to my son—if Faruk's brother gets to him—will I survive it?

"I can get to everything."

Less than three minutes later, a small piece of my world rights when I hold the new phone in my hand.

"Call Amelie. I'll try Griff again."

Endless seconds pass, our phones ringing in stereo. With each one, my panic grows. Voicemail.

"Amelie? Please call me back. Mateen...he might be in danger. I will try Laurent next, but..." The last shred of my control shatters. Sobs wrack my body. The room is nothing but a shimmering haze of gray.

Nomar tries to ease the phone from my hand, but I jerk back. "Do not touch me!"

"Fuck!" He stalks over to the window as I swipe at my cheeks. "Lisette, if I could go back to that day in Boston, I would. In a heartbeat. But you have to know... *Everything* I've done in the past two years has been to—"

His phone buzzes on the table, and he snatches it up. "Griff? Where the hell have you been?" he demands. "Mateen—"

"They took him. Shit. Stop! I'm private security—"

The line goes dead. A wail comes from somewhere deep inside, my heart shattering into a million jagged pieces. My son. My whole world.

Nomar reaches for me, but I beat my fists against his chest. He does nothing to stop my blows. I want to scream. To tell him he broke his promise. But anguish steals my words.

"We'll get him back," Nomar says. "I won't stop until Mateen is safe. I don't care how many people I have to kill. What I have to do. On my life, I'll bring Mateen back to you."

I cannot trust him. I cannot trust *anyone*. My son is gone, and I fear I will never see him again.

CHAPTER TWENTY-FOUR

Nomar

Suffering has a sound. As does despair. I should know. I've seen enough of both to last me a lifetime. Lisette's wail is so much worse. I let her hit me. It's the least I deserve. But soon, she sways on her feet, and I wrap my arms around her. She doesn't fight anymore. Doesn't say a word. I don't even think she knows I'm here.

We failed, and now that murdering asshole's brother has Mateen.

I ease her down onto the bed. "I need to get Griff back. Find out what happened."

She's too far gone to hear me. Lost to her grief. To the panic threatening to pull me down too. But I go into the bathroom, fill a cup with water, and set it on the nightstand for her. Lisette pulls a pillow to her chest, her sobs fading more and more with each passing minute.

Griff's phone goes to voicemail. Where the *hell* is he? I pick up Lisette's mobile and find Laurent's number. But he doesn't answer either. Fuck. I'm about to dial Ford when Austin's name flashes across the screen.

"About damn time. They got to Mateen."

"I know." His voice carries a deathly calm, which in my experience means he's about to blow a gasket. "Zephyr's pulling camera footage from around the observatory. She'll send it to your phone in a few minutes."

"Who the fuck is Zephyr?"

"Focus, Garcia. She's one of mine, and she can hack into anything. She and Wren together...they could take down the world if they wanted to." A horn blares over the line. "The gas pedal is on the right!" he shouts. "There were five of them. They grabbed Mateen and another boy, along with his mother. Zephyr's working on an ID for the woman and the kid now."

Fucking hell. If it wasn't bad enough he had Mateen, now he's taken *more* hostages? And then I realize who those others have to be. I lower my voice, my gaze locked on Lisette. She's still curled on her side on the bed, her shoulders shaking every few seconds. "Amelie and Philippe Dumont. I'd bet my life on it. What about the father? Laurent?"

"Shot twice. Center mass. Griff killed one and almost took down another, but it was chaos. He kept the father alive until the ambulance came. The National Police saw the dead guy and arrested him. One of my contacts is working on getting him released now."

"Other casualties?"

"None fatal."

I breathe out a sigh of relief. A single miracle in an entire night of fuckups and catastrophes. "We can't stay here. There's still at least one of Raziq's men in Toulouse. Can you get me to Afghanistan? And send someone to protect Lisette?"

"You are not leaving me behind," Lisette says, watching me from the bed with her knees pulled up to her chest.

"There's no way in hell I'm taking you to Afghanistan, sweetheart. You're safer here."

In my ear, Austin swears under his breath. "Leo's calling. He'll have an update on Griff. I'm pulling a team together. Or trying to. I'll call you back. *Sweetheart.*"

Fuck. He hangs up, and I sink against the cushions. "Raziq has Amelie and Philippe too."

Lisette covers her mouth with her hand. "No. *Mon Dieu.* This is all my fault. Faruk's brother was—is—a zealot. If he gets Mateen to Afghanistan, I will never see him again!"

I don't tell her he's probably already on a plane. "I'll get him back. I'll get all of them back."

"You cannot know that. My parents tried to get *me* back, and look at what happened…" She shrinks against the headboard, her lower lip wobbling.

I stalk over to the bed and sit close enough, we're practically touching. She doesn't move away, thank God, but she watches me warily.

"Your parents didn't have the Viper." Fuck. Even saying the name threatens to pull me back down into the darkness I lived in for two long years. "He's got contacts all over the country. If Austin can lend me a couple of his guys—hell, if he can't, I'll hire local muscle—we'll get Mateen back. Amelie and Philippe too."

"Who is the Viper?" she asks.

"Pretty sure you can figure that one out. What do you know about Raziq?" I can't talk about my past with her now. She barely trusts me as it is.

"Almost nothing. Faruk's father cut him off from the rest of the family when he took me. Raziq was older by a few years. I think he was a doctor."

Her hands shake as she reaches for the glass of water and takes a sip.

"A year before Mateen was born, Faruk went to Kabul for several days. When he returned, he told me his family had been killed, and he helped bury them. He never spoke of them again."

"If Raziq grew up in Kabul, maybe he's still there." I pull my phone from my pocket and check flights. "If I have to fly commercial, it's almost twenty-four hours to get to Kabul from here. I need to try Ford again. He can get me a private plane. You have Mateen's passport, right? I might need it to get him out of the country. Hopefully Griff can get Amelie and Philippe's passports from their hotel."

Tears gather in Lisette's eyes. "I do, but it will not help you. Mateen was born Muslim, and the dating profile Noele created for me said I was Catholic. Under Islamic law, I have no rights to the custody of my own son."

"Then we'll go through Uzbekistan."

"And what of me? I am supposed to stay here while my son is in danger? No. I refuse. I am not helpless, Nomar. I fought before. I will do it again." She stares at me with such fire in her swollen, red-rimmed eyes, I almost scoot back a few inches. "If you will not take me with you, I will go on my own."

"The hell you will." I push to my feet, but she follows me. "You don't know what I did after I left Shapur. Who I became. This is the Viper's world, Lisette. But it will eat you up and spit you out. If you even survive. I won't let that happen."

"Like you would not let anything happen to Mateen?"

Her words slice my heart into pieces. She's right. I failed once. What makes me think I won't fail again?

Because this time, I'll succeed or die trying.

A text message rattles my phone, and I turn away before Lisette can see it.

Zephyr: Install this app. Secure messaging, file, and video transfer. Firefly.

"Nomar, do not ignore me. You said in thirty minutes, you would have a plan. This is no plan. You need to come up with one that does not involve leaving me behind."

"No," I snap, then cringe at my tone. "Dammit. I'm sorry. But...fuck it. I love you, Lisette. You can't ask me to bring you somewhere I *know* you won't be safe. Griff spent more than ten years in the CIA and he couldn't stop Raziq's men. They're not amateurs. If I have to worry about you, I'll be distracted, and that could get *everyone* killed."

Lisette flinches, and she presses her hand to her heart. "Please, Nomar. Amelie is my friend. Philippe is the smallest boy in the class. I think that is why he and Mateen became such fast friends. They must be so frightened."

"Come here." I open my arms, but she shakes her head.

"Please. I have to do something," she whispers.

I stare up at the *fleurs de lis* adorning the gray molding. She's right. Having a task will keep her calm—and maybe stop her from continuing this battle she's going to lose. There's no way in hell I'm taking her anywhere near Afghanistan.

"Call Joey. See if she can get in touch with Ford. It's only a little after 2:00 p.m. in Boston. He's got no fucking business not answering my call. He can get me a plane. I need to get in touch with Austin's hacker."

It takes a full five minutes for me to install the ZEO app. Facial scan, fingerprint, passcode, passphrase...hell, I'm surprised it didn't want my mother's maiden name and my social security number. But once I'm in, I find a video file with a short message.

Footage from the attack in Barcelona. It's not pretty.

Lisette is crying as she tells Joey what happened tonight, so I put my earbud in and press *Play.*

The Barcelona street is quiet until a line of twenty kids comes into view. A woman leads the way, two more in the center, and a couple—a man and a woman—bringing up the rear. There's no sound, but the kids look like they're all talking at once.

A street light flickers. Then another. Everyone jumps as a third light explodes in a shower of sparks. The adults scramble to cover the children's heads.

The couple in back grab Mateen and another boy. Five dark-clad men race into view. Flashes of light, and the kids start running in every direction. Muzzle flares.

The guy in back falls to his knees. Laurent. Mateen wriggles out from under him as a man wearing glasses heads for the kid. Shit. That has to be Griff. He sends a powerful cross to one of the attacker's jaws, and the asshole goes down.

More flashes. One of the thugs throws Mateen over his shoulder, while another grabs Philippe and holds a gun to his head. Amelie pleads with the man, and he motions for her to follow them. Griff fires at a third, but the last man is up again. He wrenches one of Griff's arms behind his back, sending him to his knees.

A van speeds in from a side street. Griff throws himself backwards, and the guy trying to tear his arm off stumbles. It's chaos. Amelie screams. Laurent tries to get up, but his chest is soaked with blood. Another man dressed in black fires over the heads of the children, and Griff rolls to his feet.

But he's too late. Mateen, Amelie, and Philippe are already in the van. With a final shot in Griff's direction, the last man jumps into the vehicle, and it speeds away.

Griff shouts something and pulls out his phone. But three seconds later, he drops it and presses his hands to Laurent's chest.

"No..." Lisette says from behind me. "Is he...dead?"

Fuck. I didn't notice she'd hung up with Joey. I try to turn away, but she claps her hand on my shoulder.

Emergency vehicles start to arrive. Police. Fire. Ambulances. A teacher sits on the curb with a bloody arm. Children hang on to one another, crying. Griff keeps pressure on Laurent's chest until the EMTs elbow him aside. He grabs his phone and dials. But only a few seconds later, the National Police drag him away.

I stop the video and turn to her. She's too pale. Shaking, but not crying. Shock.

Until her phone rings. "It is Amelie!"

"It's not." I snatch the device from her hand. "Put it on speaker. Don't let on that anyone else is here. Keep them talking as long as you can. And get proof of life. Understood?"

She nods. I move out of camera range and switch over to the ZEO app.

Nomar: Trace the call coming into Lisette's phone.

Zephyr: On it.

"Amelie?" Lisette asks.

"You took my brother's son from him," Raziq says in refined, polished English. "You will answer for your crimes."

"Faruk is dead. Mateen is *my* son and I have done nothing wrong." Lisette's hand shakes, but she squares her shoulders and swallows hard. "And what about Amelie and Philippe? They are innocents! Let them go."

"I am a reasonable man, Lisette. I will release the woman and her son once you have turned yourself over to me. In Kabul."

Fuck.

She looks to me, panic in her eyes.

"Proof of life," I mouth and wave my hand in a circle. *"Keep him talking."*

"I need to know Mateen is safe. And that Amelie and Philippe are alive." She's on the verge of losing control. I step right in front of her and rest my hand on her hip, squeezing gently.

"Very well. You will receive another call in ten minutes. I suggest you answer it quickly. There is no point to a trace. It will come from a plane that is already in the air. The man with you may be highly trained, but in Afghanistan, *I* am the one with endless resources. You have thirty-six hours to get to Kabul. At that time, I will call with further instructions."

"Wait!" Lisette clutches the phone so tightly, her knuckles turn white, but he's already hung up.

Fuck. She's going to have to come with me.

CHAPTER TWENTY-FIVE

Lisette

THE SECONDS TICK BY SO SLOWLY, each one feels like an hour. "We have to go to the airport. Immediately. If we cannot get a flight tonight—"

Nomar stops me, his hands resting on my shoulders. "Austin's on his way to Istanbul. Zephyr's arranging a plane to take us to Barcelona. We'll meet Griff there, and the three of us will fly to Turkey together. She hasn't figured out transpo to Kabul yet, but she will."

I have no more tears left to cry. My eyes are scratchy. Hollow. "Tell Amelie I am sorry."

His fingers dig into my upper arms. "You can tell her yourself."

"Raziq will kill me," I whisper.

"He won't get close enough to even *touch* you."

"How can you say that? He knows about you! Faruk was careful. Always. He planned everything. Before he took Joey, he researched her for months. He knew everything about her. Even her bra size!"

"Fat lot of good that did him in the end. He's still dead. Raziq can join him in the afterlife. After I cut off his hands, feet, and tongue."

The visual should disgust me, but I *want* Raziq to suffer for what he is doing to Mateen. If only I believed he would.

My phone rings with an incoming video call. I can hardly breathe with how hard my heart is pounding. Nomar tugs me down next to him on the sofa and taps the screen.

My son sits in a bright blue airplane seat, his hands bound with thin ropes. A strip of black cloth gags him, and tears stain his cheeks.

"Mateen!"

His brown eyes widen, and he screams, but the sound is too muffled to make out any words.

"Let me talk to him!"

"This is all you get for now. He is alive. As are the other two," a man with a thick accent says. He pans the camera to the right. Amelie sits alone, also bound and gagged. Her left eye is swollen shut, and a cut bleeds on her forehead. In the seat ahead of her, Philippe wriggles until another man slaps him across the cheek.

I want these men to suffer. I want my child in my arms. I want to go back in time. To yesterday, when Nomar and I shared one perfect night. But I cannot have any of those things.

"Please," I manage. "Do not hurt them..."

"If your piece of shit boss expects Lisette to go anywhere," Nomar growls, "you'll let her talk to her son. Right fucking now."

For a few seconds, I hear only murmurs, the words too quiet to understand. But then the video swings back to Mateen. He shrinks against the seat as rough fingers yank the cloth from between his teeth.

"Maman," he cries. "I am scared..."

"I know, *mon chou.* So am I. But we will be together again soon. I promise. You have to be very brave for me until then."

The man shoves the gag back into his mouth, and I start to cry.

Nomar angles the phone so his face fills the screen. "Mateen, do whatever they say. *All* of you do whatever they say. Understand?"

My son nods a moment before the call drops.

My strength flees in a heartbeat, and I cover my face with my hands. Strong arms wrap around me, and for this one moment, I do not care that Nomar broke my heart. Because I have no heart left. My entire world is on that plane bound for Afghanistan.

He rubs my back, and when his phone beeps, manages to answer it without letting go.

"Griff?" he asks. "Where are you?"

We are close enough, I can hear the deep voice on the other end of the call. "On my way back to the hotel for my gear. You were my first call. What's the plan?"

I twist out of Nomar's arms, needing to know there *is* a plan beyond flying to Kabul. But the look on his face crushes that hope into dust.

"We're coming to you. ETA zero-three-thirty. Zephyr should be sending you all the details now that she knows your phone hasn't been compromised. Raziq gave Lisette thirty-six hours to get to Kabul. He won't release Amelie and Philippe until he has her. We got proof of life a few minutes ago."

"I should have been faster," Griff says. "The big one damn near ripped my arm off."

"Zephyr sent me the video. You couldn't have stopped them. Put it away. We've got work to do."

"Stay behind me, sweetheart," Nomar says as he wheels my suitcase into the private terminal in Barcelona.

"Stop calling me that." Every time he does, I wish we could be together. Truly together. But even if I could forget what he did after he left me in Boston, in thirty-six hours, I fear I will be dead. And Mateen will be lost forever.

On the hour-long flight, I could not bring myself to do more than stare out the tiny window at the darkness and the lights far below. Nomar sat next to me, tried to talk to me, but I ignored him.

Two security guards patrol, AK-47s slung over their shoulders. A man rises from one of the chairs in the waiting area. He is so young. His lip is split in two places, and a bruise darkens his jaw.

"You look like shit." Nomar lets his duffel bag slide from his shoulder and offers his hand.

The man arches a brow as the two shake. "Yeah, you try fighting off four guys at once and see how pretty *you* are when you're done. My arm is killing me. I need to catch a few hours on the flight to Istanbul."

"We all do. Griff, this is Lisette." He steps aside and I peer up at the man who tried to save my son.

"You probably hate me," he says. "And you should. I'm so sorry—"

The pain in his eyes is too much for me, so I embrace him. Griff stands stiffly for a moment, then gives me a one-armed hug.

"You tried to save Mateen. And if you had not been there, Laurent would have died." I draw back, not wishing to make him uncomfortable. "Is there any news? From the hospital?"

"He's still not breathing on his own." Griff runs a hand through his hair and shakes his head. "The man didn't think twice about shielding Mateen. Whatever he needs for his recovery, he'll have. Austin will make sure of it."

"Your plane is ready," the pretty gate agent announces. "Do you have any luggage?"

Nomar turns to her. "We're good, ma'am. Thank you."

With a rough, pained *"oof,"* Griff picks up a large black bag. He favors his left arm, holding it tight to his body. But before I can ask him if he is all right, Nomar wraps his fingers around my wrist.

"Whenever we're exposed, stay between us. You don't go anywhere alone unless we tell you to run. Understood?"

The intensity of his gaze should frighten me, but I feel nothing. Losing Mateen has left me numb. "Yes."

THIS PLANE IS LARGER. Nicer. Two flight attendants in perfectly pressed uniforms greet us, offer us water, coffee, and champagne, and show us how to recline our seats into beds. "Our flight time is four hours and thirty-two minutes this evening. As soon as we reach cruising altitude, the lights will dim and you can get some rest."

Griff asks one of the attendants for as many ice packs as they have, then sinks into a seat across from me.

"How bad?" Nomar asks as the plane starts to taxi.

"Two bruised ribs, a loose tooth, and the fucker did his damnedest to rip my prosthetic off. I'll live—"

"Your...prosthetic?" I stare at Griff, convinced my mind is playing tricks on me.

The young man takes off his glasses and pinches the bridge of his nose. "Ford didn't tell *anyone* about me, did he?"

"I do not understand."

Griff grimaces as he leans forward to remove his jacket. Under the left sleeve of his black t-shirt, his arm is...silver.

Shock steals my words, and I cannot tear my gaze away.

His hand looks real from afar, but this close, I can see the unnatural smoothness of the fake "skin."

"You fought those men with...one arm?"

Frustration simmers in his eyes. "No. I fought them with two. This is the most advanced prosthetic in the world. I have full control of all five fingers, and decent sensation. But that's not all you need to know about me." His heavy sigh twists my stomach into a knot. "I'm mostly deaf. I read lips pretty well, and those glasses are Second Sight's tech. They work with my phone. Speech-to-text. Whatever you say appears on the inside of the lenses."

"That is amazing. I did not mean to offend—"

His gaze softens. "You didn't. But Ford and I are having words when this is over. I can do the job, but it's not right you're only finding out about my...issues now."

"I would have told you tomorrow," Nomar says. "If everything hadn't gone to shit."

His voice holds so much pain, I almost reach for his hand. But the lights dim, and one of the flight attendants brings Griff several clear plastic bags full of ice.

"You can recline your seats now," she says quietly. "If you need anything else, press your call button."

By the time I turn back to Nomar, he's reclined with his beret pulled down low over his eyes. Griff unbuckles his seat belt and heads for the bathroom at the rear of the plane, leaving me to burrow under the dark blue blanket and pray.

CHAPTER TWENTY-SIX

Nomar

I squint in the bright sun, scanning the airfield for anything out of place. We're far enough from the rest of the airport the breeze carries only a hint of jet fuel.

Austin stands stiffly outside the terminal door. Two plus years retired and the man still hasn't learned to relax. Not that I'm surprised. With a curt nod, he heads in our direction.

"We're clear. Lisette, stay close."

She huffs and picks up my duffel bag. I've got her roller bag and the silver case holding Griff's arm. The former CIA officer is in a world of hurt, and removed his prosthetic right after takeoff.

We barely make it down the stairs before Austin hustles over and relieves Griff of his rucksack. "Our flight to Kabul doesn't leave until 14:30. You're going straight to the nearest health center to get checked out."

He nods, a testament to how much pain he's in. I woke up a couple of times on the flight to find him rearranging bags of ice around what's left of his arm. "If I see the asshole who jumped me, I'm dislocating his shoulder before I kill him."

"Lisette? I'm Austin. How are you holding up?"

Her gaze pings between Pritchard and Griff before she shifts subtly closer to me. It gives me hope I haven't completely ruined things between us. "Where is my son? Has he landed in Afghanistan yet?"

"Zephyr was able to track their flight. They're about ninety minutes from Kabul." Austin gestures toward the terminal. "We should get a move on. Griff needs medical, I'm on supplies, and Nomar can reach out to his contacts to see if he can pull in some local muscle. Leo—he used to work with Trevor—should be here in a couple of hours."

"You got a place I can talk in private? Or am I doing all this from the car?" I ask.

"You'll see." Austin grins, and I resist the urge to rearrange his smile. He sent me to Shapur, stalled on my exfil plan, and left his fucking post without saying a goddamn word. Maybe if he'd gotten me out like he promised, none of this would have happened.

Or maybe we'd still be here praying for a miracle.

Lisette and I squeeze into the back of the rented FIAT. I can feel her discomfort. Her fear. Everything. From the moment we met, she's been strong. But now, she's seconds away from shattering into pieces.

Austin's GPS calls out directions, and twenty minutes later, he pulls up to the Five Points Istanbul. "Zephyr should have sent you a room number, and your phone unlocks the door. She's monitoring the hotel security cameras. This is the safest place in the entire country at the moment. Food's pretty good too. Text me your shopping list, and I'll do my best."

I STAND at the window on the twenty-second floor of the luxury hotel suite, staring out over the city. Lisette picks at her pizza and Caesar salad, her gaze locked on her phone.

Zephyr's catching a couple of hours of sleep, but as soon as we take off for Kabul, she's promised to tell us everything she's found on Raziq Ali.

"Lisette, please eat more." I sink into the chair next to her and take a bite of my burger. It'll be nothing but MREs and protein bars once we get to Kabul, and I've had enough of those to last me a lifetime.

"If I do, I will throw up. Go back to your phone calls, Nomar. I cannot do this with you right now." She tries to turn away, but I cup the back of her neck and force her to look at me.

"Do what? Exist in the same room? I love you, Lisette."

"Stop," she whispers and shakes her head.

"No. After we get Mateen back, I'll walk away. You'll never have to see me again. But I won't—I *can't*—stop loving you. So for the next twenty-four hours, you're stuck with me."

"What do you expect me to say to that?" She twists out of my hold and puts as much space between us as the room allows. "You are not a parent. You cannot possibly understand what I am going through."

Fuck. A kick to the balls would have hurt less. She's right. Mateen isn't my son. But though I've only spent a couple days with the kid, I want the chance for more. For a lifetime of more.

"Tell me." I pin my gaze to hers, begging silently for the smallest opening. The slightest chance we might have some sort of a future together.

Her shoulders slump, but before she can speak, my phone buzzes on the table.

"Shit. This guy only checks his messages once a week. If I don't answer now, I'll lose him."

The relief on her face pisses me off. Though I shouldn't be surprised. She thinks I'm an asshole, and she's right.

Closing myself in the second bedroom, I tap the screen. "Aazar. *Salam.*"

"*Salam* to you as well, my forked-tongued friend. I did not expect to hear from you so soon after the mess in Lahore. Or...at all."

"I'm not that easy to kill."

He laughs, the rich sound almost enough to make me smile. The man has lost two wives and five children in his forty-three years, but when he laughs, he does it with his entire being. "I suppose not. How may I relieve you of your money this time?"

"Raziq Ali."

Only silence answers me. Fuck. Aazar is one of the few men I trust not to sell me out for a better deal. He deals in whispers. Rumors. Information no one else can get.

"I'll pay double."

"You will pay more than that. Because after Raziq Ali finishes with you, Viper, you will be nothing more than a handful of scales floating on the wind. And I will be strung up by my testicles and flayed alive."

"Are you sure we're talking about the same guy? The one I'm after is a doctor."

"I am certain. There is nothing to be gained going against this man. You will find only death. I am sorry, my friend. I cannot help you. Except to pray you live long enough to call me again."

"He's hurting women and children, Aazar. If I can't stop him... Fuck. I might as well take a megaphone into the busiest market in the city and confess to every one of the Viper's crimes."

After another long pause, Aazar sighs. "What do you need?"

"Anything you can give me. Where he lives. How many men he might have with him. Strengths. Weaknesses. All of it. Name your price. Because if I live through this, I'm out."

"Twenty. In cash."

I sink down onto the mattress. "I'll be in Kabul tonight. Keep your phone on."

"Watch your back, my friend. I am counting on that money to disappear. Do not die before you pay me."

"Leo Basher? Griff Hargrove, Nomar Garcia, and Lisette Moreau," Austin says when we board the plane.

Basher rises with a wince. "What the hell is this, Pritchard? Senior Citizens' Day Out?"

Griff swears under his breath. "I'm thirty-eight. I've got at least another decade before AARP comes calling."

"And you're down an arm. Not that I can talk." Leo gestures to his right eye. "Fake as fuck."

"My *arm* is right here. And since Austin doesn't share with the rest of the class, I'm also mostly deaf."

"Enough!" I take Lisette's arm and guide her past Griff and Leo. "Ford, Trevor, and the rest of Second Sight are ass-deep in another emergency. McCabe and his team are somewhere in South America trying to stop a goddamn civil war. And we only have eighteen hours before Raziq's deadline. Stow the gear so we can get the fuck in the air."

Austin passes the flight attendant a stack of bills. "Go home. We'll get our own peanuts."

"Of course, sir." The woman pockets the cash and hurries down the steps.

Once he secures the door, I stow the bags and retrieve bottles of water from the galley. Lisette hasn't said a word since we left the hotel. I sit across from her, silently begging her to look at me. But her gaze is locked on her phone.

She didn't see the four bags of weapons Austin *procured* from the streets of Istanbul. Or the C4. Detonators. Knives. Flash bangs.

Or the burqas. Before we land, she'll have to change. In the three years she's been gone, women have lost the few rights they once had. She won't even be able to show her face in public.

"Lisette?" Griff asks. "Do you want some coffee?"

A single tear trails down her cheek. "One cup. My...last cup."

I slam my fist down on the conference table in the center of the cabin. "I am *not* losing you, Lisette. And we're sure as fuck not losing Mateen, Amelie, or Philippe either."

The other men gather around her. The plane starts to taxi, but none of us move. "This is what we do, Lisette," Austin says. "And we're damn good at it. Leo, Trevor, and I took down an assassination plot in Panama. Griff saved his girlfriend from a trafficker with nothing but a gun and a geriatric taxi driver at his side. And Zephyr took down the Strauss cartel after convincing the grumpiest bastard on the planet she wasn't a murderer. In the face of enough evidence to convict the Pope himself. And Nomar...he's deadlier than any of us. He spent the past two years—"

"Stop," I mutter. Lisette doesn't need to know what I did. It won't bring her son back. Not yet. Not until we have a plan.

The plane lifts off, and Pritchard pulls tablets from one of the black bags. "Time to see what Zephyr's got for us."

THE WOMAN on screen looks like she belongs at a rave. Not hacking into the dark web over a bowl of Corn Flakes and the biggest mug of tea I've ever seen.

Zephyr yawns, a lock of teal hair falling over her eyes. "Wren sent over what little she could find on Raziq's financials. He's fucking loaded."

"Define 'fucking.'" Austin ambles back from the galley with a fresh mug of coffee.

"Thirty million. Give or take. He got into medical school in London, and worked for almost a decade as a cardio-thoracic surgeon. He returned to Kabul six years ago." Zephyr takes a long sip from her mug and photos of a three-story house surrounded by thick stone walls topped with razor wire stream across our tablet screens.

"He bought this property when he moved back to Afghanistan. He also has an apartment close to Salam Medical Center."

"Blueprints?" Leo asks.

She stares directly into the camera. "This is Kabul. Even if they *did* exist at one point, they don't now. Any infil is going to be blind."

Lisette

I cannot tear my gaze from my phone. From my son's smiling face. The voices around me are nothing but background noise. Mateen, Amelie, and Philippe have been in Kabul for more than six hours now. What is Raziq doing to them?

"Can you find out if Laurent has woken up?" I ask. Everyone turns to look at me. "Amelie must be frantic. She will want to know how he is..."

No one speaks for several seconds until a woman's voice

comes from the tablet in the center of the table. "I'll find out. But it might take me an hour or two."

"Merci." The word takes so much effort. Like I have not slept in weeks. A part of me is already locked away behind those high stone walls. Yet, a part of me is still here. With a cup of rich coffee in front of me. The last one I will ever have.

Will he kill me quickly? Or make me suffer? I can endure pain. As long as my son is not made to watch.

"Lisette?" Austin covers my hand with his. "He's calling."

CHAPTER TWENTY-SEVEN

Lisette

"About damn time, fucker," Nomar says.

Raziq's smile fades. He looks so much like Faruk. Heavier. Smooth skin. Perfect teeth. He stands in front of a beige wall. Dark brown shutters are partially closed over a barred window.

"Watch your tone. Or I will return the woman to you in pieces."

"I need to see my son," Lisette says. "Now."

"Say hello to your mother, Mateen."

He sits on a bed, dressed in a tan tunic and pants. He is clean, but his eyes are swollen, and his lower lip wobbles. "Maman...where are you?" he asks in French.

Raziq slaps him across the face. "This is your home now. You will speak Dari or English. No French!"

Fat tears spill into his cheeks and he curls into a ball, sobbing.

"Mateen? Look at me, please," I beg. "I am on my way, *mon chou*. But I need to know you are all right."

"I want to go home!"

"You are home," Raziq roars. "Say it!"

Mateen shakes his head. The video jerks, and a shadow looms over my son as Raziq hands the phone to another man. He grabs Mateen by the arm and yanks him to his feet.

"Say it! Or you will not eat until tomorrow!"

At my side, Nomar trembles with barely contained rage and takes the phone from my hand. "Mateen. Look at the camera, buddy. Look at me. Okay?"

Sniffling, my son lifts his gaze.

"Sometimes, we all have to do things we don't want to do. Remember when we played FIFA at the hospital and I asked you to teach me all those trick shots? You didn't want to. But you did. This is the same. Say it."

"I am home," Mateen whispers.

"Good job, kiddo. I'm proud of you." Nomar's expression hardens when the camera pans back to Raziq. "He did what you wanted, asshole. Time for you and me to have a little talk."

The anger in Raziq's eyes terrifies me. "You do not make the rules here. I do. This boy," he jerks his head toward Mateen, "knows nothing. He cannot read the Quran, he does not know how to pray—or even *when* to pray."

"He is *my son!* I decide what he learns. Not you!" I regret the words almost immediately. In the background, Mateen scrambles onto the bed and wraps his arms around his bent knees. Raziq strides from the room. The other man with him slams the door and locks it from the outside.

"You are not fit to be his mother." His snarl is so like Faruk's. My heart pounds in my ears.

"Listen, shithead," Nomar says. "The only reason I haven't hung up on you is I still need to see Amelie and Philippe. Because we don't get on our next flight until I know they're alive. We'll be in Kabul by noon—"

"Our agreement was thirty-six hours. I expect you to be at the south end of Mandai Market by 10:30 a.m. If you are not, I will kill the woman. And her son."

I turn to Nomar, burying my face against his shoulder. This is all my fault. Laurent. Amelie. Philippe. They could all die. Because of me.

The arm banding around me should bring me comfort. It would if I had any hope of surviving past tomorrow.

"Thirteen-thirty," Nomar growls. "You try getting a commercial flight out of Toulouse in the middle of the night. We flew to Paris this morning, we'll get to Istanbul at twenty-three-hundred, and leave for Kabul at oh-five-hundred tomorrow. Not all of us have our own goddamn planes. But if you don't show me Amelie and Philippe right fucking now—"

Raziq laughs. "You will do what? Kill me? I would like to see you try." He strides down the hall where another man stands in front of a door with a large padlock on it. "Open it."

"No..." I cover my mouth with my hand. The woman huddled in the far corner of the room wears a black burka. I cannot even see her eyes behind the dark mesh. Heavy manacles bind her wrists in front of her. Philippe has his arms wrapped around her waist. Dirt stains his face, though like Mateen, he wears a brown tunic and dark pants.

"Amelie? I need to know you and Philippe are okay," Nomar says. "Show me your face."

She flinches and lifts her head. Philippe presses closer to her. His bright blue eyes are dull, but he does not appear to be bound. "I cannot. He said...he would beat me again."

Again?

"That is enough." Raziq slams the door, and his face fills the screen. "They are alive. They will stay that way until tomorrow. I am a reasonable man. But if you are a minute later than thirteen-thirty, I will cut her throat."

"You fucking—shit. The asshole hung up on me." Nomar

tosses the phone on the conference table. "Zephyr, tell me you could trace that call."

On the tablet screen, she rolls her eyes. "I thought you'd been in country for most of the last twenty years. When have you known *anything* to be easy in Afghanistan? But the room Mateen was in matches the real estate photos I pulled from the archives. Minus the bars on the windows, anyway."

Austin and Nomar start talking about ingress and egress points, but I turn away. I recognized the look in Raziq's eyes. It was the same one Faruk would get when he knew he had his enemy cornered. When he knew he was going to win.

<hr>

Nomar

I glance at Lisette, curled under a blanket at the back of the plane. She fell asleep an hour ago—not long after Zephyr finished her briefing. The rest of us shared a box of cereal we found in the galley, and now we stand around one of the smaller rucksacks filled with more appropriate clothing.

Tunics, loose pants, and knit caps for us, and a full burka for Lisette. Complete with mesh to cover her eyes. I thrust the pale blue material at Austin.

"You do it. She's made it pretty damn clear she wants nothing to do with me."

"What the hell is that all about? I thought the two of you were...a thing," Griff says as he laces up his boots. He put his prosthetic on a few minutes ago and explained the science behind rewiring nerves that once controlled flesh and bone to work with titanium. Now we're staring at him tie his shoes like he's performing brain surgery.

"We *were.* Until she found out why Pritchard sent me to

Afghanistan three years ago. Human trafficking is a hard no for her. Go figure."

"For fuck's sake. You didn't have a choice," Austin mutters. "And you made up for it in spades after you sent that 'fuck you' to POTUS. Did you tell her who you've been for the past two years?"

"No. And I'm not going to. She's made it clear we're not 'together.' Once we get Mateen back and the two of them are safe, I'll disappear again. For good, this time."

Leo grabs my arm before I can walk away. "Not so fast. 'Who you've been for the past two years'? Gonna need an explanation for that one."

I shake off his hold and barely resist shoving him back. "Touch me again, Basher, and I'll knock you on your ass faster than you can say 'arthritis.'"

"You're only a year younger than I am, asshole," Leo snaps.

"Stand down. Both of you." Austin steps between us, one hand to Leo's chest, the other an inch from mine. "Tell them, Nomar. They're going to find out pretty damn quick once we meet up with your contact."

Pritchard owes me. But Griff and Leo are risking everything for a man whose entire life is nothing but secrets and lies.

I sigh and lean against the galley wall. "After McCabe and his team took out Amir Abdul Faruk, the CIA and POTUS sent me to Shapur Khan. They wanted *him* to fill the void Faruk left behind. For eleven months, I ran his whole operation. Guns. Drugs. Girls. Until I couldn't stand it any more. So I faked my own death and went rogue. Every single one of those girls has a new life now. A better one."

"Shit." Leo sinks down into one of the plush leather seats. "You're the goddamn Viper."

Griff whistles. "Holy fuck, Nomar. You have to tell her."

"No. The past few days…they were the best of my life. But last night, when she found out what I'd done, it almost killed me. She needs to focus on Mateen. On getting through the next twenty-four hours alive. And so do we. I won't lose her again. I can't. We go in, we kill this motherfucker, and we get everyone home safe. Then, I'm out. For good. Lose my number. Forget my name. Let the Viper die."

"Who is the Viper?" Lisette asks as she staggers toward us. Her eyes are bruised from crying, her hair mussed, and the knot on her temple is a deep, dark purple.

"Just a code name I used in the field a long time ago," I say and head to the galley for another cup of coffee. "We're landing in half an hour. Get changed."

Even with the sound of the engines, I hear everything. Her gasp when Austin hands her the burka. The hitch in her voice when she asks if there is any other way. The soft sobs as she pulls the nearly opaque cloth over her head.

I'd give anything to be able to comfort her. To wrap my arms around her and tell her I'll die before that bastard lays another finger on Mateen. But for the next twenty-four hours, she needs to focus on her son. On the plan none of us are sure will work. On staying alive.

***

LISETTE SITS STIFFLY in the back seat of the Land Rover. The powder blue burka covers her from head to toe. I can't even see her eyes through the mesh panel. We landed under the cover of darkness, but I wouldn't put it past Raziq to be monitoring air traffic control. Or have spies at the airfield.

"Zephyr had better be as good as you say she is." Sliding into the seat next to Lisette, I watch her for any reaction. But she's shut down again. "If Raziq finds out we landed more than twelve hours before his deadline, we're fucked."

In my ear, the hacker huffs. "You, Lisette, and Griff have seats booked on the 5:00 a.m. AirEast flight out of Istanbul. The airport cameras will record you checking in, boarding the plane, *and* sitting in your seats."

Lisette jerks and lets out a little gasp. "How can you do all that?"

"Deep fakes are one of my specialties. Along with surveillance, IDs, blackmail…"

Austin chuckles as he starts the car. "Modesty is *not* one of those specialties."

"Hey!"

"Did I say you should change? I'd be dead at least five times over by now without you," he says. "And Leo would still be in that Panamanian black site."

"So now would be a good time for me to ask for a couple new CPUs?"

Lisette turns to stare out the window. Her shoulders heave, and she brings her hand up to swipe at her cheeks. Until she finds the burka. Fuck.

I swallow hard to clear the lump in my throat. "Zephyr, if we're all headed home by dinner tomorrow—safe—*I'll* buy you those CPUs."

"Careful there, Nomar," Austin warns. "Unless you have an extra twenty grand lying around. You can't get what she needs off the shelf from Computers-R-Us."

For the next half an hour, no one says a word. Lisette's head is bowed, her fingers fluttering over the hem of the headpiece that covers her down to her thighs. The rest of us keep watch out the windows.

Twice, Austin takes a detour, worried he saw the same car more than once, but I pull out one of the mini surveillance cameras and angle it out the back window so Zephyr can run her pattern matching program on any vehicle behind us.

It's almost 10:00 p.m. by the time we get to a house on the

edge of the city. One of the Viper's contacts used to live here, but he moved to Kandahar last month and the place stands empty.

I hustle over to the gate and pick the lock. It opens with a metallic scream, but this neighborhood was bombed last year, and most of the residents left long before Farid came to his senses and bolted.

The eight-foot cement wall around the place will give us enough privacy, no one should know we're here.

Once Austin pulls in, I shut the gate and jog back to the car. Lisette opens her door, but I shake my head. "Stay with Leo and Austin, sweetheart. Griff and I need to clear the house first."

Her shoulders stiffen, and I'd bet she's angry with me, but I can't help the term of endearment. It doesn't matter that we're over before we could even begin. I love her, and that will never change.

CHAPTER TWENTY-EIGHT

Lisette

I WANDER through the old house and wonder about the people who used to live here.

The walls are painted in bright, almost feminine colors. Several throw pillows with intricately embroidered designs linger in the corners of the main room. A doll lies abandoned in the bedroom. A woman and at least one child lived here. Were they happy?

Is any woman truly happy in Afghanistan?

Griff and Leo secure black tarp over the single window. "You can take the burka off now," the younger man says. He moves carefully, and when he drops to a knee to rummage in one of his bags, lines of pain tighten around his eyes. Two broken ribs, and he has not complained once.

Ripping off the light blue material, I take my first deep breath since we left the plane. "When will Nomar and Austin be back?"

Leo checks his watch. "Couple of hours. You should try to get some rest. You too, Iron Man. I'll take first watch."

"That's Titanium Man, Grandpa." Griff unclips two bedrolls from the nearest bag and passes one to me. "If the perimeter alarms go off, my phone will vibrate and it *should* wake me up. But if not, kick my boot. Don't get any closer unless you want me to lay you out flat." He plugs his glasses and mobile into a portable battery, then stretches out on his back. "I'll relieve you in two hours."

I tuck the thin pad under my arm and start for the bedroom, but Leo calls my name. "We stay together. Sleep in here." After a beat, he adds, "Please."

Choosing the corner farthest from the other two men, I pick up one of the throw pillows and beat it with my fist. A cloud of dust clogs my throat, and my eyes water.

"Can you shoot?" Leo asks.

"Yes. But it has been a very long time."

He passes me a small pistol. "Safety's off and there's a round in the chamber. Keep it close."

The gun is heavy in my hand. Warm. Not at all reassuring. But I set it next to the bedroll.

Leo rights an overturned chair and sits facing the door, an M4 rifle resting on his thighs.

I fold the head covering over the throw pillow and curl onto my side. But every sound frightens me. The chair creaks when Leo shifts his weight. Griff lets out a single soft snore. A car passes on the street outside.

The scent of coffee fills the room, and I push up on an elbow. Leo sets an open thermos on the floor next to him.

I watch him for several minutes, wishing I could be half as calm as he seems. "Do you have paper and a pen?" I ask.

The older man points to the bag closest to me. "Front pocket. You'll find a small notebook and pen. Why?"

Tears prick at my eyes. "I will never speak to my parents or my sister again. Will you...if I write them a note, will you deliver it for me? When I am gone?"

Leo stiffens, gives the tablet screen in front of him a quick gaze, then turns to me. "You're going home, Lisette. With your son. We're *all* going home when this is done."

"You do not know that." My hands shake as I find the black notebook and pen secured with an elastic band. "You were in the CIA, yes?" At his nod, I swallow the lump in my throat. "How many times did you have something go horribly wrong?"

"I worked alone back then."

"You are avoiding the question. How many times?" In truth, I do not want to know the answer. But I need Leo to understand why this is so important to me.

The right side of his mouth twists into a scowl. "Enough. Write your letters. If the worst happens, one of us will make sure they get where they need to go."

"Thank you."

I drag another one of the embroidered pillows over next to the light Griff set up on a tripod by the kitchen.

Will I ever do something as simple as write a letter again? Raziq plans to kill me. Of that, I am certain. I can only hope he lets me live long enough to see Mateen. To hug my son and tell him how much he is loved. And how very sorry I am that I could not protect him.

Noele will blame herself. Maman and Papa will mourn me. They will try to find Mateen, but they will fail as they failed to find me all those years ago. This country is a black hole for all but the richest men. Without a miracle, my son will never see France again.

An hour—and more than a dozen tear-stained pages later —I close the notebook and secure it with the elastic band before I approach Leo. "Promise me you will not let Nomar see these."

"Lisette—"

"Promise me." A fresh wave of tears threatens. "If we fight

again, and I...die...he will never forgive himself." I stare down at my feet. At the reddish-brown flats with silver beading around the toes. "I loved him for three years. If I had a future, maybe I would love him again one day, but—"

"One day? Maybe? Bullshit. If you think you're not in love with him, you're lying to yourself."

"I do not know how to love a man who sold women. If he had done *anything* else, I could understand. But not that."

Leo shakes his head. "He's going to hate me for this, but fuck it. There are no 'good guys' in this business, Lisette. We all live in shades of gray. We lie, we steal, we kill. And sometimes, we make decisions that hurt a few people so we can save a hell of a lot more. Nomar didn't sell those women. The guy he worked for did. And when he couldn't stand it anymore, he faked his death and became the Viper."

I straighten my shoulders. Leo has a look about him that should scare me, but this may be the last chance I have to stand up for myself, and I will not back down. "You say that like it makes a difference. I do not care what he called himself."

Getting to his feet, Leo stares down at me. "The Viper freed every single one of the women Shapur Khan sold. And hundreds more. Raziq may own Kabul, but Nomar is the most feared man in all of Afghanistan. He's atoned for his sins, Lisette. Four, five times over. If not more."

"All...of them?" I ask. "Really?"

"Yes. He's been single-handedly dismantling the flesh trade in Afghanistan for two years now. He's a fucking legend." Leo shakes his head with a huff. "He did it all for you."

The horror of what I have done—how I have treated this man who has only ever cared for me—drives me to my knees. Leo grabs my arm and steadies me as he helps me up. "He tried to explain…" I whisper. "And I told him to leave. What if he cannot forgive me?"

"He loves you," Leo says. "And you haven't done anything you can't take back. Not yet. Talk to him. And for fuck's sake, tell him how you feel before the meet."

The words he did not say hang between us as Leo returns to his chair and picks up his rifle.

"Because after, it might be too late."

Nomar

I'm about to crack a molar. The headache bands around my skull, made worse by the knit cap covering my hair.

Half hidden around a corner, Austin hunches his shoulders. He's six-foot-four, almost a foot taller than the average man in this country. He sticks out like a sore thumb with his light brown hair and pale skin. At least I blend in.

"Are you sure this guy's not blowing you off?" he asks. "We've been out here for an hour."

"He'll be here." I put my back to the wall of the old building and scan our surroundings. Just a local getting some fresh air. In the middle of the fucking night.

No cars. The few street lights still standing are dark. The moon casts eerie shadows from abandoned houses and a burned-out truck a few meters away. It's quiet, only the occasional barking dog breaking the silence. "You didn't have to come."

"No one goes anywhere alone," he says. "Every time one of us steps out of that house, we're risking the whole operation. We shouldn't even be here."

"Aazar knows Kabul better than anyone. Even Raziq. And his intel is always solid. We need him."

A scooter buzzes from my right. Low, but getting louder. Adrenaline floods my veins. "This is it." Austin disappears deeper into the shadows. "Check on Lisette, will you?" I whisper.

The comms units Pritchard brought with him are twice as sensitive as the ones we used on the mission to rescue Joey. Multiple frequencies piggyback off our phones. With two taps, Austin can link up with Griff and Leo. Zephyr. Even Ford—assuming he's not neck deep in whatever shit is going on back in Boston.

Aazar coasts to a stop in front of me, a grim expression on his round face.

"*Salam alaikum.*" I place my right hand over my heart and bow my head. "But what sort of time do you call this? I've been out here for an hour."

"*Salam,* my friend." Aazar flashes me a brief smile in the moonlight. "I watched you for some time before I let myself be known. The tall American you are with draws too much attention to himself."

"Austin, get the fuck out here. You're blown." I shrug. "Sorry. He wouldn't let me come alone."

"A wise decision on his part. You have something for me?" Aazar asks. "What I have done for you...it is no small thing, Viper."

I reach into my pocket and withdraw a thick envelope. "I know. There's twenty-five in there."

Austin steps into view, and Aazar shoves the money into a small leather pouch at his waist. "I pray your death will be an easy one, my friend."

"Raziq and his men are the only ones dying today," I snap. "And they aren't worth your prayers."

"Perhaps not, but you are two. He has dozens."

"We need an exact number," Austin says as he looms over

Aazar. "For twenty-five thousand dollars, I expect better intel than that."

I force my way between the two of them. "Stand down. This is *my* meet. Not yours." Turning my focus back to Aazar, I take his arm and draw him a few steps away. "We need to know how many men he'll bring with him to the handoff and how many he'll leave at his home."

Aazar shakes his head. "You must understand, no one knows for certain. He pays for silence. And his reputation does what little the money cannot. When he travels the city, he is always accompanied by at least six. Only once did anyone try to attack him at his home. They brought eight. A dead body appeared outside his gate once a day for eight days. All had been freshly killed."

Fuck. He kept them alive to torture them.

"How did this asshole stay off my radar for so long?"

Aazar holds my gaze. "He has never taken a woman before. He is merciless with those who wrong him, but he is revered by many in Kabul. He sends men to the slums with food and medicine. He buys houses destroyed by your American bombs, then hires crews to fix them."

I feel Austin move before I see him. He jabs the barrel of his Glock 19 under Aazar's chin and shoves him against the wall. "If Raziq is such a fucking saint, why are you here? Did you set us up—?"

"No, no. I swear!" Aazar looks to me. "Viper, I have always been honest with you."

I move to Austin's side, but don't do a damn thing to call him off. "For the right price. But my American friend has a good point. Raziq owns Kabul. Stands to reason he owns you too."

Aazar holds my gaze. "He is a pestilence on this city. He will *never* own me."

I nod, and Austin lowers the gun. "Keep talking," he says.

"When Raziq came to Kabul, he hired a dozen men to build his home. He kept them inside the walls of the compound and refused to let them see their families. He sent their wages to their wives, fathers, brothers. He was even contrite. He *had* to keep them locked away so they would not reveal anything about his security measures. But he promised once the house was completed, all would be well.

"The men worked like dogs for months. Morning to night. Every day. That summer was the hottest in fifty years. Three died while putting in his *pool*." Aazar spits on the ground at Austin's feet. "When the remaining nine men finished the job, Raziq lined them up outside the gates and had them shot. My brother was the last to die."

"Fucking hell," Austin mutters and holsters his gun.

Aazar runs his hand over his beard. "It is wrong to pray for another man's death. But if you truly believe you can kill him, my friend, I will help you in whatever way I can."

His words light a fire inside me. Raziq will pay for his crimes with his own blood. For Aazar's brother. For the families of all the people he's killed. But most of all, for what he's doing to Lisette. And Mateen.

CHAPTER TWENTY-NINE

Nomar

BY THE TIME we make it back to the house, the rising sun bathes the streets in a pale orange glow. Griff opens the gate, and Austin backs the Land Rover into the carport. Aazar promised to meet us outside the market at eleven forty-five with maps showing every shortcut and side street we can take between there and Raziq's home.

No one believes he'll bring Mateen with him. And though the idea of that bastard even *looking* at Lisette makes my skin crawl, it's the only way we'll get Amelie and Philippe back.

"Zephyr's been analyzing the real estate photos of Raziq's house half the night. She sent us rough blueprints," Griff says as we trudge through the door.

Austin stifles his yawn. "That's why I pay her the big bucks. I'm taking two hours. Nomar, you should too. I want to be in position by ten."

If I don't get some sleep, I'll be a liability to the whole mission. I stagger over to my ruck and fish out a bottle of eyedrops. The cool liquid feels like heaven, but it's nothing compared to the warmth of Lisette's hand on my arm. She's touching me. Willingly. "I need to talk to you."

"I've only slept six out of the last forty-eight hours, sweetheart. Can it wait?"

She chews on her lower lip. Are those tears in her eyes? Fuck. I push to my feet with a groan. Leo catches my gaze and jerks his head toward the bedroom.

"Come on." I take her hand, surprised she doesn't pull away, and once we're shut away from the others, I realize someone moved a bed roll and a light in here. "What's wrong? Besides...fuck. Besides everything."

Lisette tugs me down onto the thick wool blanket, close enough our knees touch. I'm afraid to say a word and shatter this moment where it feels like she *wants* to be with me.

"What happened two years ago?" Her voice trembles, and I think she's on the verge of tears. But the one thing she isn't? Angry. With me.

"Leo told you, didn't he?" I should go out there and kick his ass, but I need him—and more importantly, I need *her*.

"A little. But I want to hear it from you, Nomar. I...would not let you explain last night. Or...was it two nights ago?" She shakes her head, and a tear balances on her lower lashes. "I was wrong."

I cup her cheek, desperate to soothe the pain in her eyes. "Everything was—*is*—fucked, sweetheart. We don't have to talk about this now. It can wait until we have Mateen back."

"No." Lisette swallows a sob. "I will not survive this, Nomar. Raziq will kill me. I pray you can rescue Mateen. Amelie and Philippe. But—"

I haul her into my arms and slam my mouth to her lips. She opens for me. My tongue sweeps over hers, searching and desperate. Lisette melts into my embrace. I will *not* lose her. I can't.

We're both panting when I break off the kiss, and I touch

my forehead to hers. "You *will* survive this, Lisette. You and Mateen will be free. Even if I have to take out Raziq's men one by one, with only a dull spoon, I'll do it."

Sorrow swims in her green eyes, though she manages a wobbly smile. "A dull spoon is not a very effective weapon, Nomar. Did no one teach you that in spy school?"

Laughing with her feels so right. Like we've been together for a lifetime, not a week. "Do you remember the night we spent in that old mosque?"

"You and Mateen were both so sick." She links our fingers. "You tried to be strong, but I think you were in terrible pain."

"I told you more about myself that night than I'd shared with anyone in years. And then you asked me if my job was 'really that dangerous' or if I 'simply wasn't very good at it.'"

"*Merde.* I was so rude."

Smiling, I brush my lips to hers. "That's when I fell in love with you."

Her eyes widen and she presses her hand to her heart. "Nomar! You barely knew me."

"I knew enough. I knew you were brave as fuck. I knew you were a fighter. A survivor. I could see what ten years with that asshole had done to you. But underneath all that fear, I saw *you*, Lisette. I fell in love with *you*."

The next few seconds are the longest of my life. I need to know I still have a chance with her. That my past hasn't doomed us completely.

"You saved us," she says softly. "But more than that, you saw me when I could not see myself. I needed you. That is why it hurt so much when you left."

"I'll apologize every day for the rest of my life—"

Lisette presses her finger to my lips. "If you had stayed, maybe we would have loved one another then. I cannot say. But the woman I was could not have given you forever. A lifetime should not be based on need. When you came back, I no longer needed you. I *wanted* you. I still do."

Dragging a knuckle along her jaw, I memorize the feel of her skin. The flush to her cheeks. The way her lips part for me. Even here, in this dusty room with no windows and three of the deadliest men in the world on the other side of the door, whenever I look at her, everything else ceases to matter.

"I'll tell you everything, Lisette. What do you want to know?"

"I STOLE all the data off his computer, got as far away from him as I could, and faked my own death. Blamed it on one of his rivals—Musa. The CIA had been planning to take out the guy for a year. They kept telling me they'd give me an exfil plan once they had. So I did it for them. Then started tracking down the girls.

"Wren decrypted the data for me. There were thirty still in Jalalabad. The rest were spread out across Afghanistan, Pakistan, Kuwait, and Iran. After a week, I'd freed five. But I couldn't return them to their families. They would have been shamed, maybe even killed. There was a man who helped get Joey's friends out of the country after we rescued them. I think you met him?"

"Matt? He is British?" she asks. "He helped us get from the hospital in Uzbekistan to the airport."

"That's him. Former SAS. He lives in Dubai now." Matt's face flashes behind my rough lids for a moment. "If he weren't in the middle of chemo, he'd be here. But he helped us get into the country."

Lisette tightens her fingers on my arm. "Cancer? Will he... beat it?"

"He's a lifelong spook. He could be on his deathbed and

he wouldn't say a fucking word. I hope so. He helped me set up an evacuation protocol. Five different cities, a couple dozen locals who agreed to transport the girls and keep them safe. Once they got to Dubai, Matt gave them new identities, jobs, money…"

Lisette tugs me down so we're lying side-by-side. "How long did it take to find them all?"

"Nine months, two weeks, and five days." My words are getting harder. Slower. Exhaustion threatens to pull me under. But I can't go into this op without telling her everything. A yawn pulls a crack from my jaw.

"You are exhausted," Lisette says. "Sleep with me. Please."

"Not yet. There's so much more…"

She rubs my back as she brushes her lips to mine. "I understand now, Nomar. Why you left. Why you did not call. Why you kept this from me. The rest does not matter. Not truly."

The rhythmic strokes of her hand soothe me in a way nothing else can. "I love you, Lisette," I whisper, her soft smile the last thing I see as I let myself drift off to oblivion.

Lisette

"Wake up, sweetheart."

Nomar's voice pulls me from a dream. A wonderful dream where he and Mateen wave at me from the top of the big wheel on the riverfront.

"We're leaving in an hour. Come out to the main room. You need to eat something." He cups my cheek and ghosts a thumb along my bottom lip. "We have coffee. Instant, but it still packs a jolt."

I want to tell him I love him. That I will love him for the

rest of my life—no matter how short that life may be. But Austin peers around the open door. "We're burning daylight. Come on."

Griff spins the single chair around and meets my gaze. "Sit and take off your shoe and sock," he says.

"My...shoe?"

Leo holds up a flat metal disc the size of a penny. "GPS tracker. It's a safe bet Raziq or one of his men will search you, but no one ever checks the bottoms of the feet. We'll hide it under a Band-Aid."

"When is Second Sight going to make these damn things injectable?" Nomar asks.

"They already did." Austin rubs his hip with a grimace. "McCabe shot me up with one in Venezuela a couple of years ago. But the batteries only lasted two, three days max. And they hurt like hell going in. These are functional for months."

I will not survive for months. But if I die, the tracker could still help them recover my body and find Mateen. As long as Raziq does not kill me before he lets me see my son.

Griff presses the metal disc to the bottom of my left foot and covers it with a bandage.

"Stepping on it will not break it?" I ask.

"Even if you had flat feet—which you don't—these are practically indestructible. Try walking around? We need to make sure it doesn't irritate you so much you limp." Griff offers me his hand after I pull on my sock and slip my foot into my shoe.

Once I leave this house, no one will show me such kindness again. I let him help me up, pace the room a few times, and look to Nomar.

"You're good, sweetheart. Get comfortable. We need to go over the plan."

Nomar and I get out of the Land Rover a few blocks from the market. The light blue burka is suffocating me. Long sleeves cover my hands, but I still twine my fingers together beneath the cape that flows from the top of my head almost down to my knees.

"Breathe," Nomar says and squeezes just above my elbow. "In six hours—maybe less—we'll be on the plane home. All of us."

"You cannot promise that." For the first time, I am grateful my eyes are covered. He cannot see my tears.

"I'm not leaving here without you." He scans our surroundings every few steps. "Zephyr matched the wall behind Mateen to the house Raziq bought when he returned to Kabul. He's on the top floor. From the shadows, we *think* we even know what side of the building he's on. Aazar gave us updated maps of the side streets, so we won't get boxed in. We'll have you out of there in twenty, thirty minutes. Tops."

I wish I had his confidence. "But three men cannot fight more than a dozen."

"We were three when we broke you, Mateen, and Joey out of Faruk's compound. Men like him and Raziq think strength comes from numbers. But it doesn't. We're better trained, and we have something he'll never have."

"What is that?"

A smile plays at the corners of his lips, sad as it may be. "Love."

A short burst of static comes through the tiny speaker in my ear. "In position on the roof," Austin says. "Zephyr, is the feed working?"

"Got it. If facial recognition pings on Raziq or any of the assholes from Barcelona, we'll know in seconds."

"We're in position," Nomar says quietly. "Fuckhead better answer."

He slips my phone from his pocket and punches in Raziq's number. After two rings, the video call connects.

Mateen stands next to his uncle, chewing on his bottom lip and staring down at his feet. "Say hello to your mother," Raziq says.

"Maman, come...home." His little voice wobbles on each Dari word, and he peers up at Raziq with fear in his eyes.

"Very good, Mateen. Hamza will bring you a snack soon." After a large man with a short beard locks my son in his room, Raziq's expression hardens. "My brother had a rather distinctive birthmark, Lisette. Where was it?"

"What?" I ask.

"I cannot see your face, woman. I need to know it is you under the burka. Answer me!"

"On h-his left hip. A crescent moon." I shudder at the memory of all the nights I stared right at it while he forced himself on me.

Raziq nods. "Very good." The phone vibrates, and the screen splits with a second video call. A woman in a black burka stands in front of a group of men, her head bowed. Philippe clings to her arm. "Stop right where you are and send Lisette to the stall thirty meters ahead of you selling spices and tea. When my men have secured her, the woman and the boy will be released."

Nomar's anger is a physical presence standing next to me. "I'm staying with her until I can verify Amelie and Philippe are unharmed."

"If you take one more step, they will die," Raziq says. He nods, and one of the men with Amelie lifts the hem of her cape. A belt with several black pouches wraps around her waist. Wires extend from each one.

A bomb?

"You fucking asshole. How do I know you won't blow it anyway?" Nomar's hand on my arm tightens, almost to the point of pain.

Chills break out over my skin at Raziq's smile, despite the intense heat of the day. "You do not. I will send you the code to disarm the detonator once Lisette is here with me. I have people watching all the exits. If you or the man with the metal arm at the north end of the market try to leave at any time before then...well...you will have many deaths on your hands."

Hot tears spill down my cheeks. Amelie must be so scared. I would die for Mateen. I *will* die for Mateen. But I know he will live. His uncle will revere him, even if he is a murdering, abusive, *putain* who turns my son into a killer. Amelie has no such reassurances. She is just a woman, after all. And women are of no value to him.

Nomar mutes the call and slips the phone into his chest pocket. "Lisette, look at me." He frames my face with his hands, searching for my eyes through the light blue mesh. "This changes nothing. It might take us a little longer to get to you, but that's all. Stay with Mateen as long as you can. Keep Raziq talking. Your earbud will cut out once you get too far from your phone, but as soon as we're close to the house, you'll hear me again. Okay?"

"My patience is wearing thin," Raziq shouts.

I pull away from Nomar, rushing so I do not lose my nerve. My shoulders shake with silent sobs. "I love you," Nomar whispers over comms. "We're coming for—"

The little device in my ear dies, and my heart shatters into dust.

Four men fall into step around me. They herd me under the brightly colored umbrellas lining the side of the market. "I need to go to the spice stall!" I protest. But one of them grips my arm so hard, my knees buckle.

"You go where we tell you, *kuchnay*."

Whore.

They drag me deeper into the stalls. Under the metal roof. Behind tables stacked high with burkas and tunics. A curtain falls, hiding us from view.

"Check her," one of them says. The man gripping my bicep shoves me against the wall, face first. Rough hands run up and down my arms, my back, and between my legs. He spins me around to squeeze my breasts.

I sway, the room starting to spin.

Raziq is the one who will kill me. Not these men.

The one giving the orders unzips a black pouch and withdraws a syringe.

Fear paralyzes me. My lungs refuse to draw in air. I can only watch them push my sleeve up. The needle stings as it pierces my skin.

"What did you give me?" My heart races. I cannot feel my fingers. Their smiles terrify me. "Whaaa....ivvve...eeee?"

I slide down the wall, and as I hit the floor, I realize I never told Nomar I loved him.

CHAPTER THIRTY

Nomar

"I can't see Lisette. Pritchard, tell me you still have eyes on her." Turning in a circle, I clock at least five men watching me.

"They took her inside. I'm blind here. But Amelie and Philippe are headed your way. Zephyr?"

"Her GPS has been stationary for the past two minutes." The hacker's voice in my ear brings little comfort. Why would they hide her away if not to hurt her?

Griff swears under his breath. "Two hostiles coming in fast."

"Four," Austin says. "Leo, get in there."

"No." After a grunt, Griff adds, "He hasn't made you or Leo yet. Keep it that way. I got this."

I clench my hand hard enough my knuckles crack. "If you're wrong..."

"Not...wrong."

He's too far away. The crowd presses in on me. People everywhere. A fist slams into my side. I pivot and drive the heel of my hand up into a bearded chin. The man's head snaps back. Before he can recover, I sweep his legs out from under him.

"Help us!" a woman screams. Amelie. A low whistle stirs the air, so close to my cheek, I feel the heat a second later. The guy on the ground jerks, and a knife falls from his hand.

Fuck. The blade was only inches from my femoral artery.

"You're welcome," Pritchard says over comms.

Amelie stumbles, practically collapsing into my arms. "We have to get out of here," I snap. "Follow me."

"The belt...he said he would set it off!"

"GPS is on the move," Zephyr says.

My fingers tighten on the back of Amelie's neck. "Five minutes. Keep your shit together for five more minutes and I'll get that fucking thing off you. But if we stay here, we're dead." I grab Philippe's hand and meet his terrified gaze. "I'm going to get you and your mom back home, kid. But you have to do exactly what I say."

He nods so hard, his head is practically a blur.

"Headed for an empty stall. My two o'clock. Griff? Status report!"

"On my way."

Thank fuck. "Zephyr, how are you with remote detonators?"

"I only work with code," she says. "But I'm deep in the bowels of the dark web. Get me better visuals and I might be able to talk you through disarming it."

We pass under a large red umbrella, and I tip it onto its side. It's more than ten feet across and should hide us from view. "Philippe, go stand against the far wall and don't move. Amelie, lift the cape so I can see what I'm working with."

The belt wraps around the undermost garment that covers her from shoulders to ankles. She turns in a circle as I take a video to send to Zephyr. Six pouches, evenly distributed, one holding a black plastic box with a red light blinking on top.

The fucking wires are wrapped around the belt so tightly, there's no way to get it off her without cutting them.

"Don't shoot me," Griff says in my ear, then slips past the umbrella.

The man's jaw sports a fresh bruise, and a bit of blood stains his pants. Amelie shrieks when she sees him. "He's one of the good guys," I say. "Got two more outside the market. Hold still now. I'm going to slice some of the nylon away from the C4."

Griff positions himself between me and the kid, then taps the temple of his glasses. "Camera on. Zephyr can see what we see," he says.

The minutes tick by so slowly, they feel like hours. Sweat trickles down my back. Amelie's breathing is getting more and more erratic. Each block of plastique has a secondary tripwire coming from *behind* the explosive, and we have no way of knowing if removing them will set off a chain reaction. "How long has it been, Zephyr?"

"Twenty-one minutes. Lisette's GPS signal stopped moving. She's at Raziq's house now."

Austin breaks in. "At least a dozen men searching for you up and down the stalls. You've got five minutes. Max."

That asshole could be hurting her already. *Killing* her already. My hand shakes, and I sit back on my heels. Twelve wires disappear inside the detonator box through a hole in the back. "I don't see any fucking screws."

"Pry it open," Zephyr says. "But for fuck's sake, be careful."

"Griff? Need your bionics here."

He urges Philippe to sit with his back to us and wrap his arms around his head. It won't save the kid if the whole belt blows. But if I can neutralize even half of it, he might have a chance.

"Hold the detonator steady. If I fuck this up…"

Amelie whimpers softly. "Take Philippe and run. Please. Leave me."

"No." I push to my feet and stare through the fine black mesh covering her eyes, "The man who took you is going to die today. Painfully. You and your son—along with Lisette and Mateen—are going home. Your husband's asking for you. We're doing this."

"L-Laurent? He…is alive?" she squeaks.

"He is. He lost a lot of blood, and he'll be in the hospital for a few weeks, but he should make a full recovery."

Amelie's hand covers her mouth—or where I think her mouth should be—and she nods. "Go on, then."

I adjust my grip on the multitool and look to Griff. "If the box slips…run."

"It won't." A muscle in his jaw flexes as he closes his left hand around the detonator. "Prosthetic fingers don't sweat."

The flat of the blade slides under the cover. For the first time in decades, I pray.

With a loud *snap*, a piece of plastic flies halfway across the empty stall. Inside, the wires wind around a circuit board in a demented maze of bright, happy colors. "Zephyr, tell me this makes sense to you."

"Give me a minute. Maybe three," she says in my ear.

If we have three more minutes, it'll be a fucking miracle.

Shouts come from the other side of the overturned umbrella. "What the fuck is going on, Pritchard?" I ask.

"Leo's providing…a diversion."

The angry curses fade, replaced by the dull hum of a crowded market day, and Zephyr comes back online. "Okay. Here goes nothing. Clockwise from the top left, cut wire three, eight, two, six, and five *in that order*. Fuck it up, and it'll blow."

Austin snorts over comms. "No pressure."

I can't tear my gaze away from the circuit board. "Get the hell out of here, Griff. Take the kid. And tell Lisette—"

He backs away and takes Philippe's arm, helping him up and leading him back toward the market. "I'm not your answering service, Nomar. Tell her yourself."

"I love you, Philippe," Amelie says. "Always."

The boy doesn't want to go, and tugs against Griff's hold, but disappears around the umbrella with a shrieked, "Maman!"

"It's going to be okay, Amelie." Fuck, I wish I believed my own words. Nothing will ever be okay again until Lisette and Mateen are safe. "Deep breath in with me. Good. Let it out slowly. Here we go."

The scissors are both too big *and* too small, but I maneuver them around the shielded wire.

Lisette, I'm coming for you. I promise.

The subtle *click* is one of the sweetest sounds I've ever heard. "Three. Check. Moving onto eight."

Two, six, and five fall without incident, and the glowing light on the circuit board winks out. My ass hits the ground. The multi-tool clatters across the concrete. "Zephyr? What now?"

"Cut the belt and get to the transpo," she says. "If it didn't blow already..."

"Holy shit. Did you have *any* idea if that was going to work?" Austin asks.

"Nope. But it did. I'll send you the bill for those two new servers I've had my eye on. Or is Nomar paying for this one?"

I retrieve the tool, slice through the black nylon cinched tight around Amelie's waist, and offer her my hand. "All done. Let's get out of here."

Lisette

A bead of sweat rolls down my back. I force my heavy lids open, but the sun burns my eyes, and I clamp them shut again.

Why is it so hot?

Fabric rustles as I shift my legs. Something is different. Wrong. I try opening my eyes again—only to slits—but do not see the light blue of my burka.

Panic tightens my chest. Someone...undressed me. Rough pants cling to my legs. I can feel my bra. But I have no shirt under the heavy black burka. The mesh over my eyes is askew. My entire body is soaked with sweat. Raziq's men did this. After they drugged me.

How long has it been? Where is Nomar?

My eyes are adjusting, and I raise a hand to shield them.

"I hope you enjoy the view," Raziq says. "From this far up, you can see all the way to the mountains."

Up?

I scramble to my feet. The world spins around me. I am too dizzy to remain upright. Stumbling away from Raziq— or where I think he is, as my vision is still blurry—I slam into a railing and start to fall forward. The metal burns my hands.

With a scream, I stare at the ground far below.

Someone jerks me back by one arm, then shoves me to my knees. I am on a roof. At least three stories up. I blink hard. An awning extends a meter from the rest of the house. Lush potted plants surround a wicker chair and table with an icy pitcher of water sitting in the center of it.

I lick my lips. The terrible, bitter taste in my mouth is nothing compared to the dehydration. It is unseasonably warm today, and in the hot sun, wearing all black, how long before heat stroke sets in?

Raziq steps out from the shade of the canopy, his hands loose at his sides. He looks so much like his brother. Older. A bit heavier. Streaks of gray in his beard. But the same wild eyes. A voice so similar, fear floods my body when he speaks. "Lisette. Wife of Amir Abdul Faruk. You are guilty of adultery, kidnapping, and child abuse."

I gape at him. *Adultery? Child abuse?*

"I am guilty of nothing. I *never* cheated on Faruk. He would have killed me for even *looking* at another man. I took Mateen from Afghanistan because he would have died here! I kept him safe. And Faruk is dead. You have no claim on my son!"

Stars explode in front of my eyes. My cheek throbs with each beat of my heart. Raziq steps back and uncurls his fingers. "You have no say here, *whore*. My brother sent me the security footage from the night you stole Mateen. You were sleeping with the man who helped you commit that crime!"

"Nomar? I had never met him before that night—"

The second punch is not a surprise. But it hurts no less. I taste blood. "You will stay quiet unless I ask you a question. Though now I know your lover's name."

I shrink back against the metal railing and drop my gaze. This is Afghanistan. I have no rights here. I cannot travel alone. I cannot speak unless spoken to. I cannot even show my eyes. I am nothing. No one. Not even a person.

"These are grave charges, Lisette. By rights, I could have you stoned."

I choke back a sob. Would he truly do it? Bury me up to my chest and throw rocks at my head until I die? One look at his face, and I have my answer. He would.

"But that would be a merciful death, and I am not a merciful man. You will not be stoned. Your punishment will be forty lashes every day for forty days. After that, I will decide if you have suffered enough."

Tears stream down my cheeks. Forty lashes is survivable. Forty *every day?* I will be dead in less than a week. The scars on my back ache with the memory of Faruk's braided leather whip. Of my wedding night when they were so fresh, they bled as he forced himself on me.

Nomar, where are you?

I dip my hands under the cape to wipe away my tears. The little device in my ear is gone. Flexing my toes, I do not feel the bandage. They took the GPS tracker too. This house is far from the city. If they think I am still in Kabul...they will never find me here.

"Mateen," I whisper. "You said I would be with my son."

Raziq looms over me. "I said you could *see* your son."

"Please. I am...yours." The word sticks in my throat, but the only hope I have is to tell him what he wishes to hear. "I accept my punishment. I will not fight you. I only want to see my son."

"Watch her," he says, then disappears through a heavy wooden door. Two men take positions on either side of me. One, I recognize from the market. My stomach pitches. The memory of his hands on me is still so fresh.

Several minutes pass. I peek over my shoulder, but the dizzying height is too much. Does he know that it frightens me? He must. He knows everything else.

The door opens, and Mateen jerks free from the hold his uncle has on the shoulder of his tunic. "Maman!"

He throws his arms around my neck, knocking me back against the railing.

Holding him soothes a fraction of my panic. He is safe. Whole. "I love you, *mon chou.* I am sorry it took me so long to get here."

"Can we go home now?" he asks.

Over Mateen's shoulder, Raziq's expression hardens.

My heart aches, but for as long as I am alive, I will protect my son. "This...*is* home now. Remember?" Pressing my lips to his ear through the fabric, I switch to French and whisper, "You must do whatever your uncle tells you until we find a way out of here."

"Okay," he says and draws back to tug at the burka. "Why are you wearing this?"

"Because it is the law. Whenever I am outside or around men who are not family, I must cover my face." I squeeze his arms, then run my hands up and down his back to check for bruises. He does not flinch, and I take comfort knowing he has not suffered...much. "I think you have grown in the past week. You will be taller than I am soon."

"Enough!" Raziq snaps. Mateen presses closer to me with a tiny whimper. "Mateen, Hamza will take you to make wudu. It is almost Asr and you must wash first. When I am done here, I will join you for prayers."

"I want to stay with Maman!"

Before Raziq can touch him, I curl my body around my son and turn away. "You must do as your uncle says, Mateen. Wudu is important. You must be clean to pray. Go with Hamza. You will see me soon."

A man—Hamza, I assume—takes Mateen's arm and pulls him from my embrace. He starts to cry. I try to get to my feet, but the men on either side of me clamp their hands on my shoulders to push me back down again.

"It will be all right," I call as my son is dragged through the door. "I love you!"

Raziq nods to the men holding me. One of them grabs my arms and pushes the cape back to expose my wrists. I flinch at a metallic clank from my right and turn my head.

The other man wraps a chain around the top of the railing. At the ends, thick iron manacles radiate so much heat, I can *see* it.

"No. Please," I beg. "You do not need those. I will not run."

"You are my property, Lisette. My responsibility. You will suffer for your crimes. Greatly." Raziq moves to the table and opens a long, wooden box. Before I can see what is inside, the man holding my hands spins me around so I am forced to stare out over the barren landscape. The other locks the cuffs around my wrists. The metal burns my skin. I clench my teeth so I do not scream. That is what he wants. I know it. To break me. I pull at the chain, but it is so short, I cannot lower my arms more than halfway.

"You will take your first forty now," Raziq says. "The remainder will come every day after the Sunrise prayer."

I twist, desperate to know where he is. To see the whip. Faruk favored braided leather. His brother lifts a long, thick rope attached to a wooden handle. He snaps it so close to me, I feel the stir in the air, even though the burka.

"Turn around."

What choice do I have? I do as he says, kneeling and resting my forehead against my bent arms. My heart pounds so hard, it is all I can hear.

The first strike lands along my right shoulder. After the sharp sting, my entire back starts to burn.

The second is lower. I wrap my fingers around the railing with a whimper. My vision through the black mesh tunnels.

Three. Four. Five. I cannot help the wail spilling from my chapped lips. The agony spreads to my arms and legs. Only the cuffs stop me from collapsing onto my side.

I lose count. There is nothing of me left. Only pain. Bile coats my tongue. Sweat and tears soak the cloth over my face. How many more?

My head is wrenched away from my arms, and I stare up into Raziq's wild eyes. Cold water splashes over me without warning. The fresh welts burn with each cough as I fight to breathe. To swallow even a drop.

And then it stops. His hand falls away. Footsteps recede, and the door slams shut behind me.

They left me out here in the sun. Alone. Bound. Unable to do more than cry.

CHAPTER THIRTY-ONE

Nomar

After more than twenty years in the field, I'm used to the waiting. The endless hours of nothing. The muscle cramps. The sweat gathering at the base of my spine.

Though I'm not usually stuffed into the trunk of a car.

Aazar parked this piece of shit sedan two blocks from Raziq's house at dusk, but according to his intel, the man doesn't go to bed until close to midnight. "Remind me again why I'm the one passing the time in a small, metal box?" I ask.

Austin chuckles. "You're the only one who'd fit."

He's relaxing on a roof two houses away. Hell, he probably has a cold soda and a picnic basket in front of him.

"Blame your friend," Griff says. "He could have stolen a bigger car. Maybe then the shortest guy on the team would have drawn a longer straw."

"I'm busting a gut here. You should retire from wet work and get a job as a comedian."

"Maybe I will. It'd be a hell of a lot more fun than hiding

in a drainage pipe half the fucking night. At least your ass isn't wet. Most of the residents of this city have no water, and this neighborhood's drowning in it."

My watch face glows pale green as I check the time. "Five minutes. Zephyr, any movement on Lisette's GPS tag?"

"It's shifted a few times in the past hour, but no more than a few feet. She's still in the north-west corner of the house."

"Thermals show two heat signatures in the top floor bedroom with one guard outside the door. It'd make sense those are Lisette and Mateen," Austin says. "Can't get a read on the first and second floors from here. You'll need to do that when you go over the wall."

Austin has a clear view of the hallway outside where we *think* Lisette and Mateen are, but no one's gone in or out of that room since he got into position. And the GPS only tracks lateral movement. They could be on any one of the three floors.

I slide my hand over the night-vision goggles clipped to my belt, itching to move. Our entire plan hinged on us getting to Raziq's house *before* his men arrived with Lisette. Once that was blown, Austin insisted we had to regroup. I don't care that he was right. The waiting is killing me.

Raziq's had Lisette for more than nine hours. He's hurt her by now. He made it very clear he was going to punish her for whatever "crimes" he thinks she's committed. But she's smart. Determined as fuck. She'll find a way to survive until we get her out of there. She has to.

"Three minutes," Griff says over comms. "Thank fuck."

I kick my legs out straight, and the rear cushions collapse into the back seat. Thirty seconds later, I crouch on the floor and ease the door open.

"Pritchard? Status report on the guards."

"Asshole Number One is leaning against the tree at the south-east corner of the property. Asshole Number Two is walking the perimeter. He'll pass Asshole One in approximately ninety seconds."

I'm coming, Lisette.

Creeping around the front of the car, I settle the NVGs over my eyes. They bathe the world in a bright green glow. Details I could never see without them come to life. The slender, needle-like leaves of the cedar trees. A piece of trash crumpled next to the gate. A rat scurrying across the street.

What I wouldn't give to have Leo with us. But someone had to stay with Amelie and Philippe, and we sure as shit weren't going to leave them with Aazar. He's given us more than I expected, but he's not a fighter. Not trained. Not ready to die to protect someone he's never met.

"Go," Austin says.

I take off at a sprint, covering a hundred feet in less than ten seconds. Griff rounds the corner and braces himself against the stone wall.

Cupping his hand together, he nods, and my boot lands dead center of his palms. The boost is all I need to reach the top. Razor wire catches on my sleeve, but with a hard tug, it rips and I'm free.

The first guard lights a cigarette as the second turns toward me. I pull a silenced Beretta from the holster at my thigh and fire. Head, heart. Head, heart. The two men collapse without a sound.

One of them has a radio and a beat-to-shit Markov pistol, but the other guy's pockets are empty save for a bag of nuts. Arrogant fuckers.

"That was too easy," I mutter and creep around the rear of the house to find the hardline. Got it. Right where we expected it to be. "Zephyr, talk me through this."

"Strip the shielding, then take the cables from my little magic box and connect the alligator clips to the wires. I'll do the rest."

"Seriously?"

"Let the master work, Nomar. Go open the gate for Griff."

"Not with the security system online," I mutter. "If they hear us coming—"

"I just disabled it. Get a move on."

Holy fuck. She's definitely getting a new computer when this is all over. Or three.

"Told you," Griff says when I meet him at the gate. "You owe me fifty bucks."

"I'm good for it. Switching to thermals." With one tap, my view changes. Griff and I circle the house, scanning up and down. Red, vaguely human-shaped blobs move here and there. Four gather in a downstairs room with a diffuse glow coming from one wall. Kitchen. Another two are stationary in what Zephyr thinks is a bedroom.

The second floor is almost as crowded with five separate heat signatures. Fuck. With the assholes we took down at the market, we thought we'd find only seven left at the house. Not more than a dozen.

"Got six on the first floor. Five on the second. With the three up top..." I shake my head. "Even if two of them are Lisette and Mateen, we're fucked."

"Coming to you now," Austin says.

"Hurry. Before someone asks one of the dead guys to check in." I flatten myself against the house, Griff at my side.

Less than two minutes later, Austin sprints through the gate and joins us. "Plan M?" he asks.

I raise the NVGs. "Are you fucking kidding me? Raziq lives in Plan M. We're going with Plan C."

"Follow my lead." Austin climbs the steps to the front door and pulls his weapon. He'll take the main floor, Griff will head to the second, and I'll retrieve Lisette and Mateen.

"Unless you have no choice, leave Raziq for me," I hiss

seconds before Austin breaks down the door with one well-placed kick.

We sweep through the house with practiced precision. The dull *plunks* of silenced rounds are like the popcorn machine at a movie theater. At the top of the stairs, I draw down on a man in a dark blue tunic and pants. He reaches for the gun at his hip, but my shot drops him first.

"Lisette? Mateen?" I bang on the locked door. "It's Nomar. If you can hear me, get back." There's no response, so I holster my weapon and slam my shoulder into the wood. It splinters easily, but inside sitting on the bed are two local kids. One of them has a bruise the size of a fist darkening his jaw.

"Who the fuck are you?"

The older one's gaze lands on the closet. I yank the door open and find nothing.

Shit.

"Lisette and Mateen!" I whirl around to find the kids hovering in the doorway. "Where are they?"

Before I can take two steps, they're running. "Something's fucked here! Stop the kids coming down the stairs!"

I thunder after them, but they have youth and bravado on their side. The younger one—he can't be more than seven—veers off on the second floor, while the teen vaults over the railing. He lands three feet in front of Griff and keeps going.

We race down the stairs together, and almost run right into Austin as he pokes his head out of the kitchen. The kid turns down a hallway to the rear of the house. "What the fuck?"

"He went down here," I call. Concrete steps lead down into total darkness. "There's a basement in this place?"

Zephyr breaks in. "Not on the blueprints I found. Watch your six."

The light secured to my shoulder bobs and winks in and out. Why didn't I think to check the goddamn batteries?

Because you haven't run an op like this in forever.

The stairs open up to a large, empty room. The smell of sand is so cloying, I'm surprised the floor isn't covered with it. At the far end, the kid waves, then darts through a narrow door. It swings shut with a loud *bang.*

I slam into it, but the damn thing doesn't budge. No handle. No hinges. And it's metal. The sound it makes under my fist? It's a good two inches thick.

"Get out!" Whirling around, I shove Griff and Austin back the way we came. But a second door slams in Austin's face, sealing us in the room. "Fuck. Zephyr! Need an assist here!"

"What's—" Static drowns her out, so loud it *hurts.* Austin and Griff wrench their comms devices from their ears, pained expressions on their faces.

"Fuck! Signal jammer?"

"I've got nothing," Austin says, peering at his phone. "We're a good ten, fifteen feet underground."

Griff pounds on the closest wall. "Metal. Like the doors. It's some kind of safe room."

My hands shake. "This was a goddamn trap. It all makes sense now. How easy it was. Did any of the fuckers you took down fire a single shot? Throw a punch?"

Austin shakes his head. "Not a one."

"Raziq, Lisette, Mateen...they're not here. They never were." I stagger back until I hit the wall. "He still has them, and now he has us too."

Tapping the temple of his glasses, Griff stares off into space for a full minute. I'd worry about the guy if he weren't angry as fuck and getting angrier by the second.

Another couple of taps, and he hands me his phone. "I set the glasses to record video before we breached. What do you see?"

Three men fall before I catch it. "Their clothes don't fit. They're dirty. These aren't Raziq's men."

Austin, watching over my shoulder, curses under his breath. "That's not all." He backs the video up thirty seconds, then draws his fingers across the screen to zoom in. "Look at that guy's gun."

"Holy shit. No magazine." I tug off my cap and run my hand through my hair. "These were all locals he paid to sacrifice themselves. But what's his end game? Leave us in here to die of dehydration? Is the room air tight?"

"Zephyr will know something's wrong. Leo will be here in thirty minutes, max," Austin says.

"Raziq isn't the type of guy to leave anything to chance. Leo outed himself at the market. This doesn't end well for us." Griff sinks down onto his ass, phone in hand, and pulls up a photo. The woman is beautiful. A tall, willowy blond with a brilliant smile and love reflected in her eyes. "At least I called Sloane before we left the safe house and told her I loved her."

Next to me, Austin rubs his fist over his heart. "Mikayla left me a message early this morning. But I didn't want to wake her up."

My legs go weak, and I drop to my knees. These two men are going to die because of me. Leo too. What about Amelie and Philippe? They won't get out of Afghanistan without a male escort and a hell of a lot of cash to pay off the border guards. They're dead too.

I failed everyone. Lisette and Mateen most of all. Raziq will kill her. Slowly. Painfully. And Mateen will grow up with his fanatic uncle as his only role model.

Minutes pass, each one seeming to last an hour. Austin and Griff record messages for their women—in case our phones make it out while they still have battery left. But I can't. Even if Zephyr gets in touch with Ford. Even if Second

Sight or McCabe's team searches for Lisette. She won't live long enough to hear it.

"Nomar?" Austin grasps my shoulder and points to the door the kid ran through. "Look."

Curls of smoke seep around the edges. An orange glow starts to appear in the top corner.

"Suffocation, then." The first whiff hits my nose. "Wait. That's not a house fire." The diffuse glow gets brighter. More distinct. It spreads in a line all the way down to the floor. "Someone's cutting through."

"Friend or foe?" Austin asks.

"Leo couldn't get here this fast. And while your 'retail therapy' in Istanbul was extensive as fuck," I say, holding Pritchard's gaze, "a thermal lance wasn't on the list." I grab my M4 and take aim. Behind me, Austin and Griff mirror my movements.

Three minutes. Four. Five. The door gives off so much heat, sweat stings my eyes.

"Get ready." I adjust my grip, my finger resting lightly on the trigger.

The metal creaks and moans, an old ghost searching for someone to haunt. A loud bang follows and, as if in slow motion, the door falls inward like a domino.

"Identify yourself," I shout. "Or we start shooting."

"All the trouble I went through to save you, Viper, and this is how you repay me?" A man lingers behind the wispy smoke, nothing but a silhouette backlit by the glow of the cutting tools. "I suggest we hurry and—as you have always been so fond of saying—get the fuck out of here. Unless you are somehow immune to the three rather large explosive devices set to go off any minute now."

I step forward, unwilling to believe *this* is the man saving my life. But the smoke clears, and I lower my weapon.

"Holy fuck. Shapur."

CHAPTER THIRTY-TWO

Lisette

THE STARS WINK OVERHEAD. Such beauty in the harsh loneliness of this country that has taken everything from me. I stare up at them. Counting. But I never get higher than thirty before I drift on a sea of exhaustion and sorrow.

I have not moved in hours. I am not sure I can. Every muscle aches, the pain bone-deep when I breathe. My hands are numb, but as the shadows started to fall over the roof hours ago, the first blisters appeared on my fingers. I tried to pull my sleeves over the cuffs many times, but I failed, and the sun beat down on my skin for hours.

I never thought I would be happy for the burka. But at this moment, I think it is the only reason I am still alive. The whip did not break my skin, and the material saved my entire body from burning.

Kabul is so far away. Lights glitter in the distance. The city is dying, men like Raziq adding to the despair. But still, it holds on.

It must be close to midnight. Will he leave me out here

until morning? Until I die? For all the heat of the day, after dark, the winds picked up, and I start to shiver. Nausea crawls up my throat. I feel the pain all the way down to my toes.

Eyes closed, I rest my forehead on my arms. I should sleep. Or try to. Is Mateen tucked in a comfortable bed with a full belly? His uncle will revere him for the rest of his life. He will not torture him as he does me. But the sweet, sensitive boy who cares for others will soon be gone.

The door behind me opens. I flinch and try to turn, but my vision tunnels from the effort. Someone unlocks the cuffs. My arms fall, my hands hitting my thighs. Before I can flex my fingers, a man hauls me up and throws me over his shoulder.

"Where are you taking me?"

He says nothing, only carries me down two flights of stairs with an arm banded around my legs. But I am no longer chained, and the scents of spices and fresh naan reach my nose. My mouth waters. The last thing I ate was half an MRE early this morning.

In a brightly lit room with warm, orange walls and a thick rug spread out over the tile floor, a dozen cushions border a long, low table.

"Put her down," Raziq orders.

I manage to stay upright for several seconds before the room starts to spin. My knees hit the carpet.

"If you expect to eat, you will take your seat right now." He points to the far corner of the room. "Hamsa is bringing Mateen down for dinner. He defied me all afternoon and refused his prayers. Your presence ruined all the progress I have made with him the past three days."

My heart leaps into my throat. I crawl toward the cushions, nauseous and dizzy. "Let me talk to him." Lowering myself down, head bowed, I scramble for anything that might diffuse some of Raziq's anger. "The failure is mine. I understand now. Why you brought him here. Mateen needs you. He spent the last three years without a father. You can be that to him."

The words leave a bitter taste in my mouth, but through the black mesh, I think I see Raziq's expression soften.

"But he needs time. If you let me stay with him...I can help ease this transition. Help him see you are doing what is best for him."

He stalks over to me, and I curl my shoulders inward. "This will not change your punishment."

"I would never ask for that. I deserve my sentence." If he could see my face, he would know I am lying. That I wish he would drop dead in front of me. Or that I could be the one to kill him. But this country used me and left me to die. Twice. It is time I used *it* for something.

"Very well. You will be allowed to stay with him in his room tonight. Tomorrow, I will move him into one of the larger suites with multiple rooms."

"Thank you for your...generous gift." The words stick in my throat, and I imagine them like knives piercing his chest.

"Maman?" Mateen races into the room and throws himself against me. Adrenaline floods my limbs, easing the pain of the welts across my back. "You smell bad."

Laughing, I press a kiss to his cheek. "I know, *mon bébé*. I spent the afternoon in the sun and I need to wash. But we will eat first." I look to Raziq. "He is still young enough to eat with me. But if you want him at your side..."

With a wave of his hand, Raziq dismisses the implied question. "I have already eaten. He may eat with you until his next birthday."

I take my son's shoulders and hold him at arm's length. "Mateen, sit on the cushion with your legs crossed. Do you remember all the meals we had in Papa's home?"

He shakes his head and tugs at the burka. "How will you eat with this on?"

Two men approach Raziq, crouch down, and talk in low tones. Leaning close to Mateen, I whisper in his ear. "Do not ask questions now. After the meal, he said he will let me stay with you in your room. Until then, it is very important you do exactly as I tell you."

His brown eyes well with tears, but he nods. Finding my hand under the black cape, he squeezes so hard, I bite the inside of my cheek to stop myself from crying out.

A woman in a pale blue burka comes into the room carrying a tray laden with steaming plates of food. With the grace of a dancer, she sinks to her knees and arranges the dishes in front of us.

My gaze lands on the pitcher of water, and suddenly, I am so thirsty, nothing else matters. It is barely cool, and I spill half the glass trying to maneuver it under the cape, but I do not care. Until Mateen tugs at my sleeve.

"How do I eat this?" he whispers. "There is no silverware."

His uncle's stare makes my skin crawl as I explain how to take the naan and use it as a spoon. He struggles at first—as do I—but soon is so focused on the meal, I think he has forgotten Raziq is even in the room.

Watching him smile up at me between bites is a joy I feared I would never have again. But if Nomar cannot find us, it will not last long. I can barely keep my eyes open. The meal and the warmth of the room conspire with my injuries. My mind wanders to Nomar. I hope he knows I love him.

The serving girl clears away the mostly empty dishes, but as she returns with a pot of tea, three of Raziq's men crowd through the doorway, and she flees with a quiet whimper.

"It is time," the tallest of them says. The other two take up positions close to me.

Raziq gets to his feet. Bile rises in my throat at his gleeful smile. "Bring them."

"I can walk on my own," I snap when the closest man grabs my arm. In truth, I am not certain I can, but I have to try. "Mateen, give me your hand."

He chews on his lower lip, but slips his fingers in mine. His hold gives me the strength to get to my feet.

We walk down a dim hallway, one guard ahead of us and two behind. Around a corner, we enter a sitting room. I gasp when I see video of Raziq's Kabul home on the large wall screen.

"You were smart," he says, "to hide the GPS tracker where you did, Lisette. But I am smarter. It has been transmitting from my *former* home all evening. And ten minutes ago, your lover and his friends attempted to rescue you."

Horror washes over me. My heartbeat thunders in my ears. He is too happy. Smug. Triumphant, even.

"Wh-what did you do?" I do not want to hear the answer. But Nomar saved me. He loved me. I owe him this much. I owe him so much more.

"Three of them are locked in an inescapable room under the kitchen. Two minutes ago, the fourth man entered the house." Raziq slips his phone from his pocket and makes a call.

A fireball explodes on the screen. Then another. And another. The flames lick up the walls. Windows shatter. In seconds, the blaze is so bright, it hurts my eyes. "No!"

I drop Mateen's hand and lunge for Raziq. But one of his men shoves me back.

"You killed them!" My grief is a physical weight, stealing the only shred of hope I had left. Mateen throws his arms around my waist. His body shakes with each noisy sob.

"The punishment for adultery is stoning," Raziq says with a shrug. "I merely carried it out in a unique manner."

I rub my son's back. The blisters on my fingers tear open. The tiny shards of pain are so much less than I deserve. Leo. Griff. Austin. Nomar. They are dead because of me.

"You did not need to make your nephew watch!"

"He needs to learn that actions have consequences. Stop crying, Mateen. You are almost a man and you will act like one."

Mateen swipes at his cheeks, but his tears do not slow. "Nomar was nice," he says softly. "I wish *he* was my uncle, not you."

The sliver of my heart not already broken shatters into dust. Nomar could have been so much more to my son. Maybe even a father one day.

The anger etched on Raziq's face terrifies me. "Do not make him watch any more of this. Take us to his room. Please."

"No. He will watch until he can do so calmly." Raziq crosses his arms over his chest, ignoring the horrors behind him so he can glare at Mateen.

I should say something. Try to calm my son, but I cannot tear my gaze away from the fire. The house yawns, the walls expanding for a brief moment before half the structure collapses.

A flicker of movement at the corner of the property distracts me. Then another. Four shadowy figures creep along the outside of the stone wall. The first one is a full head shorter than the others. Nomar?

Raziq turns toward the screen. If he sees them—if I am right and they are alive—he will never stop hunting them.

"I thought my husband was a monster," I say sharply. "He was a saint compared to you."

His hand flies, catching me across the cheek with such force, the room spins, and I fall to my knees.

"You will respect me or you will never see your son again!"

No!

I cannot let him separate me from Mateen. "I am sorry. Please, forgive me. I will do anything to stay with him. Anything!" Bowing my head, I extend my arms and prostrate myself in front of him. The act of submission revolts me, but what choice do I have?

"Get up," he orders. When I do, he steps so close, I can smell the garlic on his breath. "I am a man of my word, Lisette. So I will let you stay with Mateen tonight. But if you ever raise your voice to me again, it will be the last time."

Mateen buries his face against my side and I put my arm around him.

"Take them to the boy's room. Fajr is in five hours. He needs his rest." With a wave of his hand, Raziq dismisses us. His men herd us back down the hall, up a flight of stairs, and into a bedroom. The moment the lock *thunks*, Mateen throws himself onto the mattress and starts to cry once more.

I RIP the cape from my head and toss it into the corner. Dark spots float in my vision. My back burns with every breath, but I cannot let the pain stop me. Not yet. My son needs me.

"Mateen? Look at me, *mon bébé*."

"Uncle Raziq killed Nomar," he wails.

Easing my hip onto the bed, I squeeze his shoulder and drop my voice to a whisper. "I am going to tell you a secret, but I need you to promise me you will never tell your uncle or any of his men. Can you do that?"

He rolls over to peer up at me, a solemn look on his face. "Yes, Maman. I promise."

"I do not think Nomar is dead." Saying the words makes it

real, and I pull Mateen into my arms. I need his solid weight against me. To smell his hair. To anchor myself to this moment in case we do not have many more together. "I came here with Nomar and three other men. And after the explosions, I saw four people moving quickly away from the fire. I think one of them was Nomar."

"Is he going to save us? Like he did when we lived with Papa?"

Tears well in my eyes. "If he can find us, I know he will."

CHAPTER THIRTY-THREE

Nomar

Austin grabs my arm. "Shapur Khan? What is he doing here?"

I glare over at him. "How the hell should I know?"

Clearing his throat, Shapur steps back through the glowing hole in the door. "If you wish to die, by all means, remain here. I, however, prefer to see the dawn. Stay close to the wall. There is a camera across the street. I believe Raziq wants to witness your deaths."

He and his men take off. I wouldn't trust Shapur with the life of a flea, but he could have left us here to die. "Fuck. We can ask questions later. Come on."

Austin and Griff follow me out the door and up a long set of stairs to the rear of the property. Shapur climbs a ladder braced against the wall, and waves at us before he jumps down to the street. When did he turn into an Afghan action hero?

Halfway up the ladder, I tap the comms unit in my ear. "Leo? You better not be headed to the target location."

"Thank fuck," Leo mutters. "We weren't sure he was going to make it in time."

"The hell? You *knew*?" Austin leaps off the fence, with Griff at his heels.

"Hurry, hurry," Shapur says, ushering us around the side of the house. "Stay west of the wall."

"What then? You finally going to explain how you found us? And who the hell told you I'm the Viper? Because I'm going to hunt them down and pull their nuts out their nostrils."

"That's something I'd pay to see," Austin mutters. "But—"

"Talk later," Shapur says and shoves me forward. "Run, but stay low."

The first percussive wave drives us all to the ground. Sparks singe the back of my neck. Fuck. I catch a whiff of burning hair, and pat my head down, praying it's not mine.

The second blast is hotter. I can't hear anything but a dull roar. Shapur tries to get up, but I slap my hand down on his back until the ground shakes for a third time.

I spring onto my toes and stare back at the house. The windows on the top floor shatter. The roof is next, exploding into flames thirty feet high.

"Fuck. We would have either cooked or suffocated in under ten minutes." Bending over, my hands on my knees, I try to force a couple of deep breaths, but they won't come.

"We need to get out of here," Griff says. "If Raziq suspects we didn't die in there, he's going to get a hell of a lot more volatile."

And Lisette will pay the price.

Austin runs a hand through his hair and scowls. "Son of a bitch. How bad is it?"

I peer up at a patch of singed skin behind his left ear. "Well, you're not bald."

"Fucking hell. When we find this murdering asshole, promise me I can shave his beard off before you kill him?"

"I'm much more concerned with *how* we find this murdering asshole."

"Soon, all will be revealed," Shapur says with a smug smile.

That's it. He's severed my last fucking nerve. I lunge for him, grab his tunic, and slam him back against the wall. "Listen, you piece of shit. Raziq has the woman I love *and* her son. He's had her for—" I check my watch "—almost eleven hours now. If he hasn't hurt her, he will soon. And we don't have a fucking clue where they are."

Shapur shoves me back. "*You* do not have a 'fucking clue' where they are. *I*, however, know the precise location of Raziq's second home. In the next few hours, Darius will launch a drone to fly over the area. That should give you the confirmation you need."

"Who the hell is Darius?" Griff asks.

Shapur looks from me to Austin to Griff, baffled. "He is one of yours. Central Intelligence Agency Officer Darius Bakir."

THE RIDE back to the safe house passes in silence. Shapur's guys—Arash and Javed—take their own car, but he rides in the Land Rover with us, staring out the window at the slums along the way.

There aren't many lights in this part of Kabul. Aren't many people either. Most fled to rural areas years ago after one too many mortar blasts destabilized the electrical grid.

When we approach the gate, I peer over at Shapur. "Your guys coming in?"

"No. They have family here. They will wait for my call.

What we have to discuss is not for them to know. Surely you remember them? Arash and Javed were never...bright."

"Loyal as fuck, though."

He nods, and I study him as he climbs out of the Land Rover and follows Austin to the door. This isn't the same power-hungry man-child I left in Jalalabad three years ago. Shapur carries himself with a seriousness at odds with the man from my memories.

Leo meets us at the door and pulls Austin in for a quick, one-armed hug. "Don't do that shit again, man. I mean it."

"Wasn't planning on doing it this time," he says. "Spineless piece of shit."

I check the bedroom. Empty. "Where are Amelie and Philippe?"

Another man—Bakir, I assume—steps out from behind Leo. I'm on him in a heartbeat. Shoving him against the wall, I press my forearm to his throat. "Explain yourself right fucking now, asshole."

He doesn't flinch. Doesn't fight back. Doesn't seem to care that I could snap his neck in seconds. "They are on their way back to Toulouse. Or will be very soon. A colleague of mine took them to the airfield twenty minutes ago."

"Back off, Nomar." Leo grabs my wrist, and I cringe. Great. Now Shapur knows my real name. Then again, the likelihood we all live to see tomorrow is so low, it doesn't matter. "Darius is a boy scout. I should know. I trained him. For a while."

"Until you lost yourself in a bottle of rum," Darius says. "I was happy to learn you are sober now."

He speaks with precision. English isn't his first language. I look the man up and down. Six-foot-five, two-ten, with smooth amber skin. He runs a hand over his trimmed beard and mustache. If it weren't for his close-shorn, tight black curls—and his height—he could pass for a local.

"Saudi?" I ask.

He straightens his shoulders. "Egyptian."

"And you're here because?"

"Because the CIA has had our eye on Raziq Ali for the past five years. So when he started spending money at a *very* accelerated rate, we paid attention." Darius stares down at me like it's my fault Raziq kidnapped Lisette. "Imagine our surprise when we heard a rumor two of our *former* officers hired a private plane to fly them and the Viper from Istanbul to Kabul."

"That was none of your goddamn business. Or don't you know what 'former' means?" Griff asks. "My SSO locked me to a desk because he didn't think a deaf guy with only one arm could still throw a punch. Want to see how wrong he was?"

"Enough!" I wedge myself between Griff and Darius before they start wailing on one another. "All I care about is getting Lisette and Mateen away from that fanatical, delusional asshole. Once they're safe, I don't give a shit what happens. You can take down the whole goddamn agency for all I care, Griff. Hell, I'll have your back. But until then..."

The two men retreat to separate corners of the room. Austin grabs the jug of water from the kitchen and refills his canteen. "Nomar's right. We barely got out of there alive. Assuming Raziq thinks we're dead, he'll lower his guard. So all we need—" he turns to Shapur "—is the man's location. And a goddamn plan."

"We need a hell of a lot more than that." I glare at Shapur, and whatever he sees in my eyes must convey my anger, because he shifts his gaze to the floor. "Before I trust a word either you *or* Darius has to say, I need to know why *you* were the one to break us out of there. Why didn't the CIA do it?"

Darius snorts. "Because the United States government cannot—in any official capacity—put boots on the ground in Afghanistan. I'm here in an advisory capacity only."

"That doesn't explain how *you* got connected with *him*."

The CIA officer strides over to me, hands on his hips like I'm some petulant child who needs to be punished. "I thought you were a smart guy, Garcia. After all, you're the one who set all this in motion."

I whirl around and shove Shapur halfway across the room. "You refused every single meet I tried to set up. For eleven months. You're the reason I lost Lisette in the first place. If you'd gone to even one..."

"Yes, I know." He tucks his hands into the pockets of his tunic. "I have done many things I regret over the years, *Nomar*. But I am trying to atone for my mistakes. If we are all still alive tomorrow, I hope you will let me explain myself to you. But for now, time is of the essence, is it not?"

"You will pay for your crimes."

If Lisette suffers for even one extra minute because I refused to trust this guy, I'll never forgive myself. "Fine. Tell us what you know."

Shapur looks from me to Darius and back again. "He has a second home an hour outside of Kabul. At least twenty men on site. The house is three stories tall with two .50 caliber machine guns mounted on the roof. A stealth approach is impossible, as he can see for ten kilometers in every direction. It is rumored to be surrounded by land mines, and the roads are patrolled regularly."

"And the interior?" Austin asks.

The young warlord shakes his head. "All I know is what I have been able to see from a distance. But even on the roof—where Raziq spends several hours each morning—he is never alone. He has men with him at all times."

I put my back to the wall and sink to the ground. "Next you're going to tell me the entire floor of the house is electrified unless we can fake voice prints and retinal scans."

Shapur chuckles, but quickly sobers. "Raziq may be rich, but he prefers the old ways: murder, torture, intimidation…"

Torture.

The darkness I've carried for more than twenty years threatens to drag me under. Imagining all the things he could be doing to Lisette will break me if I let it. But I can't pack it all away. Not anymore.

"So how do we get in?" I check my watch. It's almost 2:00 a.m. "Sunrise is in less than four hours. If we leave now, we'd at least have the cover of darkness."

"It's almost a full moon," Austin says. "It's bright as fuck out there. How the hell didn't you notice that on the way back from the world's worst BBQ?"

Darius clears his throat. "One of our assets is sending up a drone in a few minutes. After that, we will hopefully know more."

"How? It's the middle of the fucking night. Even if we get a visual, we still don't know the layout or where Lisette and Mateen might be." Resting my head against the wall, I stare up at the ceiling. Water stains spread out from a crack near the kitchen. "Raziq is asleep. Along with half of his men. If we wait until morning prayers, *everyone* will be awake. There are five of us. Seven if Shapur lends us his two guys."

"Why do you think I am here?" he asks. "Raziq's brother tried to have me killed. If it were not for you, Nomar, I would be dead. And we will be ten. Four of my men, and me."

"Do not count me in that number," Darius says. "Advisory capacity only, remember?"

Leo arches a single brow at the CIA officer. "Cut the shit, boy scout. You're here to kick some ass and you know it."

The speaker attached to Leo's tablet crackles. "Um, guys?" Zephyr calls. "How much do you love me?"

Austin grins. "You're the single most valuable member of the team and I will tell you that every day for the rest of my life, without fail, if you have the smallest bit of good news for us."

Even *I* feel a bit lighter as her musical laugh spills from the device. "Damn straight. I got you a flyover from a Turkish AWAC with one of the most advanced thermal imaging systems in the world. In four hours, we'll know *everything* there is to know about that house, and Raziq won't suspect a thing."

"Four hours?" My heart sinks, even though Zephyr just worked a fucking miracle. "What if...?"

Austin claps his hand on my shoulder. "You said it yourself, Nomar. Everyone's asleep right now. Fajr is at 4:45. Sunrise is ninety minutes after that. He's a fucking zealot. He's not going to do a damn thing during prayer time."

I nod, though his words bring me little comfort. Once the sun comes up, Raziq will hurt her again. If he hasn't killed her already.

CHAPTER THIRTY-FOUR

Nomar

Austin, Darius, and Leo close themselves in the tiny bedroom for two hours of shuteye. Griff takes the chair, his gaze locked on the camera feeds with his M4 at his side.

Shapur sits cross-legged on a dusty red cushion and stares at his phone while I mix up packets of instant coffee.

"Mind if I join you?" I ask, offering him one of the collapsible metal cups.

"You Americans do love your coffee." He accepts the beverage and inhales the rich scent. "I have never understood the allure."

"I feel the same way about tea."

His laugh hasn't changed. It shakes his entire body. Like he's just heard the ten funniest jokes in the world all at the same time.

"How did you choose the name Guillermo?" he asks when I sit down. "It never suited you."

"My handler picked it for me. Twenty years ago. I always hated it. Why not something short? Like Raz or even Pedro?"

The first sip of the bitter brew calms my nerves. It tastes like shit, but it's a tiny bit of home in this godawful place. "What happened after I left, Shapur? How did you get...here?"

His bone-deep sigh takes me by surprise. "I mourned you, my friend. Musa's men died most painfully."

"How many did you have killed?"

Black brows knit together, he stares at me in disbelief. "All of them."

"Wh-what?" The coffee burns as it sticks in my throat. "You didn't..."

"Did you think I would not avenge you?" The man turns to face me. "I loved you like a brother...Nomar. I destroyed his entire organization—or what was left of it after you killed him."

Fuck. I thought he was just using me. Paying me to do what he couldn't. To be the bad guy. I didn't see the loneliness. How isolated he was. How I quickly became the only one in his inner circle. But looking back, it's all I remember.

"Shapur, I'm sorry. I wasn't supposed to leave...like that. My assignment was to help you for six months. Get you to agree to a meet. Gather intel on the other warlords. The CIA promised me *they'd* take out Musa. That once he was dead, I could come home. But month after month after month...they kept me there with no exfil plan. I couldn't wait any longer."

"And your woman—Lisette?—she was waiting for you?"

"No. Maybe. Not waiting. Hoping. But after all the shit I did for you, I couldn't face her. You traffic women, Shapur. And she was Faruk's *wife*. The bastard kidnapped her from France thirteen years ago, brought her to Afghanistan, and forced her to marry him."

His eyes widen. "That is why Raziq took her son. *Faruk's* son."

"Fucking shitstain thinks it's his *responsibility* to raise Mateen the way Faruk would have wanted." The rage that has been simmering inside me all week threatens to boil over. "He's convinced Lisette has committed some sort of crime and she needs to be punished."

The look on his face doesn't reassure me. "She stole a male child from his father and took him to another country. Presumably she is not raising him as a Muslim?"

I shake my head. "She's not."

"Then it does not matter that Faruk is gone. She is still guilty of kidnapping—"

"Mateen would have died if they hadn't escaped. She was a prisoner for ten years. He beat her, raped her, and when the child he forced her to have needed medical care, he kidnapped an American doctor rather than take the kid to a hospital." I'm done with this conversation. I was wrong. Shapur is still an asshole. Even if he did...*mourn* me.

He dismisses my rage with a wave of his hand. "Faruk was the worst of us. But he was a moderate compared to his brother."

"Not helping."

Another sigh, and he leans back against the wall. "For several years, I had hope for this country. Our women were working. Going to school. Even teaching. But now...none of that is possible." After a sniff of the coffee, he tries a sip. "How do you drink this shit?"

"Give me that. I'm not letting it go to waste. Not when we're probably breaching Raziq's fortress in broad fucking daylight."

Shapur shakes his head and pulls the cup close to his chest. "As you did not see fit to bring even a single tea bag, I am drinking all of this, despite the taste."

"Whatever, man. I need some air."

"Did you know," he asks before I can get up, "that it took almost a year for me to believe you were alive? That you had stolen my files and decrypted them? I was assured the security was almost unbreakable."

"If it makes you feel any better, the woman who hacked them said it was a challenge. And she's one of the best in the world." I let the coffee smooth the raw edges of my anger. "What finally tipped you off?"

"My Hajira convinced me." A little smile tugs at his lips. "She is brilliant, Nomar. Smarter than me. With the kindest heart. 'Shapur,' she said to me, 'the Viper has stopped every auction in the country for six months. He clearly knows you. Are you certain Guillermo is truly dead?'"

"She was what? Nineteen at the time?" I marvel. "And she figured it out."

"She did. And because of her, I stopped trafficking in women completely."

Holy shit.

How did the Viper miss one of the richest warlords in the region *getting out of the game?*

Because the auctions didn't stop. Only the supplier changed. I missed it because I didn't give a flying fuck who took the girls. My job was to save them.

"Did I surprise you?" he asks. "I did not think that was possible."

"Neither did I."

Shapur unlocks his phone and stares at the screen. "Hajira spent eighteen years with a father who thought she was worthless. He sold her to me for thirty thousand dollars. I sent him away the night you left and brought her mother to live with us a month later. We have a family now."

In the photo he pulls up, Hajira smiles at the camera, wearing a golden hijab over a deep blue dress, and holding a babe in each arm.

"Twin girls. Farah and Bibi," he says with a wide smile and a hint of awe in his voice.

"I'm happy for you, Shapur. Truly."

His joy fades, sapped away in a heartbeat. "They will be a year old next month, and I fear for their future. Hajira is expected to hide away from the world for the rest of her life. To let her brilliant mind go to waste. Our daughters will not be allowed to go to school. To walk through the markets alone. To be anything other than wives. If they are mistreated by their husbands, they have no recourse. Not even I could help them."

He's right. Those two girls will don burkas by the time they're twelve, and never see the world through anything other than mesh again.

"You have money, Shapur. Leave. Take them and run. Find them a better life. Hell, when this is all over, I'll even help you."

The gratitude in his eyes shouldn't affect me. He was a target. Nothing more. He understands now—how fucked his world truly is—but I'd bet he loves those girls like they're his everything.

He lowers his voice and glances at the closed bedroom door. "If Darius had not called me yesterday, we would already be on our way. When Lisette and Mateen are safe, we will disappear."

"Holy fuck. Get out of here." I get to my feet and offer him my hand. "I'm serious. Go home. Get your wife and your children and disappear."

"I will help you, Viper. Or Hajira will never forgive me." He must sense my confusion, because he chuckles and bats my hand away. "I tell her everything. She is my most trusted advisor in all things. And when we find a new home, she will be free. I will need to beg her to stay with me."

I nod at the photo on his phone. "I don't think you'll have to beg, Shapur. That look in her eyes? That's love."

Lisette

Someone bangs on the door. I jerk up with a whimper. The bone-deep bruises across my back ache, and tears burn my eyes.

"The boy needs to be ready for Fajr in ten minutes!" a man shouts.

Mateen sits up and rubs his eyes. "Maman?"

"You need to wash, *mon chou*. Hurry. Your uncle will be upset if you do not make *wudu* before prayers."

My hands shake as I lay out fresh clothes for Mateen. The little dresser has six identical tunics, six pairs of pants. All shades of brown. All the right size, down to his socks and underwear.

"Put these on," I say when he trudges back into the bedroom. His hair is still damp, and sleep blears in his eyes.

"Maman?" He reaches up to touch my shoulder. "What happened?"

Even the light pressure from his fingertips is too much. I shrink away and blink back tears. "It is nothing. Get dressed."

"Uncle hurt you." His lower lip wobbles, and he throws his arms around me so quickly, I cry out. Mateen only tightens his grip.

"Please, baby. Let go," I manage. "My back."

"No. I am not going to pray. I want to stay with you." His voice carries an edge of anger.

Fear floods my limbs. My hands shake. "Mateen, you cannot disobey your uncle. Not now." I grab a clean tunic and slide it over his head. "He only let me stay with you because I told him it would help you. If you fight him, he will lock me away and I will never see you again."

"I hate it here. He prays and asks for help doing good

things, but he hurt you and Philippe's mom and he tried to kill Nomar and—"

"Shhh. I know. Put on your pants. Quickly."

Tears shimmer in my son's eyes. How much longer do we have? One minute? Two? Three?

"Are all Muslims bad?" he asks.

I sink to my knees, too exhausted to stand, and wrap my arms around him. "No, Mateen. Most Muslims are peaceful, wonderful people. Like Madame Garnier. She is one of your favorite teachers, yes?"

He nods, his cheek resting on my bruised shoulder.

"Raziq does terrible things in the name of Islam. But that is because he is a bad man. If he were Catholic or Episcopalian or even Buddhist, he would still be evil."

"So praying will not make me do bad things?"

My son is so insightful sometimes. So very smart. But also kind. Gentle. Curious. My heart swells with pride, even as I fear for his future.

"No, it will not." Rising, I blink back tears. "I do not know when your uncle will send for me, Mateen. I hope we will be able to have breakfast together. But if I am gone when you return, do not worry."

"But..."

Someone pounds on the door. Mateen's eyes widen, and he shrinks against me. "Go. I have not covered my head, so I cannot be seen. I love you."

He offers me a watery smile. A single tear tumbles down his cheek. "I love you too."

"Follow me," a man says to him, then slams the door and locks me in.

My knees go weak, and I stumble into the bathroom. I am safe for now. Through the bars on the small window, the sky is only starting to lighten.

"Your punishment will occur every day after sunrise prayers."

Will he chain me again? Leave me out in the sun to burn?

I run cold water from the tap. My eyes and lips are still so dry. I need to drink as much as I can.

My blistered hands shake. I bring them to my lips again and again until the very idea of another drop is too much.

Last night, I was too exhausted—and afraid—to remove the burka's long under-dress and the rough pants *someone* put on me. But my skin is scratchy and I smell. With the men praying, I should have fifteen or twenty minutes to shower without worrying someone will come for me.

I strip out of my clothes, then look at my reflection. Angry purple bruises curl over my shoulders. When I turn, craning my neck to see my back, I cry out.

There is not a single inch of unmarked skin. Yellow, blue, and a black so deep, I fear the damage may be permanent. Only the burka stopped him from breaking the skin. But how will I survive another day of this?

The shower is both blessed relief and agony. The pressure of the spray is too much, but it feels so good to wash the salt from my skin and hair.

Drying myself off sends darkness flooding my vision. I stumble to the bed and collapse onto my stomach until I can see again.

Get up. Get dressed. Be strong for Mateen.

I pray Nomar is alive. That he will come for us soon. Before there is nothing of me left to be saved.

CHAPTER THIRTY-FIVE

Nomar

Shapur and Darius co-opt one of the bed rolls for a prayer rug. Griff takes the other and is out in seconds. Austin and Leo pull up satellite scans of Raziq's home and debate which roads are best for approach. But I can't sleep. Every time I close my eyes, I see Lisette afraid and in pain. I can't remember her smile. Her laugh. Only her tears.

"You're not doing her any favors," Leo mutters when they break for more coffee. "Get some rest."

"When it was Domina, did you sleep?" I run my fingers over the tattoo on my arm. It's all I have of her. What if it's all I *ever* have of her?

"Yes. I did." He casts a quick glance over his shoulder. "Though Austin and Trevor practically had to beat me over the head to get me to lie down."

"Don't even think about it."

One corner of his mouth quirks up. "Wouldn't be a fair fight. I've got six inches on you."

"Yeah, but I've got two working eyes." It's a low blow, and I hold up my hands before he can call me on it. "Sorry, man. That was a shitty thing to say."

"I said my share last year. But I was serious about the shuteye."

"We don't even know if she's still alive." I don't mean to say the words aloud. But now that I have, they're all too real. "Fifteen hours. That's how long it's been."

Austin joins us and runs a hand over two days of rough stubble. "Assuming he's not an idiot, he knows you care about her. He'd have made sure she was alive to see us die."

"Is that supposed to make me feel better?" I shove at him, but he outweighs me by at least seventy pounds, and all I manage to do is spill his coffee.

Austin wipes his hands on his pants and glares at me. "It's supposed to be the truth. Leo, Griff, and I have all been in your shoes. Our women are safe because we had help. We had family. We *listened* to the men and women who dropped everything for us. You aren't in this alone, Nomar. But you have to trust us. Take two hours. Consider that an order."

"You're not my boss anymore, Pritchard." I should listen to him, but I need to hit something, and he's the closest target. If he takes the bait.

He squares his shoulders and stares down at me. "Oh no? Griff, Leo, and Zephyr all work for *me*."

"What? I thought...Ford sent them. Who's footing the bill for all this shit?" As soon as I ask the question, I shake my head. "No. Not you."

"Why *not* me? For fuck's sake, Nomar. I'm the one who sent you to Shapur. Who kept delaying your extraction. The President put me on that goddamn publicity tour, then there was all that shit with Trevor and Dani, Pakistan, Griff..." Austin rubs the back of his neck and stares over my shoulder at the closed bedroom door. "He lost his fucking arm."

"That wasn't your fault," Leo says sharply. "You didn't set off that bomb. The Taliban did. Stop blaming yourself."

Guilt swims in Austin's gaze. He can't. He won't. He'll carry that burden for the rest of his life. "I *am* the boss here, Nomar. When this is all over, Rescue Operations Group has a place for you. If you want it."

This is too much. "I work alone."

"Not anymore." Austin claps a hand on my shoulder. "As much as I resisted it at first—hell, even the *idea* of it—my team is a family. Along with Second Sight and Hidden Agenda. Huge. Dysfunctional as fuck. But definitely a family."

"Wait. That makes you the dad, doesn't it?" Leo asks. "Tell Griff to stop calling me Grandpa, will you? Threaten to ground him or something."

Laughing feels wrong with Lisette and Mateen still out there. Scared. In danger. But it's also a reminder of what's waiting for me on the other side of this mess. A life. One where maybe...I don't have to be alone.

"I already sent him to his room," Austin says with a chuckle. "You too, Nomar. If you won't follow orders, maybe you'll listen to old Pops here. Get some rest. In two hours, we'll come up with a plan."

"Pops?" I shake my head. "You're two years younger than I am."

"Could be worse," Leo says. "He could have asked you to call him Daddy."

I MANAGE an hour before I'm so wired, I can't lie still. Griff, the bastard, doesn't hear the low murmurs of the men in the other room. Not being able to understand what they're saying through the door sets me on edge, but if I show my face, Pritchard is going to start spouting off about family again.

Leo's pack is propped against the wall. I saw a notebook in there earlier. It's been years since I left a letter in my foot-locker. Years since I thought anyone would care if I didn't come home.

But this whole situation is FUBAR, and if shit goes sideways, there's no one left to send in. So I find the notebook, sink down across from the door, and start flipping to find a blank page.

Lisette's flowing script stares back at me. Letters to Noele, her mother, father, and...me.

I should put the damn thing away. Pretend I never saw it. But when have I ever done the *right* thing?

Dear Nomar,

I am afraid. Raziq will kill me. Of that I am certain. If I am lucky, I will see Mateen again. Hold him. Tell him how much I love him. But I have only been lucky once in my life. And that is when I met you. I fear it is too much to hope fate will smile upon me a second time.

I believe you will save Mateen. I believe you will not stop until he is free. I take comfort in that.

I wish we had more time. I wish for so many things. Dinners and movies. Strolls along the riverbank. Kisses and touches and everything that comes after. But you will laugh when I tell you I also wish to sit with you in the rain, shivering, while we watch Mateen play soccer.

I hope when I am gone, you will not disappear from his life completely. He needs you. I would never ask you to love him. But if I am right, you already do.

You showed me I could be brave. That I could be strong. But you also showed me I could be weak, and someone else would shoulder the burden for a time.

I could not say any of these things to you face to face. I wanted to. But I did not know how. Please forgive me.

I love you.

Lisette

Tears cool on my cheeks. My battered heart aches. I didn't know what love was until I met her. Now, I'm terrified I'll fail, and I'll never be able to tell her that I didn't save her. She saved herself. But that's not all.

She also saved me.

"Heads up." Austin raps on the bedroom door. "The thermal scans are coming in now."

I scramble up, then remember Griff can't hear the knocking. Kicking his boot, I wait for him to look at me. "It's time."

He fumbles for his glasses. "Fuck. Go. I'm right behind you."

Not going to argue with the man. I need to know what we're dealing with. If Lisette is there. If she's still alive.

Austin has all our tablets propped up on the stained kitchen counter. The red blobs don't look like people at all, given that the camera is three miles up. But with each passing second, the images change. Small details emerge. Arms and legs. Subtle differences in size.

"It'll be another ten minutes before we have the full picture," Zephyr says, her voice spilling from a tiny speaker on one of the tablets. "But I count twenty-two distinct heat signatures."

I zero in on the smallest one. "Mateen's on the first floor. One other man in the room, two in the hall. Want to bet that's Raziq next to him?"

"Two women," Austin says. "One in the kitchen, and the other on the second floor. That's got to be Lisette."

The urge to touch the screen—to touch *her*—is almost too much. "The rest of the men are spread throughout the house and grounds. Looks like six on patrol, one on the roof."

"What I wouldn't give for McCabe's tactics guy right about now." Austin rubs the back of his neck, his gaze pinned to the center tablet. "Sampson's a fucking genius at infil and exfil. It's going to be damn near impossible to get the drop on these assholes."

"Harder than that, boss," Zephyr says. "Check out the wide shot."

The image shifts, the house shrinking to a square in the center surrounded by a hundred small, round dots. "What the fuck are those?" I ask.

She pauses for so long, the answer can't be good.

"Zephyr?"

"Those are land mines."

HALF AN HOUR LATER, we're no closer to a plan. The AWAC's cameras gave us a hell of a lot more than just thermals.

We have rough specs on every room, and from the dead zones directly behind them, the front and back doors are likely reinforced.

"Top speed on any piece of shit motorcycle we could find around here is one-fifty, but I wouldn't trust them not to fall apart at half that. Plus, we'd have to double-up, so a hundred? They'd have us in their sights the moment we crested that hill."

"What about a helicopter?" I turn to Darius. "Are there any SOG teams in the area?"

"Perhaps you did not hear me before," he says, his eyes flashing with anger. "The United States cannot put boots on the ground anywhere in Afghanistan. We would start a war."

"Who said anything about *your* boots landing anywhere *near* the ground? We don't need the bird to land. Just give us a ride."

Griff stares at me. "My glasses must be malfunctioning. Because it sounds like you want Darius to commandeer a SOG team, ask them to risk their lives—and a thirty- to forty-*million*-dollar aircraft, so we can all jump out of the damn thing into the middle of the most heavily fortified fortress since...the dawn of time."

"Yep."

"With at *most*, eight people." He scoffs and looks to Austin. "You're not seriously considering this, are you?"

Pritchard sinks down into the single chair with a heavy sigh. "You have a better idea? The sun's been up for half an hour. My guess? Raziq sends someone to check out last night's fireworks soon, and he's going to figure out pretty damn quick that we're not dead. After that, our job gets a hell of a lot harder."

Darius mutters to himself as he paces the room. "They could have picked anyone else for this. Saxon. DeMarche. Williams. But no. They pick me. Because my skin is brown. Because I made one mistake that I will never be able to atone for."

Leo starts for the man, but I slap my hand to his chest. "I got this."

The look Darius gives me is nothing short of murderous, but I'm beyond caring. "Follow me, boy scout. Outside."

The second the door closes, I lay into him. "What the fuck are you even doing here, Darius?"

"Saving your ass," he snaps.

"No. That was Shapur. All you did was call him. Could have done that from Langley. Instead, you flew halfway across the world. For what? Just to get in our way? Because that's a shitty fucking thing to do if you ask me."

Darius leans against the carport and stares up at the bright blue sky. "My first year at the agency, I wrote a paper on Amir Abdul Faruk. My SSO decided he hated me the moment he found out I was Muslim, and I had to prove my worth."

I gesture to my face—dark eyes, light brown skin, distinctly Latino features—and sigh. "My first couple of years, they only sent me to Mexico and South America. I speak six languages. But not a word of Spanish."

"Do you think that makes us equal?" He shakes his head. "The prejudices against you do not stem from a terrorist attack that killed three thousand people."

Shit.

"I'm sorry, man. You're right. That was a stupid fucking thing to say. About as stupid as lumping all Muslims in with Al-Qaeda and the Taliban. I've been in and out of this region for more than twenty years. I should have known better."

He studies me, still wary, but appears to accept my apology.

"Faruk was highly intelligent. Perhaps even a genius. His brother makes him look like an idiot," Darius says. "I flew to Oxford to interview Raziq—I paid for the ticket myself—"

"Wait. You've met him?" Of everything I expected him to say, that was nowhere on the list.

"Yes. I wanted to know what he thought of his brother's endeavors. Even then, he was...fanatical. Extreme in every way. I remember thinking, 'It is good he is a doctor. If he were ever to join his brother, they would be unstoppable.'"

"Fuck. Why did he come back to Kabul, then? He's not running drugs, guns, or women. I'd know."

Darius holds my gaze, the gravity of his stare a physical weight pressing down on my shoulders. "Power. Money. Control. With the Taliban takeover, Afghanistan is becoming the country he always wanted it to be. One where men are revered, women are invisible, and he who has the most cash is treated like a king. Raziq could destabilize the entire region with a single word. He does not *need* to traffic in any of the usual ways. He controls those who do. Shapur is the lone holdout, and why the CIA is so interested in keeping him safe—and doing his job."

An uncomfortable silence stretches between us. Shapur won't be doing his job much longer. No wonder the man swore me to secrecy.

"If you're here to protect Shapur, get us that ride. It's the only way we live through this."

Hell, even if we could somehow teleport into the house and right back out again, we might not survive.

Darius rakes his fingers through his dark hair. "If the operators engage, there will be hell to pay."

"They won't. I've got an idea that should keep Raziq's men distracted. Make the call."

He nods and pulls out his phone. "The Viper's reputation is legend. As is yours. But my trust only goes so far. Break it, and you will find out who I truly am."

My respect for him rises a notch or two. I'd love to unpack his cryptic statement, but there will be time for that later.

Or we'll all be dead, and I won't give a damn.

CHAPTER THIRTY-SIX

Lisette

SUNRISE HAS COME AND GONE, and I am still alone. I had hoped Mateen would return. Hoped for even a few more minutes with my son before Raziq orders me to the roof for my punishment.

The closet held an assortment of plain, serviceable clothing to wear under the burka. Most of it black. I am a widow, I should not be surprised he would choose that color. The long-sleeved t-shirt will be stifling in the sun, but I hope it will provide at least a small bit of protection from the whip.

I sit on the bed, my hands folded in my lap, and try to stay awake. But the dark mesh over my eyes conspires with my exhaustion, and I nod off more than once.

The door slams open with a loud bang. I shoot to my feet. One of Raziq's men glares at me, and I think he is disappointed he did not catch me with my face uncovered.

He does not speak as he grabs my arm and pulls me from the room.

"Let go of me." I twist out of his hold. "There is nowhere for me to run. I am no threat to you."

His wild eyes terrify me. For a moment, I fear he is going to strike me. But he merely points down the hall. "Go."

I swallow my fear and hurry ahead of him. The house slippers make almost no noise on the polished tile floors. He directs me down the stairs, and around several corners before stopping me outside an open door.

"When will the contract be completed?" Raziq asks, his phone pressed to his ear. Papers are spread haphazardly over a dark wood desk. After a pause, he slams his fist down, rattling his tea cup. "You were supposed to deal with that particular *problem*. Why is she still making trouble?"

My *escort* shoves me into the office and points to a chair. I sit, pulling the sleeves of the burka over my sunburned hands.

"I cannot leave Kabul for another thirty-nine days." Raziq glares at me. "I have responsibilities here. But after that, my nephew and I will spend a month in Dubai. The heiress has been a thorn in my side for too long. If you do not deal with her soon, I will."

Throwing the phone onto the desk, he launches into a string of Dari curses so vile, I cringe. But then his words sink in. After thirty-nine days, he is taking Mateen out of Afghanistan. Without me.

Because I will be dead.

Tears prick at my eyes and clog my throat. If Nomar cannot find me, I have only weeks left to live. Only weeks left with my son. How can I teach him everything he needs to know when we have so little time together?

The phone buzzes. Raziq snatches it up and snarls, "If you do not have good news for me, hang up now."

A moment later, he strides out of his office and shouts for

several of his men. His footsteps slap against the tile, growing fainter and fainter.

He left me alone. In his office. I scan the desk, praying for something—anything—I can use as a weapon. But there is nothing. Not even a pen.

Quickly, I move some of the papers. A woman's photo stares back at me from the corner of one of them. She is beautiful. A shimmering silver headscarf covers most of her hair. Dark eyes, skin like fine burnished clay, and full lips.

Amani Skye.

I cannot make out most of Raziq's terrible handwriting, but one word leaps out at me.

Termination.

Folding the paper several times, I slip it under the burka and into the pocket of my light pants. And then I see a glint of metal. A paper clip securing a stack of balance sheets.

Faruk spent years locking me away. After he forgot me in a closet for three days, I taught myself how to pick locks. I do not know what good that will do me here, but closing my fingers around the twisted metal gives me a burst of hope.

I am no longer helpless. Trapped, yes. Terrified, yes. But this one small act reminds me who I have become.

I am Lisette Moreau. I am a mother. A florist. A French citizen. And I will fight for my life and that of my son for as long as I am able.

"Get up and follow me!" Raziq snaps from the doorway.

The paper clip almost tumbles from my shaking fingers, but I manage to slide it into my bra as I hurry after him.

Two of his men lead him down the hall and two more crowd me from behind. In the room where he made us watch the explosion, Mateen sits cross-legged on a cushion with the Quran in his lap. Bags swell under his eyes. He reads in Dari, but struggles with all but the simplest words. Until he sees me and throws the book aside.

"Maman!"

Raziq grabs his wrist when he jumps to his feet. "You do not disrespect the Quran. And I told you that you could have breakfast *after* you read five pages in both English and Dari. You still have half a page to go."

"But I am hungry!" he whines.

"Finish reading and you may eat."

Mateen looks to me and my heart aches. "Do what your uncle says. I can help you, if he allows it."

Raziq pushes Mateen back toward the cushion. "The boy will do this on his own. Naveed, stay with him until he finishes, then take him to the kitchen."

"I want to eat with Maman!" he says.

"Your mother is fasting today. And every day until I decide otherwise. You will see her at dinner. *If* you complete your lessons." He points to the discarded holy book. "Pick it up. Now."

"Please," I say softly. "Give me a moment with him."

He considers, then huffs. "One. And then we go to the roof."

Dropping to my knees, I smooth my hands down Mateen's arms. "Remember what we talked about last night, *mon bébé*. Your lessons are important."

"But why can't you eat with me?" He sits on the cushion with all the weight of pre-teen rebellion and crosses his arms.

"Your uncle wants me to fast. So I will fast. He is the head of this household and he makes the rules. We have to do what he says." I lean in so my lips brush his ear through the burka. "For now."

Mateen picks up the Quran and starts to read. Before he makes it through a single sentence, Raziq wraps his fingers around my upper arm and drags me from the room.

My muscles tremble with each shallow breath. Blood plasters the t-shirt to my back under the burka. At least three times, I felt my skin tear under Raziq's repeated blows.

He left me chained, on my knees, my arms mostly numb, with two of his men standing guard. Why? I cannot escape. After so long kneeling, I do not even think I can walk.

Tomorrow will be worse. How much more of this can my body take? I wanted to curse Raziq with each strike, and I fear I will soon be unable to pretend I deserve this fate.

It has been hours, and my mind wanders. Did Mateen get to eat? Where is he right now? Will his uncle let him play? Read anything besides the Quran? Rest?

The sun is almost directly over me, chasing the shadows away. Sweat stings my wounds. My hands are bright red. How much longer until fresh blisters form?

Through my tears, I watch a vulture soar across the sky. For a moment, I can almost hear its wings beating.

A dull whine from my left draws my gaze. Another bird? This one is smaller. Low to the ground.

One of the men jogs over to a rifle mounted on a swivel and peers through the scope. "Drones. Two of them. Tell the boss."

My heart leaps into my throat. Could this be Nomar? With my next breath, I give up on that brief moment of hope. Drones will do nothing against so many men. Against the twin guns on the roof.

Another drone approaches from the right. Still another skims the landscape directly in front of me. Four. Five. Six.

The first shot is so loud. My scream sounds far away. Muffled. The closest drone shatters into dust. The second swoops up so high, I have to crane my neck to see it, then plummets to the ground.

A plume of fire explodes from the impact, followed by dark smoke. The building shakes.

A second explosion. Then a third.

More shots. I cannot cover my ears. The chain between my wrists is too short.

The low *thump, thump, thump* of the vulture's wings returns. No. Not a bird. A helicopter.

Nomar

"She's on the roof," Austin says in my ear.

I raise the binoculars in time to see one of Raziq's men jerk Lisette to her feet and toss her over his shoulder. She struggles weakly as he disappears through a door to the house.

"Fuck. Not anymore." Passing the binoculars to Leo, I heft the Kestrel onto my shoulder. "Count it down, Sergeant."

The SOG team leader's focus is locked on the .50 caliber guns pointed right at us. "Thirty seconds."

Austin, Griff, Leo, and Darius shoulder their packs.

"Four kilometers away," Shapur says. He and his men are in an armored van barreling toward the house. Our backup if everything goes to shit.

Zephyr—and a couple of her friends—pilot one drone after another, driving them into the land mines surrounding the house. The explosions hid our approach for almost a full minute. But the gunners have spotted us now.

"Evasive maneuvers," the pilot snaps.

The Blackhawk banks steeply, then straightens out. Austin takes aim at one of the shooters. "Hold steady!" He fires three shots. "One down."

If I had any idea where Lisette and Mateen were, I'd send this rocket to the roof and take the rest of those fuckers out.

But instead, I point the sights at the twelve-foot wall surrounding the house and pull the trigger.

With a loud whistle, the payload screams for its target.

"Ten seconds! Get ready to drop." The man in black fatigues without a single insignia jerks his thumb toward the back of the beast. "Thank you for flying 'We Were Never Here' airlines. Take care with that first step. It's a steep one."

I hand him the rocket launcher and tug on the heavy welder's gloves.

Leo and Darius toss thick, weighted ropes off the sides of the Blackhawk.

Here goes nothing.

Bracing my feet on the edge of the deck, I grip the rope loosely. Across from me, Austin mirrors my position.

"See you on the other side," he says and jumps.

The rope slides through my loose grip, the ground racing up to meet my boots.

I tighten my fingers at the last minute. My body jerks. I jump the last four feet and pull my M4. A shot whizzes by my shoulder.

Tucking and rolling, I come up a dozen steps closer to the front door. Griff and Leo lay down cover fire until I get there. "Pritchard, tell me you're in position."

"On your mark," comes the reply in my ear.

I slap a charge around the door handle and set the timer. "Ten seconds. Starting now."

My boots slap against the hard-packed dirt as I book it around the corner of the house. Twin explosions shake the structure.

"Back door is down. Griff and I are going in," Austin says.

Darius slams his back into the wall next to me. "What are you waiting for, Viper?"

I take off at a run. "Not a damn thing."

Hold on, Lisette. I'm coming.

CHAPTER THIRTY-SEVEN

Lisette

THE FLOOR SHAKES AGAIN. Nomar found us. But Raziq has so many men. I cannot count the number I have seen, but it must be at least twenty. There are a dozen rooms on this floor. At least half as many above and below.

I need to get to my son. But one of the guards threw me back into Mateen's bedroom and locked the door. My blisters tear as I dig my fingers under the burka and pull the paper clip from my bra. It takes me precious seconds to straighten the metal and break it in two.

My legs are still numb, my arms not much better, but I drag myself to the door. Searing pain snakes around my torso as I reach for the knob.

I can do this.

The first piece of metal scrapes against the tumblers. Quiet pops and dull bangs sound every few seconds. Tears clog my throat. Nomar could die. Austin. Griff. Leo. Because of me. The last tumbler falls, and the knob turns so quickly, I lose my grip and collapse to the floor with a whimper.

But the door swings open.

Muffled shouts come from down the hall. I cannot make out the words.

Pulling myself up is the hardest thing I have ever done. Until I try to take a step. Dizzy, I collapse against the door jamb.

The black mesh over my eyes is suddenly so claustrophobic, my breath catches in my chest. My hands shake, but I rip the cape from my head. Whatever Raziq does to me now, I do not care. I need to see. To be...*me* again.

A man rushes out of one of the rooms by the stairs and heads down to the first floor. He did not see me, and I creep closer. My muscles tremble violently. There are so many steps, and no bannister.

Mateen is down there.

I can do this. For him. Bracing my hands against the walls, I try to hurry. But halfway down, my foot catches in the too-long burka. I fall—in slow motion until the last second. Then everything moves so quickly. My wrist cracks against one step. My head hits another. Whimpering, I draw my knees to my chest.

"Get the boy!" Raziq shouts. "Bring him to the garage and start the Hummer."

The garage. If he takes Mateen away from this place, I may never find him again. Using the wall for support, I push to my feet and chance a quick look out of the stairwell. Raziq's office is to the left. Two men stand in the doorway, arms crossed, guarding their boss.

"Let me go! I want to see Maman!" Mateen cries from my right.

One of the taller guards—Naveed, I think—strides from the sitting room at the end of the hall with my son thrown over his shoulder. "Quiet! Your mother is not coming with us."

He screams so loud, it hurts my ears. Naveed slaps his bottom, hard.

"No! Stop!" I come within a few steps of them before Naveed whirls around, his gun pointed at my head.

"The boss wants you dead, whore," he says with a sneer.

"Maman!" Mateen twists and digs his fingers into Naveed's black hair, pulling hard enough, pain crinkles at the corners of the man's eyes. His legs flail, one foot catching the guard's arm.

The gun clatters to the floor between us. I dive for it. My fingers close over the handle. It is so heavy.

Naveed slams Mateen into the wall. His body goes limp.

No!

I aim for his leg. He still holds my son. The shot hits him in the calf. Blood stains his brown pants. He drops to one knee with a groan. Mateen slides off his shoulder and curls into a ball on the ground.

His eyes flutter open, then lock on me. Tears slip down his cheek.

"Run!"

Naveed lunges for Mateen, and I fire again. This time, the shot hits his chest. He curses under his breath. Weaker this time.

"Go, baby. Nomar came for us. Hide somewhere until he finds you. Or I do. Please!"

He nods and backs slowly down the hall.

"You are both...dead," Naveed wheezes.

I should be scared. My son was within reach, and I sent him away. But in my heart, I find only determination. Staring at the man who felt me up in the market, who probably stripped me down to my bra and panties, who locked me to that railing until I burned, I smile at him. "Then I am taking you with me."

This close, I cannot miss. Two shots pierce his heart. His

eyes widen. One hand presses to the wound, but it is no use. There is too much blood. He falls seconds before footsteps sound from behind me.

A rough hand grabs my hair. I am flying. My body hits the wall. Darkness curls around the edges of my vision. The gun. Where is the gun? My fingers won't move. My arms. My legs. I cannot feel anything but pain.

Raziq's face swims in and out of focus over me. "Mateen will watch you and your lover die. And then I will take him somewhere no one will ever be able to find him."

He steps away, and one of his men flips me over. My arms are pinned behind my back. Something hard wraps around my wrists.

I only have one thought running through my head.

Did Mateen get away?

Nomar

The shot grazes my hip. It's not serious, but pisses me off enough, I grab an expensive looking vase from a table and lob it at the two assholes shooting at us from behind twin pillars at the end of the hall.

It shatters into dust. Leo pops up from behind a heavy table, fires twice, and sinks back down onto his ass. "This is fucking ridiculous."

Austin's voice in my ear agrees. "We're pinned down in the northeast corner. Haven't made it more than thirty feet. There are too many goddamn blind spots in this place."

Leo pulls a grenade from a pouch on his hip. "I can clear a couple of those right now."

"No!" I glare at him. "We don't know where Lisette and Mateen are. No explosives."

With a muttered curse, he hefts his M4. But then he pushes to his knees and fires at the door behind us. A body hits the polished tile. "I thought Shapur was supposed to be watching our six."

"We are trying to get into the garage," Shapur says over comms. "Do you want him driving out of here? With your woman and the boy?"

"Need a little help out here," Darius calls. "Another six men just arrived."

Leo holds out his hand. "Give me the fucking grenade. I've been itching to blow something up all day. This is my chance."

"Fine. I'm done with this shit. Take 'em all down. I'm going to get Lisette back."

"Not alone you're not," he mutters, but I'm already bobbing and weaving toward the pillars.

Another explosion rocks the ground. Behind me, a piece of the ceiling crashes to the floor. Just the distraction I need. With my M4 held like a club, I corner the pillar and slam the rifle into the nearest asshole's face. His nose shatters, and blood spurts down his shirt.

Before the second man can raise his weapon, I pull my Beretta and fire two shots between his eyes. "I'm in. Proceeding to Target A."

A high-pitched scream sends ice flooding my veins. Mateen.

"He got away!" someone shouts. "Find him!"

The kid was in some sort of large space on the first floor this morning. Zephyr thought it was a sitting room. But there are half a dozen other rooms between here and there, and I have to clear each one of them. Precious minutes tick by. Minutes Raziq could be using to kill Lisette. Or get away.

Darius meets me back in the hall with Griff on his heels.

"Leo went to help Austin. They are clearing the east wing now. No sign of Lisette and Mateen?"

"No. The kid screamed, but that was at least two minutes ago. Shapur, tell me you got into that garage."

Another explosion, and his voice over comms is strained. "We did. There was a Hummer running inside. We have... disabled it."

The target room is just up ahead. Cushions line the walls. Blankets are piled haphazardly in the corner. A low table sits in the center, holding a copy of the Quran along with a tea pot and several cups. I lift one of the cups to my lips. "Still warm."

"Raziq's office is around the next corner," Griff says. "Go. We've got your back."

A quiet sob stops me before I make it back into the hall. Fuck. It came from the far corner of the room. "Mateen? Kiddo, it's Nomar."

Silence. I look to Darius. He nods. I didn't imagine the sound.

"Firefly?"

The blankets move.

"Cover me."

Griff aims at the pile, while Darius keeps watch at the door.

"Mateen? It's okay. You can come out now." I start pulling the blankets off one at a time, until his black curls peek through. He wriggles free and throws his arms around my waist.

"You came! Maman knew you were alive! She told me so. Did you find her? Uncle Raziq hurt her. I told him I wanted *you* to be my uncle, not him."

The lump in my throat makes it hard to speak. "I want that too, kiddo. Do you know where your mom is? When did you last see her?"

His lower lip wobbles. "I...maybe that way?" He points to the left. "She told me to run and I did, but then some of Uncle's men came and one of them grabbed me, but I kicked him and he let me go."

"Good job." I ruffle his hair. "I'm going to find her. But I need you to go with Griff and Darius."

"No! I want to stay with you!" he whines.

Over comms, Austin breaks in. "The first floor's clear. They must have gone up."

"Up? Why the hell would they do that?" I turn to Mateen. "Is there another way out of here besides by car?"

"One of Uncle's men said the garage was too dangerous and he should go to the roof and wait for a helicopter." The kid presses closer to me. "Is Maman with him?"

Leo rushes through the door. "I saw them. Raziq and three of his men. One of them was carrying Lisette. They were headed to the stairs."

"Mateen," I kneel in front of the boy and rest my hands on his shoulders. "Go with Griff and Darius. They'll keep you safe."

Griff holds out his left hand. "Nomar said you liked robots, right?" he asks. Mateen nods, and Griff uncurls his fingers. "Touch 'em."

"Whoa. Are *you* a robot?" His wide eyes stare up at Griff like he's found a new hero. I'm almost jealous.

"Nope. But my arm is titanium. I'll tell you how it works if you come with me while Nomar gets your mom back."

Zephyr breaks in over comms. "Another three vehicles just showed up. Shapur's got his hands full. One of the assholes blew out the tires on the van and you've got six men headed for the front door."

"Fuck." I meet Mateen's terrified gaze. "Change of plans. We're *all* going to get your mom. But you need to stay by Griff's side no matter what. Okay?"

He nods so hard his curls bounce. "Okay. You won't let him hurt her again, right?"

"No, Mateen. I won't."

Leo and Austin take the second floor, clearing one room at a time while Darius, Griff, Mateen, and I climb the last flight of stairs. "What's up here, Mateen?" Griff asks.

He shrugs. "Uncle only brought me up here once. Yesterday. Maman was outside. She was scared."

I'm going to kill Raziq. Slowly. Painfully. For everything he's done to her—and for making Mateen see his mother's fear.

Austin jogs around a corner, Leo on his heels. "We doing this?"

"We're doing this." I meet Griff's gaze. "Keep the kid safe. Leo? If anyone comes up the stairs, shoot them. Blow them up. I don't give a fuck."

"Chopper incoming," Zephyr says over comms. "It's eight minutes out."

Eight minutes.

Austin and Darius take positions on either side of the door. They draw their Berettas and look over at me. "On three."

I count it down, and Austin yanks on the handle.

Bright sunlight hits my face. Two fig trees in large pots sway in the gentle breeze. A metal railing surrounds an almost luxurious outdoor space, with a pair of shackles glinting in the sun.

A flash of brown to my left. I drop to my knee and fire, taking out one of Raziq's men. His pistol bounces and tumbles through the slats of the railing. Austin's rifle blast obliterates a second asshole's face. One left.

"Lower your weapons or she dies!" Raziq shouts.

The three of us turn in unison. At the far corner of the roof, a set of steps leads up another ten feet to a large, empty space. We should have known it was a helipad. Every insane megalomaniac has one at their disposal.

Raziq presses himself to the corner of the railing, Lisette held in front of him. A dark bruise swells on her cheek. Another creeps up her neck. Raziq bands an arm around her waist. I can't get a shot off. The man's only an inch taller than she is. A few feet away, the last of his goons points an AK-47 at us.

"Not going to happen, asshole. Lisette goes free, or I'll burn down the world—and you with it."

Lisette mouths, "*Mateen?*"

I give her a tiny nod. Her shoulders slump. Tears shimmer on her cheeks.

"Shit!" Griff says over comms. "There's a fucking elevator! We're in trouble here. Sending the kid to you."

Mateen slips through the door. Lisette screams, "No! Mateen, stay back!"

I catch the kid in one arm before he can run to his mother. On either side of me, Austin and Darius press closer, weapons still at the ready.

"Even better," Raziq says, a gleeful edge to his voice. He wraps his hand around Lisette's neck and squeezes. She struggles against his hold. Her cheeks turn red. "I will give you the woman. But my nephew comes with me."

I take a step forward with the kid held close. "I came here for Lisette *and* Mateen."

The dull *whomp, whomp, whomp* of rotors sounds from the east.

"You want to live? I'll let you get into that helicopter. But Lisette goes free."

"Mateen, come to me," Raziq orders. "Or I will kill your

mother." I don't have time to fire a shot. He shoves Lisette, bending her over the railing so her upper body dangles in the air.

She screams and struggles, her gaze locked on the ground so far below. Thin ropes bind her wrists. The only thing holding her in place? Raziq's weight against her legs.

If he dies, she falls.

"Please, Nomar," Lisette cries. "Take Mateen. He is all that matters."

Raziq shakes her arm so hard, her head almost hits the railing. "If you do that, she dies, *Nomar*."

The helicopter is almost here. Two minutes. Maybe three. Griff and Leo are still pinned down inside. Austin and Darius stand next to me. Their anger is a physical presence. As is mine. An energy that's either going to save us, or kill us all.

Mateen's arms wrap around my neck. "Help Maman," he whispers in my ear. "Like you did before."

God. How? I only have seconds. Raziq is at least thirty feet away. If I shoot him, she dies. If I hand over Mateen, we all die. Anything I say to Austin and Darius, he'll hear.

"He plays soccer now. He's good. Averaged two goals a match in summer league."

Ford's words from less than a week ago. If this doesn't work—no. It *has* to work.

I set Mateen on his feet, kneel, and drop my voice to a whisper. "Your mom says you have a killer back heel kick. When I tell you, show it to me and hide, okay?"

Confusion furrows his dark brows, but he nods.

Twisting one arm behind me, I make a fist, then splay two of my fingers wide and point toward the guy with the AK-47. Austin coughs. Darius is probably confused as fuck, but he'll catch on. I hope.

"I am losing my patience!" The helicopter gets louder. It's so close, Raziq has to yell to be heard.

"Zephyr, need a distraction," Austin mutters.

Shapur's voice fills my ear. "I can give you one. Thirty seconds."

After I hug Mateen tightly, I slide my pistol halfway to Raziq and straighten.

Lisette wails, "No!"

"It'll be okay, sweetheart." With a glance behind me, I give the order. "Lower your weapons." Darius tosses his M4 to the side, and Austin kicks his Beretta away.

"Pull her up, asshole."

Raziq narrows his eyes. "Mateen, come here," he shouts and jerks Lisette back in front of him.

Tears shine on her cheeks. Her entire body shakes with her sobs. The look of betrayal in her eyes is enough to destroy me.

"I love you, Lisette. With all my heart." I give Mateen's shoulder a squeeze. "Go to your uncle, kiddo. Nice and slow."

He takes two tentative steps, then glances back at me. "Nomar...?"

Fuck. If this doesn't work, I'll lose them both. I'll lose myself. "We'll play soccer—sorry, *football*—again soon. You can show me that kick you love."

The helicopter's only a few hundred feet away. The air starts to pulse around us.

Shapur counts down in my ear. "Five. Four. Three..."

"Now, Mateen!"

He takes off and drives his heel back against the gun. It spins and skitters over the concrete. A high-pitched whine fills the air. Shapur found the goddamn rocket launcher.

The helicopter explodes into flames. It spins out of control, then plummets like a stone.

I dive for the Beretta. Mateen is only a blur as he passes me. Lisette screams. Raziq tries to pick her up and *throw* her over the railing, but she plants her feet on the edge and locks her knees.

I fire.

Raziq doesn't move. His mouth opens. His arms are still tight around Lisette's torso. They fall backwards onto the concrete together. It's so slow. Like a movie played at a quarter speed. A trickle of blood stains his temple.

Austin jogs over to the stairs. I didn't even notice who shot the last of Raziq's men. Didn't hear the shot. I don't give a fuck who did it as long as he's dead.

I drop the gun and scramble for Lisette. Behind me, Darius tells Griff he's coming to help.

Snapping the thin cord around her wrists, I pull her into my arms. She cries out, her entire body going rigid before her head falls onto my shoulder and she collapses against me. Boneless. "What's wrong? What hurts?"

"Mateen?" she whispers.

"He's safe, sweetheart. You're both safe. But I need to know where you're hurt."

She doesn't answer.

Fear wraps around my heart, squeezing so hard, I can't breathe.

I lower her so I can see her face. She's so pale. Bruises mar her jaw. Her cheeks. Dark circles swell under her eyes. The sticky warmth of blood soaks through my sleeve.

Mateen throws himself down next to her. "Maman? Did you see my kick?"

Lisette's weak smile is the most beautiful thing in this world. "Yes, *mon bébé*. You...were so...brave."

"Time to go!" Austin calls. "The house is clear, but we've got two vehicles approaching at high speed from the south."

"What about the van? Zephyr said it was toast." Griff staggers over to us, rubbing his left shoulder. Behind him, Leo wipes blood from his cheek and slams a fresh magazine into his pistol.

Shapur chuckles over comms. "We will travel in style, my friends. Come to the garage and see what I have prepared for you."

CHAPTER THIRTY-EIGHT

Lisette

THE ELEVATOR JERKS TO A STOP, and I bury my face against Nomar's neck so I do not cry out. He cradles me carefully. One arm under my knees, the other pressing to the middle of my back.

I tried to walk on my own, but my legs would not support me. Mateen holds Griff's hand. In front of us, Austin, Leo, and another man I do not know stand ready to fight.

The doors slide open. The scent of blood, harsh and metallic, fills my nose. Griff turns Mateen to face him. "I'm going to carry you, kiddo. Close your eyes until I tell you to open them. Okay?"

"With your robot arm?"

Griff chuckles. "Yep. Hold onto me." He picks my son up and totes him down the hall, stepping over bodies every few feet.

Nomar follows Griff—with me still in his arms. He tries to be gentle, but each step is pure agony on my abused back.

So many of Raziq's men. Most still clutch their automatic

weapons, even in death.

The enormity of what Nomar and his friends have done washes over me. They risked their lives for me. For Mateen. And they won. Raziq is dead. Along with most—if not all—of his men.

"Come, come, my friends!" a man with a local accent calls. I stiffen.

"It's okay, sweetheart. Shapur's with us," Nomar says.

Shapur. I know that name. The man he worked for when he left Boston. The man who sold women.

"What...is he...doing here?" I manage.

Nomar peers down at me. His eyes hold so many emotions. Pain. Worry. Love. "He saved our lives. Broke us out of the house in Kabul minutes before Raziq blew it up. And he got out of the flesh trade. Hell, he's practically legit now."

"Excuse me," the man next to Austin says. "Did I do *nothing* for you? May I remind you who called Shapur in the first place?"

"Darius, you need anything—ever—the Rescue Operations Group is at your disposal," Austin says.

With every passing minute, less and less of what is happening around me makes sense. Darius called Shapur. Shapur saved Nomar's life.

"You can open your eyes now." Griff sets Mateen on his feet inside a large garage. Wide doors at the far end of the space open to reveal a road stretching toward the city.

"Whoa!" Mateen's gaze sweeps over a dozen different vehicles. A large HumVee smolders to my left. Several trucks with shattered windows do not look drivable.

Shapur waves us over to the largest SUV I have ever seen. "Is that a *stretch* Escalade?" I ask. The man chuckles.

"We're not outrunning *anyone* in that thing," Nomar says.

"In this, we do not need to." Rapping on the door, he grins. "Bulletproof. And look." He reaches inside and flips a switch on the dashboard. The roof opens, and a very large, very lethal-looking machine gun rises from within.

"I'm convinced," Griff says, opening one of the back doors. In the distance, dust swirls from the road where two black spots grow larger and larger.

Austin slides behind the wheel. "We're going to have company soon. Everybody inside. Now. I don't know how the hell we're supposed to get this thing through the streets around the safe house, but—"

"You go right to the airport," Shapur says. "Arash's brother will get your bags and meet us there."

Austin starts the engine. "You're a lifesaver."

Nomar settles me in the center of the front row of plush, leather seats, and Griff lifts Mateen up so he can climb in next to me. As soon as my son snuggles to my side, I start to cry.

"Maman? What's wrong?" He reaches up to touch my cheek. "Nomar came like you said he would. We can go home now, right?"

Does he know that his uncle is dead? He must. He is a smart boy.

"We are," Nomar says as he takes a seat on my other side. His voice is not steady, and when he wraps his arms around us, he starts to shake. I do not understand until the first tear hits my neck.

"Hang on," Austin calls. "This is going to get bumpy."

Darius climbs over the last row of seats, braces himself against the opening in the roof, and runs his hand over the weapon. "I have always wanted to fire one of these."

Nomar straightens and drags the back of his hand over his cheeks. "Mateen, cover your ears, buddy. This is going to be loud."

My son stares up at Darius in awe. "He's going to shoot that big gun?"

"Not until you cover your ears," Darius replies with a wink.

The SUV bounces over the uneven road, and soon, I slip away on endless waves of pain. I cannot feel Nomar's arm around me. Darkness steals the sight of my son's messy curls. Gunfire is all I can hear. And then suddenly, it is quiet. A welcome warmth spreads through my limbs.

I take a shuddering breath. The world lightens until I can see Mateen's worried face peering up at me. "Better?" Nomar asks. "Griff gave you a shot of morphine."

So that is why everything is softer now.

"You were crying for a long time," Mateen says. "And Nomar could not get you to stop."

"I am so sorry." For the first time in two days, the sharp edge of pain lessens, and I wrap my arms around my son. "You have been very brave, Mateen. So much braver than me."

"We're ten minutes from the airfield," Austin calls over his shoulder.

Ten minutes? I blink away the last of my tears and stare out the front windshield. We are back in Kabul. "How...we only just left..."

Nomar cups my jaw, his thumb skating over my cheek. "It's been almost forty minutes, sweetheart. You wouldn't answer me or Mateen. Wouldn't even open your eyes. I thought—"

I cannot stand the pain in his eyes. Leaning closer, I brush my lips to his. It is barely a kiss. A single moment of connection. But it settles me in a way I did not know I needed. I think it settles him too.

But when Austin slows and pulls through a gate, I grab Nomar's arm. "I am not covered. My face...my hair. We will be stopped!"

Across from us, Shapur chuckles. "You are with the great

Shapur Khan. No one will dare."

"And if they do," Leo says, "they can have a nice little talk with my new friend Kalishnakov." He pats the automatic rifle on the floor in front of him. "Kali can be very persuasive."

"You *named* the gun?" Nomar scoffs. "Does Domina know you're cheating on her with an AK-47?"

"Domina knows she's it for me. My relationship with Kali is purely platonic."

"What does...platonic mean?" Mateen asks.

Nomar's cheeks turn a dark red. "Shit. Uh...shoot. It's when a man and a woman don't hold hands or kiss, kiddo. When they're just friends."

"Oh." He nods solemnly, then snuggles closer to me.

The SUV glides to a stop. Leo and Griff get out first, followed by Darius.

"Lisette?" Shapur holds out his hand. "It was an honor to meet the woman who brought the Viper into being. He loves you very much, you know."

I nod as Shapur brings my fingers to his lips. He is so different than I expected. This is no warlord. He has more in common with my father than Faruk or Raziq. But then I notice the simple silver band he wears. Perhaps marriage softened him.

Nomar nudges Mateen's shoulder. "Go with Griff, kiddo. He'll let you pick any seat on the plane you want. Your mom and I will be there in just a minute."

Your mom and I.

It sounds so right when he says those words.

Dropping his voice, he leans closer to Shapur. "Take Hajira and the girls and run, my friend. Half of Kabul knows Raziq is dead by now. If you don't get out soon..."

"We are leaving tonight," he says. "Hajira has been packed for a week."

"I owe you everything, Shapur. When you're clear, you

know where we'll be."

***

Nomar

Mateen presses his forehead to the window and watches the city fall away. Zephyr worked a small miracle getting us *another* last-minute flight.

"Are we going back to Turkey?" Lisette asks. Her pupils are half blown from the morphine, but she's no longer sobbing in pain, so I'll take the win.

"Not this time. In three hours, we'll be in Dubai. It's another seven to Toulouse from there."

"Dubai?" She fumbles in her pocket and pulls out a folded piece of paper. "I...Raziq had this in his office. He said he was going to take Mateen there after...after..." Tears fill her eyes.

"Shhh. He's right next to you, sweetheart. No one can touch either of you here."

I smooth the paper out on my thigh. The woman in the photo is stunning. Smooth skin, glossy black hair under a glittering headscarf, and kohl-lined eyes. "Amani Skye? Who is this?"

"What did you say?" Across the aisle, Darius unbuckles his seatbelt and jerks to his feet. "Give me that." He stares at the paper like he's seeing a ghost. "It cannot be."

"Darius?"

If Lisette weren't squeezing my hand so hard my fingers ached, I'd get up and shake the man. He can't take his eyes off the woman's picture.

"Pritchard?" Darius turns to Austin, and the desperation in his voice is one I know all too well. "I am in need of that favor. Now."

LISETTE FELL asleep as the plane crossed into Pakistan. After the fifth time Mateen asked me if she'd be okay, I pulled him into my lap and wrapped my arms around him. Now, he snores softly with his head on my shoulder.

I couldn't give him an answer. I don't even know what she's been through the past twenty-four hours.

The comms device in my ear crackles to life as the plane starts its descent. "There's an ambulance waiting for you on the tarmac," Zephyr says. "They'll check Lisette out while the plane refuels. If she needs medical care immediately, she'll have it."

I'd thank her, but she's already moved on. "Darius? I got you a car and a hotel room at the Five Points Dubai. A laptop, encrypted burner, and clean ID will be delivered before midnight."

"I can never repay you for this."

"Anyone Raziq wanted dead is worth saving," Austin replies. "Are you absolutely sure you don't want us to stay in Dubai for a few days? Nomar needs to get Lisette and Mateen home, but Griff, Leo, and I can hang out until you know what's up."

"No. I need to do this on my own."

He won't tell us who the woman is—or how he knows her. Only that she's "important."

"Darius?" I pull out my phone and text him a number. "I trust Matt with my life. Tell him I sent you, and he'll hook you up with anything you need."

"Thank you. I admit, you are not what I expected," he says. "I hope they will be all right."

The plane touches down, and I tighten my arms around Mateen.

"I hope so too."

Three Days Later

MATEEN THUDS DOWN THE STAIRS, his hair standing up in all directions. "Nomar?"

"In the kitchen, kiddo. You want pancakes or bacon and eggs this morning?"

"Pancakes. Is Maman going to come down today?" He stares up at the second floor and worries his lower lip between his teeth.

"I don't know. But if anything can help her feel better, it's a batch of chocolate chip pancakes. Want to help?"

"Okay." He climbs up on the stool next to me, and I hand him a bowl. "Crack the eggs in there, then use the whisk and beat them until they're all one color."

He focuses intently on his task while I measure out the dry ingredients. Someone cleaned up the mess I left in Lisette's entryway and fixed her door, so for the past three days, we've been holed up in her house pretending to be a family.

The EMTs in Dubai stitched up five deep wounds across her back and gave her a portable CT scan. She was damn lucky. No internal bleeding. Nothing broken. But they warned me she'd take weeks to fully heal.

Mateen didn't blink an eye the first night when he climbed into bed with Lisette and found me next to her. He simply lay down between us and fell asleep.

He laughs for the first time when I flip the pancakes over and he sees the chocolate chips arranged in a smiley face. I have to rummage in the small fridge for a moment so he doesn't see me with tears in my eyes.

Even with everything he's been through in his short life, he's still kind. Sensitive. Observant. He understands more than the average nine-year-old. Maybe that's why he hasn't asked when I'm leaving again.

Because he knows I'm not going anywhere.

Once he's settled on the couch with his plate and Panama vs. Brazil on the TV, I carry a tray upstairs to Lisette's bedroom.

She's managed to sit up on her own, though from the lack of color in her cheeks, it cost her. "Fuck. Use the bell, sweetheart. I would have come right up."

"It was going to hurt either way," she says simply. "And I am not helpless."

"No. But you *are* injured. I'll get you a pain pill."

She catches my fingers in hers before I can reach for the bottle on the nightstand. "They make me dizzy, and I want to talk to you."

I set the tray on her dresser and crawl back into bed next to her. She's slept so much since we got back, and Mateen hasn't wanted to be far from her side. We've played *a lot* of FIFA in this room. I even taught him how to make a blanket fort.

Lisette snuggles against my chest. One of her hands slides under my t-shirt to play with the barbs piercing my nipples.

"Fuck, sweetheart. We can't. Not yet."

"I know." She smiles, and though her eyes are wan, she looks more like herself than she has since she was taken. "But I can dream. In a few days, maybe."

Lisette wraps her hand around the back of my neck and pulls me close to kiss me. She's slept in my arms. Cried in them when the pain got to be too much. I've helped her to the bathroom. Held her in the tub. Washed her hair. But doing more...felt wrong. I needed her to take that first step.

"Nomar, before we went to the market, I was so scared. I *knew* Raziq would kill me, and I thought...if I told you I loved you, it would make everything worse. That if I held onto the words and kept them only for me, that no one could take them from me. Not even him." A tear shimmers in her eye. "But as soon as his men grabbed me, I knew I had been wrong. Because I do love you. I should have told you then. And every day since."

"I love you, Lisette. I've loved you for three years, and I don't plan on stopping. Ever." Sliding a hand into her hair, I touch my forehead to hers. "I want us to be a family. I want dates, long walks along the river, and hours spent in bed exploring one another. But, I also want pancake breakfasts, parent-teacher conferences—do they have those in France?—and all those cold football matches in the rain."

Her eyes widen. "You read my letter."

"I wanted to write you one of my own. I didn't mean to pry. But...I want all of it, Lisette. With you *and* Mateen."

She chews on her lower lip, and I start to panic.

"This is all too fast. I'm sorry. Forget I said anything." I start to pull away, but Lisette grabs my arm.

"It is not too fast, Nomar." She winces but manages to straddle me. "I love you. And I want all those same things. Except for the parent-teacher conferences. They are so boring. Almost painful. I want as few of those as possible. But Mateen is a good student who loves school. We will be lucky, I think."

I press my lips to hers. Lisette drapes her arms around my neck, her nipples hardening to tight nubs under the silky t-shirt. The little moan she makes promises more, and I draw back to meet her gaze.

"Oh, we're definitely lucky, sweetheart. We found each other. Twice. That's the luckiest damn thing in the world."

EPILOGUE

Two Months Later

Lisette

THE BELL over the flower shop door jingles, and I float out of
the back room, dancing on anticipation.

"Are you ready, sweetheart?" Nomar unbuttons his leather
jacket in the warmth of the shop. His dark blue dress shirt is
open at the neck, several whorls of ink peeking out.

"Fleur? I am leaving. I will see you in the morning!"

"Have a good night, honey," the older woman calls from
behind the counter. "And you should take tomorrow off. In
case you need to rest." She winks at me, and Nomar chuckles.

"I'll make sure she doesn't get out of bed until at least
noon," he says. "Thanks, Fleur."

Not long after we returned home, Fleur showed up at the
house with so many flowers and plants, they filled every flat
surface. She'd only stayed for an hour, but in that time, I'd
cried on her shoulder and found a small bit of *me* again.

My phone buzzes, and I glance down at the screen.

Noele: Are you certain you do not need me to cook for Saturday?

I stare at the message for several seconds before I reply.

Lisette: Nomar is making tamales. He says the recipe serves at least ten people.

Noele: Very well. Marcel and I will arrive at seven.

My sister and I have barely talked since she listed my profile on EuroMatch. She blames herself for everything that happened, and though I wish I could tell her it was not her fault, I have yet to be able to say the words. Because they are not true.

Raziq would have found me eventually. He was too rich. He had too many resources at his disposal. But as he was whipping me the first day, he confirmed he found me through that one photo.

"What's wrong?" Nomar asks.

I show him the phone.

"Are you sure you're ready?" He wraps his arms around me, and I snuggle against his chest. My back still twinges from time to time. Five fresh scars pull tight when I reach for a vase on a high shelf.

"I miss her," I say softly. "I do not know how to forgive her, but maybe in person, it will be easier."

Nomar threads his fingers through my hair, tips my head back, and slants his lips to mine. The kiss is all-consuming, his tongue seeking entrance. I melt against him, letting him take, not caring that Fleur is only a short distance away.

The older woman clears her throat as my hands slide up Nomar's chest, finding the nipple piercings through the silk blend of his shirt.

"Sorry, Fleur. This is a big night for us," Nomar says, his cheeks a dark crimson.

She shuffles over with a single red rose in her hand and offers it to me. "I know, dear. So get to it."

With his arm around my shoulders, we stroll down Rue du Parc to the first restaurant we ever visited together. We have not been back since, and I am surprised when the maître d' leads us to the same table with rose petals scattered over the table cloth.

"Someone planned ahead," I tease.

Nomar's dark eyes hold the same intensity that drew me to him the very first time we met. When I was terrified my son would die, that my husband would kill me, that I would never escape. But now, the emotion behind them is not fear. It is love. The kind of love that is so rare, when you find it, you do *anything* to nurture it, to keep it safe. The kind of love that lasts a lifetime.

"There is nothing I won't do for you, Lisette." Nomar lays his hand, palm up, on the table, and waits for me to drape my fingers over his. Suddenly, he is uncertain. Worried, even. "We never talked about...what happens long term. For the first month, I stayed because you needed me. You were in so much pain, Mateen was having nightmares, we had to make sure no one from Raziq's empire was left to ever come after you again. But now, every morning I wake up and wonder if this is the day you'll decide you need space—space you have every right to—and you'll ask me to leave."

"Nomar!" I grasp his hand tightly so he cannot pull away. "I love you. Mateen loves you too. Why would I ever ask you to go?"

The relief in his eyes would break my heart if I were not so certain of his love for me.

"Because everything moved so fast. Especially for Mateen. I disappear for three years, he gets kidnapped, and then suddenly, I'm back again. Moving in. Playing house. Being..."

"A father?" The first tears burn my eyes, lending a shimmer to the candlelight flickering around us. "He loves you, Nomar. You are his hero." A smile curves my lips. "Though I suspect he wishes *you* were the one with the 'robot arm' and not Uncle Griff."

Nomar laughs, and the tension in his shoulders melts away. "I can't believe Griff FaceTimed his visit to the prosthetics clinic in Bethesda."

"Mateen is still talking about that." I keep hold of Nomar's hand. My sleeve rides up, the burn scars around my wrist shiny. A flash of memory darkens the mood. The hot sun beating down on me. My hands blistered and bright red. But I blink it away. This is a time for happier things.

"He invited us to San Diego for Thanksgiving," Nomar says, bringing me back to the present. "Austin and Mik will be there, and I think Leo and Domina are coming too."

"That is...in a couple of weeks? American Thanksgiving always confuses me. It changes dates, yes?"

"Two weeks from Thursday. Mateen would have to miss a few days of school. Would his teachers be okay with that?"

I love that he always thinks of my son. In two short months, he has become a father, whether he believes it or not. "After what happened, they will understand. And Mateen is a good student. If he falls behind at all, we can find him a tutor over the holidays."

"Okay. I'll book the flights tomorrow," he says. There is still a hint of uncertainty in his voice, and I tug his hand closer.

"Are we done discussing foolish things?"

"Foolish?"

"Yes. You leaving? You believing I would ever ask you to go? You doubting the family we have made together? You are mine, Nomar. And I am yours. That is all that matters."

NOMAR ENTERS the twelve-digit code on the keypad, and the light blinks green. Only days after we arrived back in France, a small team of women showed up to install a state-of-the-art security system. Panic buttons in each room, cameras over every door and window, and remote monitoring capabilities.

It helped me feel safe when every noise frightened me. When I still worried I would wake up one day and Nomar would be gone. Or worse—that someone would come after my son once more.

But there has been no threat, and Mateen is at Philippe's house for a sleep over. His first since he was taken. I have lunch with Amelie once a week, and Laurent—after a month in the hospital—is even back to work.

Someone—Nomar would not tell me who, but I have my suspicions—paid all of their medical bills *and* arranged for counseling.

"Do you want a glass of wine?" he asks me once he has armed the system again.

"I want you." His jacket lands on the floor as I run my hands down his arms. "This is our first night alone in... months. No one to hear us."

"You mean hear *you*." He presses a kiss to the curve of my neck. "You aren't quiet when you come, sweetheart. I should probably find someone to soundproof the bedroom walls..."

"Enough talking." I cup the back of his neck and pull his head down so I can claim his mouth. Sucking his lower lip between my teeth, I bite down gently until his arousal strains his zipper.

He groans. His hips grind against me, and then his hands are in my hair. Taking control of the kiss in a way he knows I love. That I *need*.

We stagger together toward the stairs, still connected, desperate, as if we have been apart for months—even years—rather than the short hours of the workday.

His hands wrap under my thighs, lifting me, and I drape my arms around his neck. I love it when he holds me. When he carries me like I weigh nothing at all.

In our bedroom, he strips off my red sweater. "My God, Lisette. You look…"

"Do you like it?" I finger the strap of the black lace bra. "You should take off my pants then."

"I love it. I love…*you*." He drops to his knees, flicks open the button at my waist, and slides the linen pants to the floor. His nose presses to my mound, inhaling deeply through the lace thong. "I can taste you already, Lisette. How long have you been wet for me?"

"All day."

Nomar pinches one of my nipples, and I cry out, my arousal flooding the thin scrap of fabric between my thighs. He tongues the lace, then slides a finger under the hem to swirl around my channel and ghost over my clit.

The light pressure is almost too much. I buck against his hand, needing more. Needing *him*.

My hands shake when he stands and lets me unbutton his dress shirt. I shove it off his shoulders, trapping his arms so I can have my way with him—if only for a few minutes before I need him to take control once more.

I flick one of the thick barbs with my tongue, and his nipple hardens. His groan spurs me on, and I suck the hard nub between my lips. "Fuck. Yes."

Seeing him like this, head tipped back, goosebumps rising along his arms, is intoxicating, and I move lower, kissing a trail down his chest, to the *V* of muscle disappearing below his belt.

He steps free of his pants. The black briefs do nothing to hide his need, or the heavy ring piercing his crown.

"I need you inside of me," I whisper. "Please."

His eyes flash, dark and dangerous as he eases me down to the bed. "Soon." With a twist of his fingers, he unhooks the bra, and my breasts spill free. "I want to taste you first."

He feasts on me, licking, sucking, kissing my thighs, my mound, my lower lips. I writhe on the bed, dew covering my skin. He has kept me on the edge for what feels like forever.

I can no longer beg. Or speak. Only desperate whimpers and mewls.

Pausing the rapid strokes of his tongue, Nomar peers up at me. "I love you, Lisette. With everything I am."

Before I can find the words to reply, he plunges two fingers into my channel and takes up a punishing rhythm against my clit.

With a scream, I fly off the cliff, the pleasure consuming me. There is nothing left but him. Us. Together.

One Month Later

THE PATTER of rain on the umbrella is a calming backdrop to the chaos all around us. Some of the parents call out to their children, trying to coach them from the sides of the pitch. Others cheer and clap. Or talk amongst themselves.

Nomar returns to my side with two cups of coffee in his gloved hands. "This should help," he says and brushes his lips to mine.

"The coffee? Or the kiss? Because only one of those things truly warms me."

"Let me guess. The coffee." He grins, and we both laugh. "I think you might love it more than you love me sometimes."

I take a sip, savoring the rich flavor tempered with a hint of milk. "Never. But after you and Mateen...coffee might be my third love."

He scans the pitch, and his entire body tenses with coiled anticipation. "He's got the ball." Standing, his free hand clenched into a fist, he watches Mateen with such focus, my heart swells with love. "He's going to score!"

Mateen veers off to the side of the pitch, looking around as if he is about to kick the ball to someone else. The two opponents closest to him turn their attention to other players, and my son takes off once more. Seconds later, he skids on the wet grass and drives his heel backwards against the ball.

It sails, fast and true, into the net as the clock hits zero.

Nomar cheers louder than anyone else in the stands. But as soon as he turns to me, fear churns in his eyes. "Lisette? What's wrong?"

"Nothing," I choke out over my tears. "This...is what I dreamed of. When I thought I was going to die. When I thought I would never see you again. *This* is all I wanted, Nomar. To be wet and cold and so very happy. With you and Mateen. As a family."

Nomar kisses me, one arm around my back, and I melt against him.

The kids form a circle with Mateen at the center, jumping and cheering. Slowly, the parents clear from the stands, collecting their children before hurrying out of the rain.

Mateen and Philippe help their coach collect the balls and penalty flags from the field while we stand on the side-lines, my hand tucked in the crook of Nomar's arm. Amelie and Laurent huddle under their own umbrella next to us.

"You played so well, Mateen," his coach says. The woman used to play for Division 1 Féminine, and has taught her players so much in the past two years. "Tell your maman and papa you should have extra dessert tonight."

Nomar flinches almost imperceptibly, his gaze locked on Mateen.

My son—soon to be *our* son once the two-month waiting period for adoption passes—grins. "Philippe and his parents are coming over for dinner tonight and Papa Nomar is making his *grand-mère's* chocolate cake. It is *three* layers!"

Coach Bernard laughs and waves to us. "*Magnifique!* You have earned it. See you at practice on Tuesday."

The boys run over to us. Nomar bends down and scoops Mateen into a hug. "Good game, kiddo. You ready to go?"

Nodding, Mateen leans over to plant a kiss on my cheek. "Can I help make the cake when we get home?"

Nomar raises a brow at him. "Only if you promise not to steal any of the chocolate once its melted. I'm onto your tricks, you know."

He sighs with all the drama of youth. "Okay. But I still get to lick the spoon when you are done."

"Deal." Nomar holds up his hand, and Mateen gives him a high five. "Are you ready, sweetheart?"

My heart is so full, I blink back tears. "*Oui.* Let's go home."

THANK you for reading Rogue Operator. Nomar and Lisette (and of course, Mateen) have a special place in my heart. I didn't expect their story to be *this* intense. This special. But here we are. I hope you love them as much as I do.

If this is your introduction to the Gone Rogue series, you might be curious about the other men (and women) who helped Nomar, Lisette, and Mateen along the way.

Austin - Rogue Protector

Griff - Rogue Officer

Leo - Rogue Defender

Zephyr - Protecting His Target (Away From Keyboard series)

Ford - By Lethal Force (Away From Keyboard series)

Trevor - Call Sign: Redemption (Away From Keyboard series)

Next up, you can find Darius and Amira in Rogue Redeemer!

ABOUT THE AUTHOR

Patricia D. Eddy is a USA Today bestselling author who writes romance for the beautifully broken. Fueled by coffee, wine, and *Doctor Who* episodes on repeat, she brings damaged heroes and heroines together to find their happy ever afters in many different worlds. From military to paranormal to BDSM, her characters are unstoppable forces colliding with such heat, sparks always fly.

Patricia makes her home in Seattle with her husband and very spoiled cats, and when she's not writing, she loves working on home improvement projects, especially if they involve power tools.

Her award-winning *Away From Keyboard* series will always be her first love, because that's where she realized the characters in her head were telling their own stories—and she was just writing them down.

facebook.com/patriciadeddyauthor

x.com/patriciadeddy

instagram.com/patriciadeddy

bookbub.com/profile/patricia-d-eddy

tiktok.com/@patriciadeddyauthor

ALSO BY PATRICIA D. EDDY

Away From Keyboard

Dive into a steamy mix of geekery and military prowess with the men and women of Hidden Agenda and Second Sight.

Breaking His Code

In Her Sights

On His Six

Second Sight

By Lethal Force

Fighting For Valor

Finding Their Forevers (a holiday short story)

Call Sign: Redemption

Braving His Past

Protecting His Target

Defending His Hope

Trusting His Instincts

Guarding His Heart

Gone Rogue (an Away From Keyboard spinoff series)

Rogue Protector

Rogue Officer

Rogue Survivor

Rogue Defender

Rogue Operator

Rogue Mission

Dark PNR

These novellas will take you into the darker side of the paranormal with vampires, witches, angels, demons, and more.

Forever Kept

Immortal Hunter

Wicked Omens

Storm of Sin

By the Fates

Check out the COMPLETE By the Fates series if you love dark and steamy tales of witches, devils, and an epic battle between good and evil.

By the Fates, Freed

Destined: A By the Fates Story

By the Fates, Fought

By the Fates, Fulfilled

In Blood

If you love hot Italian vampires and and a human who can hold her own against beings far stronger, then the In Blood series is for you.

Secrets in Blood

Revelations in Blood

Holidays and Heroes

Beauty isn't only skin deep and not all scars heal. Come swoon over sexy vets and the men and women who love them.

Mistletoe and Mochas

Love and Libations

Restrained

Do you like to be tied up? Or read about characters who do? Enjoy a fresh COMPLETE BDSM series that will leave you begging for more.

In His Silks

Christmas Silks

All Tied Up For New Year's

In His Collar